# HOUSE OF BLOOD AND BONE

Kimberleyjward.co.uk

The right of Kimberley J. Ward to be identified as the Author of the Work has been asserted by her in accordance with the Copyright, Design and Patents Act 1988.

First published 2020.

UK English Edition.

All rights reserved.

No part of this book may be used or reproduced in any manner whatsoever without written permission from the author except in the use of brief quotations in articles or reviews.

All characters in this publication are fictitious and any resemblance to real persons, living or dead, is purely coincidental.

Cover Image Copyright © Kimberley J. Ward
Text copyright © 2020 Kimberley J. Ward
Re-covered 2022 – cover by Getcovers
The moral right of the author has been asserted.

ISBN: 978-1-5272-7246-0
*Also available as an ebook.*

www.kimberleyjward.co.uk

THE WYRD SEQUENCE BOOK 2

# HOUSE OF BLOOD AND BONE

## KIMBERLEY J. WARD

৪০ ✦ ৫৪

ALSO BY KIMBERLEY J. WARD

*The Wyrd Sequence*
House of Fear and Freedom
House of Blood and Bone
House of Gore and Gold
House of Dreams and Dragons

*The Otherside Chronicles*
There is Only Darkness
As Darkness Gathers
When Darkness Devours

*To those who were mad enough to have waited so long for this damn thing...You rock!*

# PART I

# Chapter I

The darkness was a sanctuary to him. It was a blanket of cover that concealed him from prying eyes, wrapping around him like an old friend, like a long-lost lover. Not that he had to worry about being seen, considering what he was and what he could do. Still, one couldn't be too cautious, especially at times like these.

Change was coming.

He could smell it in the air. He could sense it in his bones. His blood thrummed at the promise of war, and his wings burned with the need to take to the air, ready to bring him face to face with his destiny. It would be too dangerous for him to fly now, though.

He looked to the north, where the moon hung heavily in the sky, a watchful eye that surveyed the forest that stretched out almost endlessly in all directions. It would be full in a couple of nights.

For some reason, that sat ill with him.

His eyes lowered and locked onto the creature that was far in the distance, its mighty wings beating at the air with purpose, taking itself and the man upon its back further and further away.

There had been a time when he had looked upon such a sight with amazement, with wonder. That was a long time ago, though. A time when he had been young and foolish, blind to the ways of mankind. Now, he simply stared at the dragon and its Rider, feeling nothing but anger, anger when he remembered what he and his kind had been reduced to by the Dragon Riders in years gone by.

He pulled his stare away from the dragon as it disappeared behind the sharp shapes of the Cléa Mountains. He knew that it was no threat to him. He knew that it was too far away to sense his presence. He knew where the dragon was taking its Rider; he knew that they had received their summons from the king.

King Kaenar was calling his Dragon Riders back to his golden palace.

The king had heard the whispers and he knew what they meant for him.

A metamorphosis was on the horizon for the Twelve Kingdoms, rising like a reborn phoenix, all fire and glory.

With his gaze drifting down to the ruins of what had once been a castle of breathtaking magnificence, he watched and waited.

Sorrow bred there.

Few remembered that place and even less knew of its past.

It was cursed, they said. Haunted.

He knew, though. He remembered, as did the trees

and the earth. They spoke to him, telling him things that few could hear. Secrets, both beautiful and tragic. They were his to keep now, a handful more to add to all the others.

Secrets and lies. Promises and vows. They were consuming him slowly. He was sure they'd get the better of him one day soon and swallow him whole.

He was beginning to welcome the idea.

There was a chill in the air, and he pulled his cloak tighter, huddling deeper into it, seeking warmth and comfort.

His eyes ran over the castle's ruins, taking in the sight of crumbling walls of weathered stone, the tangles of vicious briars. Trees grew where towers had once been, and the acres of carefully tended gardens had been devoured by the wild forest long ago. Nothing remained. Not the pale gravel paths nor the heavenly roses which had climbed around the castle's doors and windows, framing them in lush leaves and enchanted blooms. The air had once been sweet with the scent of a thousand different flowers. Now, the air reeked of desperation and anguish.

Little of the castle above ground remained. However, it seemed that the cellars and tunnels below had escaped the castle's destruction. In fact, despite no one living there for hundreds of years, with no one seemingly daring enough to venture to that desolate place, the castle appeared to be in use. People were far beneath the rubble and earth, locked away in cells, chained and imprisoned. Most were of no interest to him. No others were of importance except for one.

All along he had known where she had been taken, although he had kept that information to himself. He'd had to be patient, to wait and bide his time.

Everything needed to be just right. Otherwise, all he had been working for would be for nothing. All the sacrifices he had made over the last eighteen years would be rendered pointless.

He couldn't let that happen.

He wouldn't let that happen.

His attention went to a door, new and at odds with the ruins surrounding it, framed by the remains of the tower. Leading away from it was a path, muddied and littered with the first fallen leaves of autumn, connecting it to a nearby clearing that was just big enough for a dragon to land and take off from.

The door opened.

Although he knew who would emerge, it was still a shock to see them.

The man stepped out onto the pathway, carrying something in his arms, holding it tight to his chest. The man looked around, searching the tree line, the sky above.

The man did not sense the pair of glacial-blue eyes on him. The man did not see the figure, hooded and cloaked, trail silently behind him as he slipped through the castle's ruins, making his way into the darkness of the forest.

The figure trailed behind the man, nothing more than a ghost in the night, and found himself wondering why the man was there, of all places. He wondered if it troubled the man to return there after so long, to see the place that had once been so close to his heart lying in pieces, little more than a memory. He wondered if the man remembered that place at all, or if he had forgotten it, too broken to remember anything from *before*.

The man went deep into the forest, where the trees

were tall and silent, and where much of the ground was covered in a dense thicket.

All the while, the man carried something in his arms. Someone.

It was a girl, asleep or unconscious, small and fragile, with long hair trailing over the arm of the man who carried her. Whilst he couldn't see her face, he knew that it was *her*, the one he had come to collect now that the time was right. She was much changed. Just as he had known she would be.

Just as she needed to be.

He watched, bemused, as the man did something unexpected. Slowly, carefully, the man kneeled and laid the girl on the ground, setting her down between two trees that had grown close together, offering her some shelter from the brisk breeze that was coming in from the mountains.

The man stood, uncertainty on his face, eyes running over the girl's thin form. Then, as if he wasn't quite sure of himself, like he was taking himself by surprise, he hesitantly unclasped his overcoat.

The man placed it over the girl, swiftly tucking it around her like a blanket, and then quickly backed away. He looked spooked, like he wanted to run. The man didn't, though. He lingered for a heartbeat, his sapphire-blue eyes sparkling with something that was eerily akin to fear. He whispered something, the wind whisking the words away before the hooded and cloaked watcher could catch what he had said, then he turned and slipped away, disappearing into the trees, little more than a shadow amongst shadows.

Wings itching with growing misgivings, the watcher stepped forwards, moving to stand over the girl. His head tilted to the side as he stared down at her, and he wondered… He wondered about a great many things…and lost the battle of keeping his wings pressed flat against his back.

They snapped open, spreading wide, buffeting the air with mighty beats as he shot upwards, shooting into the sky like a fired arrow, a black spot against the all-knowing moon.

# Chapter 2

The girl ran through the forest. Brambles snagged her clothing, tearing at the already shredded fabric. Tree branches reached towards her like grotesque claws. Seeking her. Trying to ensnare her. Her heart hammered in her chest, fast and wild, and her blood roared in her ears, drowning out all other sounds.

Was she being followed? Hunted?

The girl didn't know.

She didn't know anything. Not anymore.

So she ran, propelled forwards by the sense that something terrible loomed behind her.

How had she got there?

Where *was* there?

She had awoken on the ground, cold and alone, swallowed by the darkness of night. An overcoat had been thrown over her, acting as a makeshift blanket. Whilst it had made a valiant effort, it hadn't been able to stay the chill for long. That was what had eventually made the girl stir, forcing her from the blessed calmness of sleep. Shivering, she had sat up slowly, finding herself to be fuzzy-headed and weak. The girl's thin arms had trembled at the strain of pushing herself upright.

Slipping into the overcoat—the colour too dark to distinguish easily, perhaps a deep blue or black—she had leaned back against a tree, uncertain of what she was meant to do. She had cast around, searching for answers, for some form of help. Neither had been found.

The forest had been still and silent—no whisper of wind or rustle of stirring leaves. It had felt as if something unseen had been watching, waiting. Unease had crept over the girl. She had needed to get away from there. Far away. She had started to run, not thinking about what she might be running from or why. The girl had acted on instinct, dashing blindly through the dark forest, twigs slapping against her like whips, thorned undergrowth ripping her tattered dress-top and leggings beneath her overcoat, slashing her skin.

The girl ran until she could run no longer, until the forest wasn't quite so silent and the sense of being watched had eased. It felt as if she had been going for hours. Her legs shook and her breaths rattled in her chest. The girl allowed herself to slow and stumble to a stop, and before her legs could collapse beneath her, she settled down against a tree, pressing her back against its rough bark, huddling between its gnarled roots for shelter, for some semblance of safety.

Pulling her knees to her chest, the girl wrapped the long overcoat snugly around her, desperate to find some warmth. It was a cold night, and the threat of a frost hung in the air. Though sleeveless, the overcoat was thick and covered her from shoulder to ankle. She looked up, peering through the forest's canopy. The sky was clear; the stars, bright specks of light, were twinkling like the finest of diamonds, and the moon was heavy and low, half-hidden behind the mountains in the near distance. The moonlight was pale and ghostly, trailing over the forest's floor in a gentle caress, struggling to break through the leaves that still lingered on the trees, not yet ready to join their brethren on the ground.

The girl peered into the gloom around her with wide, brown eyes, trying to make out any details of her surroundings, trying to figure out what she should do next, where she should go.

In every direction, there was nothing but the dark, twisted shapes of trees. Unable to bear being still any longer, the girl stood on unsteady legs. The need to get moving, to put as much distance between her and what was behind her, burned strongly. Unable to summon the energy to run, the girl settled for a slow, limping walk.

Without fear pushing her forwards, the girl's mind began to wander, drifting off into a twilight zone between conscious thought and daydreams. Something slowly awoke within her, uncoiling and rising from a place unknown to her.

Warmth bloomed in the girl's chest. Her right forearm and hand tingled as a peculiar sensation filled her head. It was as if someone else was there, another mind rubbing against her own.

It was strange but not entirely unwelcome.

The girl reached out to it, pushing her mind towards it.

Whoever, whatever it was startled into awareness. Its shock, its surprise, coursed through her body as if it were her own.

Shaken, the girl fell to her knees, overwhelmed by powerful emotions that weren't hers.

The other mind abruptly withdrew, severing whatever connection there was between them. The sudden silence in her head was deafening. It felt wrong. The girl was incomplete.

Panicked, desperate, she cast out her mind, searching for the presence. She found it, could sense it in the distance. The mind was no longer open to her, shielded behind walls of solid amethyst.

The girl closed her eyes and concentrated, trying to locate it, trying to pinpoint its whereabouts. Her breath left her. It was near, only a few miles away. But it was moving rapidly, heading in the opposite direction to her.

It was leaving her behind.

All sense of rationality deserted the girl. She scrambled to her feet, racing in the direction of the *other*, the distance between her and it becoming greater as the mind grew ever fainter.

The girl sprinted through the dark forest with reckless abandon, distressed beyond reason at the prospect of losing the *other*. She narrowly avoided careening into tree trunks and barely avoided tripping over roots and fallen branches.

The wind picked up, blowing in from the mountains which were steadily getting closer, pushing against the girl, making her hair fly around her as if possessed. The wind carried something with it, a sound, a whisper. She slowed for a heartbeat and turned her head, her eyes searching the darkness for any hint of movement.

At first, the girl saw nothing. Then, when she was about to turn away, she caught sight of something in the corner of her eye: a glint, a brief shimmer in the sinister gloom, gone before it was ever really there.

The girl paused, her heart racing, her large eyes scanning her surroundings, watching, waiting for it to show itself again.

It revealed itself in brief flashes here and there, disappearing before the girl could identify what it was. Misgivings fluttered in her stomach like butterflies, a gentle warning. She spun around and began running once again, chasing after the amethyst-shielded mind. It was so far from her now. She could hardly sense it. Fearful that she would lose it, the girl pushed herself harder, forcing herself to go faster, further.

A shape hurtled out of the darkness, heading straight for the girl.

She tried to skid to a stop, but damp leaves slipped beneath her bare feet, throwing her off balance. She fell to the side, and the ground suddenly vanished.

The girl was airborne for a heart-stopping second. Then her descent came to an abrupt and bruising end as something hard smashed against her chest.

The girl lay there, stunned and breathless, her ribs aching. Slowly, she came to realise that a fallen tree had stopped her fall. She had come to a painful rest at its base. The ground around her tilted down at a steep angle. The darkness had concealed the drop.

Shaking, the girl pushed herself up and discovered that she was nearly at the bottom of the slope. On unsteady legs, she clambered down the rest of the way, finding herself standing in a long, narrow gully. The girl looked around, trying to spot the creature that had sprung at her, and there, sitting on a branch above her head, she spied a bird.

A raven.

Its black feathers gleamed in the ghostly moonlight, and its vivid, blue eyes seemed all too bright in the darkness around them.

They stared at each other, eyes locked, and a peculiar feeling settled over the girl, one that made goosebumps rise on her forearms. She frowned up at the bird, and for some reason lost to her, she reached out to it.

The raven fanned its wings and uttered a piercing *caw*!

The girl jumped and pulled back her hand. She didn't like the look of its beak, large and sharp. Blinking, trying to clear away the fuzziness that lingered in her head, she began to slowly back away.

With an angry *caw*, the raven took flight, heading straight for the girl. She ducked, feeling it shoot over her head, only just missing her, and she heard the sound of hurried wing beats. The girl didn't turn to see where it was or what it might be doing. The girl didn't wait for it to return, talons bared and beak aimed with intent.

Once again, the girl found herself running, barrelling through the dark forest at a breakneck speed. Through the gully she sprinted, the earthen banks rising up on either side of her, too steep for her to clamber up in a hurry. The ground was slick with leaves and muddied water, and it was hard for the girl to stay upright. The raven was behind her, beside her, its wings flapping furiously.

Then it wasn't.

The girl slowed and turned, ready to run at the slightest noise, the faintest flicker of movement, and peered into the gloom. The raven was nowhere to be seen. All was still and quiet. The girl let out a shuddering breath and leaned against a tree, trying to calm her racing heart. She didn't understand why the raven had singled her out, corralling her through the forest.

As the din of panic began to recede, the girl cast out her mind, searching for the mind shielded behind amethyst walls.

It was gone, too far away for the girl to sense anymore.

Pain tore through the girl as her heart was split in two.

She had lost it. She was alone. It had abandoned the girl to the darkness and the cold. She fell to her knees, unsure as to what she should do, where she should go. Tears welled in her eyes, and she sobbed, her voice broken from disuse. The girl buried her face in her hands, flinching as tears made the fresh scrapes on her palms sting.

A twig snapped, and the forest became eerie once more. The wind stilled, and the trees stopped their whispers, becoming watchful, curious.

The girl's head whipped up like that of a startled deer: eyes wide, darting this way and that.

Another twig snapped.

Some leaves rustled.

Hastily, the girl stood and pressed herself against a tree, hiding as best as she could. She inched around it, treading softly, hardly daring to breathe, too scared of making a sound.

The bark was rough beneath her hands as the girl steadied herself, as she gripped onto the trunk whilst she leaned to the side, peering around it. The sound of movement paused for a heartbeat, then resumed, slow and quiet. It was the footsteps of someone trying to make as little noise as possible.

A voice floated on the air, softly calling a name. A name that reverberated through the girl.

Her legs twitched with the need to run, but by some miracle, she held herself still. Her eyes scanned the forest, drifting over the twisted shapes of knotted branches and thick tree trunks.

Although the girl knew that someone was out there, she could see nothing, but she knew they were slowly drawing closer. She could hear them, sense them somehow, and she waited.

A shape moved out from the darkness, the moonlight revealing nothing more than that they were tall and armed. In their hand, shining malevolently, was a hunting knife.

The girl's eyes locked onto them, keeping them in her sights. They crept through the trees, quiet and alert, their feet carefully placed, their head swivelling as they looked all around. The girl knew that they were searching for something. The girl knew they were searching for her.

Her blood turned to ice.

What did they want with her?

Were they going to take her back? Take her back…where? The girl couldn't remember what she had been running from, only that she couldn't go back, couldn't let herself be captured. Not again. Never again.

Whoever they were, they were surely a foe. Why else would they have their knife out? They must mean to use it, right?

The girl held herself as still as she could, hardly daring to breathe, not wanting to draw their attention. She was weary, her strength all but spent. She wouldn't be able to outrun them. The girl could only hope that they'd move past without discovering her. Perhaps then, she'd make her escape once they were gone.

The girl rested her cheek against the tree, the bark as

coarse as sandpaper against her delicate skin. Her rapid breaths burned her painfully dry throat as she struggled to keep them hushed, and she couldn't help but be aware of the tremors that raked her body, threatening to send her to the ground in a boneless heap. The girl prayed to the gods, whose names she couldn't quite recall, that her presence would go undetected.

Her prayers, though, were in vain.

Despite holding herself as still as she could, barely making a sound, the foe's head snapped up, his eyes seeming to lock with hers regardless of the barrier of night between them.

Whilst she knew that her legs wouldn't be able to carry her far, the girl made to run. The foe was fast. Before the girl got more than a few steps away, they were nearly upon her. Having no desire to feel their blade in her back, she spun around with one hand held out as if she could ward them off. The foe skidded to a stop, knife poised to strike, feet spread apart for balance.

The trees around them sighed, branches shuddering and parting above their heads as if moved by hands unseen. Moonlight came spilling down like an ethereal waterfall, pooling around the girl and the foe.

They were revealed to one another, the pale light just enough for them to see the barest of details.

The girl's gaze ran over the foe, taking in his mop of messy hair, the baggy tunic and trous that partially concealed his tall, lean frame. His boots were unlaced as if he had put them on in a hurry, and as her eyes locked with his, trying to catch a glimpse of the thoughts whirling around in his head, she witnessed a shockwave course through him. His amber eyes widened and his lips parted, shaping soundless words as he took a stumbling step forwards. His hunting knife fell from numb fingers.

"Nessa?" he breathed, his voice hushed with astonishment, with disbelief.

The girl's eyebrows pulled together, and her heart skipped a beat.

"Nessa," he said again, sounding surer of himself, "is that you?"

The girl shook her head.

"It is," he whispered, his amber eyes shining with emotion. "Come on, Nessa. Don't you remember me?"

# Chapter 3

The girl began backing away from him. She didn't know who the foe was or why he talked as if he knew her. He was someone who skulked through the woods at night, armed, no less. That couldn't be good—even if he had dropped his blade on the ground.

The foe frowned as he took in the girl's wide eyes and her slow retreat. "You do remember me, right?"

No, the girl didn't remember him. She didn't remember a time before waking up on the ground, cold and alone. Her head was empty of anything and everything.

"Nessa?" The foe hesitantly stepped forwards, inching towards her as if he feared he might scare her away. He wasn't wrong. The muscles in her legs twitched with the urge to flee, to run and hide.

"I don't know you," the girl croaked, shaking her head frantically, tangled wisps of hair falling across her face, her chapped lips. "I don't know who you are." Her throat hurt, dry as sand, and her words were little more than a hoarse whisper despite her desire to scream them.

"Of course you do," the foe insisted, shooting her a small, uncertain grin, teeth bright and white in the moonlight. "I know I look a bit worse for wear, but it's me, Hunter. I'm your friend."

"I don't know you," the girl argued, stumbling away from him in earnest. She felt dizzy and weak, and the ground seemed to roll beneath her, threatening to unbalance her and swallow her whole.

"Ness—"

"Stop calling me that," she cried. "That's not my name."

"Yeah, it is," the foe—Hunter—said soothingly.

The girl froze.

Hunter crept closer to her.

"It's alright," he murmured. "You're safe now, Nessa."

*Nessa.* Was that what she was called? Was that her name? The girl didn't know. She didn't remember.

She couldn't remember anything. She was no one.

The girl swallowed nervously, her throat burning as she did so. "I'm Nessa?"

Hunter nodded, messy locks of dark hair falling across his forehead.

Something deep within her clicked into place, and she didn't feel quite so hollow, quite so incomplete. A soothing calmness settled over her, over *Nessa*, and she found herself stepping forwards, closing the gap between Hunter and herself.

Hunter held himself still as she looked up at him, scrutinising his features in the moonlight. His hair looked like it hadn't seen a comb in a couple of days, and he had a dusting of stubble on his jaw that still held the soft touches of lingering youth. Whilst his amber eyes were bright, weariness was etched across his face. Worry had been eating him alive for some time.

Hesitantly, Nessa reached up and cupped his cheek, his skin heated beneath her cold hand. As soon as their skin touched, she knew that his words were true: he was a friend. Any distrust and fear she felt towards him dissolved to nothing. He was a safety and certainty. He would do her no harm. Nessa sighed, relieved beyond measure.

"You've been searching for me?"

Voice thick with emotion, he said, "For months."

"You've found me."

His hand went over hers, holding it against his cheek, keeping it in place. She could feel his growing solace, his long festering weariness. "Finally."

"Hunter...?" His hand. It was so, so warm against hers. So pleasant.

"Do you remember," he whispered, earnestly hopeful. "Do you remember me?"

"I...I..." Nessa wanted to lie. She wanted so desperately to lie, to tell him that her memories had come flooding back and save him from the painful truth. But she couldn't lie, not to him. Not now. Not when he was all she had. "I don't," she said weakly, mournfully. "I'm sorry, but I don't. I remember nothing beyond waking up here. In this forest."

At first, Hunter was disappointed; then her words sank in, and he became worried. Very worried. Scared. Nessa could sense all of it. She could feel the churning thoughts in his head. She could practically taste them, see them. A little perturbed, she pulled her hand back, slipping it out from beneath Hunter's.

"I'm feeling a bit dizzy," Nessa confessed.

"Oh?"

"The world is spinning."

"That's not good."

"I think I'm about to faint," Nessa said just as her legs buckled and black motes swam across her vision.

"That's not particularly helpful," Hunter mumbled, catching her before she hit the ground. With one arm around her back and the other under her knees, he swung her up, holding her tight against his chest.

As weak as a newborn kitten, Nessa wrapped her arms around Hunter's neck as he set off with purpose. The black motes were fading, but all her strength seemed to have fled. Nessa was sure that if he were to set her back on her feet, she would simply collapse. Besides, Nessa didn't want to be put down, even if she were strong enough to walk. Hunter was warm, so very warm against the chill of the night. His body heat seeped through the layers of their clothing, and Nessa found herself to be cosy and comfortable for the first time in hours.

"Where are we going?" she asked, her cheek coming to rest on his shoulder. The rocking motion of his steps was lolling, the softness of his tunic soothing, almost homely and familiar. It swiftly became a struggle to keep her eyes open.

"The others and I set up camp a few miles to the east," Hunter said, voice low and quiet, and tinged with gentle optimism. "I'm taking you there. Then I'll get you something to eat and something warm to wear, and when you're too full to even think of food for the next week, you'll snuggle beneath a pile of blankets and can sleep for the next two days straight."

"That sounds rather nice," Nessa murmured, losing the battle of keeping her eyes open.

"Well, I think you deserve it."

"I do?"

"Yes," Hunter said, a smile colouring his voice. "Sleep, Nessa. When you wake up, we'll be at camp. Then we'll get this mess all figured out."

"Food and piles of blankets?" Nessa said wistfully.

"Food and piles of blankets," Hunter promised.

# Chapter 4

Although exhausted to a near-painful degree, sleep eluded Nessa. All she could manage was an unsettled doze. There were too many things coursing through her mind, too many unsettling thoughts. Hunter was mostly silent during their trek through the forest, concentrating on not tripping on the uneven terrain. However, the few times he had caught her looking around nervously, he would talk to her, his voice low and gentle, as if he could tell that she was uneasy and in need of soothing.

It was during the quiet interludes that Nessa wondered if her tired mind was playing tricks on her, making her hear things, strange things. She swore that she could hear whispers, voices that were too quiet for her to heed the words, voices that belonged neither to her nor Hunter, or to any physical being. Nessa felt as if the wind and trees were trying to talk to her, trying to tell her something. What they might have to say, she didn't know. She couldn't even guess.

Worse than the whispers, though, were the occasional beats of wings sounding out behind them. The few times Nessa had managed to pluck up the courage to peer over Hunter's shoulder, she would see nothing but the forest's darkness staring back at her. There was no sign of the blue-eyed raven anywhere. But she knew. Some part of her knew that it was there, following, watching. It was a shadow in a shadow.

The moon was inching behind the mountains to the north as their journey neared its end, their peaks haloed in fragile light, just visible through the trees' branches. They were tall, stabbing high into the sky, jagged like claws. They were proud sentries, guarding over the land and forest, and as it appeared, Hunter's campsite.

Three small tents sat nestled amongst a group of mighty trees that towered over them, tucked into the wide space between their trunks. A campfire, a handful of small flames clinging to the last few scraps of firewood, cast a warm circle of illumination in the centre of the clearing, the light only just reaching the canvas tents, making them look like strange ghosts.

Hunter carried Nessa over to the fire and carefully set her on her feet. She wobbled, unsteady, and he put a hand on her arm, supporting her, steadying her as she lowered herself to the ground. The fire was so warm on her face, on her hands, her feet. She shuffled nearer, sitting as close to it as she could, savouring it, bathing in its heat. Hunter ducked into a tent, and when he reappeared a mere moment later, he was holding a couple of blankets. He swiftly draped them around Nessa's shoulders, bundling her up tightly. He crouched beside her and busied himself by building up the fire.

There was a pile of wood nearby, already split into manageable logs. Hunter selected a couple and placed them on the remains of their predecessors. The flames quickly caught, eager and hungry, devouring their fresh meal. Lively light flooded the campsite, making it feel a lot more welcoming. Homely, even.

Hunter stood, dusting off his hands, and gazed around the campsite. "Right," he said, more to himself than her, "now for the food. I wonder where Orm has squirreled away the good stuff?"

"Orm?" Nessa enquired.

Hunter blinked, momentarily taken back. "Oh, yeah. I forgot you have no idea who he is. I'll explain after I get you something to eat. You look like you're about to keel over."

"Alright," Nessa murmured. *Orm.* Was this another friend she couldn't remember?

Hunter disappeared into one of the tents, a different one this time, and she could hear him rummaging around inside.

Nessa's eyes ran over her surroundings, taking them in, trying to find some kind of familiarity, a hint of recognition. The campsite itself wasn't situated in a clearly defined clearing, she realised. The forest was too old to have such a thing, but between the wide gaps of a handful of mighty oaks, their trunks at least ten feet in diameter. They towered over their younger companions, a collection of their offspring, their lower branches as thick as the middle of a grown man. The tents were small, bell-shaped, and made from a heavy canvas to ward away the chill of the autumn nights. Nessa guessed that they were just big enough to fit one person and their supplies inside.

Off to one side was a large patch of trampled earth, flattened in the centre as if a large beast had slept curled up there, not unlike a cat. A hole in the tree canopy was directly above it, twigs and entire branches snapped off. They had been dragged a short distance away, bits and pieces hacked up for firewood. An axe was embedded in one, ready to be called into action should they run low on logs.

Hunter reappeared, carrying a drawstring bag and a wooden plate.

"The cheeky git tried to hide all the food under his pillow," he said, sitting down beside Nessa. "Now, we don't have much, seeing as I didn't get around to setting up my traps today…yesterday?" He looked in the direction of the moon, which was now behind the mountains, completely hidden from sight. "Definitely yesterday."

Opening the bag, Hunter pulled out several cloth-wrapped bundles and set them down on the plate. Even before she knew exactly what was offered to her, Nessa's mouth began to water. She watched eagerly as they were unwrapped, revealing a selection of berries, hard cheese and some strips of jerky.

"Here," Hunter said, sliding the plate in front of her. "Start with the berries and see how you feel. We don't want you being sick, now, do we?"

Nessa only half-heard him, fingers plucking at the berries as soon as she saw them, plopping them in her mouth. They were juicy and sweet, ever so sweet, and her taste buds were flooded with the most glorious of flavours. Nessa's eyelids fluttered shut as a wave of euphoria washed over her. Hunter handed her a waterskin, and when the cool liquid hit her throat, Nessa thought that she had died and gone to heaven. Water and berries, such simple things, yet at that precise moment, they felt more precious than all the gold and jewels in the world.

As the worst of Nessa's thirst and hunger abated, she became keenly aware of a pair of eyes watching her every move. She slid a glance to her left, catching Hunter staring at her with a level of nervousness that was almost palpable. Nessa paused, a piece of jerky poised at her lips, and raised her brows in question.

Hunter blinked, shaking himself, and grinned with a touch of embarrassment. "Forgive me. I don't think I've ever seen a girl eat so much food so quickly."

"I'm starving," Nessa mumbled, embarrassment making her shoulders hunch beneath her cocoon of blankets. She looked down, finding that she had eaten the berries and was finishing off the last few pieces of jerky. Guilt grew. "Sorry. I should have saved more for you…and the others?"

"No worries." Hunter batted her apology away with a wave of his hand. "Eat it all if you want. The others and I can go foraging for something later."

"Foraging?"

"Yeah. Find some nuts and whatnot."

"Nuts?"

Hunter shrugged. "Or mushrooms. You never know what you might end up finding when you forage."

Nessa supposed she'd just have to take his word for it. She suddenly noticed her appetite had now fled, and she lowered the piece of jerky, no longer desiring it.

Hunter sighed. "If you're hungry, then eat. It's okay. Don't feel bad. The others won't mind. Orm can whip us up something if need be. It would give him something useful to do."

"I'm not hungry," Nessa said softly, setting the jerky down on the plate. "Not anymore."

She spoke the truth, kind of. She was full. The pangs of hunger were gone, but they had been replaced by another form of discomfort. She was convinced that the food had turned into a hard ball in her stomach, heavy and unpleasant.

"You sure?"

Nessa forced herself to smile. "I'm sure."

Hunter looked unconvinced, his eyes uncertain.

"Who are the others?" she asked quietly, changing the subject. "Orm and…?"

Hunter shifted position, sitting cross-legged. "Orm and Chaos. They're my friends, our friends. Well, Orm's a friend. Chaos is more of a companion. One who can barely stand the sight of me or Orm."

"If this Chaos person can't stand the sight of either of you, then why is he travelling with you?"

"Because he wanted to help us find you, of course. He pretty much hates Orm and me, but he seems to care about you."

Nessa blinked, surprised. "Really?"

Hunter nodded. "The three of us have been looking for you since you were taken. We've searched half the world trying to find you."

"Since I was *taken*?" Nessa whispered, latching onto that sinister word. "Why was I taken? Who took me?"

"Well, um…" Hunter floundered. "It's…err…a bit of a long story."

"A long story?"

Hunter nodded uneasily, unable to look her in the eye. Nessa began to worry. Her heartbeat sped up. Had she upset him? Asked too many questions?

"Come on," he said gently, clearing his throat. "Let's get you settled into bed. I promised you a pile of blankets, so a pile of blankets you shall get. It's probably best that the others are here when you're told what happened."

"Is it so bad that you can't tell me now?"

"No." Hunter tried to be reassuring. "But it's something that should be discussed when both of us are well rested. I haven't had any proper sleep in days and I could really do with a nap before I explain."

Nessa's shoulders sagged as disappointment crept up on her. She didn't want to wait for answers. Nor did she want to argue. Not right then, not when she was so tired, and not so soon after being found. The idea of a pile of blankets to sleep under was a small consolation. One she might be glad to take. Nessa eyed the bell tents, thinking that they did look rather cosy.

Hunter helped Nessa to her feet and shepherded her over to a tent, the one nearest to the area of flattened ground. She watched as he tied the door flap open, ducked inside, and began moving things around.

"This is my tent," Hunter said over his shoulder, pulling some clothing from a bag and stuffing other things in. "But you can have it now. I'll bunk with Orm for a while. It will be rather snug, seeing as they're only little tents, but I'll make do." He grinned mischievously. "After a couple of nights, Orm will get fed up and go sleep outside like the dog he is."

"Umm...?"

Hunter smoothed out the sleeping bag and plumped up the thin pillow, then grabbed his bag and exited the tent. "Well," he said, "I'm afraid you'll have to borrow some of my clothes for the time being. I swear they're clean, though. Warm, too. Just let me grab you some more blankets for that pile I promised, then I'll leave you to get changed and rest."

Nessa nodded, her poor, tired mind unable to form any words, as she clutched the blankets that were wrapped around her like a cloak. She watched silently as Hunter crossed over to the nearest tent and flung his bag inside. He was swift to return, handing her a couple of thick blankets that he had just swiped. "I'd imagine that Orm and Chaos will return soon. We'd split up to search for you when we heard—" His mouth snapped shut, trapping the rest of the sentence behind his teeth before it had a chance to escape. "Well, in any event, they should be back soon. Don't worry if you hear a ruckus later. It'll just be them."

"Okay."

"Okay," Hunter murmured, running out of things to say. "Sleep tight then, and I'll see you tomorrow."

"Thank you, Hunter," Nessa whispered. "Thank you for everything."

Hunter's smile was small—small and weary—but sincere. "If you need anything else, I'll be just over there." He nodded to the tent that was just a stone's throw away. "Give a shout and I'll be here before you can blink."

"Good night," Nessa said, ducking into the tent as he hesitantly turned away. She sat down on the sleeping bag and deposited the blankets beside her as she untied the front flap. It slid closed, sealing her in. Her last sight was of Hunter doing the same, an odd expression on his face, one that was a peculiar mixture of elation and fear.

The firelight made the canvas' sides glow, and it was just bright enough for her to discern the vague details of her surroundings, both inside and outside the tent.

Too tired to make the effort of changing her tatty attire, Nessa moved her loaned clothes out of the way and slipped into the sleeping bag. It was heavy and warm, the inside lined with soft fur. She quickly arranged the blankets around her and snuggled deep into her little nest, curling up in a ball on her side. She could hear Hunter moving around in his tent, arranging things and muttering under his breath. Orm's name was mentioned a few times.

With the weight of the blankets making her feel safe, and the sound of Hunter reminding her that she wasn't alone, Nessa smiled and closed her aching eyes.

଼ଡ଼✦ଔ

Nessa's head was filled with a pleasant sort of haze when she heard the others return. She was half-asleep, her eyes closed and her body relaxed. She was warm and comfortable, her mind at ease. She heard murmured conversations, the sound of people moving around the campsite, Hunter being called a "pillow-stealing bitch" by, she presumed, Orm.

Everything eventually fell silent as everyone drifted off into an exhausted sleep, all except for Nessa, who was slowly drawn into a sinister world of dark previsions. Her nest of safety was unable to keep them away for long.

She was running through the forest again, lost and alone. Something was after her, hunting her. She could feel its breath on the back of her neck, could feel the air stirring behind her as it drew ever closer.

She could not run fast enough to escape it.

She could not hide.

The ground turned to quicksand between one step and the next, and she was trapped, stuck in its unforgiving grip. The trees shifted, looming over her, their branches reaching towards her like twisted talons, and from the darkness, a shape emerged, eyes ablaze with green light.

Somewhere in the forest, a raven cried a warning.

༄ ♦ ༄

With sunlight dancing on the tent's canvas, Nessa stirred, drowsy and confused, still caught in the clutches of dreams she couldn't quite remember. She was warm and comfortable under the pile of blankets, her cheek cradled on a soft pillow. Through sleep-clouded eyes, she watched the play of light around her for a moment.

Forced by her grumbling stomach, Nessa slowly, reluctantly, sat up. She wrapped a blanket around her shoulders, keeping the cool air at bay, and rubbed the tiredness from her face, forcing herself to feel marginally more alert. Nessa went to stand when something made her pause.

Frowning, Nessa held up her hand, turning it this way and that. Beneath all the grime covering her skin, sitting amongst the multitude of cuts, scrapes and bruises she had accumulated during her mad dash through the forest, was a peculiar mark.

It held a faint, purplish sheen, an iridescence that made it shimmer gently with the slightest of movement. It curled around her forearm, a thin line at first, which then widened at her wrist, with two lines branching out to run beside it. The mark continued over the back of her hand and ended on her palm. Nessa thought it looked remarkably like a silhouette of a dragon diving in mid-flight.

The sound of voices reached her ears, drawing her attention. Nessa clutched the blanket tightly and stood, the tent's low ceiling forcing her to stoop, and pushed the door flap aside. She shuffled outside, her muscles stiff, protesting after the abuse of last night. The voices quietened and Nessa looked around, spying Hunter and another man sitting by the campfire, using a couple of stumpy logs as stools.

A few hours of sleep had done Hunter some good, and he appeared considerably less weary and dishevelled. His hair, an earthy-brown colour that fell nearly to his shoulders in careless waves, had been brushed, and he had found the time to shave, his stubble gone. Dressed simply in a dark linen tunic and trous, boots reaching to his calves, loosely laced, he looked at ease with the day, suited to a life in the woods.

Nessa's eyes drifted away from Hunter and settled on his companion, who was staring at her with surprised whiskey-coloured eyes. He was tall, taller than Hunter by at least a head, and muscular, his biceps on display since his tunic's sleeves had been removed, the deep red of his top complimenting his golden skin nicely. The chilled autumn air didn't seem to bother him. His head was shaved smooth and his face was characterised by a nose that would be called hawkish when he's older.

Painfully aware of their gazes on her, Nessa hesitantly approached, pulling the blanket tighter around her as if it could protect her from their scrutiny.

"Well, look at you," Hunter said in welcome, grinning up at Nessa as she joined them by the campfire, which was burning happily away, small flames licking at the frying pan nestled amongst them. "You're finally up and about."

"Good morning," she murmured shyly, moving to sit beside Hunter on the ground, her eyes darting between him and his companion.

"Morning?" Hunter laughed. "More like afternoon. You've slept most of the day away."

"Well, you did promise me a pile of blankets and two days' worth of sleep."

Hunter blinked, his grin growing. "So I did. And yet here you are, up and about when there's still another full day of sleep to be had."

Nessa chuckled, the long disused sound bubbling up, dislodging from where it had been hidden. "Tempting as that is, my stomach is growling too much for me to fall back asleep."

"Well, your timing is fortuitous," Hunter said, nodding to the frying pan. "Orm was just whipping up some of his infamous scrambled egg."

Nessa sneaked a glance at Orm, who rolled his eyes and jabbed the anaemic looking scrambled egg with a spatula. "I think you're getting famous and infamous mixed up."

Hunter winked at Nessa. "No, I'm pretty sure I'm not."

"I can't tell you how glad I am that we've got you back, Nessa," Orm said. "This one," he pointed his spatula at Hunter, "has been driving me mad."

Hunter pretended to be outraged. "I have not."

"You have and you know it."

"Rubbish."

Orm shook his head. "As I was saying. I'm glad you're back, safe and relatively sound."

"I'm glad to be back, too," Nessa murmured

uncertainly. She found their familiarity with each other and her to be a little overwhelming. She didn't know where to look: at them or the ground. Her eyes darted between both options.

"Now that he has someone else to annoy," Orm said, "he might leave me alone for a bit."

"He lies, Nessa," Hunter told her in earnest. "He is spinning malicious lies about me. Tell him off and make him see the error of his ways."

Orm reached over and cuffed Hunter around the head. "See what I've had to put up with? He's near impossible to bear when he gets like this."

"Like what?" Hunter scowled. "Happy? Am I not allowed to be happy?"

"You can be happy. Just be happy in silence."

"Happy in silence?" Hunter pondered. "That's like telling someone to have fun in silence."

Nessa watched them banter with one another, her head swivelling from side to side like their exchange was a tennis match. She was at a complete loss for words and was grateful when Orm dished up the scrambled egg, handing her a plate piled high with it. Hunter too, was handed a plate, although he looked down at his meal with distaste.

"You know," he said contemplatively as Orm rose, standing over him, "for someone who makes so much scrambled egg, I'd have thought you'd be able to make it at least half-decently by now."

"I'm going to be kind and forget that comment, Hunter, my dear boy." Orm turned, heading over to his tent. "But only because I don't want to upset Nessa by having her witness you being beaten into a bloody pulp."

Hunter laughed and stabbed his scrambled egg with

his spoon, then set the plate down and picked up a cloth-wrapped block from the supply bag beside him. "If we cover the eggs with cheese, it might disguise the taste long enough to swallow."

Nessa scooped up a spoonful. "It can't be that bad," she said, peering at it. Admittedly, it didn't look particularly appetising: burnt yet somehow unusually jiggly.

"If you don't believe me," he said, pulling out a knife and whittling thin slivers of cheese onto his unappealing meal, "then take a bite. Go on, I dare you."

Nessa could see the mischief shining bright in his amber eyes, and deciding against his dare, she held out her plate. Hunter topped it in a healthy covering of cheese, smirking as he did so. Only when the eggs were completely hidden was the cheese stowed back in the supply bag.

Picking up his plate, Hunter shovelled a heap of cheesy egg into his mouth, grimacing. "If you pinch your nose while you chew," he advised. "It won't be quite so bad. Possibly."

"I heard that, you swine," Orm called from the other side of the campsite. A rucksack was slung over his shoulder as he stood by Nessa's tent, holding the clothing that Hunter had loaned her last night. Seeing them, Nessa wished she had gone to the effort of changing. Though the blanket partially cloaked her, it didn't cover her completely, and some of her clothing was visible. The half-dress, dirtied and ripped, at odds with the plush overcoat she still wore, peered out through the gaps in the material. Nessa felt a touch embarrassed at her bedraggled appearance. Orm strode off into the trees, leaving the camp, cursing Hunter under his breath as he went.

"Where's he going?" Nessa asked, also wondering why he'd taken her change of clothes.

"Oh, he's just adding a few finishing touches to a little surprise we've whipped up for you," Hunter said. "He'll be back soon to collect you, so you'd best eat up."

Nessa ate her meal as fast as possible, largely in part so that she didn't actually have to taste it. Contrary to her prior belief, the scrambled egg was as bad as Hunter made it out to be. Not even the pile of cheese helped.

"So, what's the surprise?" Nessa enquired, stacking her almost empty plate on top of Hunter's.

He smiled. "It wouldn't be a surprise if I told you about it, now, would it?"

"Can I have a hint?"

Hunter shook his head.

"Not even a teeny-tiny one?"

"Not even a hint of a hint shall be given."

"Hmm." Nessa looked over her shoulder, trying to spy Orm, but he was out of sight, the trees hiding him away.

"So," Hunter shifted on his makeshift stool, leaning his elbows on his knees, "did you sleep okay?"

Nessa blinked up at him. "I think so."

"No bad dreams? No being able to remember what happened?"

"I had a dream." Nessa frowned. "I think. I can't recall what it was about, though."

"Oh? Well, maybe that's for the best."

"Yes," Nessa agreed, "maybe."

Her attention slid over to the mysterious third tent, the one furthest away. She could see movement within it, someone bumping against the canvas as they shuffled around the cramped space. Nessa thought for a moment that they were about to come out. However, no one appeared. Instead, they seemed to settle back down, probably going back to sleep.

"That's Chaos," Hunter said, following her gaze. "He's been acting oddly the past couple of days. Well, *odder*. Keeping to himself even more than usual. Thank the Creator. Having him around makes me uneasy."

Nessa looked up at him, surprised. "Uneasy?"

"Yeah, uneasy. And that's the polite way of putting it. You'll understand when he decides to show himself. Although I hope that's later rather than sooner. He's a freakish sight to look upon. He also threatens to kill me on a regular basis. That hasn't particularly helped endear him to me."

"He threatens to kill you?"

Hunter nodded cheerfully. "He also threatens maiming as well. He often reminds me that maiming is always on the table."

Nessa was horrified. "Why are you even travelling with him?"

Hunter shrugged. "He's unpleasant company, but he has his uses. He did help us find you, after all."

"Oh?"

"Yeah. It was him who urged us to come westward. Orm and I wanted to go either east or southeast. Chaos, though, said to come this way, said that he could "feel it in the wind". Whatever that means. So here we are. We searched around the Cléa Mountains first, and when we found no sign of you there, we headed deeper into the forest. We set up camp here whilst we searched around the nearby area. Been here about five days before, as if by magic, you turned up. Just in time too, because we were about to pack up camp and head further north."

"How fortuitous," Nessa murmured, her eyes locked onto the tent. There was an air of otherness around it, both alarming and comforting.

Quiet footsteps sounded behind Nessa, and she turned, finding that it was Orm returning from wherever he'd been. For such a large man, he moved with an impressive amount of stealth.

Orm grinned and extended a hand to Nessa. "Your surprise awaits."

With a mixture of excitement and nervousness, Nessa took Orm's bear paw of a hand, and he helped her up, swiftly ushering her from the campsite. She glanced over her shoulder at Hunter to see if he was following, but he hadn't budged.

"Enjoy," he said, giving her a small reassuring grin.

Nessa allowed herself to be led away, tree trunks quickly concealing Hunter and the bell tents. Intrigued as to what the surprise might be, she looked all around, searching for any clues. The trees towered around them, growing closer together than the ones by the campsite, a few leaves still clinging to the lower branches in enchanting shades of orange and red. Here and there were light patches of undergrowth.

The ground sloped downwards gently, becoming rocky underfoot, and the sound of running water soon reached Nessa's ears. Orm headed towards it, pulling Nessa along behind him, his hand wrapped around hers, holding it like she was a small child who might wander off and get lost. He pushed past a bush with flame-esque leaves and Nessa's surprise was suddenly revealed to her.

*Oh!* What a surprise it was.

# Chapter 5

It was something from a fairy tale, a dream, one built from a river of crystal-clear water and sparkling waterfalls.

The river ran calmly downhill, edged on either side by natural bedrock capped with young trees. Branches reached over the river, raining down dappled shade. A collection of small pools made up a section of it nearby, ringed with boulders and dark earth covered in a carpet of lush moss.

Nessa's eyes were drawn to the pool closest to her.

Larger than most of the others, it was deep and round. A long, wandering waterfall cascaded down from the pool above it. Dotted around, peppering the rocky banks, lining the sides, were hundreds of tiny flames. At first, Nessa mistook them for small candles, but she was quick to realise that the flames hovered an inch or so above the ground, appearing out of thin air. Their light danced across the water's surface, golden and magical, and caught on pockets of rocks and moss, highlighting them with an ethereal quality even in the daylight.

Nessa looked up at Orm. "What's this?"

"It's your surprise."

"A chance to look at a pretty river and some floating flames?"

Orm laughed.

"No, silly." He nodded to where her pile of loaned clothes sat alongside a couple of other items by the pool. "It's a relaxing bathing session that's guaranteed to make you feel like a completely new person."

"Oh."

"It was thought up on short notice. It's the best we could do to right now to, ya know, make you feel better and stuff." He helped Nessa navigate over the mossy rocks, stopping her from slipping as they neared the water's edge. "We've got you clean clothes, soap, a comb and," he let go of her hand and kneeled beside the pool, dipping a finger into the water, "a nice, hot bath." His fingertip glowed red and the water rippled, steam rising in a rapidly growing circle until the whole pool was steaming.

Nessa gasped. "How did you do that?"

Orm stood and grinned. "It's just a little thing I can do." He snapped his thumb and index finger, and a flame sprang up between them, red but flickering with hints of green. "A gift graced to me by my father's lineage."

"It's amazing."

"It comes in useful every now and again. But I can't hold it for long, so I suggest you hop into the pool whilst it's hot. The campsite's not too far away, so if anything happens, just holler. Not that anything should happen. Everything is perfectly safe."

"Okay," Nessa murmured, her eyes wide with wonder even as Orm waved the little flame away.

"You know which way to go when you've finished?"

Nessa nodded.

Orm started to walk away. "Then I'll leave you to it."

"Thank you."

He gave her a small smile from over his shoulder as he disappeared into the trees. "Think of it as a welcome back present," were his parting words.

Nessa stood on the riverbank for a second, drinking in the sight of the natural pools; the carpet of moss; the warm, welcoming water; Orm's little magical lights. It was a dream, surely, a beautiful one, granted, but a dream regardless. She was imagining it all. Be that as it may, it didn't stop the blanket from slipping from her shoulders, nor did it prevent her from freeing herself from her dirtied clothes, throwing them to the ground with distaste. Nessa could tell that they had once been something lovely to wear, but now they were barely more than rags, riddled with holes and ominous red-brown stains.

Tiptoeing over the ring of dancing flames, Nessa stood at the lip of the pool, watching the steam curl over the water's surface in rolling waves. She dipped a toe into the water, testing the temperature, testing to see if it was part of her reality.

It was perfection. The dream remained unaltered.

Nessa carefully entered the pool, finding it deeper than she had first thought. The shallowest part reached up to her knees.

Nessa waded further into the pool, curious as to how deep the centre was, and she smiled as tropical water closed over her shoulders, hot and oh-so soothing. Her muscles began to relax, and she tilted her head back, letting the water soak into her hair.

Already, Nessa felt like a completely new person.

She pulled her legs up, feet leaving the bottom of the pool, and allowed herself to just drift in the water, letting it gently pull her this way and that, the slow current tugging her around in a gentle circle as the pool was filled and emptied in equal measure. Whatever magic Orm had spun, the temperature remained the same, even with the continuous flow of fresh water. Nessa briefly wondered how long it would last for, then made her way over to the soap.

Soon clusters of bubbles shimmered iridescently in the firelight as Nessa scrubbed herself with relish, rubbing at the stubborn grime until it either came off or was revealed as bands of dark bruises. Every time soap came into contact with a cut or a graze, it would sting violently, but seeing as most of her was covered in some form of wound, she swiftly got used to the hum of pain. Nessa didn't really have much of a choice, not if she wanted to be clean.

She wanted to be clean.

So she persevered.

In the end, with her skin free of dirt, Nessa was able to see the true extent of her ordeal.

Around each wrist and ankle was a thick band of raw flesh, a sickening collection of fresh wounds mixed with half-healed scabs and pink scar tissue. Nessa washed them carefully, trying not to open any of the lesions, wondering bleakly as she did so of what had caused such injuries. It was as if she had been chained hand and foot, struggling endlessly to get free. *Was that what had happened?* If so, Nessa couldn't help but feel that maybe it was a small kindness that she couldn't remember.

Nessa's attention drifted to the rest of her body, fingers gently skimming over the bloody grazes on her knees. They were new, acquired during her hectic race through the forest last night. Her palms had similar abrasions, although they were smaller and not quite as deep. Her feet, legs and arms were crisscrossed with an unfathomable number of scratches. These too had been collected during the night. Nessa faintly recalled thorns and spiky undergrowth snagging on her clothing, ripping and slicing.

Between the cuts were a handful of forming bruises, a beautiful vivid blue that was in stark contrast to the bruises that covered the rest of her in large swathes. These were older, a deep purple and tender to the touch. Nessa thought that they were perhaps a couple of days old. She was mystified as to what might have caused them.

Nessa searched her mind, her memories, for how she had got them, but came upon a void of darkness. There wasn't so much as a hint of a time before the forest.

Despite the heated water, Nessa shivered. *What had happened to me? What had been done to me? Most importantly, why can't I remember anything?*

Mulling over those dark thoughts, Nessa rubbed soapy bubbles into her hair, massaging her scalp, trying to work the worst of the knots from her tresses. Foreseeing a fair bit of work ahead of her, she moved over to the side of the pool and leaned back against the rocky ledge, resting in a small fork in the waterfall, water cascading down on either side of her.

It was shallower there, and Nessa was able to sit on the pool's floor, the water reaching almost to her shoulders. She pulled her knees to her chest and reached for the comb that Orm had left on top of her change of clothes. It was made from metal, pewter being her guess, and had fine detailing on the front and back. Her thumb caressed the shapes of antlers and runes meditatively for a second. Then she began to run the comb through her hair, slowly loosening the knots and snags, slowly transforming herself from a wild thing back into a girl.

Steam drifted over the pool's surface, curling tendrils that seemed to hold an ethereal quality. They defused the firelight, softening it, making the flames appear as delicate floating orbs. Everything was so dreamy...so calming... Magic had been used to heat the water, and Nessa couldn't help but wonder if Orm had added some healing qualities to it as well. Whilst the bruises and cuts remained unchanged, the aches and pains gradually faded. With the absence of those discomforts, Nessa found herself at peace, her muscles relaxed, the inner turmoil forgotten.

She sank deeper into the water, only keeping the top half of her head above the surface. Her hair drifted around her shoulders in a dark cloud.

*Oh*, Nessa thought, *this is perfection.*

She allowed her eyes to drift shut.

There was a splash.

Nessa's eyes snapped open.

Everything seemed as it should.

The little flames danced happily away, undisturbed, and the forest was calm, the trees whispering quietly, sleepily.

Then, on the other side of the pool, Nessa spied something a little strange. The water rippled, a ring of small waves spreading outwards as if someone had thrown in a stone. Nessa looked around, expecting Hunter or Orm to be standing nearby, about to tell her that she was taking too long. No one was there, though. Nessa turned back and stared at the wavelets, peering at the spot they originated from.

As Nessa watched, an object moved in the water, gliding beneath the surface for a second. It drew closer. Closer. Then a little humanoid creature cautiously revealed itself.

Its head breached the water only a few feet away from Nessa, just out of reach. Small and delicate, all graceful limbs and alien features, it couldn't have been more than ten inches in height, no bigger than a child's doll. Its skin was a pale green and its hair was a deep emerald, drifting around its form like dark silk. The little creature was as beautiful as it was strange.

They stared at each other, neither seeming to know what to do.

"Hello," Nessa said gently, voice barely above a whisper, fearful of scaring it away.

The creature blinked.

"Do you understand me?"

Its head cocked to the side, its overly large eyes, the colour of peridot, running over Nessa's face. For the briefest of moments, Nessa felt a flicker of a memory, a ghost of one. She closed her eyes as if she would be able to see it against her eyelids, but it was gone before it had a chance to show itself.

A wave of disappointment, of loss, crashed over her.

Nessa fought against the prickling of tears and focused on the little creature. Who, she saw, was slowly inching closer. Nessa eyed it with a touch of suspicion.

"Have we met before?" she asked. "Do I know you?"

It shook its head.

"But…"

The creature paddled closer, tiny webbed hands working at the water, long hair flowing behind it in a cloud.

It slowly dawned on her. "I haven't met *you* before," Nessa murmured thoughtfully, "but I've met one of your kin, haven't I?"

The creature gave a little nod.

Nessa couldn't help but smile. "I almost remember, but it's like something's keeping the memories at bay. Every time I try to unlock them, I seem to hit a wall of solid darkness."

A shrug of a small, green shoulder.

"Will I ever get them back?" Nessa wondered. "My memories?"

It nodded

Hope flared to life. "Really?"

It gave another nod.

"How?"

The little creature came to a stop just in front of Nessa and raised a hand. A charge filled the air, static and heavy. Magic was being drawn upon, ancient and wild. Nessa braced herself, half-expecting mystic lightning to shoot down from the clear sky and strike her.

The magic strengthened.

An angry caw sounded out, loud and jarring. Nessa jerked back, the rocky ledge digging into her spine. The little creature's head snapped to the side, its eyes growing frantic and wide. Nessa followed its gaze and a shiver of unease crawled over her skin.

There, sitting on a nearby branch, was the blue-eyed raven.

It had appeared suddenly and silently, as if conjured from nothing, and watched Nessa keenly. It cawed again, with its wings beating at the air in a threatening manner. Nessa flinched and the little creature emitted a sound of distress. In the blink of an eye, it vanished, diving beneath the water. Nessa was left to face the raven alone. She sank lower into the water, never taking her gaze off the bird, hoping that it wouldn't attack her again.

The raven's blue eyes locked with hers, conveying a wordless message that Nessa was unable to decipher. *Could it be a warning? A threat? A promise?* Then, with one last *caw*, it simply flew away, shooting through the trees as a dark shadow until it disappeared from sight.

Nessa let out a shaky breath and abruptly decided that bath time was over.

She was quick to dress, hardly taking the time to dry herself off, and found that Hunter's clothing was almost comically too big. The cream-coloured shirt reached almost to her knees, the sleeves hanging past her fingertips, and the brown trous were far too long, forcing her to hastily roll them up to avoid tripping over.

Nessa scooped up her discarded clothing and Orm's comb, then hurried into the trees, heading back to the campsite. The raven had scared away the sense of security, and once again everything seemed sinister. The woods filled with menacing shapes and eerie whispers. The path was fairly easy for her to follow. The way appeared often traversed by Hunter and Orm, used as a route to the river for collecting water and bathing—hopefully not at the same time—and because of this, the fallen leaves had been kicked out of the way to reveal the earthen floor.

Voices from the campsite could be heard before it

came into sight, and Nessa breathed a sigh of relief, glad to be back in the safety of Hunter and Orm's company. Just as the tents came into sight, her name was uttered. Nessa paused. The voice was unknown to her. It wasn't Hunter or Orm.

The wind moaned softly and the trees chattered quietly, and Nessa ducked behind a wide trunk before she was spotted. Their discussion was hushed, their voices faint. Once or twice Nessa heard her name floating on the breeze. They were talking about her. She strained to hear what they were saying, curious and a little bit perplexed. The tone was one of disagreement.

*Were they arguing about me?*

"Something isn't right," Hunter insisted.

"I know," Orm said. "I've had three of these joints now and I'm barely feeling a thing."

"I thought the whole point of smoking those was to not feel anything."

Orm huffed. "Usually yes. But I mean that I'm not feeling any effects from them. They're not working."

"Oh no," Hunter's voice oozed with fake sincerity. "Whatever are we to do?"

"Well—"

"Enough, you fools," someone hissed, cutting off Orm's response. It was the voice that had made Nessa pause. "We need to decide what we're going to do with the girl."

"What do you mean?" Hunter asked, sounding uncertain.

"We need to decide what we're going to tell her. Are we to tell her the truth or do what I suggested?"

Hunter snorted. "The truth, obviously."

"Are you sure?"

"Yes."

"Think about it, Chaos," Orm spoke up. "What if her memories come back? What if the memory loss is just caused by trauma and is temporary?"

"Don't talk down to me, boy!" Chaos snapped. "And stop looking for false hope. I taught you better than that. Someone has tampered with her mind. Her memories have been locked away. They will never return. Heed my advice and save the girl a lot of unnecessary pain."

"You mean lie to her?" Hunter growled.

"No, I mean to simply give her a different version of the truth. She has a chance to start again. To have a fresh start. You would be cruel to throw away the opportunity of saving your friend from all the confusion and fear she's carried for so long. Do not be stubborn and blind with this decision. For this is your decision to make, human, seeing as you have known her the longest."

Hunter grumbled something under his breath, too low for Nessa to hear. There was the sound of retreating footsteps, then the rustle of canvas rubbing quietly against canvas. Nessa guessed that someone had just entered a tent and closed the door flap behind them.

There was a heartbeat of loaded silence.

"Hunter—" Orm began.

"No, this doesn't sit right with me. None of this is right. And what he says is most definitely not right."

"Maybe he's onto something—"

"You can't be serious?" Hunter spat.

"We'd be fools to not at least consider what Chaos suggested."

Hunter grunted.

"I can't help but think that maybe it would be kinder for her to start anew…"

Nessa couldn't bear to listen anymore, fearful of what she might hear next. She stepped out from behind the tree, making sure she trod on a few twigs as she did so, and continued along the path.

༄ ✦ ༄

If Hunter and Orm were troubled about what they'd just been discussing, they were swift to cover it up, donning relaxed smiles when Nessa entered the campsite. She hastened to join them by the campfire, pretending that she hadn't been eavesdropping, trying to conceal her troubled thoughts by averting her eyes.

"Hey," Orm said brightly. "Look at you, all cleaned up and whatnot."

Nessa plastered what she hoped was a sincere looking smile on her face as she sat down between them, sitting as close to the fire as she dared, needing it to warm her bare feet and dry her wet hair. It was making her shirt stick uncomfortably to her back.

"And feeling like a completely new person," she muttered. "Just as you promised."

"I'm glad to hear it."

"We have to get you some clothing of your own," Hunter said, his eyes twinkling as they ran over her. "You're practically swimming in those."

"Mm," Nessa held up her old clothing, "I suppose so, seeing as these aren't particularly salvageable."

"I doubt they were worth salvaging in any condition," Orm mused, plucking them out of her hands and throwing them onto the campfire. They were engulfed in flames almost instantly. Nessa gazed at Orm, wondering if he was mad. He arched a brow and raised an odd, flaky cigar to his lips, the tip flaring green as he inhaled.

"Boring colours," he explained. "You deserve something a lot nicer."

"If you say so."

"A rich colour, perhaps. Maybe red or purple?"

"Purple sounds nice."

"The nearest village is small," Hunter warned. "I doubt they'll have anything particularly fancy. We're also poor, so the budget is kind of limiting."

Orm waved a hand. "Technicalities."

"You could send Chaos to a larger town," Hunter suggested, his eyes bright. "He could do something useful for once, and we could have a break from his charming company."

Orm rolled his eyes. "You mean *you* could do with a break from him."

"He keeps threatening to kill me."

"He does not."

Hunter looked at Nessa and said, "He threatened to kill me not even ten minutes ago."

"That was only because you were sat on his stool stump," Orm interjected. "What else was he meant to do?"

"Ask me politely to move?"

"As if that would have worked."

"It might have."

Orm snorted.

As they bickered, Nessa peered at the third tent, the one belonging to Chaos. She wondered why he kept to himself so much. It was like he was trying to avoid her. It seemed such a silly thought, though, and Nessa flung it aside as soon as it popped into her head. *What possible reason would he have to hide from me?* Anyway, it wasn't like she particularly wanted to meet him just yet, Nessa told herself, not after what she had heard him say. She needed time to digest his words, their possible implications. At least, Nessa thought, she could trust Hunter. He had been on her side, arguing against Chaos' suggestion of telling her a false truth...

"Anyway," Orm said, picking up the overcoat that she'd awoken with last night. "This is good quality. We could sell it and use the money to get Nessa something nice to wear."

"What I have on is fine," Nessa said softly. "There's really no need if you don't have much money for new clothing."

Orm didn't seem to hear her as his fingers caressed the overcoat, feeling the texture of the soft velvet and the fine, silver trim. "This is really good quality," he mused. His eyebrows pulled together as he looked at Nessa, his whiskey-coloured eyes filled with careful contemplation. "How did you come by this?"

Nessa grew uncomfortable under both his and Hunter's gaze, feeling like she may have done something wrong. "I woke up with it. It had been placed over me. I was cold, so I put it on."

"And you don't remember who gave it to you?"

Nessa shook her head. "No."

"You don't remember anything before waking up in the forest?"

"I've told you all of this," Hunter interrupted, cutting in before Nessa could form a response.

Orm glared at him. "Well, *I* want *her* to tell *me* what happened, not what you've assumed. I need to know. We need to know." He turned to Nessa, beseeching. "Please, tell us everything you can. Right down to the smallest of details."

Nessa peered at Hunter, seeing no reason why she shouldn't tell them what she remembered. After all, there was little for her to recount. Orm asked for the details, so she gave them, digging up even the smallest of things. She told him how, at first, the forest had been so old and unnatural, and that it had felt as if the trees had been watching her, waiting for something. Nessa shivered at the memory, feeling like she was there all over again, lost and alone, not knowing who she was and why it seemed as if the trees were whispering to her.

She fiddled with her sleeve, pulling at a loose thread, twining it around her finger with nervous energy, finding herself unable to continue with her tale. The words hid from her.

Orm shifted, uneasy, and took a long drag on his cigar. "And then, by chance, you ran into Hunter?"

Even as doubts began to creep up on her, Nessa swallowed and nodded. *Was it by chance?* Because the more she thought about it, the more it started to feel as if the raven had forced her towards Hunter. Otherwise, she might have ended up going in a completely different direction.

Nessa looked up at Hunter, who had been painfully quiet. He was biting his lip, his gaze darkening as he stared down at her hands. Nessa realised that as she'd been fiddling with her sleeve, it had slid back to reveal the band of scarring and half-healed contusions around her wrist.

Nessa went to shove the sleeve back down, hiding it from sight, but Hunter took her hand in his, stopping her from doing so. His throat worked as he struggled to keep his emotions in check, and his other hand came to hover over Nessa's wrist as if he was going to brush his fingers over the wounds, like he didn't quite believe they were real.

"These must hurt," Hunter murmured, his eyes hard, jaw clenched.

"Not really," Nessa whispered, watching his fingers ghost over her wrist. "I think I've grown used to the pain."

"And you don't remember how you got them?"

"No, I remember nothing." She pulled her hand from his and tugged down her sleeve, concealing the wounds. "But looking at them...I'm almost glad that I don't remember what happened."

Hunter watched her for a heartbeat, the tension draining from his hunched shoulders. He then shared a loaded glace with Orm.

Sagging just a little, with weariness beginning to weigh him down, Hunter sighed. "Six months ago," he said quietly, "you and I had just arrived at The Hidden City. We were paying Orm a visit. Then it came under attack. Margan and Shadow, along with their dragons, razed the city. In the mayhem, you were separated from us, and one of them—we're not sure who—took you. We searched everywhere for you, but without any success. They had hidden you away somewhere we couldn't find."

"But why?" Nessa asked, bewildered. "Why did they take me?"

Orm put a large hand on Nessa's shoulder, warm and steadying. "Hunter's got a bit ahead of himself. Let's start from the beginning, shall we?"

# Chapter 6

"We do not know your origins," Orm murmured, his voice dropping mesmerisingly low. "But we do know that there's more to you than meets the eye. This, we believe, is one of the reasons why Margan and Shadow targeted you."

Nessa sat quietly with wide eyes, clinging to each and every word.

"You see, you're like me. A person born of magic. Only instead of being a half-blood such as me, you're a pure-blood. Now, I'll tell you the truth in this matter, because you deserve that, but we're not entirely sure what you are, just that you are an Old Blood. Potentially a very powerful one."

Nessa frowned, "An Old Blood?"

"They are ancient beings, powerful beings. Some of the Old Blood's descendants inherited their gifts, although often weaker and diluted by generations of interbreeding with humans. What people refer to as 'magic users', such as witches, are in fact either halflings or have an ancestor who is an Old Blood. There are many types of Old Blood, different species, if you will. Water sprites and nymphs to name a few, for example. Some Old Bloods look more animal than human, while others look more human than animal. However, there is usually something that sets them apart from the mundane varieties. This, though, can often be hidden with a glamour or something of the kind. You, thankfully, look very human." Orm tried for a smile. "Imagine our surprise when we found out that you were a pure Old Blood and not a halfling like me." Orm's smile became uncertain. "Are you following me?"

Nessa blinked. "I think so? Maybe. You're telling me that, while I look human, I'm actually an Old Blood, exact species currently unknown. This, for some reason, makes me special…rare…?"

Orm nodded. "Indeedy. Now, do you want to know why being an Old Blood is so rare?"

"I guess so?"

"Because, Nessa, my dear girl, they were hunted to near extinction long ago. Any Old Bloods that have survived this long have the good sense to keep themselves well hidden. Else they'll meet their kindred's fate. None of them would have let one of their own run around the kingdoms, ignorant of their heritage and in such danger. Not when their numbers are so low."

"Was that what I was doing? Running around the kingdoms?"

"Well, *running* might not be the correct word. For simplicity's sake, though, we'll just go with that. Anyway, a couple of years ago, your path crossed with

Hunter's. The two of you became friends," Orm winked at her, "of a sort."

Nessa's lips parted in astonishment and she looked up at Hunter questioningly. He didn't notice, too busy glaring at Orm, his expression growing dark.

"Anyway," Orm continued, "a few adventures later, you and Hunter end up in Ironguard. Which, naturally, Margan is master over, what with it being the main seat of power for House Īren and him being House Īren's Dragon Rider. You, unfortunately, gained his attention. He figured out what you are. He realised that you are an Old Blood. We don't know what his motives were, but we assume that he wished to use you—your power—for his own gain. You and Hunter, crafty as you are, managed to escape from Margan. You both came to me seeking answers and such, which is how Chaos got involved.

"Being an Old Blood himself, I thought he might be able to shed some light onto the matter. Before he could, the city came under attack from Margan and Shadow. We fled, but in the process, you became separated from us. They captured you, hiding you away from us. No matter how hard we searched, we could not find you, not until Chaos heard a whisper of your name on the wind and brought us here."

Nessa didn't know what to make of Orm's tale, what to think or what to feel. "So..." she said slowly. "So, what you're saying is that I'm an Old Blood, a creature belonging to a long lineage of magical beings? Because of this, this Margan fellow kidnapped me and...and..." Nessa struggled to find the words, her thoughts in turmoil. "I don't understand. Even if I am an Old Blood, which I struggle to believe, what does he want with me?"

"I don't know, Nessa," Orm sighed. "We don't know. He's unpredictable. Maybe he hoped to turn you to his side, use your powers to aid him in a secret plan or something. Maybe he planned on making a gift of you to King Kaenar, trying to get into his good graces, if the king has any. We can only speculate on the reasons behind Margan's actions. All we know for certain is that he demolished an entire city to get to you before the king discovered your existence."

"He destroyed an entire city to get me?"

Orm nodded gravely.

Nessa found it difficult to grasp that someone could do such a monstrous act—that they *would* do it—just to get to her. "But what powers do I have for him to want me so badly?"

"We don't know. We never had a chance to find out before they took you."

Nessa turned to Hunter. "But if we've known each other for years, surely you must know something?"

"I'm sorry," Hunter said, gazing down at his feet, his voice barely above a murmur. "I thought you were completely human until Margan revealed otherwise."

"Well," Nessa grimaced, "I don't suppose Margan would be kind enough to answer some of my questions if we were to meet him, would he?"

"No, I don't think he would," Hunter grumbled, his expression becoming ever darker as he stared downwards, not looking at either Nessa or Orm.

"Are we likely to see him again?" Nessa was forced to ask as the cold hand of dread settled upon her. "Will he come for me?"

Both of them were slow to answer, as if the notion had only just occurred to them.

"I'd imagine so," Orm said grimly. "In fact, I'd say that it's quite certain we haven't seen the last of Margan. He'll be desperate to get to you before King Kaenar finds out about his involvement."

"What would happen if the king was to find out about me?"

"Nothing particularly good."

"Oh?"

"Best case scenario: death."

*"Death?"* Nessa shrieked. "Death is the best thing that could come from the king finding out about me?"

Orm put it bluntly. "Yep."

"Lovely." Nessa's sense of dread and alarm morphed into pure fear. Her heart did a strange dance in her chest. "Best to not get caught by either of them, then."

Hunter leaned over and captured her trembling hands in his. "Don't worry, Nessa. We'll keep you safe. They'll never find you unless you want to be found."

Nessa's laugh was a forced one. "And why would I ever want them to find me?"

"Because, one day, you might be powerful enough to take them down."

"Take them down?"

"He means to kill them," Orm summarised simply.

Nessa felt like she could have been knocked over with a feather. She looked at them, wondering if they were joking. They appeared to be perfectly serious.

"But—I—Why?"

Orm shrugged. "Because you might be the only one who could."

"The only one?"

"King Kaenar is more powerful than you could ever imagine. He is cruel and a tyrant. We suffer under his rule, just as our forebearers had. For near on five hundred years, the king has been hunting the Old Bloods. They—we—are now approaching extinction. He will burn entire cities to the ground if he hears so much as a whisper of discontent, will kill thousands of innocents on nothing more than a whim. You and you alone might be able to free us from his dark hold. You might be able to save us."

"If the king's able to kill Old Bloods and destroy entire cities, then what makes you think I'd stand a chance against him?"

"Because you are something more than just an Old Blood," Orm said with something akin to reverence, slipping one of her hands out from Hunter's hold. He pushed up her sleeve to reveal the strange mark of a dragon's silhouette. "This here bears testament to what you are and what you could become."

"And what exactly," Nessa asked nervously, "is that?"

☼✦☾

The air sang, vibrating in a slow beat, almost humming. Nessa looked upwards, trying to identify what was causing such an odd sound. Through the tree branches, some with leaves and most without, all she could see was the blue of the sky and the watchful peaks of the nearby mountains.

Nessa, alongside Hunter and Orm, stood near the odd patch of flattened ground at the edge of the campsite, with the broken hole in the tree canopy above them. Their gazes too, were cast up, although theirs were free from the bewilderment that filled Nessa's. She wondered why they couldn't simply tell her what was happening, what the mark around her forearm and hand meant and why it had started tingling. Nessa didn't understand why they insisted on theatrics instead.

The deep thrum in the air grew, beginning to sound rather like the slow, methodical beat of a mighty creature in flight, with its strong wings working at the air in an unhurried pace. Nessa turned to Hunter and Orm, beginning to feel a bit panicked, and saw that they were relaxed, like this was a usual occurrence for them. Nessa's eyes went to the flattened ground, starting to think that maybe it was.

A peculiar sensation rolled through Nessa like a lulling wave, calm and soothing. Her eyelids fluttered closed and her unease faded away. Warmth bloomed in her chest and her marked hand itched fiercely. It was then that she realised something: she had felt this before. Instantly, Nessa pushed her mind outwards, quickly encountering the foreign mind that was carefully shielded behind amethyst walls. This time, instead of being startled, fleeing from Nessa, it was more welcoming of the connection, hesitantly embracing it.

Nessa sensed it was close, very close, and looked to the direction it was approaching from. Eagerly, she waited, watching for it. Her heart felt like it was about to burst from anticipation.

A creature glided over the campsite, blocking out the sun for a spellbinding moment, throwing the forest floor into shadow.

Its scales glittered and gleamed in the light, sparkling like the finest purple gemstones, and its huge membranous wings glowed almost black as the sun shone through them.

The creature hovered for a second, its wings buffeting the air, stirring up gusts of wind that swirled around the campsite like a tornado, kicking up loose leaves and bending tree limbs. It then swooped, diving through the hole in the tree canopy and landing with a mighty thump, flattening the ground just a little bit more.

Pushing back the damp hair that had blown across her face, Nessa stared.

A dragon stood before her.

Snapping its wings closed, folding them tight against its body, the dragon held itself still as Nessa's gaze ran over it, her wide eyes taking in every single detail: its delicate build, all graceful limbs and lean muscle, its shoulder coming to stand level with the top of Nessa's head; its arching neck and angular face, with a sharp jawline and elongated snout; and the petite spikes that ran down its spine, from the base of its head to the tip of its tail, pure white and shimmering like pearls.

Nessa stumbled forwards, and the dragon's nostrils flared, breathing in her scent, learning her in a primal way.

Snaking out its neck, the dragon lowered its head until they could see each other eye to slitted eye, knowing that the missing piece of their souls had been found. All sense of caution was thrown to the wind and they became one, their minds joining together, the dragon's amethyst shield falling away, crumbling to dust.

*Oh, my little Rider,* an otherworldly voice spoke in Nessa's head, *how I've longed for you to be by my side.*

Nessa raised her hand, the one bearing the mark representing their tie to one another, and pressed it against the dragon's nose.

"Aoife," Nessa whispered.

For the first time since waking up in the forest, alone and lost, her memories gone, did she finally feel a semblance of peace settle over her. After six months of being separated, dragon and Rider were finally together. They were complete.

# Chapter 7

The stars glittered and gleamed like diamonds, a hundred thousand watchful eyes that turned their gazes downwards to peer at Nessa and Aoife as they sat together, learning everything they could about one another. Admittedly, it was rather one-sided, taking into account that Nessa couldn't remember anything from before last night.

Aoife didn't seem to mind, though, and shared some of her memories with Nessa, offering her a glimpse into the life she'd been trying to recall. Inside the dragon's mind, Nessa experienced Aoife's first flight. She felt Aoife's exhilaration as her own, seeing the earth from a thousand feet above it, a patchwork quilt of fields and forests, towns and mountains. She witnessed herds of wild horses running through meadows, their manes flowing out behind them, and saw the slow change of seasons, the patterns of migrating birds.

Flowing alongside these visions were memories of

Hunter and Orm. Aoife delighted in showing Nessa the sparring sessions between them, which usually started in a serious manner only to swiftly descend into a rowdy wrestling match filled with underhanded moves and insults. They were Aoife's more light-hearted memories, and brought a smile to Nessa's face. Even so, she could sense the undercurrents of sorrow and incompleteness that had been Aoife's constant companion.

*Although I had Hunter and Orm, Chaos too, our separation was almost unbearable,* Aoife said softly, curling her long tail protectively around herself, keeping Nessa tucked up against her scaled side. *There is no substitute for the loss of a Rider. Nothing and no one can fill that void.*

"I'm sorry to have caused you so much pain," Nessa murmured.

*It was not of your choosing, my little Rider. I blame you not. You are with me now. That is all I care about.*

"I'm never leaving you again."

*As if I would ever give you the chance,* Aoife chuckled. *With our bond, I'll be able to sense where you are at all times. If you're ever in danger, I'll swoop in and whisk you away.*

Nessa had to admit that the idea of being protected by a dragon was a rather pleasant one. However, she couldn't help but ask, "Then how come you couldn't before?"

Aoife exhaled. *You were hidden from me. Margan and Shadow are both experienced Dragon Riders and have had much time to learn magic. They must have shielded you behind spells and wards. Through the bond, I could sense that you were alive, but not much more than that. I could not find you or tell how you were faring. It was as if a wall of darkness was between us.*

"So, being a Dragon Rider gives the Rider the ability

to use magic?"

*Indeed it does, amongst other things.* Aoife winked. *Just one of the perks of being bonded with a dragon.*

"Does that mean I'll be able to use magic as well?"

*All in time, my little Rider. Although, even without me, you'd still be able to use it.*

"Because I'm an Old Blood?"

*Yes.*

"Do you know what kind I am?"

Aoife ruffled her wings, settling them into a more comfortable position. *I do not, my little Rider. But even amongst the Old Bloods, you are something special. I am sure of that.*

"Hmm." Nessa sighed and shifted, turning her head to rest a cheek against Aoife's shoulder, the scales were hard and surprisingly warm against her skin. She tapped a fingernail against one, amazed by its depth of colour. Even in the semi-darkness of the gathering night, the campsite lit only by the stars and the campfire, Aoife was a beacon of splendour, her scales ablaze with an inner glow.

As Aoife continued to talk, telling her not to worry and other inconsequential things like that, Nessa's gaze strayed to where Orm and Hunter sat on their makeshift stools, the firelight caressing their faces. They were trying to decide what should happen next, their voices a low murmur as they debated where they should go, where the safest place was.

Nessa could only hear bits and pieces of their conversation, and she couldn't help her mind going back to the last time they'd had a hushed discussion. She had to wonder. Which story they had decided to tell her? Had they told her the truth about her past, her abduction? Or had they sowed the seeds of a deception? How would she know?

Aoife could sense Nessa's growing discontent and looked down at her. *You can trust them, my little Rider. They only want what's best for you.*

"Do you?" Nessa turned to Aoife. "Trust them, I mean?"

*With my life.*

Nessa pushed aside her misgivings and forced out a small smile. "They did look after you, so I guess I owe them for that at the very least."

*You trusted them before, surely that stands for something?*

"I suppose it should."

Aoife touched the tip of her snout against Nessa's forehead, a dragon's version of a kiss. *Give them a chance, my little Rider. They care about you more than you know.*

"Because I might be powerful enough to kill the king one day?"

*Because they're your friends.*

"Mmm."

*Besides, if you want to run around killing kings, then you had better eat your dinner. Right now, a leaf could knock you over.*

"Ha." Nessa grinned. "If Orm's cooking scrambled eggs for dinner, then I'll happily let a leaf best me."

*Fear not,* Aoife said, sniffing at the air delicately. *That isn't on the menu tonight. Smells like pheasant to me.*

"Pheasant?"

*Yes. Chaos snuck away a while ago and seems to have been successful in his hunt.*

"Oh. Well, pheasant sounds a lot nicer than the monstrosity Orm likes to call scrambled eggs."

Aoife laughed, a rough chuffing sound, and jerked her

head. *Here he comes. And look, I think he's brought you some boots.*

Nessa peered in the direction that Aoife had nodded to, and at first, saw nothing but the gloom of the forest. Then, she spied a shadow of movement from between the tree trunks, and a shape detached itself from the darkness, entering the campsite. Nessa blinked several times, wondering if her mind was playing tricks on her. It appeared that Chaos had *wings*.

Large and bat-like, with frightfully sharp talons peeping above his shoulders, they were a scary sight to behold, just as he himself was. Chaos was tall, almost as tall as Orm, and his black hair fell as straight as a pin to his waist. He wore a leather surcoat that came to just below his knees and heavy looking boots, thick-soled with metal caps over the toes. As he neared, Nessa saw that in one hand he held a brace of pheasants, already plucked and gutted, and in the other, he carried a pair of old boots.

Chaos flung the pheasants onto Hunter's lap. "You may cook these," he said, his frigid tone leaving no room for argument.

"Considering you've got them all ready," Hunter murmured, "I'm more than happy to."

"I am not the one who prepared them."

Hunter frowned. "Who did then?"

"One of the somebodies these used to belong to." Chaos held up the pair of boots.

"Ah," Orm murmured. "Stealing, I see."

"I did not steal them," Chaos sneered. "They were given to me when I asked for them."

"With great haste too, I imagine," Hunter said with a smirk.

Chaos inclined his head. "And quite a lot of screaming."

Nessa couldn't tear her wide-eyed stare away from Chaos. *Aoife?* Nessa said, hesitantly planting her words directly into Aoife's mind, just as Aoife does when she speaks. *Chaos is an Old Blood, isn't he?"*

*Indeed he is.*

*Does that mean I'll grow wings? Because looking at his, I'd prefer to go without.*

Aoife laughed quietly. *Fear not, my funny, little Rider. You are wingless.*

Nessa breathed a sigh of relief.

Chaos' head snapped to the side, only just noticing that Nessa was there. Eyes the colour of glacial ice ran over her and Aoife. Nessa barely stifled a gasp of horror. Around them was a thick ring of white scars, a ghastly mockery of a mask. They were deep and jagged. It looked like something had tried to claw Chaos' eyes out.

*Don't worry*, Aoife said calmly. *He is no threat. I've already warned him that if he's mean to you, I'll eat him.*

*Oddly enough, that really isn't a comfort right now.* Nessa could feel the energy coming off him in waves, almost dizzying in strength.

Nessa forced herself to stand when she realised that Chaos was making his way over to her, and rested a hand on Aoife's shoulder, reminding herself that she wasn't alone anymore.

"Finally, you have been found," Chaos said in way of greeting. He came to a stop an arm's length away from her. Nessa couldn't quite tell if he was happy or irritated about that. His lips were a thin line and his jaw hard. "Seeing as you have no clothing of your own, I took the liberty of collecting these for you." He held out the boots.

"Although, judging by the state of your feet, my efforts have come a little too late to be of much use."

Peering down at her bare feet, which were bruised and cut much like the rest of her, Nessa gladly took his offering. "Well, I suppose something's better than nothing, right?"

Giving what Nessa assumed was his best attempt at a smile, Chaos turned around and stalked over to his tent, swiftly disappearing inside.

Nessa looked at Aoife, stunned by his abrupt departure. "That wasn't too bad."

*No?*

"I feel perfectly at ease with him now."

*Oh, really?*

"Nope. I'm lying. He's scary."

*You'll get used to him, given time.*

"I hope not," Nessa mumbled. If she ever felt at ease with someone, *something* like Chaos, it would be a clear sign of madness. She gave the boots a quick inspection, seeing that they were well worn, the toes scuffed and the laces close to snapping in places, then stepped over Aoife's tail and placed them by her tent. She made her way over to the campfire, deciding that it was time to join Hunter and Orm, but also because she felt Aoife's encouragement silently urging her, through their bond, to spend more time reacquainting with the others. When she looked over her shoulder, Nessa saw that Aoife had curled up into a ball, her head tucked neatly under a wing, her tail coiled tightly around her body.

Nessa sat cross-legged between Hunter and Orm, her long overcoat pooling around her like a blanket. When she stood, the hem reached almost to her ankles. The pheasants, she saw with pleasure, were already positioned over the fire, skewered on a metal spit. Her stomach clenched in anticipation, eager for the meal.

"Fancy that," Hunter said to no one in particular. "Chaos does know how to be civil. Although I must admit, he seems to be a little out of practice."

"It's the trying that counts," Orm said.

Nessa smirked.

"Maybe he should try a little harder," Hunter suggested. "And more often. He's always welcome to practice with me."

"He's scary when he's being polite," Nessa said with a wry grin. "I dread to think what he's like when he's angry."

*"Terrifying,"* Hunter and Orm said in perfect harmony.

"I bet."

Hunter reached out and turned the spit, letting the pheasants cook evenly. "Now you can see why I don't enjoy his death threats very much."

"You must have nerves of steel."

"Or a rock in his head instead of brains," Orm quipped.

"How dare you say that," Hunter said. "Each and every one of his threats was completely unprovoked and unnecessary."

Orm cocked an eyebrow. "Oh really?"

"Yes."

"So you never go out of your way to wind him up?"

"Never."

"You haven't jumped at every opportunity to make fun of him?"

"Of course not."

Orm snorted and turned to Nessa, peering down at

her with amusement. "He gets a weird thrill in angering Chaos, and endeavours to irritate him on a near-daily basis until there's a reaction."

"Lies," Hunter mock-whispered to her. "He tells you lies. I'm nothing but polite to Chaos. It is he who takes offence at the slightest thing."

Nessa laughed, not quite sure what to make of either of them, yet somehow feeling at home with them, their easy banter the perfect balm for her near-constant jitters of unease. "So, while I was with Aoife, did you manage to decide what we're doing next?"

Hunter rested his elbows on his knees, watching the pheasant's browning meat with hungry eyes, firelight showing him in warm hues. "It's best not to linger here any longer than necessary, especially when we don't know who might be nearby. Margan or Shadow could discover that you've escaped at any time, if they haven't already. We'd be foolish to stay here."

"So we're going somewhere else?"

Hunter nodded.

"And our destination is?"

"We haven't decided yet."

"Excellent."

"We'll go to Ellor," Chaos declared, leaving the confines of his tent and coming to stand over them.

"Who's Ellor?" Nessa asked.

"Not who, but what," Chaos corrected sharply. "Ellor is a place, a city."

"Not just any damn city, though," Hunter said heatedly. "It's the bloody capital. Ellor is the last place we should go."

Chaos growled low in this throat and fixed his glacial eyes onto Hunter. "It is the best place for us."

"Yeah?" Hunter smirked. "Care to share the reasoning behind your wacky idea?"

Chaos looked just about ready to murder Hunter, and Nessa was starting to see where Orm was coming from. Hunter had the gift of annoyance, and he wasn't afraid to use it. He knew exactly how to get under Chaos' skin.

"What Hunter means to say," Orm interjected calmly, "is why should we go to the one place that naturally needs avoiding?"

Nessa was quizzical. "Why do we want to avoid the capital?"

"Because of the king," Chaos snapped. "Idiot girl."

From where she rested, Aoife growled a warning, lifting her head out from under her wing. Her gaze locked with Chaos' and something passed between them. Nessa guessed that only Chaos was privy to what Aoife had to say. He muttered under his breath and cuffed Hunter around the head.

"Off my stool, peon," Chaos ordered.

Although indignant, Hunter did as he was told, moving across from Nessa on the other side of the fire. "Peon?" he mouthed to Nessa, who shrugged with an amused smile. She watched Chaos settle himself down on the log stool from the corner of her eye, curiosity getting the better of her, noticing that the bottom tips of his wings brushed against the ground.

"King Kaenar resides in Ellor," Orm explained. "It's basically his home. He rarely leaves the palace. It's a dangerous place for us to go. We really should keep as far away from him as possible right now."

"So he doesn't learn of my existence and kill me," Nessa summarised.

"Correct."

"Then why do you want us to go there?" she asked Chaos.

"Because it is the last place anyone, Margan in particular, would expect you to go. You'd be hidden in plain sight. It is also the perfect strategic position. Over the last few weeks, the king has been summoning his Dragon Riders. Margan is one of them. Why King Kaenar might be doing this, I have yet to find out. If we were to go to Ellor, we would hear whispers from the king's inner circle and ascertain what he might be up to."

"Could he have learnt about Nessa?" Hunter asked, worried. "Might that be why he's calling the others back? To see if they know anything?"

"I believe the king may have sensed a change in the kingdoms, as there is when a powerful Old Blood is about to come of age," Chaos mused. "However, I do not think he is certain, as Nessa is still a way off from this happening. No, I think he only suspects the change has been caused by a young Old Blood, not Nessa specifically, and he definitely does not suspect that there is a Dragon Rider free from his control. I have a feeling that he is preparing himself in the event of confirmation; then he will send out his Riders to deal with it, as he's done in the past."

"So we're safe at the moment?"

Chaos shrugged. "As safe as we can be given our circumstances. From our travels, we have learnt that only Margan and Shadow know of Nessa and her legacy. I am sure that neither of them will tell the king unless absolutely necessary. For now, we can assume that the king only suspects the presence of a strong Old Blood, but that is it. Because of this, I feel that it would be wise to go to Ellor."

"And spy on the king?" Hunter's grin was wicked.

Chaos inclined his head. "In a fashion."

Orm looked troubled. "You say he's summoning his Riders? Who has he called back so far?"

"Six have arrived. Tolan of House Mægen, Aggnarr of House Đunor and Braelyn of House Blēoh were the first to arrive at Ellor three weeks ago. Cade of House Eodor and Kassian of House Hālig arrived a few days ago, and Margan of House Īren flew out yesterday. He must have arrived by now."

Orm was contemplative. "What about Shadow?"

Chaos shook his head. "He is hidden to me, but I do know that he has not been called back yet. It is only a matter of time, though."

"Far too many Dragon Riders in one place for my liking," Hunter grumbled.

"Now is the best time to go to Ellor," Chaos insisted gruffly. "While Nessa is still anonymous, we must make the most of it."

"Won't the other Dragon Riders be able to sense me?" Nessa asked. "You know, since the king seems to be able to, in a way."

"King Kaenar is old, powerful and cunning," Chaos said. "But there are limits to his knowledge. He may be able to sense that there is soon to be a powerful Old Blood, but that is probably the extent of it. He won't yet know who they are, what they are or where they are. Not yet, at least. At the moment, you are practically invisible to him."

"But that won't last for much longer," Orm added.

Nessa frowned. "Because of this 'coming of age' thing that keeps being mentioned?"

"When an Old Blood reaches the age of eighteen or

so," Orm said, "their power, which has slowly been building up since birth, surfaces. Basically, they 'come of age' when their power surfaces and they can use it fully."

"And I haven't 'come of age' yet?"

"Not yet."

"But I will soon?"

"We have a few months, by my guess," Chaos answered, "which is why we need to go to Ellor while we can. Otherwise, the king will easily learn of your presence, and we will have missed our only opportunity to find out what the king is doing."

"Well," Nessa murmured, "I suppose we should make the most of the limited time we have."

Hunter's eyebrows shot up, disappearing into the mop of messy curls that trailed over his forehead. "You actually want to go to the capital, to perhaps the most dangerous place for you to be? Where there isn't just one Dragon Rider there, but seven?"

"If Chaos thinks it's the safest place for us, then yes, I'm all for going to Ellor," Nessa argued. "You—we—might be able to learn something useful. And don't look so gutted, you looked excited a moment ago at the prospect of spying on the king."

"Indeed I did," Hunter admitted.

"What about you?" Nessa asked, gazing up at Orm. He sat leaning forwards, elbows propped on his knees, his hands held together in a thoughtful manner. At Nessa's enquiry, Orm's eyes darted amongst her, Chaos and Hunter.

"The idea does have many benefits," he admitted. "But it also has many risks."

"Every path we choose is filled with risks and rewards," Chaos said dismissively. "The benefits of going to Ellor now outweigh the risks. If you have any hope of Nessa defeating the king, then you have to learn as much as possible about his stronghold whilst you can."

"That's a valid point," Hunter said. "We do need to learn everything we can. It will be of use to us later on."

"I'm so glad you agree with me," Chaos said dryly. "I can now die happily with the knowledge that a *human* approves of my plan. My life goal is now complete."

Hunter glared at him. "You son of a bi—"

"So," Nessa turned to Orm, ignoring Hunter and Chaos' quarrelling, "are you in agreement with going to the capital?"

"I'd hate to get in the way of a unanimous vote," Orm said, raising his voice to be heard over the death threats that were being hurled across the campfire. "So I guess we'll be going to the city of Ellor."

# Chapter 8

Having come to some kind of tentative agreement over their course, Nessa and her companions were swift to settle down for the night, eager for a decent amount of sleep before they departed in the morning. With Chaos unable to locate Shadow, it was deemed too much of a risk to linger any longer. They wanted to leave before their camp was discovered. Nessa, doubtful she'd be able to make it any great distance, had voiced her worry. The others didn't seem too concerned, saying that covering even a couple of miles was better than nothing.

Burrowing deeper into her sleeping bag, Nessa pulled it tight around her shoulders. There was a chill in the air that not even the tent's thick canvas could keep out. After realising she had most of the camp's blankets, Nessa had given them back to Hunter, seeing as he didn't have a sleeping bag anymore. He'd taken them, but only after Nessa had insisted she'd be warm enough in the sleeping bag and in her loaned clothes. She may have been wrong. The cold air seemed determined to caress the back of Nessa's neck no matter what she did.

Sleep was elusive, and Nessa's mind drifted, restless and more than willing to dwell on the matter of the king.

Hunter, Orm and Chaos unanimously agreed with each other that King Kaenar was someone Nessa didn't want to cross paths with. But why? What kind of threat could she, a seventeen-year-old girl with no memories, pose against him? Her dragon was young and she herself was still months away from coming into her Old Blood powers. Did being an Old Blood really warrant a death sentence? Nessa had done nothing wrong. She had not broken any laws or hurt anyone. It was daunting to think that the most powerful man in the world would have her killed simply because of the blood that ran through her veins.

Nessa rolled onto her side, troubled.

The others said the king would kill her simply for existing, but would he really? For all she knew, she could march right up to him, and he'd welcome her with open arms. Did Nessa have any right to kill him over something he *might* do? It sat uneasily with her that she had to rely on other people's words, even if they were her friends.

Nessa wanted her memories back.

She needed them back.

Chaos seemed inclined to believe that they were gone for good, but the little creature from the river appeared to disagree. Was there a way for Nessa to regain her memories? Could she use magic or witchcraft or…or…sorcery?

Outside, the fire was burning low, ruddy light

brushing against the canvas of her tent. Nessa watched the dance of shadows for a time. Aoife was asleep, curled up in her nest of flattened earth, her thoughts slow and soothing against the edge of Nessa's mind. Naturally, Nessa assumed that the others would be asleep as well, so it came as a surprise when she spied movement.

Propping herself up on an elbow, Nessa observed their dark shape tiptoeing past her tent, heading out into the surrounding forest, moving as silently as a ghost. She waited for them to return, thinking that if it was Hunter or Orm, she might call out to them and spend a few minutes in their company. Perhaps they knew a trick or two to help quieten a noisy mind. As time passed, though, measured by the steady beat of Nessa's heart and the crackle of the fire, she grew concerned.

Concern soon gave way to suspicion.

Who was creeping around an eerie forest in the middle of the night?

Wide-eyed and with a great deal of caution, Nessa poked her head out of the tent. She saw nothing stirring in the gloom. The campsite was still and calm, bathed in muted darkness, the circle of firelight only just reaching to the tents. Nessa crawled forwards with as much stealth as possible, grabbing her overcoat as she did so, and stood. She wrapped the overcoat around her like a capelet, the velvet warm and heavy on her shoulders, staying off the cold. With her gaze darting all over the place, Nessa inched closer to the other tents.

The nearest one, which belonged to Hunter and Orm, appeared to be occupied. Twin snores could be faintly heard, and the bottom edge of the tent bulged outwards as someone was squished against it.

"If they're there," Nessa murmured, "then the creeper

is..." Her eyes landed on Chaos' tent.

Listening for the faintest sound of rustling leaves or footsteps, anything that might indicate that someone, namely Chaos, was approaching, Nessa made her way over to the tent. She used her foot to nudge the door flap aside, and when she saw no one in there, she reached down and pulled it back completely.

Chaos definitely wasn't there. His sleeping bag was in disarray and his bag a mess, clothing spilling out in a jumbled puddle. It looked like he'd made a half-hearted attempt at shoving some of it back in. About to let go of the tent's door flap, Nessa paused. The campfire's light glinted dully on a partially covered object. Curious, Nessa crouched down and reached out, pushing aside the tangle of socks and sleeves that were trying to conceal it.

Heavy and made from metal, Nessa at first thought that it was a small box. She balanced it on her knees as she ran her fingers over the top, feeling etched details that were impossible to see in the gloom. As her fingers moved around to the box's sides, the metal gave way to a soft, uneven surface. Nessa turned the box and realised that she was holding a very peculiar book.

Soft, vellum pages sat between the metal covers, their edges worn with age and use. Sections of the book were comprised of pages varying in thickness and size, thus explaining the uneven texture. It was as if bits and pieces had been added slowly over time. An odd lock held the covers closed, keeping the pages pressed tightly against one another, not allowing the book to be opened even a fraction of an inch. Nessa didn't have the faintest idea of what might be written on those rough pages.

"What a strange thing," Nessa whispered. She rested a hand on its metal cover, her fingers drumming as she turned a contemplative eye to Chaos' bag. *What other intriguing things might he be hiding?*

Nessa didn't get a chance to find out.

The book grew hot, the metal almost scalding her palm. Alarmed, Nessa jumped up. It tumbled to the ground, landing with a dull *thud*. She stared at it, breathing hard, holding her hand to her chest, more in shock than from any real pain. She had relinquished her hold before it could burn her. Wearily, Nessa stood over the book, half-expecting it to burst into flames or for the cover to start glowing red. The book did neither. It lay on the ground just as any normal book would, still and silent, and with no hint of doing anything unusual.

Nessa didn't trust it, not one bit. It wasn't a normal book. It wasn't normal at all. She didn't know what the book was about or what it might do next, and before it could give her any more unwanted surprises, she hastily stowed it back in Chaos' bag and hurried back to her tent. Nessa lingered there just long enough to grab her sleeping bag, and then she crossed over to Aoife on the far side of the campsite.

Nessa needed her dragon.

Aoife stirred when Nessa stepped close, her tail moving away from her body and her wing lifting a little.

*What's wrong, my little Rider?* Aoife asked sleepily.

Nessa ducked under Aoife's wing and positioned the sleeping bag close to Aoife's side. She then swiftly snuggled into it, folding the overcoat into a makeshift pillow.

*I can't sleep,* Nessa said, keeping her misgivings to herself. Something about Chaos didn't bode well with her; something about him and that strange book made her increasingly uneasy. Nessa couldn't quite put her finger on what it was, though.

Aoife's tail curled around Nessa and her wing dropped back down, sliding over Nessa to form a living tent. *Is something troubling you?*

*No,* Nessa lied. *I'm just excited for tomorrow's adventure.*

*Are you, now?* Aoife was barely awake, her words distant and faint. *It will be nice to leave this land. Sorrow breeds here. It makes my hide itch.*

*What do you mean?*

*I don't know, not really. Something happened here a long time ago. Something terrible and tragic.*

*Oh?*

*Come,* Aoife murmured, *let us not dwell on such dark thoughts. We are together and safe. Tonight, we shall sleep and dream of pleasant things.*

*Pleasant things, hmm? Like what?*

*Like...like...*

Aoife's thread of consciousness through their bond dwindled to little more than an impression of thoughts, and Nessa realised that Aoife had fallen back to sleep.

Rolling onto her side and closing her eyes, Nessa tried to quell the whirlwind of questions that grew with each passing hour. She buried her face in her makeshift pillow, the velvet soft and comforting. The scent of the forest still clung to it—earth and moss—and there was an underlying essence of something else, something more familiar: a hint of sandalwood and *otherness*. Brows furrowed, Nessa breathed it in, wondering if it was just her troubled mind playing tricks on her.

Did the scent really stir up a memory? A disjointed one filled with sadness and hope, darkness and despair, and the most beautiful blue eyes she'd ever seen?

༄༅༆

They gripped her like talons. Strong. Unyielding.

And ever so cruel.

The dreams, the nightmares, swirled around her like a whirlwind, a tornado, a hurricane.

Nothingness swallowed her whole, heavy and sinister, and filled with mocking laughter.

A speck of light appeared, small and weak, flickering like a candle flame. She went to run towards it but realised that she couldn't. She was stuck, trapped, tied down. She struggled and strained against her bonds, but she was only rewarded with the clatter of unbreakable chains.

The laughter grew louder, a sharp edge entering it, and someone leaned over her, their icy eyes staring into hers, shimmering with madness.

*"Even from the roughest of iron ore,"* they whispered, *"can the finest blade be made…"*

# Chapter 9

Nessa's eyes snapped open, wide and staring. Sweat peppered her brow and her heart thundered away, as fast and frantic as a galloping horse. She placed a hand on her chest and struggled to calm herself. The dream, the nightmare, had felt all too real, and it took a few shuddering breaths before Nessa was sure that she was free from it.

Aoife was curled around Nessa, her wing stretched over the both of them, acting like a tent. Sunlight shone through the membrane, highlighting the tapestry of delicate veins that sat beneath the fine surface. It was just bright enough for Nessa to see, her little space drenched in a deep-purple light.

Nessa rolled onto her side and jumped, surprised at the sight of a large, slit-pupil eye staring at her from a foot away.

With a strained chuckle, Nessa tried for a small smile, her thoughts still a little preoccupied by the lingering grip of her nightmare. "I assumed you were asleep."

Aoife blinked slowly, as if trying to convey something, the delicate scales around her eye twinkling as they shifted with the movement. Nessa frowned, wondering why Aoife didn't just speak directly in her mind. Then she realised that Aoife couldn't. Nessa had shut her out with a wall of amethyst bricks, hiding her thoughts, her feelings behind it, just as Aoife had done before their reunion.

"Sorry," Nessa murmured, letting the wall fall away. "I didn't mean to lock you out."

*Fear not,* Aoife said. *You are allowed to have privacy in your own mind when you want to. We don't want to be in each other's minds all the time, now, do we?*

*I guess not. But surely there's a happy medium between locking you out completely and sending you every single thought?*

*Of course there is. We just need to practice and grow our connection more.*

"Of course," Nessa muttered, pushing herself up and rubbing the sleep from her eyes. "Are the others awake?"

*Yes. They have been for almost an hour. I told them you were getting some much-needed rest, so they've been as quiet as possible.*

"A shame, then, that my rest wasn't particularly restful."

*You only just started to have the nightmare. I was about to wake you, but I didn't get the chance to.*

"Mmm."

*Come on, my sleepy little Rider,* Aoife said. *You'd better get up before the others eat all the food. They've already packed most of the camp, and Orm keeps eyeing the food they've saved for you.*

"I suppose he won't be able to resist the temptation for much longer."

*Probably not,* Aoife said, sounding faintly amused. *And threatening him wouldn't do any good. That one has no fear.*

"Oh dear." Nessa smoothed a hand over her hair, trying to tame some of the wildness that reached past her waist in a dark spill, and tugged at her baggy clothing, hoping to make herself look at least moderately presentable.

*I wouldn't worry too much about looks. Chaos has wings, Orm's bald at the grand age of twenty-something and Hunter always has the appearance of one dragged through a hedge backwards.*

"Well, I can't really worry about my looks all that much considering there's no mirrors around," Nessa mused as she slipped into the overcoat, which was a little worse for wear after being used as a pillow, crumpled and wrinkled.

*In any event, I'd get a few decent meals in you before you go in search for a mirror,* Aoife advised as she pulled back her wing.

Bright sunlight assaulted Nessa's eyes, dazzling her for a second, forcing her to squint as they slowly adjusted. She spied Hunter dismantling a tent nearby and Orm sitting by the fire, staring forlornly at a plate of leftover pheasant that was beside him. Both were dressed as they were yesterday, which made her feel slightly less insecure. Hunter still wore his dark tunic and trous, and Orm was dressed in a similar fashion but with his favoured sleeveless top.

Nessa joined Orm before he had a chance to help himself to her breakfast, picking up the plate and perching on the wooden stool. "If you're that hungry," she said, nibbling at a piece of meat, "then you could always whip yourself up some scrambled eggs."

Orm shrugged, looking dejected. "I'm not really in a scrambled egg kind of mood."

"He's also already eaten," Hunter remarked as he grappled with the tent. He'd managed to fold down the frame and tie up the guy lines so that they were out of the way, and was now trying to roll the canvas neatly so that all of it would fit into its valise. He wasn't having much luck. "Orm, come here and sit on this whilst I do up the bag's straps. It keeps popping open."

Orm sighed theatrically and ambled over to Hunter, begrudgingly lending him a helping hand.

Nessa looked around, discovering that the other two tents were already packed and sat in a pile with the other supplies, including their blankets and sleeping bags, personal effects and cooking equipment. It appeared that they were almost ready to depart. Strangely enough, Chaos was nowhere to be seen. Nessa wondered if he had even returned from his late-night sneakings.

Finishing her breakfast, Nessa rose and rinsed her plate off using the waterskin, then crossed over to the pile of bags. It took a bit of rummaging, but Nessa eventually found where the cutlery was stashed, and tucked her plate alongside the others.

"This is an awful lot of stuff for us to carry," Nessa mused, counting the bags.

Hunter grinned. "Good thing we're not carrying all of it, then, isn't it."

"Huh?"

*They strap them onto my back,* Aoife explained, casting out her words for all of them to hear, not just Nessa, *and I carry them.*

"It's been bloody useful having a dragon around," Hunter said, finally winning the battle against the tent, trying up the valise's straps.

Aoife snorted. *These poor, feeble males can barely carry anything, and if they do, it just slows them down. Before I was big enough to carry all of the kit, progress was painfully slow.*

"It wasn't that slow," Hunter argued.

*It was slow enough, and you didn't even have tents until recently. Without me, you'd be slow and tentless.*

"We didn't need tents until last month, and I've said on numerous occasions: if we simply got some horses—"

"No horses!" Orm interjected. "You are not to be trusted with horses."

"Why do you say that?"

"Because you lost the last horse that was in your care."

"I didn't lose Betty. She was stolen."

"Oh, stolen? That's so much better."

"Yes, it is," Hunter fumed, standing with his hands on his hips. "Having the horse stolen was out of my control. There was nothing I could have done."

"You could have tried to retrieve it."

"I was outnumbered. Tell him, Nessa." Hunter turned to her. "Tell him how we were outnumbered by the bandits."

Nessa blinked. "Umm, I don't really—"

"Remember," Hunter finished glumly. "What a bugger. I fought those bandits so valiantly too."

Nessa smirked. "Of course you did."

"Yes, I did. It made you swoon."

"Swoon," Nessa laughed. "I don't think so."

"How would you know?" Hunter quirked a brow. "You have to take my word for it."

"I don't think I'm the swooning kind of girl."

"Perhaps not," Hunter admitted. "But you were very impressed."

"Was I, now?"

"Indeed, for I was very impressive."

Chuckling, Nessa shook her head. "As you've just said, I'll have to take your word for it. Unless, of course, Orm or Aoife have something to add to your tale?"

*Alas,* Aoife said, deeply amused, *that happened before I hatched.*

"However, if he'd fought half as valiantly as he said he did," Orm mused, crossing over to the pile of bags, carrying the packed tent, "then he would have been able to retrieve the horse. So if I were you, Nessie, I'd take his story with a pinch of salt."

*Oh, Hunter, you are a silly human,* Aoife said. *And you do entertain me so well.*

Glaring at them with false hurt, Hunter grumbled, "At least the oversized lizard appreciates me."

*Careful,* Aoife murmured, eyes twinkling, *or this oversized lizard will tell Nessa all the embarrassing things you've done over the last few months, giving her ample opportunity to tease you whenever she feels like it.*

Hunter's response to the threat was a roll of his eyes. "Come on, bullies. If we want to cover any decent amount of distance today, then we should head off as soon as we can."

"Always so eager to move on," Orm sighed. "Live in the here and now, Hunter, my boy. Stop wishing your life away."

"I'm not wishing my life away," Hunter said, unstirred by Orm's words of wisdom. "I would just like to make it to the nearest village by noon. Then we can get

Nessa some clothing and buy more food."

Orm shook his head. "Chaos said we should forget about the villages and spend a night or two in a town. That way, Nessa can get a proper night's sleep in an actual bed, and we'll have a better chance of getting proper supplies and whatnot."

"And have a greater chance of someone recognising and reporting us to the authorities," Hunter added.

"A bed does sound rather nice," Nessa said with a touch of wistfulness. *A nice spongy mattress and a poofy pillow...*

"Come on, Hunter," Orm urged as he organised the pile of bags, checking that they were fastened and accounted for. "A town is bigger and has more options than a village, more people coming and going. No one would remember a small group of travellers. We'd fit right in with the other visitors. There's no harm in it. Not really."

"The nearest town is Arncraft. We won't reach it till almost nightfall. If we're lucky"

"And that's a problem how?"

Hunter shrugged. "It will be a long day of marching, that's all. Nessa might not be up to it." He smiled at her apologetically.

"I don't mind the trek," Nessa said. "If I get tired, I'll just make one of you give me a piggyback."

"There," Orm grinned and clapped Hunter on the back, "we have decided. We're going to Arncraft. I reckon we'll get there in time for me to win a few card games and get some money to fund a visit to the markets before the day's end."

"Wow," Nessa murmured. "Sounds like you have everything planned out."

Orm nodded, his whiskey-coloured eyes twinkling at the prospect of gambling.

"Come on," Hunter sighed, "let's load all of this onto Aoife. Then we'll be ready to head off, provided Chaos returns soon."

"Where is Chaos?" Nessa asked.

"He's scouting ahead," Orm said. "Making sure there's nothing bad hiding around a corner, waiting to jump out at us."

"Chaos is trying to discover how Shadow is hiding from his sight, and where Shadow is," Hunter explained. "He's also listening for any word of the other Dragon Riders being summoned back to the capital. He likes to go off by himself. Says that he needs peace and quiet in order to concentrate."

"Apparently, Hunter and I are too annoying for him to be anywhere near," Orm added, picking up a couple of bags and moving them over to Aoife.

"Is that so?" Nessa chuckled, grabbing an armload of light supplies and following after him.

"Oh yes," Hunter agreed. "We are very annoying when we want to be."

"And even when they're not trying," a voice intoned from behind them, "they are still incredibly annoying."

Nessa turned and spied Chaos making his way out of the trees, approaching them in a leisurely manner, the silvered caps of his boots glinting with each of his steps. Strapped over a leather-clad shoulder was a duffel bag. Nessa recognised it and eyed it with suspicion, trying to spot the shape of his unsettling book, but it was concealed, tucked away in the middle of the clothing.

Chaos' gaze shifted from Hunter and Orm, and came to rest on her. Hastily, Nessa dragged her eyes away from his bag and said, "By your relaxed demeanour, I assume we're safe from any beasties that may be lurking about?"

"Our path is clear," Chaos said. "For the time being, at least. I still cannot find Shadow, but I do know that King Kaenar has sent word for his return, and that it has been answered. I presume Shadow is now making his way back to the capital."

"When did he get his summons?" Hunter asked.

"Within the last hour."

"Has the king called back any of the others?"

"Not yet, but I'm sure he will soon."

*Have you heard anything about why he's calling them back?* Aoife enquired.

"I've heard a few whispers on the wind," Chaos answered. "They are little more than suggestions and ideas. Guesses, really."

"A stab in the dark," Hunter supplied helpfully.

*And which whisper is the loudest?*

"There are rumours of discontent amongst a small number of the populous. What happened at The Hidden City sits ill with them, particularly with those who had links with the black trade or had friends and family who lived there."

"This can't be good." Hunter looked worried, his eyes troubled. "The last time there were rumours of this nature, an entire town was destroyed."

"Don't fret, Hunter," Orm said. "I'm sure that won't happen again. Not in your lifetime, at least."

Hunter was silent as he grabbed a couple of bags and loaded them onto Aoife's back. She crouched down, making it easier for him to reach and position them comfortably between the spikes that ran down her spine. Using a length of sturdy rope, he tried them into place, and then with his foot braced against her foreleg, he clambered up Aoife's side. Orm passed the other bags to Hunter, and they too were tied securely in place.

Nessa eyed the bags and the giant spider web of crisscrossed rope. *Doesn't all of that make it difficult to fly?*

*No, my little Rider. When Hunter ties them just right, I barely notice them. And anyway, I like to count the extra weight as practice for when we'll fly together.*

*Fly together?* Nessa murmured, recalling the memories Aoife had shared with her, the ones where Aoife had been soaring a thousand feet above the ground, higher than any bird would dare to go. Nessa felt a little nauseous. *When will we be flying together?*

*Not for a little while yet,* Aoife chuckled, sensing Nessa's trepidation and finding it amusing. *I still have a bit of growing to do before it's safe.*

*Safe? Why is that? You can carry all those bags?* Nessa wondered. *I'm pretty sure that they weigh a lot more than I do.*

*Indeed they do, but it's not just about weight,* Aoife explained. *It's to do with the space between my spikes. While I could easily bear your weight, it would be far too dangerous because if we were to hit an up or downdraft, or if I dived or landed too roughly, you might accidentally impale yourself. As I grow, the space between my spikes will widen, and you'll be able to sit between them without the risk of being skewered.*

*I would rather not be impaled,* Nessa mused.

*As would I, my little Rider.*

"Right," Hunter said, giving the rope one last tug, knocking Nessa and Aoife from their silent conversation, "how does that feel?"

*Perfect,* Aoife said, rolling her shoulders. *Is that everything?*

"Yep, that's all of it." Hunter hopped down from her shoulder. "You're all set."

Nessa looked around and realised that as she and Aoife had been talking, Hunter and Orm had finished loading the bags. Well, all except for one. Chaos still carried his.

"Don't you want Aoife to take that?" Nessa asked him. "It doesn't look very comfortable to carry."

"I prefer to carry it myself," Chaos said. "I was raised in a time when dragons were considered to be more than beasts of burden. The very least I can do is carry my own clothing."

*Ignore him,* Aoife murmured in Nessa's mind. *He gets a little peculiar when it comes to his personal belongings and the olden ways from when he was young. It's best just to leave him be.*

*If you say so.* Nessa had the impression that Chaos just didn't want anyone to stumble across his weird book. She kept her suspicions to herself, though. "So, are we off to Arncraft now, then?" she asked in way of a distraction, wanting to steer her mind away from Chaos and his secrets.

"Once you've put on your lovely second-hand boots and we've put out the fire," Hunter said, ambling over to the fire in question. With a few deft kicks, he covered the flames with earth, smothering them. He grinned at her from over his shoulder. "Now we're just waiting for you to put on your boots."

Nessa looked at her bare feet and wiggled her toes. "I think I need some socks."

"Already thought of that." Hunter nodded to the boots, which were resting beside one of the log stools. "I've kindly lent you some of mine."

"Clean ones, I hope." Nessa crossed over to the boots and sat down on the stool. The socks, she saw, were shoved into the boots. She put them on without inspecting them, deciding that an "ignorance is bliss" view was perhaps best.

"Of course, they're clean." Hunter smirked. "Although I can't say the same for the boots. I wouldn't sniff them if I were you."

Nessa, reaching for one, paused. "You sound like you know not to do that from experience."

Hunter shrugged. "Curiosity killed the cat."

Nessa grimaced as she slipped her feet into the boots, careful not to breathe in too deeply just in case she caught a whiff, and did up the laces, which were nearing the end of their lifespan, frayed and stretched.

"Is it too much to ask for a pair of new boots when we reach Arncraft?" Nessa asked, standing. The boots were a little on the large side, and even though Hunter's chunky socks helped to stop her feet from sliding around too much, she couldn't help shake the feeling that the boots were making her feet dirty.

"Clothing and new shoes? Gosh, you are a demanding girl," Hunter remarked. "What do you say, Orm, oh mighty gambler? Are new shoes and clothes on the cards this day?"

Orm's eyes were bright and eager. "Oh yes, I reckon so."

Hunter clapped his hands together. "There you have it. Looks like you'll be doing rather well this afternoon."

"Not if the lot of you keep dithering around," Chaos growled. "Get a move on. You're wasting time."

"Dithering?" Orm rolled the word around in his mouth. "I do like that word. Dithering."

Chaos turned and walked away, heading into the trees with a muttered, "Idiot."

Nessa watched him go for a second, expecting him to stop and wait for them. To her surprise, he didn't, and his long-legged strides soon carried him out of sight.

"Well," Hunter sighed, "it seems that Chaos is eager to get to Arncraft."

"Indeedy," Nessa murmured.

"Come on, you two," Orm called, heading after Chaos. "Stop *dithering* around."

Nessa laid a hand on Aoife's side, her fingers idly tapping against scales. *I guess you won't be able to walk with us, will you?*

*No, my little Rider,* Aoife told her, voice tinged with a small amount of regret. *The forest is too dense, and I must fly high in the clouds to avoid anyone seeing me.*

*It's a shame. I like having you nearby.*

*I'll never venture too far away,* Aoife said. *And we can view this as an opportunity to practice communicating with each other over larger distances.*

*I do need to learn more about this bond we have and what it really means.*

*Of course you do. We can talk about it later if you want?*

*I look forward to it.*

Aoife snorted softly and brought her snout down, brushing the top of Nessa's head gently in a dragon's version of a goodbye kiss. *I'll see you later, my little Rider.* Aoife looked to Hunter and Orm. *I'll be close until you leave the forest. Then, I will have to stay near the mountains; otherwise, I'll risk being seen.*

"Sounds fine," Hunter said. "We'll meet up with you a couple of miles outside Arncraft and unload you, then rejoin you in the morning once we've got everything we

need."
*Sounds like a plan.*

# Chapter 10

Sunlight rained down, threading its way through the tree branches, bringing out the browns and oranges of the fallen leaves that covered the ground in a whispering carpet. Lichen and soft moss covered the lower halves of the trees' trunks, and spread amongst their knobbly roots, growing in little clusters, were small mushrooms. They were unusually coloured, their caps a riot of vivid reds and purples, blues and greens. Many of them featured a scattering of large, rounded spots of a different colour to that of their caps, often clashing with them. They were fun, quirky and also, apparently, deadly poisonous.

Nessa wanted to take some with her. Because what girl doesn't desire some wildly colourful and poisonous mushrooms upon her person? Orm was all for it, even suggesting that they could find a way of preserving them, turning them into little mementoes. The idea of terrarium pendants and charms was thrown around. Orm seemed inclined to create a jewellery empire that specialised in poisonous fungi.

"We'll put the 'fun' in fungi," Orm said meditatively.

Nessa laughed. "We have to work that into our shop slogan."

"Agreed." Orm linked arms with Nessa. "Now, what do you think our marketing strategy should be?"

"You're forgetting a couple of important factors with this idea of yours," Hunter said mildly, walking a couple of steps behind them.

Orm cocked a brow. "Oh?"

"First of, it seems a wee bit dangerous to sell poisonous mushrooms as pieces of jewellery."

"Jewellery with a touch of danger." Orm shrugged. "People love having a bit of danger in their lives."

"Anyway," Nessa added, "they'll be encased in, like, mini glass bottles or something."

"Excellent," Hunter said dryly. "Second of all, you can't pick them now because you have nothing to put them in."

"That is a bit of a problem at this precise moment in time," Orm admitted.

"And if you touch them with bare skin, you'll die within a matter of minutes. That kind of makes them rather hard to pick."

"Gloves," Orm sighed. "Gloves will help with that little problem."

"Will gloves help with the little problem that we are wanted fugitives? I'd imagine it's rather hard to set up a business with a bounty on you."

"You and Nessa are wanted fugitives," Orm corrected him. "And technically, you're secret fugitives. Only Margan has issued warrants for the two of you, and he's going to keep the search rather quiet, lest the king finds out about his shenanigans."

"Secret fugitives?" Nessa snorted. "That's a bit of an oxymoron, isn't it?"

Orm frowned, and looked down at her. The top of Nessa's head barely came up to his shoulder. "Or is it ironic?"

"I have no idea." Nessa peered behind her, wondering if Hunter would know, but he was just looking at them blankly, shaking his head slowly in minor despair.

"How did we even end up in Ironguard?" Nessa asked, curious as to what kind of mischief she and Hunter had got up to in order to be imprisoned.

"Oh," Orm smiled, "you and Hunter broke into the castle to try and kill Margan."

"What!" Nessa stumbled, only stopped from tripping over by her and Orm's linked arms. "I tried to help kill someone?"

Orm patted her hand reassuringly. "What are good friends for if not to help each other enact revenge?"

"There's having each other's backs," Nessa croaked, "and there's being an accomplice to murder."

"Revenge," Orm corrected. "Revenge and murder are very different from each other."

"Umm."

"Ignore him," Hunter told her, glaring at Orm, who merely rolled his eyes and looked away. "It wasn't like how he's telling it."

"So we didn't try to kill Margan?"

"No, *we* didn't," Hunter murmured. Nessa started to relax before he added, "I did, though."

Nessa was shocked, not quite able to wrap her mind around the fact that one of her friends had tried to kill someone. "Why do you want to kill Margan?"

Blood leached from Hunter's face. "I have my reasons."

"Good ones?" Nessa whispered. "I hope?"

Hunter nodded stiffly.

Nessa abandoned the subject, wishing that she'd never brought it up to begin with. Whilst Hunter's face was pale and impassive, it was the look in his eyes that gave Nessa pause. They shone brightly with emotion, burning with a mixture of anger and pain. He had his reasons, although Nessa wasn't sure if she ever wanted to know what they were.

Margan must have done something to Hunter. Something bad. Awful. Why else would Hunter be driven to try and kill Margan? Whatever it was, it couldn't have happened all too long ago. The pain in Hunter's eyes was still too fresh, the wounds too raw.

Floundering, not knowing what to do or say, feeling as if she had done something wrong, Nessa reached out her mind. *Oh Aoife, I think I've brought up something I shouldn't have.*

*Don't worry, my little Rider*, Aoife said, her tone wise and soothing. *He has a few devils he needs to battle, but he will tell you what they are when he is ready.*

*Do you know what these devils are?*

*I do. They were told to me in confidence. I promised I wouldn't tell a soul. They are his to bear and his to share if he so wishes to.*

*Hmm.*

*Don't dwell on it*, Aoife told her. *You've done nothing wrong.*

*I feel like I have.*

*You haven't.*

*If you say so.*

*I do.*

*Okay then.*

*Okay.*

Nessa resisted the urge to sigh—just. She didn't want to alert Orm and Hunter to her silent conversation. A large part of her found the idea of being able to speak mentally to someone else rather strange. The fact that she was speaking telepathically with a dragon, *her* dragon, still hadn't sunk in fully.

*How's flying?*

*The weather today is perfect. I can't wait until it's you on my back instead of all these bags. I'll be able to show you the world in a way few can even imagine, let alone experience.*

Nessa gazed upwards, trying to peer through the tree branches and amber leaves, her eyes searching for a shimmer of purple in the sea of blue above. *I can't see you. Where are you?*

*I'm a few miles north of where you are. Mist is rising from the base of the mountains. I'm hiding in that.*

Nessa looked over to the mountains, unable to see much more of them other than their snow-covered peaks. *I still can't see you.*

*I do believe that's the whole point of hiding.*

*Ooh, a sarcastic dragon.*

*Quiet you,* Aoife said, her amusement reaching Nessa through their bond. *If you spend six months with Orm and Hunter, sarcasm is just something that develops of its own accord. I was powerless to stop it.*

*Were you, now?*

*Oh yes. The sarcasm is strong with those two. Just you wait. A few more weeks and then you'll be joining us in our sarcastic ways.*

*I can't wait.*

*See?* Aoife snorted. *Only a couple of days with them and it's already happening.*

Nessa chuckled and clamped a hand over her mouth, embarrassed at being caught laughing at herself.

Orm raised his brows, peering at her, then looked over his shoulder at Hunter. "I have a feeling someone's talking about us behind our backs."

Hunter smirked. "Or she's simply realised how absurd your poisonous mushroom jewellery idea is."

"The mushroom jewellery is an amazing idea," Nessa argued. "I was just laughing at…"

"Us," Orm finished.

"You were merely mentioned in passing."

"So we're not even worth a good gossip between you and your dragon?" Orm shook his head. "Are you hearing this, Hunter? And to think I was about to set up a jewellery empire with you. Tut-tut, Nessa. Tut-tut."

"What is going on?" Nessa asked, bewildered at the conversation's sudden change of direction.

*He's mad,* Aoife explained. *Completely mad.*

*I agree.*

"You're doing it again, aren't you?" Orm's eyebrows rose. "Talking to that dragon of yours. Chitchatting."

"Am not."

"Are too. You kinda get this zoned out expression like you're thinking really hard about something."

"I don't get a 'zoned out' look." She turned to Hunter. "Do I?"

Hunter raised his hands in surrender. "Believe it or not, but I don't really know. I'm behind you, so I can't actually see."

"Oh, right. Of course." Nessa slipped her arm free

from Orm's and fell into step with Hunter. Whatever had been troubling him only a minute ago wasn't anymore. The colour was back in his face and his eyes were cheerful as he gazed down at her.

"And what, pray tell," Hunter said, "were you and Aoife talking about if it wasn't about me, Orm or poisonous jewellery?"

Nessa shrugged. "I was merely checking up on her. Making sure she was alright."

"And is she?"

"Yep. She's having some fun flying around the mountain foothills. Apparently, there's mist for her to hide in."

"Ooo, mountain mist," Orm remarked dryly. "How exciting."

"And how are you?" Hunter asked, giving Orm's back a withering glare. "Are you alright?"

"Oh, I'm more than alright," Nessa said brightly. "I'm enjoying this walk quite a bit."

"Really?"

"Yes. The sun is shining, there are colourful mushrooms dotted around and I have fantastic company."

"Hear that Orm? We're fantastic company."

Orm grinned. "Indeed we are."

"Now," Hunter said to her, "you keep hold of those happy thoughts. You'll need them in mind later when you're sick of walking and want to curl up in a ball on the ground, having no intention of ever moving again."

"I don't think I'm going to do that when I'm fed up with walking."

"No?"

"Nope. Orm will be giving me a piggyback long

before that happens."

Hunter threw back his head and roared with laughter. Nessa smiled as Orm sputtered with indignation.

"Anyway," Nessa added. "We've been walking for a while, and I'm doing fine."

"Feet don't hurt?"

"Not yet."

Hunter gazed upwards, tracking the pace of the sun. "That's impressive. We've been walking for a couple of hours."

Nessa was surprised. "Really? That long. It feels like only half that."

"Mmm, we must have covered a few miles."

"And yet there's no end of this forest in sight."

Trees surrounded them, mighty oaks, thick-trunked and with twisted branches that reached far overhead. Small clusters of hawthorns and maples grew here and there, tall and spindly, barely more than saplings. Whilst there was no sign of the forest coming to an end anytime soon, there was a change within it.

It was beginning to *feel* different.

Back at the campsite, the air had held an ominous quality, a warning. The trees had been watchful, waiting for something. Now, though, they were silent and sleepy, just as they should be, growing further part, the gaps between them slowly getting wider and wider.

It was peaceful.

Calm.

Normal.

"This land is wild and the forest old," Hunter said. "It stretches far and wide, but we are nearly free from it. I'd imagine Aoife would be able to tell you how much further we have to go, if you ask her. Bird's-eye view and all that."

Orm sniggered. "Ha, more like a dragon's-eye view."

"Why don't you ask Aoife?" Nessa said. "I think the information would be a lot more useful to you than me. I have absolutely no idea where Arncraft is."

"I can't," Hunter murmured. "It doesn't work like that."

Nessa was confused. "Well, how does it work? Aoife's talked to you before."

"Yes, Aoife and I talk. Quite often too, I'd like to add." Hunter's brows pulled together. "It's just…"

"Hunter's mind doesn't work like ours," Orm said, saving Hunter from having to explain. "Therefore, he has to play by a different set of rules when it comes to magic-related issues."

"Why's that?"

"Because he's a human through and through," Orm clarified. "You and I, we're Old Bloods. We have magic. Hunter, bless his poor, bland soul, doesn't have a drop of magic in him."

Nessa peered at Hunter, wondering if he took offence at his friend's less than complimentary description of his humanness.

Hunter shrugged nonchalantly. "It's something I'm eternally grateful for." At Nessa's questioning look, he added, "In my opinion, magic is a lot more trouble than it's worth."

"That's just because you don't have it," Orm said, a little smug.

Nessa could sense Aoife listening in on their conversation. She could feel the tug on their bond, the strange sensation of Aoife's mind brushing against her own. Whilst Aoife was listening, she didn't seem inclined to join in with the conversation, so Nessa asked, "What does having magic have to do with Hunter being able to talk to Aoife?"

"Oh, he can talk to Aoife," Orm said, "but only if she wants to talk to him in the first place." He gave up his slight lead, and Nessa found herself sandwiched between the two of them, Orm on her right and Hunter on her left.

"You see," Orm continued, "as beings of magic, we are of a different mind. And I mean that in quite a literal way. Hunter's mind is, shall we say, *fixed*. It's there to stay, never venturing outside his physical form. But Nessa, our minds are different. They are *fluid*. With the proper tutelage, we can cast them out, send them beyond our physical forms. With this ability, we can communicate telepathically with others, unhindered by the constraint of distance."

Nessa frowned, struggling to digest what Orm was saying. "So, because we are Old Bloods, and because our minds are *fluid*, we could stand on the opposite sides of the world and have a nice chat?"

"Well, theoretically yes."

"But Hunter and I can't because I'm an Old Blood and he's not?"

"You can reach your mind out to his," Orm said, "and then you can talk with each other. However, you would always have to be the one to initiate it, not him, because his mind is fixed and he cannot cast it out to you."

For a second, Nessa could feel Aoife's agreement trickling through their bond, and then she felt Aoife withdraw, having grown bored with the conversation. Nessa was once again left alone with her thoughts. Questions arose.

"If what you say is true," Nessa said to Orm, "then

doesn't that mean you and I could have a telepathic chat right now?"

"Well, I suppose we could," Orm mused. "However, you don't have the knowledge of how to do so, so you'd probably have to rely on me to keep our minds connected."

"But I can communicate with Aoife without a problem, so why would it be any different with you? Or anyone else, come to think of it?"

"Because it's different when it comes to you and Aoife."

"Of course it is," Nessa muttered.

Hunter snorted, his lips twitching with a barely suppressed smirk.

Orm pulled Nessa to a stop and reached out, pushing back her sleeve. Surprised, Nessa offered no resistance. Soft sunlight caught on the iridescent mark that curled around her forearm, wrist and hand.

Tapping it with a large, broad-tipped finger, Orm said, "This here is evidence of how you are different to me. This is the physical manifestation of the connection between you and Aoife. You and Aoife are bound together, body and soul. Your minds are melded together in a very intricate way. Someone like me, no matter how much practice, will never experience the level of ease that you and Aoife will have in anything related to magic. With as much energy as blinking, you can reach out to each other and know what the other is thinking, what they are feeling. You need to understand that while other magic users *can* cast out their minds, with years of practice and patience, it isn't an easy or natural thing to do. The connection you share with Aoife is something only experienced between a dragon and their Rider.

While you are an Old Blood, you are also a Dragon Rider. You are something that this world has never seen before. I fear that the rules that govern me and my gifts, along with those of others, aren't quite the same for you."

Nessa tugged her arm free and stared at the mark. "So, what you saying is: I'm weird and it's like the blind leading the blind when it comes to me, Aoife and magic?"

Orm nodded slowly. "Pretty much."

"Fantastic."

Placing a hand on the small of her back, Hunter urged her forwards. "Think of it as venturing into uncharted territory," he murmured to her as they started walking again.

"When we're safely tucked away somewhere in Ellor," Orm said, "I'll help you discover what you can do, teach you all that I know about magic. If you want me to?"

"I'll take you up on that offer," Nessa said with a sigh, pulling down her sleeve, hiding all of the mark save for the part that ran over the back of her hand. "The other Dragon Riders…do they have marks like mine?"

"Yes." It was Hunter who answered. "The mark you bear is like those of any blood vow: the visible manifestation of the unbreakable bond between you and Aoife, between dragon and Rider. All Dragon Riders have one, although there are slight variations between them, like size and colour."

Nessa peered at hers, twisting her hand this way and that, watching as it shimmered faintly with different hues of purple, not too dissimilar to Aoife's colouring. "Huh. Cool."

☼✦☙

The spacing between the trees grew ever wider as the day gradually passed, and the leaf litter slowly gave way to a carpet of fine grass and moss. Much to Nessa's disappointment, her colourful and deadly mushrooms dwindled in number until they disappeared altogether.

"How many Dragon Riders are there?" Nessa asked quietly.

"In the good old days, there were twelve Dragon Riders," Hunter said. "One dragon and Rider per House. One for each of the twelve ruling families. However, since King Kaenar came into power, things got a little complicated."

"Excluding you," Orm did some quick counting with the aid of his fingers, "there are currently fourteen other Dragon Riders."

"So there's only two more Dragon Riders than there should be?" pondered Nessa. "That doesn't sound too complicated."

"Three if we count you," Hunter added. "And if we want to get really particular, then there are four extra Dragon Riders thanks to the king's meddling."

Nessa sighed and tapped her temple as a subtle reminder. "I'm not really following."

"Before the king came into power, there were the twelve ruling families, the Twelve Houses."

"Right."

"Each of the Twelve Houses had their own Dragon Rider. This Rider would govern the lands, protect them and such."

"I'm with you so far."

Hunter nodded. "Great. Now, five centuries ago, there was a terrible war. In the aftermath, King Kaenar rose up and claimed the lands for his own. Many of the Houses followed him out of lust for more power or out of fear."

"That's not very good."

"No, it isn't," Hunter agreed. "Lingering stories tell of a House that tried to stand against him: House Fæger. They fought him with everything they had, but alas, it was all for nothing. They lost. In revenge for their rebellion, King Kaenar destroyed them, killed every last one of them. While all of us know of the Twelve Houses, House Fæger is nothing more than a memory."

"So, no more Dragon Riders for House Fæger then."

"No more Dragon Riders for House Fæger. But there's still another eleven Houses, all of which have their obligatory Dragon Rider. A couple have more than one."

"Oh?"

"Before King Kaenar, no House ever had more than one Rider at a time. There was never an exception to this, not even in times of war. It just wasn't done."

"And then the king came along and…?"

"And somehow he changed things. Two of his most loyal Houses both had twins in line as their next Riders, and when their predecessors passed away, he bequeathed both sets of twins with their own dragon eggs. When those eggs hatched, there were four Dragon Riders when there should have only been two."

"You need to understand that the bond between a dragon and their Rider isn't a naturally occurring thing," Orm added. "It was something that came about thousands of years ago by magic. The spell used to create the Dragon Riders prevented each House from having more than one Dragon Rider at a time."

Nessa frowned. "But if the king managed to gain extra Riders with the twins, then doesn't that mean the spell isn't working like it used to?"

"It's more likely that he's found a way around the spell."

Nessa looked at Orm, intrigued by the amount of unease colouring his words. "Your tone suggests that's not a good thing?"

"No," he said quietly, "that's most definitely not a good thing."

She turned her gaze to Hunter, wondering if he would shed some light onto the matter, but he just shrugged. "Not my area of expertise."

"Magic is an old thing," Orm murmured. "It was around long before mankind existed, and it will be around long after it's gone. Magic is old, and it is also wild and unpredictable. It has taken thousands of years for us to weave spells to harness it, to have some semblance of control over it. The spell used to bind dragons and their Riders was very raw and powerful magic, practically untamed. In order for there to be more than the stipulated number of Dragon Riders, the king must either be more powerful than those who created the spell in the first place or is using a *very* old form of magic to circumvent the spell."

Having no prior knowledge of magical matters, Nessa could barely comprehend what Orm was saying. "I…uh…presume both of those scenarios are bad?"

"Oh yes," Orm said brightly, as if delighted. "It's very bad. But also very interesting."

"What's very interesting?" someone asked, their voice carrying an underlying hiss to the words, making the question seem almost sinister.

Nessa jumped, startled, and turned to see Chaos stepping out from behind a tree. For someone so large and who also had wings, he moved with an unnatural degree of stealth. His footsteps were silent on the rustling leaf litter and the whispering grass.

"Ah, there you are," Hunter said blandly, pointedly ignoring the question. "I was wondering where you had wandered off to."

Chaos scowled, the ghastly scars around his eyes crinkling and deepening. "No, you weren't."

"No," Hunter agreed with a small smile, "I wasn't. In fact, I was quite enjoying not having you around."

Chaos simply grunted and moved to take the lead. Orm jogged up to his side, murmuring something that was too low for Nessa to hear. She and Hunter trailed behind them, keeping a comfortable distance away.

"You should be careful talking about magic and Dragon Riders when Chaos is around," Hunter advised quietly. "It can send him into a rage."

Nessa's eyes ran over Chaos' back, taking in the sight of his large, bat-like wings. They were folded in tight, the taloned tips rising over his shoulders and the lower points reaching down to the backs of his knees. Walking behind him, Nessa didn't think that he was quite as intimidating, not when those pale, scarred eyes of his weren't trained on her. They were unnerving, like they could look straight through flesh and bone and see the soul, laying it bare for the world to scrutinise. Without Chaos' gaze on her, his attention focused elsewhere, Nessa could almost see past the sense of warning that came over her whenever he was near. She could appreciate the strange, unearthly beauty he had.

Although his wings were quite terrifying to behold, they were also fascinating, a clear reminder that, whilst he appeared mostly human, he was anything but. And his hair, Nessa eyed it with a touch of envy, wondering if she would ever get hers to be as smooth and as shiny. She toyed with a lock of her brown tresses, pulling at a curl gently so that it became straight as she held it taut. When she let it go, it sprang back, the bottom couple of inches winding back into a loose curl, the rest falling back into relaxed waves.

No, Nessa supposed it would never be as smooth and as straight as Chaos', but that was alright. It was normal hair, mundane hair, nothing that would mark her out as anything other than human. It wasn't something that would draw unwanted attention to her. Chaos' hair was just another thing that revealed him as something other than human: too straight, too dark, such a deep black that it almost shimmered blue in the sunlight. The way he walked, that too wasn't quite right: too quiet, too fluid, like that of a cat stalking its prey, or maybe, upon further reflection, a panther.

Nessa couldn't help but wonder if all Old Bloods were like Chaos. Were they beautiful in a strange way too, inhuman in appearance and mannerisms? They said that she was one, and yet Nessa felt so very human, so very normal. She didn't have wings or the ability to see into someone's soul—not so far as she could tell—and she certainly didn't move with the grace he did. Fallen leaves whispered with each of her steps, twigs snapped occasionally too. Maybe they had it wrong? Maybe Nessa wasn't an Old Blood and was just a Dragon Rider?

*Just* a Dragon Rider. Nessa nearly snorted at such a notion. As if being a Dragon Rider wasn't enough for her to deal with.

Nessa gazed down at the mark on her hand, suddenly feeling like she hadn't even begun to fully comprehend what being a Dragon Rider really meant.

# Chapter II

Nessa tried to hold onto the memories of actually enjoying the walk, but despite them only being a few hours old, it was hard to keep a grip on them. They just kept slipping away. Gone was the enjoyment of being on the move, the exhilaration of heading somewhere new and exciting. Those feelings had been replaced by constant aches and pains.

Her feet hurt the worst, the soles tender and bruised. Hunter's thick socks did little in the way of cushioning them anymore. Nessa was pretty sure they were just acting as makeshift bandages, soaking up the blood and whatever else oozed from the popped blisters. Her calves were faring only slightly better. The tops of the boots had rubbed a band of skin nearly raw. No matter how tightly or loosely she tied the laces, they still shifted with each step. Nessa accepted that there was little she could do other than to go barefoot, which wouldn't be any good. So, persevering, Nessa trudged alongside the others, telling herself that a night or two at a nice inn with a soft bed and some decent food was well worth the pain.

She wasn't having much luck convincing herself. Especially when the muscles in her lower back protested as she stepped around a chunk of broken wall.

Nessa slowed, emerging from her little world of misery, and looked around.

The forest still surrounded her, oaks and a handful of other hardwood species growing all around, but they were small and sparsely placed. This part of the forest was young, not yet fully established. Grass covered the ground, fresh and green, not yet hindered by the encroaching winter. The juvenile trees had already given up their lot for the year, their leaves littering the floor in a patchwork of browns and oranges, building up against the remains of a wall, blown against it by the autumn winds.

The others walked ahead, not noticing Nessa's hesitation, not noticing her moving closer to the wall. It was the first thing she had seen all day that wasn't something flora related.

The wall was old and broken, what remained of it only coming up to hip height. Nessa could tell that it had once stood taller, but time had worn it down, making the top half crumble and fall around the base. It was built from pale stone which caught the sunlight, twinkling gently when viewed from different angles.

Nessa placed a hand on it, leaning against it for a second, and wondered why there was an old wall running through a forest, neglected and forgotten. A peculiar sensation settled over her, resting upon her shoulders like a fine cape. Nessa grew cold and disconcerted, then lightheaded and dizzy.

The world twisted, spinning in a sickening way, a blur of sky and trees, ground and stone.

Abruptly as it started, the spinning stopped. Nessa stumbled a step or two, steadying herself against the wall before she fell. Her stomach churned and her legs felt weak. She doubled over, praying to gods unknown to not let her be sick or faint. The gods, whoever they might be, seemed merciful, for neither of those things happened.

With her hand still braced against the wall, Nessa pushed herself upright.

She blinked and stared.

"What the…"

The forest around her was gone, replaced by far-reaching gardens of manicured lawns and flowerbeds filled with blooming roses. Twin rows of oaks lined either side of a cobbled road, disappearing into the distance. The wall beside her was new again, unbroken and standing tall. Hunter and the others were nowhere to be found.

Uncertain as to what was happening, to what *had* happened, Nessa stumbled onto the road. On either side, the wall ended in decorative piers. Carved into them was an emblem. Nessa's wide eyes were drawn to it, *she* was drawn to it, and in a blink, she was somehow standing before one of the piers without ever taking a step.

Swallowing nervously, Nessa gazed around for an explanation. She had just moved from one spot to another with the faintest of thoughts. Magic was clearly afoot. What kind, Nessa didn't have the faintest idea. She wasn't even sure if the magic was hers or someone else's, even though she couldn't see anyone.

Her eyes went back to the carved emblem, the crest. It was of a bird, a raven or a crow perhaps, perched neatly on a branch with its head turned to the side, looking back over its shoulder. A blue gem was set into the stone, acting as the bird's eye. Nessa raised a hand to caress it and reared back in shock.

She was a ghost.

There, but not entirely.

Nessa stared at her hand in horror. It was nothing more than a pale shape, all but invisible. With her heart hammering away like the hurried beats of a hummingbird's wings, she looked down, discovering that the rest of her was similarly affected. She had lost all colour, all substance. She could see the ground beneath her too-large boots.

*Keep calm... It's alright... Keep calm...* She started chanting those words like a mantra. *Keep calm... It's alright... Keep calm...*

Nessa didn't move for fear of the earth opening up and swallowing her whole, claiming her wandering soul, sending it to whatever hellish place that might hide in the earth's belly.

A voice whispered.

Two names drifted through the air, uttered almost too softly for Nessa to hear.

She turned towards the source, but the world spun again, a sickening blur of colour and disorientation. Nessa swayed, dizzy and faint, and her knees buckled.

Hands gripped her shoulders, holding her steady. Nessa blinked wearily, unsettled and confused.

Gone was the sight of manicured gardens and bird crests, replaced by the worried eyes of Hunter staring down at her.

"Are you alright?" he asked, his hands slipping from her shoulders and coming to rest on her upper arms

"You're very pale."

Nessa's gaze darted all around. She felt rather lost. The forest surrounded her once more, an endless sea of trees and fallen leaves, and the wall had reverted back to its broken state, weathered and crumbling. There was no sight of the bird emblem or the cobbled road, no suggestion of grass lawns or flowerbeds filled with roses. Nessa couldn't help but wonder if she had momentarily lost her mind, imagining it all.

"Nessa?" Hunter said, giving her a gentle shake. "Are you with me yet? You've been staring into the distance for a good minute or two now. It's a little disconcerting."

"Fine." Nessa tried to clear away the fog that filled her head. She felt like she was in two different places at once, here and there. Nothing seemed quite real. "I'm fine."

Hunter didn't look convinced. "Are you sick? Faint?" His eyes ran over her, searching for any clues as to what ailed her. "I knew we should have taken things easier. You need more time to heal and rest, and to recover from your ordeal."

*My little Rider,* Aoife called, her voice loud and urgent, drowning out whatever else Hunter had to say. *What happened just then? You were there, and yet you weren't. It's hard to describe.*

Aoife's words, her alarm, pushed aside the fog in Nessa's head. She frowned, more than a little bewildered.

"I'm fine," she told both Hunter and Aoife, her words holding a measure of assurance, of truth. "I just kind of, I don't know, slipped into this weird little daydream."

"And got lost in your little daydream," Hunter muttered. "If you ask me."

Nessa chuckled. "I guess so."

"And you're sure that you're alright?"

Nessa nodded.

"We can take a break if you're tired?" Hunter insisted.

Nessa spied Orm and Chaos standing nearby. Orm, like Hunter, looked at her with a mixture of worry and concern. Chaos, though, had something else shining in his glacial eyes, a strange kind of consideration. A shiver of warning ran up Nessa's spine. She forced herself to smile.

"A break isn't necessary," she told him, the desire to leave being stronger than her aches and pains. "And anyway, I'm eager to get my new shoes."

Hunter nodded to himself and took a step back, his hands slipping from her arms. "Your feet hurt, don't they?"

"Nope," Nessa said, trying to be believable, worried that he would keep pressing the issue. Even though she wasn't sure what had happened to her, she didn't want to linger, fearing that it would happen again. "My feet are perfectly fine."

Hunter, although looking unconvinced, thankfully didn't seem inclined to argue. Without saying a word, he turned and moved to join the others. Nessa hurried after him, her feet protesting with each step.

As soon as Orm saw that they were continuing with their journey, he started off, leading the way through the trees. Chaos hesitated for a second, and Nessa could feel his stare focused on her. She was unable to meet his gaze, knowing that he would be able to see her lies and doubts.

*I'll trust that you are okay to continue on your way,* Aoife said quietly. *However, I can tell that something has unsettled you.*

Nessa was reluctant to divulge what had happened. The whispered names she heard in the daydream echoed softly in her ears, resonating and haunting. But Aoife was her bonded partner, though, and if a girl couldn't confide in her dragon, then who could she confide in?

*I'm not sure that the daydream was entirely a daydream. It felt as if a spell had been cast over me.* It felt more like a waking dream, one that held a great and terrible secret, and quite possibly a warning too.

Aoife was quiet. If not for the tie of their bond, Nessa would have thought that she hadn't been heard. As it was, she could faintly sense Aoife's deep contemplation, her mind a churning mass of emotions and sensations.

*How very peculiar,* Aoife eventually said.

*Do you know what it was?*

*I do not.*

*Oh...* Nessa tried to hide her disappointment, but some of it managed to leach through the bond.

*You are a creature born of magic,* Aoife said placatingly, *and magic is a strange and sometimes unpredictable thing. Do not worry or dwell on what happened for long. You'll just give yourself a headache.*

Nessa took Aoife's advice under consideration. *Please don't tell the others.*

*Why not? They're concerned about you.*

*It's just something I want to be kept between us. At least for the time being.*

*If that's what you really want, then I shall keep my silence.*

*Thank you.*

*Although I do suggest sharing your experience with the others,* Aoife murmured gently. *They may be able to help.*

Nessa had her doubts. Those names...the undercurrents of warnings and secrets...they felt as if they were for her ears only.

*You fear that they will see you as weak, don't you, if you ask for their help,* Aoife mused, thoughtful. *That's why you won't tell them your feet hurt, and why you're reluctant to tell them about what happened back by that wall.*

*They worry enough about me as it is. I can feel it coming off them in waves. They already think that I'm helpless and weak.*

*No, they don't.*

*They do,* Nessa argued. *But I'm not. I'm not weak and helpless. I won't be a burden, slowing them down and causing a fuss over a few blisters.*

*Judging by your discomfort, I think it's safe to say that you have more than just a few blisters.*

*Maybe.*

*Just take a break from walking and let Orm give you a piggyback. It will be fun. You'll enjoy it.*

*I'm perfectly capable of walking, thank you very much.*

*That's just your pride talking.*

Nessa huffed. *My pride?*

*Anyway, you're not weak if you admit that you're hurt or scared. You can't be strong every moment of every day.*

Aoife withdrew from Nessa's mind, leaving her with a lot of things to mull over.

# Chapter 12

The town of Arncraft was bigger than Nessa expected. Quite a lot bigger, in fact. She had anticipated a small farming town consisting of a number of dwellings and a little marketplace. Instead, Nessa found that Arncraft had a vast selection of inns to choose from, a wide array of shops and a rather sizable market.

Arncraft was a town large enough for weary travellers to get lost in if they weren't careful.

The market occupied most of the main road that wove through the town like a snake, long and narrow, with tall buildings rising up on either side, a mixture of houses, shops, bakeries and everything in between. Most were timber framed with small mullion windows and pitched roofs, their wattle and daub panels painted a pleasant cream or yellow. The streets were crowded with people, and the air was filled with joyous noise. Arncraft was bustling and alive.

With no recollection of ever visiting a village, a town or—to be honest—*anything*, everything Nessa saw was a first. She found it to be awe-inspiring and a smidgen overwhelming.

Nessa trailed behind Orm and Hunter as they made their way down the market street, searching for an inn they liked the look of. Those two were picky when it came to a place to stay. They both carried a couple of bags each containing their clothing and a few extra things. The tents and other supplies were with Aoife, who was tucked a few miles away in the foothills of the Cléa Mountains. Through their bond, Nessa knew that Aoife was curled up comfortably on a rocky embankment, soaking up the late afternoon sun, hidden far away from prying human eyes.

They had met up with Aoife shortly before Arncraft had come into sight, relieving her of her load and taking what they needed for their short stay in the town. While Hunter and Orm were sorting through the bags that would be left behind, Nessa had sat beside Aoife, resting her hurting feet, savouring their time together. Chaos had wandered off, claiming he was going to get changed. Nessa briefly wondered why, given that no one would be looking at his clothing once they caught sight of his monstrous wings and eerie eyes.

*This is a perfect spot*, Aoife said. *I can bask and see the town from here. If anything happens, I can simply swoop down and whisk you away.*

Nessa peered at the horizon, seeing nothing other than wild meadows that slowly gave way to tended fields. *I can't see it.*

*That's because my eyesight is better than yours.*

Nessa's sarcastic response was poised on the tip of her

tongue; then she saw something that stopped her dead.

Chaos had changed alright, but not just his clothing. He had changed everything. Literally, *everything*. His wings and scars had gone, as had his long black hair.

The clothing he now wore consisted of faded robes that hung from his frame, tatty and baggy, and he carried a walking stick in one gnarled hand. Where he had got that was anyone's guess. His back was severely humped, making him hunch forwards, almost doubled over, and his black hair was now straggly and white.

Chaos shuffled out from behind a bush, tying a strip of cloth around his eyes as he did so. Nessa caught a glimpse of his face before he hid most of it, and sort of wished she hadn't. Chaos' ghastly scars were gone, which was a slight improvement, but so had his eyes. Two smooth hollows stood in their place. Gone was the winged nightmare, replaced by a deformed old man. Still, Nessa found him no less intimidating.

*Close your mouth,* Aoife advised. *Otherwise, you'll start catching flies.*

Nessa's mouth snapped shut, her teeth chinking together sharply. *What…how?*

*Chaos is old and powerful, even by Old Blood standards.*

*That's not an answer.*

*Some more—how do I put it—inhuman species of Old Bloods have two sides to themselves, like that of a coin. This is one side of Chaos, the blind seer, and the other, which you are more familiar with, is the harbinger of truths.*

*That sounds a little alarming.*

Aoife laughed. *At least he doesn't have wings now. He'll draw less attention when you're in town.*

*I'm not so sure about that.*

Yes, Chaos appeared more human without the wings

and the glacial eyes, what with the strip of cloth hiding the hollow sockets, but he wouldn't pass completely as a human. There was still an aura of danger and otherness about him. Nessa could feel the power coming off him in waves, a deep thrum that was felt in her bones.

*He knows what he's doing,* Aoife assured her. *He's done this many times before.*

*I guess I'll get to see for myself shortly, won't I?*

But Nessa didn't get to see, not really.

As soon as the crowded market came into sight, Chaos muttered something along the lines of "bloody hate humans" and slipped away, disappearing down a narrow alleyway. Those who crossed paths with Chaos before he had left had given him a wide berth, but hadn't stared too much. Nessa thought it was handy that Chaos could pass himself off as human if he wanted. She had been wondering how he was planning on going incognito when they got to the capital. Now, Nessa knew.

Just ahead of her, Hunter pulled Orm to a stop and nodded at something before catching Nessa's eye, waving her over. She quickened her pace, closing the gap between them, curious to see what had captured his interest.

On the other side of the street, sheltered under a large awning, was a booth that sold an array of colourful clothing. Dresses, capes and tunics hung on rails, and footwear covered a table top. Knickknacks such as belts and bags were to be found nestled amongst the other items, as were socks, gloves and underthings.

"There," Hunter said as Nessa came to stand beside him. "That seems like a fine place to get you a few things."

It looked a good a place as any, by Nessa's

approximation, but she had to ask, "I thought we didn't have enough money to get me things until Orm had won us some?"

"Oh, we have enough to get you a change of clothes, at the very least." Hunter winked. "And some shoes that fit too, I think."

Nessa's back straightened as she recognised the glint in his eyes. "You know my feet hurt, don't you? You've known all along. Aoife told you."

Hunter grinned, wicked. "Maybe she did. Maybe she didn't."

*Traitor!*

*I merely mentioned it in passing after he noticed you limping,* Aoife murmured sleepily. *Now, go find some shoes that fit before you get gangrene or another one of those pesky ailments.*

"Anyway," Hunter said, "Orm can get a head start on gathering some winnings whilst we get you some things. He can recoup what we spend. Can't you, Orm?"

Orm nodded, his eyes bright with excitement. "I think I've already found a likely spot. Looks just the place where gullible rich fops go to lose lots and lots of money."

"Go forth, my friend," Hunter sighed even as Orm moved away, cutting through the shoppers with ease, purpose in his step, his smooth head bobbing above the market's crowds. "Go forth and win."

Nessa cocked a brow. "Is he likely to win?"

"Orm's the finest cheat out there."

"He's going to cheat?"

"Of course," Hunter smirked. "Why, did you think he was going to play an honest game?"

"No," Nessa mumbled. Orm did not strike her as

someone who would ever play an honest game.

Hunter nudged her with an elbow. "Then don't act so surprised. Come on," he began herding her over to the clothing stall, "let's get you something that doesn't make your feet bleed or make you look like a vagrant."

Nessa looked down at herself, trying to see how she might appear to other people. Yes, everything was a little oversized, but at least it was clean. She had bathed and her hair was brushed. Surely she couldn't look *that* bad. "I think the term 'vagrant' is a little harsh."

"Mmm, I guess we'll have to see what the seamstress thinks, won't we?"

The seamstress in question milled around her stall, talking to a potential buyer. She was middle-aged, her brown hair threaded with a delicate touch of silver, and her face holding a scattering of laugh lines. Her gaze darted to them as they approached, and when she realised they were interested in her wares, she smiled warmly.

"Can I help you with anything?"

"Perhaps," Hunter replied, looking around with a keen eye. "It depends on your prices, and if you have anything that fits my wee friend here that's ready to go."

The woman took Nessa's measure, which couldn't be easy considering how baggy Hunter's clothes were on her.

"I believe I have a few things that might fit," the seamstress replied. "And I assure you, my prices are the best in town."

As Hunter and the seamstress fell into conversation, haggling on prices, Nessa meandered around, perusing what was on offer. There wasn't anything particularly fancy, but all of it was of high quality and well made.

Judging from what the other women wore, Nessa assumed floor-length dresses were the fashion. She had seen a few younger girls wearing leggings and half-dresses that fell almost to their knees, but other than that, everyone else was in a long dress, although the styles did vary. Nessa supposed that social status and age played a part in who wore what.

Those of the upper class, though rare, were easy to spot. They walked around with a confidence that few had the privilege of experiencing, oozing self-entitlement and wealth. They were clothed in velvets and silks of vibrant colours, royal reds and purples and blues. The women's dresses featured a fitted bodice and three-quarter-length sleeves that left their wrists bare for them to display an array of bejewelled bangles. A full skirt edged with delicate embroidery or decorative trim flared out from the waist, falling gracefully to the ground in an elegant sweep, accentuating their tiny waists and making them seem taller than they actually were. The men were no less splendidly attired, wearing rich brocade doublets or tunics paired with fine overcoats, their knee-high boots polished to a high shine and a dagger or two sheathed at the hip.

Those belonging to the lower and working class wore more modest, practical clothing. The men were dressed similarly to Orm and Hunter, wearing smocks, tunics or loose shirts paired with trous. The women wore linen dresses that featured slim-fitting sleeves and a bodice that laced up at the back or sides. The skirts were usually softly pleated, giving them a bit of body and movement. A matching surcoat or, like the seamstress had chosen to do, an apron was sometimes added.

Unfortunately for Nessa, who eyed the dresses of the

upper class with a touch of longing, the stall only catered to the lower classes. There was no sign of a lush velvet gown in Nessa's immediate future. Not that she had the money for one, come to think of it.

Hunter and the seamstress appeared to have reached some kind of agreement and crossed over to the side of the booth. As they began looking through a pile of folded clothes, Nessa joined them, eager to see what she would be getting.

"Since you aren't planning on staying for long," the seamstress was saying, "that limits our options. But seeing as she's small, these should be alright lengthwise. They lace up well, so they shouldn't be overly baggy with a bit of tweaking."

"Hear that, Nessa?" Hunter asked. "They won't be too baggy with a bit of tweaking."

"Some growing room, I suppose," Nessa murmured.

"Exactly. Get a few pies in you, and they'll fit perfectly soon enough."

Nessa chuckled.

"Here we are," the woman muttered to herself, pulling out a few items from the middle of the pile and setting them on top. She unfolded a dress and held it up to Nessa, checking the size. "I made these from a shipment of new fabric last month. I think they turned out rather nice."

"How very stimulating," Hunter said. "And what a fantastic seamstress you are. However, Eliza, as I've explained, dresses aren't particularly practical for long travels. Don't you have some tunics she can wear instead?"

"And as I've explained," Eliza replied, holding up another dress. "It's all well and good for young ladies to be running around in tunics and trous down in the south, but here in the midlands, that's just not the done thing. And it's certainly not acceptable in the capital, not at her age."

"It's not acceptable for her to be tripping over every five minutes whilst walking to the capital," Hunter grumbled.

Eliza glared at him. "She won't trip over." She turned to Nessa. "You won't trip over, will you?"

Nessa shook her head complacently, unwilling to be in the middle of an argument. "Since dresses are the fashion in these parts, especially in the capital, I suppose I should wear them. I wouldn't want to draw any unwanted attention to myself, now, would I?"

Hunter rolled his eyes, grumbling something uncomplimentary under his breath.

Eliza clucked like a happy mother hen and moved around her stall, searching for clothing that was within their budget, whatever that was. By the time Eliza had finished collecting and laying out Nessa's options, Nessa had six dresses to choose from. While Hunter and Nessa looked over the dresses, Eliza busied herself on the other side of the stall, selecting some shoes, socks and a few other things.

"I've negotiated for two outfits," Hunter informed Nessa. "Plus a pair of shoes and some, uh, underthings."

"Underthings?" Nessa queried, amused.

Hunter scowled. "Hush."

Nessa snorted, then looked over the dresses. "Two, you say?"

He nodded.

"Then I'd like to have the blue one and the red one?"

Hunter shrugged. "They seem as good a pair of

dresses as any I've seen before."

"They're an excellent choice," Eliza said as she rejoined them, carrying a selection of shoes and an armload of neatly folded things. Nessa presumed that they were the underthings which Hunter found too embarrassing to mention without his cheeks turning pink. "The red compliments your complexion, and the blue goes nicely with your hair." Eliza sighed as she set down her armload by the dresses on the table. "Although it is a shame that I don't have anything in purple. That would go with your eyes so perfectly. But still, the blue and the red are lovely."

Nessa felt herself blush at the compliments, knowing that she looked less than her best. She managed to squeak out a small "thank you".

Eliza smiled, the fine creases around her eyes deepening, and nodded to a nearby stool. "Why don't you sit there and try these on," she passed a few pairs of shoes to Nessa, "and see which ones are the most comfortable. I'll go wrap everything else for you."

Nessa perched on the stool, hesitant to remove her current footwear, fearful that her blisters had bled through her socks. Knowing that she needed to try on the new shoes, lest they are as uncomfortable as the ones she already had, she forced herself to bury her embarrassment. She placed the changes of shoes on the ground and unlaced her boots, slowly pulling them off. To her pleasant surprise, no blood stained her socks, and Nessa slipped on her first choice of shoes. They were soft suede, lightweight and durable. They were also a good fit. Nessa decided they would do just fine. She didn't bother trying on the other pairs.

Reluctant to put her old boots back on, Nessa decided

to simply keep wearing her new shoes, even if they did look a little odd paired with Hunter's oversized socks. She tugged the bottom of her trous down, trying to conceal the strange ensemble as much as she could. As she did so, her sleeves unrolled, falling around her fingers.

Nessa sat up just as Eliza finished wrapping their purchases. Hunter gave Eliza a winning smile as he deposited a palm-full of coins in her waiting hand and took the wrapped bundle.

Fiddling with her sleeves, trying to roll them back up, Nessa joined them, her feet marginally more comfortable already.

"Well," Eliza said, casting a warm glance at Nessa, "we've got you sorted out nicely. However..." She looked Hunter up and down, taking in his mop of messy brown hair and his lazy grin. "You could do with some new things if you want to get ahead in the big city. No one wants to do business with a scruffy southerner."

"I beg to differ, dear Eliza," Hunter remarked brightly, tucking the wrapped bundle under his arm. "I think people will love my southern charm. It seems to have worked wonders with you."

Eliza smirked. "Don't make the mistake of thinking that I gave you this bargain because of your so-called 'charm', young man. I just felt that this poor girl has enough to deal with, what with travelling and having to put up with you, that she shouldn't have to look like a vagrant."

"If that's what you need to tell yourself," Hunter sighed, "then I'm okay with that. But only because I know the truth." He winked. "Southern charm."

Quite uncharmed, Eliza turned to Nessa. "A word of

advice for the capital..." Her words faded away as her eyes were drawn down.

Nessa followed Eliza's gaze, wondering as to what had made her pause mid-sentence. She quickly realised that Eliza was staring at her hand, at the distinctive, purple-hued mark that wrapped around it. Unease fluttered in Nessa's stomach. She shoved down her sleeve and hid her arm behind her back.

Her stare broken, Eliza blinked and cleared her throat.

"Well," Hunter said abruptly, "it was a pleasure shopping with you, Eliza. Thank you for all your help. It was most appreciated. However, the time has simply flown by, and we really need to be going. Otherwise, we'll never find our companion."

With a hand on Nessa's back, Hunter steered her away from Eliza, propelling her into the tide of shoppers. They were soon engulfed by the crowd, swept away by the current.

"She saw my Rider's Mark," Nessa hissed, panicked.

"I know," Hunter said, "but maybe she doesn't know what it is. Maybe she was just taken aback by it. It does kinda look like a scar at first sight."

"Do you really believe that?"

"No, I don't. A guy can always hope, though, can't he?"

"This could be really bad," Nessa insisted. "Really, really bad. What if she tells someone?"

"I'm fully aware that this isn't good," Hunter said sharply. "But considering that this is a boring town, it's highly possible that *no one* here has ever seen a Dragon Rider before, let alone a middle-aged seamstress who sells clothing at a market stall."

Nessa could see the sense in his reasoning and tried to

push aside her concerns. Hunter clearly knew of the implications should Eliza understand what the mark signified.

"Which way did Orm go?" Hunter mumbled, his hand slipping from Nessa's back as he stood on his tiptoes, peering over the throngs of shoppers.

Nessa, too, looked around, unsure as to which direction Orm had wandered off in. Her attention elsewhere, Nessa didn't see the figure rushing up behind her, didn't sense their approach, until it was too late.

A hand clamped around Nessa's wrist and another slapped over her mouth, smothering her strangled scream of alarm. With a forceful yank, she was pulled backwards. Hunter didn't notice her being bundled into a shadowed alleyway. No one did.

*Nessa?* Aoife cried, awoken by the rush of Nessa's alarm shooting through their bond. *What's happening?*

*Uhh...* Nessa twisted, Aoife's fear giving her the strength to wrench herself free from her assailant's grip. She swung around, a hand raised, fingers curled into a fist.

"Eliza!" Nessa froze, her punch suspended in the air.

"Your secret is safe with me," Eliza gushed, her eyes wide and earnest. "I won't tell a soul."

The words were slow to register, but when they did, the tension eased from Nessa's shoulders. She could sense the truth in them. Slowly, Nessa lowered her fist.

"Thank you," she breathed.

Eliza took Nessa's hands and wrapped them around a small, soft package. "You need to be more careful. Much more careful. I will keep my silence, but there are those who would not. Perilous times are ahead. People like us can never be too careful."

"People like us...?"

Smiling coyly, Eliza peeked over her shoulder, quickly checking that no one was lingering by the mouth of the alley. When she turned back, her appearance had changed ever so slightly.

Eliza's hair was darker, the threads of silver gone, and her skin was smoother, the fine wrinkles having vanished. Her cheekbones were more defined, sharper, and her eyes...

Nessa blinked, not quite believing what she saw.

Eliza's hazel eyes now bore a striking resemblance to those of a cat: large, angled and with slitted pupils.

*Old Blood,* Aoife whispered, awestruck.

Nessa barely stifled a gasp.

As swiftly as Eliza's features had changed, they reverted back, her features softening, her skin subtly ageing, her cat eyes once again human.

"Shh." Eliza glanced over her shoulder, then held up an amulet, small and old, which hung around her neck by a leather cord. A faded runic symbol was etched into its surface. "My brethren and I are your allies. But you need to be wary around others who do not bear this seal. They are your enemies, even if they are like kin to you."

"What are you talking about?" Nessa asked. Dread bloomed like a dark, malicious flower.

Nessa received no answer. Eliza tucked the amulet back under the neckline of her dress and dashed from the alley, nearly crashing into Hunter as he rounded the corner. Before either of them could recover from their shock, Eliza slipped into the crowd and disappeared.

Hunter shook off the dismay first. He rushed over to Nessa. "Was that—"

"Eliza the seamstress?" Nessa muttered. "Yes, yes it

was."

"And dare I ask what that was all about?"

"She said that my secret is safe with her," Nessa murmured. "She also said a few other things about being careful and to only trust her brethren."

Hunter's eyebrows rose. "Oh, is that all? Glad she didn't stab you or anything nefarious like that."

"Stab me?"

"The next time someone drags you into a dark alleyway, maybe you could at least try to fight back?"

"I was taken by surprise," Nessa argued. "And anyway, I had a punch primed and ready to go. Then I saw who it was."

Hunter's eyes twinkled, his lips twitching as he fought back a grin. "You were going to punch her?"

"Maybe." Nessa shrugged. "What of it?"

"Nothing," Hunter smirked. "I'm just pleasantly surprised, that's all. I didn't think you had it in you to punch someone."

"Well, now you know."

"Indeed, I do."

"You won't be underestimating me again, now, will you?"

"I'll be sure not to make that mistake again." Hunter gestured to the alley's entrance. "Come on. Let's go find Orm before something else unexpected happens."

They left the alleyway, keeping close to the sides of the buildings, avoiding the flood of shoppers that seemed to be growing with the later hour. Freed from the shadows, Nessa was able to see what Eliza had handed her in the gloom of the alley. She carefully unrolled the small bundle of soft, dark fabric.

"What's that you got?"

Nessa held up two matching items. "Eliza just gave them to me."

"Oh, the nutty woman gave you some arm warmers? How nice of her."

"I believe," Nessa said, putting them on, "that they are to hide my Rider's Mark." Everything from her knuckles to the elbow was concealed, everything except for her thumbs and fingers.

"Well, fancy that." Hunter spared them a glance. "That *is* nice of her. Thoughtful too. What else did Eliza give you? Did she say anything useful?"

"Well..." Nessa hesitated, feeling Aoife tug on their bond.

*Careful with what you say,* Aoife warned. *Eliza said that she would keep your secret, so I think you should show the same courtesy.*

*I guess you're right,* Nessa admitted. *It's probably not a good idea to go around telling people that there's an Old Blood living here.*

*Especially since the king has a penchant for hunting Old Bloods and killing them.*

"Eliza just said that my secret is safe with her," Nessa murmured, "and that I should be more careful. Oh, and that perilous times are ahead."

Hunter's brows rose. "And I presume that you feel like your secret is safe with her?"

"Yes," Nessa said honestly. "Otherwise she wouldn't have bothered to give me something to hide the mark, now, would she?"

"No, I suppose she wouldn't," Hunter agreed. "And these perilous times ahead, did she give any insight on that, any clues or hints?"

"None whatsoever."

"How delightfully vague and unhelpful."

"And here I was thinking that you'd appreciate the vagueness."

"Oh, under normal circumstances, yes, I would. However, when a vague foreshadowing of impending doom is predicted by a stranger who knows that you're a Dragon Rider, I suddenly find myself wanting a little less vagueness involved."

"Mmm, while we're on the subject of vagueness, Orm wasn't particularly forthcoming when it came to telling us where he was going."

"I doubt Orm really knew where he was going himself," Hunter laughed. "But he won't be that hard to find. He usually sticks to the same kind of establishments." Hunter nodded to a building up ahead. "I bet my best shirt that he's in there."

"I'm wearing your best shirt, so that's not a very good bet."

Hunter snickered.

Nessa looked at the building that Hunter was betting his best shirt on. It was large, long and several stories tall. The exposed timber framework was painted a harsh black, as were the window frames and shutters. The upper floors were jettied, each one sticking out a little further than the one below it, and the steep roof had a dusting of grey soot around the clusters of tall chimneys that were dotted around, many of which spewed thin fingers of smoke.

As they drew closer, Nessa saw a sign hanging above the double front door that read "The Blackened Cauldron".

"You reckon he's in there?" Nessa asked, voicing her doubts.

"Oh yes," Hunter said, coming to a stop in front of the doors. "It's big enough to have plenty of rooms for travellers to spend the night, and it appears to be nice enough to attract more wealthy visitors. Yet it's not too nice as to prevent less well-off people from stopping by every now and again for a drink and a game of cards."

Nessa summarised, "So it has a wide variety of people for Orm to swindle money from?"

Hunter nodded. "Pretty much. Now, let's go join him."

# Chapter 13

Considering that the sun had yet to retire for the day, The Blackened Cauldron was busy. More so than Nessa had thought possible. Individuals jostled to get to the front of the large queue for the bar, eager to get a refill, and gatherings of friends milled around, laughing and gossiping boisterously. A number of tables closest to the bar and door were occupied by large groups of men enjoying their pints and a hearty meal. The windows were small and closed, and there was little in the way of natural light or fresh air. Thick wooden beams were only a few inches above Hunter's head, the ceiling perilously low, and more than a few people were smoking, thin tendrils of haze drifting up from the tips of their cigars and pipes. The smell of tobacco and more questionable substances was almost overwhelming.

Nessa's eyes watered and her nose blocked up as Hunter led her further into the tap house, winding his way around tables, servers and a few people who staggered into his path. He was aiming for a dark corner that was cloistered from the rest of the tavern by a staircase that led to the upper floors. It was a secretive, little nook that hosted a couple of round tables that men loitered around, avidly watching a number of card games being played.

Although his back was to them, Nessa instantly knew that one of them was Orm. His distinctive bald head glinted in the dim candlelight as he threw it back, laughing loudly. He was sat at one of the tables, a fan of splayed cards in one hand and a tankard in the other.

"Guess you won the bet after all," Nessa said.

"What can I say?" Hunter grinned. "I have a gift when it comes to finding my gambling friend."

"Mmm, and your gambling friend certainly has a gift for finding somewhere that isn't particularly family friendly."

"Well, Orm isn't really a family-orientated man."

In all honesty, no one in the premises really looked like a family person. Other than Nessa and a handful of other women, mostly serving girls who looked like they could hold their own in a bar brawl, everyone was male. Whilst Nessa had to admit that the inn's patrons didn't look like complete scoundrels, they didn't come across as outstanding members of society either.

*Some of the men keep looking at me.*

*They're not looking at you,* Aoife said. *They're leering at you. There's a difference.*

*Thanks for that. Really reassuring.*

*You're welcome.*

Hunter stepped up behind Orm and clapped him on the shoulder, eyeing the stacks of coins sitting in front of him. "I see you're having a winning streak, my friend."

Orm chortled, showing Hunter his play of cards. "The gods favour us this day."

"Indeed they do," Hunter murmured, picking out one card and slotting it between two others, putting them into a neat order. "But we can't trust you with all the winnings, now, can we?" He reached out and swiftly pocketed a couple of coin stacks, leaving Orm with just one. Orm pouted but then shrugged, raising his half-empty tankard to his lips, his attention sliding back to the game.

"I don't suppose Orm's booked us a room, has he?" Nessa asked as Hunter straightened. "I don't like how some of these people are looking at me."

Hunter peered around and scowled. The men in question, who—as Aoife put it—had been leering, quickly turned away, eyes pointedly focused elsewhere. "Why don't you stay with Orm for a minute? I'll go find whoever's in charge and get us a room or two for the night."

"Fine," Nessa sighed. "I'll go hide in the corner. Out of sight."

"And while you hide in corners, you can hold this." Hunter handed her the bundle of wrapped clothing he'd been carrying before ambling over towards the bar, weaving through the crowds and around tables.

Nessa hugged her arms around the bundle as if it were a pillow, holding it tight to her chest. She crossed over to the stairs, where it was quieter. In the space under them, not visible to most of the room, was a pair of small booths. One was occupied by a group of young men who appeared a little worse for wear. A mess of empty rum bottles littered their table. They seemed oblivious to everything around them, thanks to their high levels of intoxication, which was probably why they hadn't noticed the ominous figure sitting in the booth next to them.

Nessa slipped in beside Chaos, setting the packaged clothing down on the table in front of her. Chaos turned his head as if he could actually see her. Nessa found the move a little disconcerting because he was eyeless and blindfolded, but she pushed away her unease and steeled her nerves. They were, after all, travelling partners. It wouldn't do for her to be frightened by him all the time, especially not if she wanted to learn more about Old Bloods and magic. Witnessing Eliza shift her appearance had made a lot of questions arise, and since Orm was otherwise engaged, Nessa was hoping that Chaos would shed some light onto a few of them.

*Might.*

If she was lucky.

Really lucky…

"Did you have a nice wander around the town?" Nessa asked, trying for some polite small talk before launching into her inquisition.

"Not really."

That wasn't the answer she expected. Nessa pursed her lips, rethinking her approach. "Well, um…that's a shame."

"Not really," Chaos grunted. "It was what I had anticipated. Boring, little human town that it is."

"I thought the market was quite nice."

"Exactly how many markets do you have to compare it against?"

Nessa sagged back against the chair, wishing that she had never opened her mouth. "None, I suppose, since I can't remember anything."

"Precisely. So you'll have to take my word for it."

"I guess I'll have to."

"This is a very unremarkable little town. It is a boring little town that has only prospered to the state it's in because it's part of the black-market trade."

Chaos crossed his arms over his chest. "I find myself curious," he said grudgingly, unwillingly. "What do you think I was doing around the town?"

Nessa shrugged. She didn't really care. After all, she was just temporarily aiming for some small talk. "Oh, I don't know. You left us so soon that I sort of thought you were meeting up with a friend of yours. Another Old Blood, perhaps?"

"Another Old Blood?" he scoffed. "Here? Margan really has done a number on your brain if you think an Old Blood would lower themselves to dwelling in a place like this."

The mention of Margan made Nessa's spine straighten sharply.

*Ignore him,* Aoife said quickly, sensing Nessa's anger, her blossoming hurt. *He speaks whatever comes to mind. I'm sure he means no insult.*

*That was a horrible thing to say.*

*I know, my little Rider. But be the better person and don't retaliate. He probably doesn't see how that came across.*

*Bu—*

*Hush, my little one. Water off a duck's back, as the saying goes.*

"Why," Hunter said brightly, "don't the two of you look like you've been having a jolly old chitchat." He came to stand by their booth.

Nessa glared at him.

Hunter held up a key. "Room 36 is all ours."

Nessa frowned. "*Just* room 36?"

"It was the last room available. Possibly because it costs a small fortune."

"All four of us are sharing the same room?"

"It's a large room."

"This room is large, and yet it's not quite large enough."

Hunter's eyes slid to Chaos knowingly. "Well, there are beds, and I've organised for food and drinks to be brought up shortly, so you'll just have to deal."

With a sigh, Nessa rose, grabbed her bundle of clothing and crossed over to the stairs, happy to have some space between her and their unsavoury companion. "You're mean."

"I know." Hunter waved her onwards. "Now up you go. A nice, warm, comfy bed awaits you."

"Is that a promise?"

"A guarantee, apparently."

The stairs led up to a long, narrow hallway. Doors lined either side, all of them closed and with little number plaques nailed onto them. The only source of light came from a small, solitary window in the far wall.

Nessa peered at the doors closest to her, trying to see the numbers. The hallway's dimness didn't make the job easy.

"Our lovely hostess said that we're on the top floor," Hunter said, moving past her. "We have an attic room."

"Bloody damn stairs," Chaos growled. "Makes my bones ache."

Nessa looked over her shoulder, finding that Chaos was a few steps shy of reaching the top stair. For a split second, Nessa felt pity and almost went to give him a helping hand. Then she reminded herself that there was more to Chaos than the blind old man guise. For that's what it was: a guise, a cloak he wore which hid the fearsome, winged Old Blood that lurked beneath the surface. Nessa also reminded herself that he had just been particularly mean to her.

Without feeling any guilt whatsoever, Nessa turned away from Chaos and hurried after Hunter.

They went up a further two flights of stairs before they reached the end of their ascent. Nessa found herself waiting in a short entranceway while Hunter struggled with the door to their room. The lock stuck for a second, the tumblers refusing to turn.

Hunter gave the key a peculiar little jiggle, and it finally unlocked. The door swung open.

Hunter stepped into the room, looking it over with a critical eye. "Not too shabby, if I do say so myself."

"I think your opinion is a little biased," Nessa said, moving past him.

After seeing downstairs, Nessa had given up hope of having a pleasant night spent in a cosy inn's guest room. She was expecting something rather plain and basic, and probably not quite as clean as she would have liked.

However, as Nessa gazed around, she found herself pleasantly surprised.

The attic room was large and spacious, the ceiling high and sloped, the beams rustically bare. One wall was exposed brickwork with a feature fireplace, and the window seats were quaintly tucked away in the pair of dormer windows. The wooden floor was covered in a collage of different coloured rugs, and the quartet of beds were neatly made with fresh linens. The air was free from any hint of dust or smoke, which was a nice change compared to downstairs. Nessa felt her nose starting to unblock.

"Well," Hunter said, "what do you think?"

Nessa went over to the furthest bed and sat down, bouncing on the edge, testing the mattress "I think this is a lot nicer than what I was expecting."

"It should be, considering the price," Hunter mumbled as he took the bed next to hers. "I'm pretty sure you could rent a small house for a month with what this room cost for the night."

"Oh."

"You know, I think there's something strange with the women in this town." Hunter flopped back on the mattress, tucking his hands behind his head. "I can't seem to charm them like I can elsewhere. It's a real pain."

"My heart bleeds for you."

"Oi! If we were anywhere else, with a smile and a twinkle in my eyes, I would have got this room for half the price."

Nessa chuckled. "Maybe you're just not as good as you think you are, ever think of that?"

"No, I haven't. And you know why? Because the very idea is preposterous." Hunter closed his eyes and wiggled, getting comfortable. "Not as good as I think I am, what a silly notion."

The door slammed open, hitting the wall behind it with a bang strong enough to make the furniture rattle. Startled, Hunter jolted, his body leaving the mattress for a comical second, his eyes wide and staring. Nessa clamped a hand over her chest, her heart doing shocked, little spasms as she watched Chaos come to stand in the doorway, filling it with his hunched form.

"Was that really necessary?" Hunter demanded,

sitting up and glaring at Chaos.

"I don't know," Chaos growled, "was it really necessary to get a room on the top bloody floor?"

"Yes, actually, it was. The other available rooms just went to a group of traders from Vasindor. I'll take this opportunity to add that we could have had those rooms if you'd bothered to book them instead of sitting on your sagging arse over in a dim corner doing nothing particularly useful."

Nessa stared at Hunter, wondering if he had lost his mind and wanted to suffer a horrifying and painful death.

Chaos stomped forwards, shutting the door behind him violently. "I find conversing with humans who run this kind of establishment beneath me."

"You find everyone and everything beneath you," Hunter muttered, lying back down.

Nessa bit her lip, trying not to snigger, and watched Chaos, half-amazed that he hadn't flown into a rage and killed Hunter on the spot. Chaos placed his bag on the bed furthest from her and hobbled over to the fireplace, walking stick tapping quietly on the flooring as it helped to keep him upright. His lip curled with disgust and he grumbled something under his breath, too low for Nessa to hear.

Chaos held out a hand, palm facing towards the hearth.

*Wait for it,* Aoife murmured in anticipation.

There was a spark and a mighty *whoosh* of rushing air, and the fireplace was suddenly filled with roaring flames. Nessa jumped and shifted uneasily on the edge of her bed. Hunter, clearly used to the blatant display of magic, merely rolled his eyes, unimpressed.

*I love it when he or Orm starts a fire like that,* Aoife said, her satisfaction leaking through their bond. *I like fire.*

Nessa couldn't help but smile. *Do you, now?*

*Yes. Fire is wild and fierce. Beautiful too.*

*Just like dragons are?*

*I suppose. Although I've never thought of it like that. Sometimes I feel like I could stare into the dancing flames for hours.*

Nessa gazed at the fireplace, at the flames, watching them coil and twist around each other in a hypnotising ballet of yellows and oranges, and understood where Aoife was coming from. Even tamed, fire was beautiful and powerful.

*I guess that liking fire is kind of required, seeing as you're a fire-breathing reptile. It wouldn't be any good if you were scared of it.*

*No,* Aoife laughed, *that wouldn't be any good at all.*

There was a quiet tap on the door, a timid knock. Nessa looked over, expecting it to be Orm. Since the door was unlocked, she expected him to saunter in, but he didn't. Instead, there was another knock, a louder one this time.

Hunter sat up. "That must be the dinner I ordered."

Chaos grunted.

"That was an indication that I wanted you to go open the door."

Chaos made no indication of moving from where he stood.

Nessa went to stand when Hunter rolled off the bed and strode over to the door with long-legged strides.

"I've got it," he said for Nessa's benefit, casting a scowl in Chaos' direction. "You need to rest your feet. Otherwise, they'll swell up to the size of watermelons."

Nessa grimaced at her feet. "That's an unpleasant thought."

Hunter grinned at her as he pulled the door open. "Just you wait until tomorrow. You'll be wishing that you had taken Orm up on his offer of giving you a piggyback."

"Oh, I am already." Nessa was dreading the time when she was to take off her shoes to survey the damage.

"Ha, live and learn," Hunter chuckled, stepping aside to allow a woman entry.

Nessa faintly recognised her as one of the servers from downstairs, one who had been behind the bar. She was older than the others, but only by a handful of years, her hair peppered with silver, yet still thick and worn long. She was carrying a large tray ladened with everything a group of tired, hungry travellers could want for their evening meal.

"There we go," she said, placing the tray on a small table that was tucked away in the far corner. "Is there anything else I can get you?"

"That's everything," Hunter purred with a winsome smile. "Thank you, Lannie. It's much appreciated."

"And well paid for," Lannie replied with a wink as she left the room.

Hunter closed the door behind her with a grumbled, "Don't remind me."

"And what do we have here?" Nessa murmured, going over to the table, eyeing the collection of dishes wolfishly.

"We have toad-in-the-hole, mash potato, a selection of mini pies, gravy, sweetcorn and peas bathed in butter, and my personal favourite," Hunter grinned from ear to ear, "a large jug of their finest ale for us to share."

"Why, Hunter, I think you've spoilt me for choice."

Nessa set her sights on a toad-in-the-hole, fully intent on smothering it in thick gravy and mashed potato. Her stomach grumbled greedily at the very idea. She pulled out a chair and sat, sliding a plate in front of her.

Hunter followed suit and patted the third chair. "Come on, Chaos. Eat up before it gets cold."

Chaos scowled at what was on offer. "I'm not eating that. It's common human muck."

Hunter set down the serving spoon, drawing in a deep breath. Nessa quickly snapped it up, filling her toad-in-the-hole with the creamy mash, watching the ensuing argument with amusement, smiling faintly.

*All they do is fight.*

*I know,* Aoife sighed. *The animosity between them never ceases to amaze me.*

"This right here is the finest 'common human muck' that this lovely establishment provides."

"Then both it and you have very low standards," Chaos sniped.

"If it's good enough for Nessa, then it should be good enough for you."

Nessa's fork, which was heaped with food, paused halfway to her mouth. "Don't bring me into this."

Aoife was in hysterics.

"It's not good enough for me," Chaos snarled. "I prefer my meals to be less dense."

Hunter's left eye developed a twitch. "Dense?"

"And with flavour," Chaos continued gruffly. "Something like a nice soup, or maybe a vegetable broth. And some tea. I want some tea as well."

"Since you seem to know what you want, why don't you go downstairs and order yourself something?"

"As if this place serves anything that's actually edible," Chaos scoffed. "I bet their soup is only fit for animals or prisoners. Nope," he shuffled over to the door, "I shall decline your offer of dining with you and go elsewhere for my dinner."

The door slammed shut behind Chaos, and Hunter turned to Nessa with a smirk, picking up the serving spoon. "Now, we'll be able to enjoy ourselves without him."

"You orchestrated that little dispute just to get rid of him, didn't you?"

"Maybe."

# Chapter 14

Nessa sat curled up on a window seat by herself, nursing a half-pint of ale and a very full stomach, idly watching the sunset. Hunter had eaten and drank enough to send him into a coma, and was sprawled across his bed, snoring softly.

Taking a sip from her tankard, Nessa absorbed the sight of the clouds turning pale pink. The advantage of having a room on the top floor was the view. While the inn wasn't the tallest building in all of Arncraft, its attic room still presided over most of the surrounding buildings, allowing Nessa to see over many of the town's roofs.

Much of Arncraft was shown in silhouette, a dark sea of pointed roofs and tall chimneys. Windows had their shutters pulled closed, but even so, here and there, thin seams of light could be seen, indicating that someone was home. Unlike in larger towns and cities, there were no large lamps in the streets. That fact didn't close the market for the night, though, nor did it stop people from venturing from their homes in search of a meal or an evening of entertainment.

Nearly all of the market's stalls had their own little lanterns, and light streaked across the street from the windows and doorways of other inns, taverns and shops that were still open for business. It was quieter than it had been earlier, but not by much, and even though Nessa had the window shut, the sound of laughter and conversation seeped through the window's thin glass. There was an air of celebration about.

The light from the street didn't reach further than the first floor, and the attic room was only lit by the glow coming from the fireplace. Without Chaos' magic keeping the fire lively and bright, it had dwindled in size and ferocity, and had slowly climbed over the logs that Nessa had fed it a short while ago. The room was warm, and the subdued light made it feel cosy and snug.

Nessa took another slurp from her tankard, unable to decide if she loved or hated ale. It was malty and bitter, and yet heavy and warming. In any case, Nessa found herself continuing to drink it, even after Hunter had stopped urging her to.

The sky darkened to a deep-cobalt blue, and then eventually turned black. A scattering of silvery stars was visible, pinpricks of light that accompanied the luminosity of the moon, which sat heavily in the sky, low and full, a watchful presence over the town and its inhabitants.

Leaving her roost, Nessa went over to the table, wondering if there was any ale left. She was in need of a top up. She doubted it, though, considering how much Hunter had drunk. By the end of their meal, he should have just done away with his tankard and drank straight from the jug.

Whilst not desperate for more ale, Nessa needed something to do, not yet tired enough to snuggle into bed. Her companions were either asleep or absent. Nessa found herself growing bored and a little lonely. Aoife was fast asleep. Nessa could sense this through their bond, the quiet hum of Aoife's dreams brushing gently against her mind. No one should ever wake a sleeping dragon. She contemplated going downstairs to see what Orm was getting up to, but didn't think that was the best of ideas. She was also unwilling to negotiate with that many stairs. Her feet had only just stopped hurting. Her new shoes, having only been worn for a couple of hours, were already moulding to her feet. The leather was soft and forgiving.

On her way over to the table, something caught Nessa's eye. A bag sat on a bed. Chaos' bag. The one with that strange book of his.

Nessa bit her lip, her eyes darting amongst a comatose Hunter, the door and the bag. She wondered if it was a good idea to have another look at it.

Probably not.

Nessa found herself going to the bag anyway.

Listening for any sound of approach from the hallway, Nessa kneeled down and opened Chaos' bag.

The book was tucked safely in the middle of the bag, wrapped in a couple of shirts to hide its distinct shape. Nessa pulled it out and carefully rearranged the bag so that it appeared untampered with. Taking the book with her, she hurried over to the fireplace, sitting down cross-legged in front of it.

With the book resting on her lap, Nessa ran her

fingers over the metal front cover, her fingertips brushing against decretive ridges and dips. An image was intricately etched onto it, no inch left unadorned. There were plants and flowers, and a variety of fungi, including some that Nessa had seen earlier during the journey to Arncraft, small and spotted. Ones she had yet to see were amongst them, fanciful ones with wide brims and curled tips. Scattered around, hidden in the wild collection of flora were skulls: mice skulls, bird skulls, deer skulls and even a human one.

Nessa searched for any sign of a name, a title, anything that might give a clue as to what was written on its soft vellum pages.

There was nothing obvious.

Turning the book, Nessa peered at the lock, intrigued by it. *How was it meant to be opened?* There was no keyhole, just a little indentation in its place. By accident, one of her fingers grazed over it, dipping into the hollow just a little. A sharp stab of pain pierced her fingertip.

Nessa jumped, startled, almost dropping the book.

She looked down and found a small bead of blood gathering on the tip of her finger, a pinprick of vivid red.

Nessa stared at the scarlet droplet, feeling a peculiar silence settle over her, a silence that steadily grew, devouring the room, enveloping the town.

Everything had fallen eerily silent. The low murmur from the marketplace had ceased.

Frowning, misgivings growing, Nessa stood, quickly tucking the book into her bundle of wrapped clothing, and hastened over to the window. Opening it, she poked her head out.

The street was crowded with people, but they were still, quiet, peering at each other and up at the dark sky questioningly. Nessa listened intently, wondering as to what had captured so many people's attention. At first, she didn't hear anything notable, just the occasional hushed whisper from below.

Then a sound reached her ears, a deep *thrum* that resonated through the air, coming and going in a leisurely beat.

Nessa scanned the sky for the source, but nothing obvious showed itself.

There was something about the sound, something that was almost ominous.

Her Rider's Mark started to tingle, cutting off her train of thought. Nessa reached out her mind, thinking that Aoife was behind it, only to find that Aoife was still fast asleep, oblivious to the world around her. Then, it dawned on Nessa. The sound was remarkably similar to that of a dragon in flight, large membranous wings working the air in a slow, unhurried pace.

But if Aoife was fast asleep, then that could only mean...

Nessa left the window, dashing to Hunter's side, her heart practically in her throat.

*Please let me be wrong,* she prayed as she shook Hunter, trying to wake him even as the sound grew ever closer. *Please let me be wrong.*

Hunter's eyelids fluttered and he groaned. A hand swatted at her weakly. Nessa easily avoided his half-hearted blows as she continued to shake him into alertness.

The wing beats were growing frightfully close, the very air trembling with their strength.

Empty dinner plates and cutlery began to rattle, falling off the table one by one, landing on the floor with blunt bangs.

The glass windowpanes started to quiver.

People in the streets shouted and cried out.

There was a mighty roar of wind, the sound of something huge— monstrous— hurtling through the sky at an alarming speed.

Hunter leaped up, his eyes wide. The blood left his face, turning it bone white.

"I know that sound."

The pressure in the room changed, making Nessa's ears pop. She turned to the window just in time to see a huge dragon soar overhead, blotting out the moon and stars.

That's when the screaming started.

And the town began to burn.

# Chapter 15

The flames were quick to spread, catching on exposed timber frames almost immediately. Any buildings with thatched roofs were incinerated in a heartbeat, standing no chance against Dragon Fire. Within seconds, much of the town was engulfed in a blaze that burned hotter and stronger than any normal flame could ever hope to, hot enough to melt glass windowpanes. Great plumes of putrid smoke rose high into the starry sky, swiftly creating a cloud of cover that reflected the firelight grotesquely.

It was by no small miracle that Nessa and Hunter managed to make it out the attic room before the dragon did another flyby, fire blasting from its mouth in a manifestation of the beast's hatred and anger. Hunter pulled Nessa down the stairs at a break-neck speed, hurtling around corners and careening into walls with bruising force. Nessa clutched his hand, letting him propel her forwards, preferring to be bruised than burned alive.

The Blackened Cauldron was filled with smoke, thick and choking. With her free hand, Nessa pulled her shirt up over her nose, trying to create a pocket of fresh air to breathe. Judging by the burning in her lungs, she wasn't very successful.

They made it to the ground floor in record time, accompanied by a panicked group of people who sped past them as soon as they were free from the stairs, knocking into them when Hunter pulled Nessa to an abrupt stop. He turned towards the nook where the card game had been held, his bag acting as a crash mat as Nessa skidded into him, a corner of Chaos' book digging painfully into her shoulder. As they'd fled their room, Hunter had the sense to grab his bag and shove her bundle of clothing inside it, seemingly not noticing the book in his haste.

Tables and chairs were overturned, knocked aside as people fled the roaring flames that now swallowed the far wall, devouring wooden beams and bricks alike, almost liquidising them. The bar was reduced to little more than a pile of spitting embers, and hissing fingers of flames streaked across the floor and ceiling, hungry and vicious.

*Get out of there before you pass out!* Aoife ordered, her urgency crashing through Nessa's mind. *Orm's outside! Find him before he gets caught up in a stampede!*

*You've talked to him?*

*Yes, and I still am. He's trying to convince me not to come and help you.*

*No!* Nessa shrieked. *Don't come here. There's another dragon! It doesn't seem to be a very friendly one either!*

*I know there's another dragon. I can bloody well see him*

*from here. He's setting the entire town on fire.*

*Oh, really? I hadn't noticed.*

*Now is not the time for sarcasm.*

*If I can't be sarcastic when it feels like my blood is boiling, then when can I?*

*After you've got out of the burning town.*

Nessa tugged on Hunter's hand, shouting, "Aoife says Orm is outside."

Hunter looked confused. Nessa wasn't sure if he could hear her over the howling of the fire, the wails of people in the streets. She sucked in a breath. Instead of air though, she breathed in smoke and ash. Her lungs screamed in protest, her chest contracting. Nessa was gasping, her body rebelling against her, coughing and choking with enough force to rattle her bones.

Hunter abandoned his search of the room and grabbed Nessa's wrist, pulling her along behind him.

They burst out onto the street as beams and parts of the inn's upper floors collapsed behind them, screeching and thundering in protest at their destruction. The heat was unimaginable. Unbearable.

Nessa swiped her cheeks and rubbed her eyes, trying to clear them of tears and ash. She only managed to smear the black concoction more. Her vision was cloudy, blurred. Soot scratched against her eyelids as she forced her eyes to focus.

Anarchy. That was what Nessa saw.

Arncraft was in ruins, the marketplace destroyed, booths and stalls standing no chance against Dragon Fire. Buildings fared no better. Almost every one of them was ablaze. Flames devoured roofs and upper floors, quickly spreading, creating a crown of angry crimson claws that reached high into the sky. The air was thin, the fire hungry for it, consuming it greedily. Embers and ash rained down, gentle and soft, a cruel imitation of snow.

People were everywhere, running and screaming, standing and gawking, not knowing what to do or where to go. Some were gathered in groups here and there, pointing and shouting, armed with buckets of water. Nessa thought that it was a futile and pointless venture, dangerous too, for them to even attempt to save their homes. Then she caught sight of movement from within a building, and she realised that they were trying to aid those trapped.

With his hand still firmly clasped around Nessa's wrist, Hunter hurried away from The Blackened Cauldron, his eyes sweeping over the faces of the bodies on the ground. Nessa gagged as the stench of burnt flesh reached her, as she caught sight of charred limbs. She kept her gaze locked onto Hunter's back, unable to bear seeing any more horrors. Hunter was taking them down the street they'd come up earlier, retracing their steps in the hope of being able to escape quickly.

"Keep your eyes open for Orm," Hunter shouted over the wails of the injured and the dying, over the keening of those who were witnessing their entire world going up in flames.

*He's about a hundred yards ahead of you,* Aoife informed them. *He says he's standing next to what used to be a bakery.*

"Thanks, Aoife," Hunter murmured, picking up speed. "Having a dragon locate your missing friend is remarkably helpful."

*Glad my efforts are appreciated,* Aoife remarked dryly.

Wagons and tables littered the street, overturned and in disarray having been shoved aside by people fleeing. It was carnage and made for a slow and tedious passage.

The people around them, panicked and many of them wounded, didn't help matters, pushing and shoving past or standing in the way, shell-shocked and unable to move.

A chorus of screams came from a short distance away, high pitched and filled with terror. Nessa looked over, but something rolled underfoot and she tripped, falling to the ground. Hunter's grip was broken and he stumbled forwards, catching himself against a fallen beam.

Nessa landed on something oddly soft.

Arms trembling, she managed to push herself up onto her hands and knees, only for her gaze to meet that of another.

She was staring into eyes that were large and angled, like those of a cat, slitted pupil and all. They were eyes that had once been full of secrets and knowledge. They were the eyes of an Old Blood. A dead Old Blood. Gone was the spark of life, replaced by glazed surprise.

A scream rose in Nessa's throat as she flung herself backwards, away from Eliza's body.

The body she had fallen atop.

Nessa's back hit a wooden cart that was overturned, resting on its side, one wheel still spinning slowly, flames licking the spokes. She huddled against it, unable to tear her gaze away from Eliza, from the blackened mess that used to be her torso.

Hunter turned, about to dash towards her, when the screams of a crowd reached a fevered pitch. People came spilling out from an adjoining road in a frenzy, a mad rush, cutting across his path. Hunter reeled back, trying to avoid being trampled in the stampede. Nessa cringed beside the cart, pulling her knees up to her chest.

*Beware!* Aoife cried. *The beast is heading for you.*

There was no time to run.

There was no time to hide.

A shadow detached itself from the sky, hurtling towards them at a startling speed. The stampede suddenly made sense to Nessa: they were fleeing the dragon. In a suspended moment, her and Hunter's eyes met through the crowd. They knew there was nothing they could do. They were utterly and completely helpless.

Hunter mouthed two words. *Take cover.*

Nessa lost sight of him.

The dragon swooped low overhead, uncaring about the flames that caressed its black scales, or the tempest of cinders and smoke that were stirred up by its passing. Nessa was bewitched, unable to look away even as the dragon opened its jaws, fire glowing red at the back of its throat.

It was a monster, but a beautiful one. Nessa couldn't deny it.

At least five times the size of Aoife, the dragon was huge, its muscles strong and defined, pearlescent spikes running down the length of its spine as sharp as swords. Its scales gleamed in the firelight, black but glinting with flecks of reds and greens, and its venomous eyes shone brightly with terrible glee as it beheld the destruction it had created. Upon its back, sat in an unusual saddle, was a man.

Although dwarfed by the beast he rode, he was somehow as equally intimidating.

Dressed in black armour with red inlay, the man was a likeness of his dragon, a villainous pair. His head was concealed by a decorative helm, leaving only his eyes and mouth visible. Despite this and the distance between them, Nessa somehow knew that he was smiling, laughing.

Whilst they were a fear-inducing sight, their appearances weren't the most terrifying thing about them. It was the power that came off them in waves, a dark and intoxicating magic which drifted through the air, thick and syrupy, heavy and oppressive. It brushed against Nessa, wrapping around her for a heart-stopping moment before slithering elsewhere.

She sagged against the wooden cart, feeling sick and dizzy, choking back sobs.

*The magic...there was something about it...something not quite right...*

Fire burst forth from the dragon's mouth, so hot it burned a blinding white. The force of it sent shockwaves through the air, sending lighter objects flying and knocking Nessa over. She curled into a ball with her arms wrapped around her head, waiting for it to end, for it all to stop. The heat from the Dragon Fire was staggering, overwhelming. Even though the overturned cart and her clothing sheltered her from the worst of it, it was scalding.

Nessa could sense that Aoife was poised to take off, ready to come to Nessa's aid. Aoife was watching through Nessa's eyes, their minds melding together as if they were one soul.

*If you come here,* Nessa murmured, struggling to breathe, ash and burning air catching in her throat. *Then they will see you. They will kill you.*

Aoife didn't respond, but Nessa could feel Aoife's bleak agreement.

*I'm not hurt,* Nessa continued. *Petrified, yes, but not hurt. The best thing you can do right now is to stay where you are and keep an eye on Hunter and Orm. You can help us get out of this mess from where you are.*

*I'm already doing that,* Aoife said tensely, painfully alert. *Orm's nearly outside the town and Hunter's on the other side of those flames. Only the gods know where Chaos is.*

*Tell Hunter to get out of here!*

*I have. Multiple times. He won't listen. Although I've told him that you are unsinged, the idiot is still scared for you.*

Aoife's alarm spiked as, with a shrug of its wings, the dragon changed direction. *Watch out! He's going to land behind you.*

Nessa twisted and crawled to the side of the cart, keeping close to the ground, trying to stay clear of the torrent of Dragon Fire. She watched, trembling, as the black dragon dropped down, forelegs outreached. It landed on the roof of a tall building that was faring better than those around it, and snapped its jaws closed, bringing an end to the violent stream of flames. Tiles were knocked free as the dragon's claws grappled for purchase, and its wings buffeted the air for balance, fanning the flames, encouraging them to burn brighter and stronger.

The dragon was facing away from Nessa, both it and its Rider's attention focused on something in front of them. Nessa saw it as her chance to run, to get to Hunter without being noticed.

She'd need to be quick about it. She knew that. Quick and silent. Otherwise, her spirit would be joining Eliza's, wherever it had gone.

*Careful,* Aoife whispered.

Nessa peered down the street, trying to plan a route through the burning wreckage of the market. Thanks to the latest dose of Dragon Fire, everything was alight.

*Everything.* Tables, wagons, buildings, people, even the damn cobblestones.

*This is going to be difficult.*

*You'll have to go a different way,* Aoife told her, *and circle around.*

*And what about Hunter?* Nessa asked, trying to catch sight of him amongst the growing destruction. There was a handful of survivors, a few who had managed to take cover in time. *Is he alright? Where is he? I can't see him.*

*He's safe,* Aoife said soothingly. *He's alright, but he's been forced to go further down the street. The buildings around him were starting to fall. Their roofs are collapsing. He didn't want to be squished.*

*Can you persuade him to get out of the town and find Orm? I can't concentrate when I'm worried about them.*

*Oh, give me a second,* Aoife sighed. *I'm having three separate conversations at once. It's hard work keeping track of what everyone is saying.*

Aoife's mind drifted away from Nessa's as she endeavoured to persuade Hunter to get to safety. Nessa kept an eye on the monstrous dragon as she tried to figure out which direction she should go in. In all honesty, her options were rather limited, and none of them were particularly promising.

The black dragon prowled over rooftops, only a street or two away from Nessa. The distance was rendered almost meaningless given the dragon's size. As buildings gave way under its weight, timber and bricks snapping and crunching, the dragon stretched out its wings further, keeping itself steady. The right wing, although only partially extended, still reached over Nessa, a living canopy that blotted out the sky and trapped smoke and heat beneath it. With fires raging all around her, the heat was already stifling, but as soon as the dragon's wing came over the street, it became horrendous. The air wavered and shimmered before her eyes, scorching her throat and lungs with each laboured breath. Sweat beaded on her forehead, only to instantly evaporate.

*I've managed to bully Hunter to go after Orm,* Aoife told Nessa, *but he says that if you're not out of the town in ten minutes, then he's coming back for you.*

If her eyes hadn't been so dry, Nessa would have rolled them. *So I have ten minutes to get out of here before he does something stupid?*

*Pretty much. I suggest you get a move on.*

*Which way do you think I should go?* Nessa looked around in despair, allowing Aoife to survey the street through her eyes.

*Over there,* Aoife advised, *to your right.*

*Are you sure? That would take me awfully close to the dragon.*

*I think he's moving towards the square or something. Maybe a park? I've seen him head in that direction a few times. It's like he's herding any survivors that way.*

*Why would he do that?*

*I don't know, my little Rider. I cannot fathom why any dragon would want to cause such harm and destruction, even if their Rider wanted to.* Sorrow and anger seeped through the bond. *Now go! Before they take off for another loop of the town.*

*I'm going. I'm going.*

*Remember, you don't have much time before Hunter tries to be a hero.*

*You don't have to remind me of that.*

*No, but I warn you, he will be accompanied by me.*

*Well, when you put it like that, I had better hurry.*

*Indeed.* Aoife's mind withdrew to the very edge of Nessa's mind with a whispered, *Be careful.*

Without the distraction of worrying about Hunter and Orm, and with Aoife keeping her distance, silently watching and waiting, Nessa tried to calm the swarm of butterflies in her stomach. Slowly, carefully, she crept out from behind the cart.

With the dragon so close, its wing only twenty or so feet above her head, Nessa couldn't help but feel all too exposed. It didn't help that the street was now suddenly deserted. Nessa was the only person there; she couldn't see another living soul nearby. The stampede that had filled the street only a few minutes ago was gone. They had either ran for cover or had succumbed to the Dragon Fire. More than a few had been caught by falling wreckage.

As quietly and as timidly as a mouse, Nessa tiptoed forwards, never taking her eyes from the black dragon for more than an instant, fearful that it would turn around at any second. Thankfully, as Nessa wormed her way around flaming wagons and tables, their former wares scattered across the ground, the dragon slowly prowled away, skulking across the rooftops, its gaze fixed elsewhere.

As Nessa turned a corner, entering a narrow alleyway, she was momentarily freed from the oppressive shadow of the dragon's wing. With only small piles of smouldering timber and tiles, the path was mostly clear. Nessa paused quickly and glanced up, making sure that nothing was hanging loosely overhead. It would be rather bad luck if she was killed by a falling bit of debris, especially after managing to escape from a burning building and having narrowly missed being roasted alive by Dragon Fire.

Her eyes ran over looming buildings, finding that the jettied floors, which had appeared quaint upon arrival, had now turned sinister. They reached towards each other, unstable and broken, holes rapidly forming even as she watched, ash and embers gently raining down. Fire was steadily devouring them. Soon it would be impossible to tell that they had once been people's homes and businesses.

Despite the hazard of falling rubble, the alley was still the quickest and, ironically, the safest route. Wasting no more time, Nessa dashed down it, hopping over the growing mounds of smouldering rubble.

The alley opened onto a street much like the one she'd just come from, wide and filled with burning debris. Most of it appeared to have come from the buildings, many of which were slowly falling down, their roofs caving in and their walls crumbling. Having a dragon clamber over them was only speeding up their ruin.

The dragon wasn't far away. It had only stepped over a couple of rows of houses and was stood to Nessa's right, tail whipping overhead, twitching and jerking from side to side like that of an angry cat.

Nessa watched the beast for a second, trying to gauge if it was likely to change course, and then darted to the other side of the road. She would be less visible there should the dragon and its Rider glance in her direction. Nessa prayed that they wouldn't. She kept as close to the buildings as she could, but flames climbed out of empty doorways and windows, keeping her at arm's length, spitting and hissing, reaching out hungrily as she made her way closer to a junction, a fork in the road where it split into two. The left road, Nessa presumed, would link back to the town's main street. And hopefully back to Hunter, Orm and her beloved, non-murderous dragon, whose watchful presence hovered at the edge of Nessa's mind.

Excited at the prospect of nearly being free from Arncraft, Nessa hastened towards the split in the road.

The air above her stirred and whistled. Nessa barely had time to flinch before the dragon's tail smashed into a nearby building, the spiked tip catching against the unstable remains of a chimney stack.

Wooden beams splintered and snapped, and masonry was sent flying. The building, already weakened by the ravaging fires, began collapsing, each floor falling down onto the one below it, the walls folding in on themselves.

The building tumbled down like a house of cards.

Nessa flung herself forwards, landing jarringly on the ground, narrowly avoiding being struck by some of the larger pieces that were launched like cannonballs. A cloud of smoke, dust and smaller pebble-sized lumps of brick engulfed her.

Arms wrapped protectively around her head, shielding it from the worst of the falling debris, Nessa waited for the pieces to settle, for the cloud to dissipate. It wasn't doing so in a hurry.

The heat was sweltering, and the soot made it near on impossible to breathe. Nessa clamped a hand over her mouth, trying to smother the coughs that tickled and caught in the back of her throat. The dragon was still too close for comfort. Nessa could hear the whistle of air as its tail jerked from side to side. She could feel the ground quiver with each of its steps, crushing roofs and walls alike. It was as if the dragon didn't even notice them.

Nessa wasn't sure if the dragon would be able to hear

her cough over the noise of its passage and the roaring fires, but she wasn't going to risk it. Not when she heard the growls growing in its chest, deep, low and hair-raising.

*What's happening?* Aoife demanded.

*I was almost squished by a collapsing building.*

*But you're unsquished, right?*

*My heart is beating so fast that I think it's about to burst, and I'm pretty sure I have a whole, new collection of scrapes to add to the ones I already have. But yes, I am unsquished.*

*Surely, you're just one big walking wound by now?*

*Ha, it certainly feels like that.*

*Hmm.*

Aoife was about to say more but was interrupted by a mighty *thud* that made the earth rumble and shake.

There was a pause.

*Thud.*

Another pause…

*Thud…*

Slowly, hesitantly, Nessa uncurled from her protective ball and pushed herself up onto her knees, wide eyes sweeping over the buildings. Well, what remained of them.

*Aoife, where's the dragon? I can't see the dragon.*

Nessa twisted around, searching for the slightest glimpse of a wing or tail. The buildings and far-reaching fires made the task impossible.

*I don't know,* Aoife said. *He must be in a larger street, walking behind some of the taller buildings.*

*Have we seriously lost sight of a giant bloody dragon?*

Nessa could sense Aoife's displeasure as she mumbled, *It would seem so.*

Clambering to her feet, Nessa peered at the walls of

fire around her, at the dust from the building's collapse that had yet to settle, spinning in a circle.

Thuds continued to come in a steady beat. It slowly dawned on Nessa that they were, in fact, the dragon's steps, filled with purpose and weighted with malice. She tried to identify the direction from which they came. The entire ground rattled and shook ferociously, such was their strength. She couldn't tell where they originated from.

*Can't you see the dragon at all?* Nessa enquired, lurching forwards, stumbling towards a gap in the wall of flames, determined to continue with her escape.

*No,* Aoife said shortly. *I thought I did for a second, but many of the fires are burning taller than he stands, and the colour of his scales makes him blend in all too well. They reflect the light perfectly. The distance between us is making the task a lot harder too. If I were to take flight and view the town from above, then I'd be able to spot him without a problem.*

*But you'd run the risk of it seeing you.*

*Him,* Aoife corrected. *He is a him.*

*How do you know that?*

*Because of his build and facial spurs.*

*Facial spurs?* Nessa kept the conversation going, genuinely intrigued but mainly using it as a distraction.

Magic was once again floating through the air, heavy and syrupy, sickly. It weighed down on her, flowing against her, around her, slowing her down. Each breath, each step, suddenly seemed to take an inordinate amount of effort. A headache formed behind Nessa's eyes, and she found it ever harder to listen to what Aoife was saying.

*Yes, facial spurs,* Aoife murmured, seeming not to notice Nessa's difficulties, her voice fading to the back of

Nessa's mind.

Nessa was grateful because she knew that, without a doubt, if Aoife sensed that she was struggling, she would come flying no matter the danger. *Males have them along their jawline,* Aoife continued, *and they have extra pairs of spikes atop their heads. The strongest males have up to four pairs.*

*You only have one pair of head spikes,* Nessa said as she clambered over a mound of rubble, broken bits of brick and tiles slipping underfoot, releasing little plumes of smoke and lively embers, *and they're only little.*

*That's because I'm young and not anywhere near being fully grown. Once I reach my first year, mine will have grown quite substantially.*

*I think you've got quite a lot of growing to do before you're as big as the other dragon.*

*Indeed, but it will take a few hundred years, by my estimate.*

Nessa blinked in surprise. *It's going to take that long before you'll be big enough to match him in a fight?*

*Not necessarily,* Aoife mused. *The first few years are when we grow the most. After that, while we still continue to grow, it's at a much slower pace.*

*Huh.*

Nessa battled against the sickness rising up inside her, pushed against the current of warped magic that wanted to send her to her knees and staggered down another street. She had no idea where it might take her, or what might be waiting for her at the end. For all she knew, the dragon could be sat there, patiently waiting for her to venture closer. Or the street could come to a dead end, blocked by either fire or collapsed buildings. Maybe both.

*Oh, the joy of surprises.*

The occasional *thud* of the dragon's steps came every now and again, shaking the earth violently, seeming to come from all directions, offering no hint of the dragon's whereabouts. Nessa eyed the buildings on either side of her with trepidation. The fires had eaten much of them; the roofs and upper floors were gone completely. Riddled with holes where the wattle and daub had burned away, or where bricks had been knocked loose, what was still standing didn't look like it'd be for much longer.

Nessa hurried forwards, her eyes running over the flame-licked walls, watchful for any sign of an imminent collapse. With each shaking dragon step, small cascades of glittering cinders would come spilling from cracks, raining down like delicate waterfalls before floating away on a rush of sweltering air.

Managing to make it to the end of the street without incident, the dragon nowhere to be seen, Nessa paused briefly, peering around. Any hope she felt faded to nothing as she realised that she was well and truly lost.

*Right or left?* Nessa asked.

*Left,* Aoife said hesitantly. *No, wait. Maybe right?*

*That's not particularly helpful.*

*Well, my guess is as good as yours. I have no idea where you are. And before you ask, no, I don't know where the other dragon is. I still can't see him.*

*I'll go left, I think. Left looks like a decent option.*

*Right or left, they both look identical. But whichever one you take, I would advise you to hurry up. You only have another six minutes before Hunter and I come charging in there for you.*

With the reminder that she was working with a deadline, Aoife withdrew to the edge of Nessa's mind, leaving her to navigate the burning maze.

There was a gust of hot air, a breeze of sorts, carrying the hiss of flames and urgency. And something else…something that was rather out of place…

Nessa turned her head and listened. It was faint, nothing more than a whisper. It came from somewhere ahead of her.

At first, it kept itself hidden from Nessa, staying just far enough away that the fires and buildings concealed it, but close enough that Nessa could hear it, just. Then, as if it knew that it was being followed, it revealed itself in tantalising flashes, the briefest of glimpses, a tip of a wing here and there, a gleam of deep-blue eyes.

Misgivings fluttered in Nessa's stomach, the gentlest of warnings. For a second, she felt something niggling at the edge of her mind. It was the sense of familiarity, of recognition, a ghost of a memory. As soon as she reached for it, though, the feeling vanished, slipping through her fingers like a shadow, vanishing as if it had never really been there.

Cool air brushed against her cheek, as soft as a brush of a feather.

Nessa blinked, roused from a daze she didn't recall slipping into. She found herself standing at the edge of a wide square.

The raven was the first thing that captured Nessa's attention, what with it being the one from the forest, the one with the blue eyes. It was perched on a branch of a burning tree, a limb yet untouched by the flames. Briefly, Nessa wondered how it had come to be there, *why* it had come to be there. Of all the places in the world it could have flown to, it had decided on a burning town. Her queries were quickly forgotten when the raven let out a piercing *caw!* and turned its gaze away from her.

Nessa followed its stare.

It took a second for her to realise what she was seeing, for her to fully comprehend what was happening. When the scene finally sank in, horror rooted Nessa on the spot, a wordless scream rising in her throat. She wanted desperately to run, to hide.

It was too late for that.

The black-armoured Dragon Rider turned around.

And his eyes locked with Nessa's.

# Chapter 16

His gaze cut through her like a spear, sharp and hard, painful and jolting, his eyes glimmering like diamonds, like the finest black opal. They were beautiful. They were terrible, filled with menacing truths and sinister deceptions. Those dark eyes ran over Nessa, examining her, scrutinising her. They missed nothing, not even the smallest of details, from the smudges of soot on her face to the rips and holes in her baggy clothing.

Nessa had been found, discovered by one loyal to King Kaenar.

Terror flooded her veins, terror and a sad sense of finality, of defeat.

*What will he do?* Nessa wondered bleakly. *How is this to end?*

Escape seemed like a pointless venture, futile. It could only lead to humiliation and death. Would her demise come by his hand, or would he let his dragon do the deed, swallowing her whole or incinerating her with Dragon Fire? Maybe he planned on presenting her to the king like an offering, a gift of sorts.

Nessa wasn't quite sure which scenario was the worst.

The Rider's gaze lingered on Nessa's face, committing her features to memory. He smirked, his perfect lips curving mockingly before his black eyes went skywards and locked onto the moon hanging low overhead, heavy and full. His syrupy magic brushed against Nessa, wrapping around her stupefied form like a boa constrictor, tight and crushing.

He wanted her to watch, to witness something.

Nessa searched for help, an escape, anything.

She was alone, save for a raven and an enemy Rider, ensnared by ropes of malevolent magic, immobile and spellbound.

There was no escape.

Aoife's mind brushed against her own. Before she could ask anything, say anything, Nessa slammed up her walls of amethyst, shutting Aoife out. It may not have been the best idea, but it was the only thing Nessa could do. She had to protect her dragon, her bonded partner, by any means possible.

Their bond would allow Aoife to sense that Nessa was alright, that she was alive and, so far, unhurt. But with the walls around Nessa's mind, Aoife was locked out, unable to talk to her, but also unable to see what was happening. That was what Nessa wanted. That's what Nessa needed. Nessa knew that if Aoife saw what she had stumbled into, then Aoife would come to her rescue in a blink of an eye, no matter the danger, no matter the practically nonexistent chance of them making it out alive.

Nessa felt that there was no point in both of them dying needlessly. Anyway, there was a tiny voice of optimism that told Nessa that she might be able to get out of there alive. Granted, it was a very small, incredibly quiet voice, but it was there nonetheless. That's all that mattered. That tiny voice gave Nessa hope. Nessa clung to that hope with everything she had.

But the hope was short-lived.

The earth rumbled and shook, and a shape detached itself from the ground, standing tall and strong, its venomous, red eyes trained on Nessa. She trembled, redoubling her struggles against the chains of magic that twisted around her, dismayed to realise that the Rider's dragon had been there all along, hidden in plain sight.

The dragon's scales, surrounded by the chaos of raging fires and broken buildings, offered a strange kind of camouflage, drinking in the light and offering nothing but darkness. When the dragon had held himself still, he was almost unnoticeable amongst the ruin and flames, his scales reflecting what was around him. Uncurling from where he had been lying, coiled around his Rider and what he stood upon, it was as if the dragon had emerged from the earth itself, manifesting from nothing more than shadows, fire and wickedness.

Upon stumbling across the square, Nessa's attention had immediately gone to the raven, and then the Rider. She hadn't had much time to look at her surroundings. Not once she realised what the Rider was standing on; not once he had turned, and his eyes had locked with hers. Trapped as she was, Nessa couldn't shield herself from the horrors in the square.

The Rider was standing atop a towering mound of bodies. The number of people resting beneath the Rider's feet must have been in the thousands. The scale of the pile of charred limbs and departed souls was revealed as the dragon shifted.

Stepping around the bodies, the dragon circled the dead, coming to stand proudly behind his Rider, the king of anarchy and destruction. Together they openly displayed the carnage they'd so happily brought about.

Nessa's eyes ran over the heap of bodies, over the blackened and twisted limbs, over the outstretched hands that had been reaching for mercy. People who had escaped the initial attack, those who had fled from their burning homes, had been corralled there, herded like a flock of sheep to slaughter. The dragon's path, the pattern of destruction, had all been strategic. They had wanted as many people as possible in one place.

Tears ran down Nessa's face, blurring the image, but not getting rid of it entirely. The sight was imprinted in her memory, there forever. Every time she blinked, she saw burnt, twisted forms with haunting detail, with savage clarity.

The dragon ruffled his wings, settling them comfortably against his side as if preparing for an arduous chore, and turned his venomous, red eyes upwards, following the gaze of his Rider.

Nessa couldn't help but glance up as well, wondering what had captured their attention, why the moon held such interest to them. Whatever it was, it wasn't obvious to her, at least not yet.

The Rider flung up his arms, spreading them wide like he was about to embrace something unseen. His dark armour glinted, the firelight accentuating the red inlay perfectly, highlighting a slim waist and broad shoulders. His eyes and mouth were all that was visible to Nessa, the rest of his head and face concealed by his helm, but it was enough for her to see his evil delight, his ecstasy. It was clear in the way that his lips curled, the way his eyes shone.

He was saying something, chanting, his words a hum in the hot breeze, indecipherable over the hiss of angry flames and the clatter of falling bricks.

A charge filled the air, static and heavy, sweeping over the ruined square like a thunderstorm. The smoke was pushed away, dissolving into nothing.

Nessa's Rider's Mark tingled in warning.

The Rider's chant grew in strength. The charge began to crackle. And the Mark started to itch and burn.

She looked down at it, only to find that it was hidden by the arm warmer Eliza had given her. A saving grace, Nessa thought faintly. Otherwise, the Rider would have seen it, would know without a doubt what she was.

The possibility, the hope that he didn't know, at least not fully, sprang to mind.

But if he didn't know, then why was she still alive?

Why wasn't she like the others in that square, broken and burned, trampled beneath his feet?

Was it little more than a game to him? Did it give him a sick thrill to have a witness?

The charge continued to strengthen, growing more powerful with each word the Rider uttered, as did the pain coming from Nessa's forearm. It felt as if her Rider's Mark was coming alive, ripping at her skin to free itself, clawing and biting. The sensation wasn't contained to just the mark for long.

Nessa stared, alarmed, as the ghastly feeling steadily slithered its way up her arm. For a second, she wished that she could see what was happening. But then, when it seemed like her veins were writhing beneath her skin like worms, like snakes, she was immensely relieved that she couldn't. There was no telling what she might have seen if she wasn't so well covered. Ignorance is bliss, as they say, and right then, Nessa desired to be as ignorant about her predicament as possible.

Something entered the ruined square, swooping down with a gust of unnatural wind that blew Nessa's loose hair across her face, into her eyes. Blinded and afraid, she shook her head, trying to shake off the tresses so that she could see. She was met with some success. Only a handful of strands remained stuck to her cheeks, adhering to the tears that streamed down them.

Nessa blinked, disorientated and sick, and more than a little panicked. The Rider's dark magic battered against her, crashing down on her like waves caught in a fierce storm, relentless and merciless. It was unstoppable. There was no point resisting it, in fighting against it.

Peering through strands of hair, Nessa searched for the source of the unnatural winds. They blew around and around the ruined square, never flattering or shifting course. They stirred up ash and embers, creating a tempest of glinting disorder. There was no one but her, the Rider and the black dragon.

No one alive, that is.

The magic, Nessa was sure that it was the Rider's. She could feel it coming off him, almost powerful enough to be visible, the air wavering and shimmering around him. But the wind…the static charge…that was not of his doing. Not entirely. He was summoning something, awakening an entity that shouldn't be.

It was a force unseen. A force to be reckoned with.

Although hidden from the eyes of mankind, Nessa

could sense it all around her, a creature as old as time, one that whispered dark secrets and promised terrible things. It was filled with wrath and loathing, and had an insatiable hunger for *more,* a greed that would never ebb no matter how much it fed.

Intangible fingers brushed against Nessa's cheek, pushing back a stray lock of hair. She shuddered and renewed her struggles against her bonds, desperate to get away, to get far, far away.

The magic strengthened to an overwhelming degree, pushing against Nessa, holding her down. Nessa felt as if a cyclone was bearing down on her, one that would destroy everything she had ever known, everything she held dear. The sensation of her Rider's Mark clawing, ripping at her skin, reached the top of her arm, spreading across her shoulders, and down her other arm. It seeped into her chest, her heart. It was taking over her, changing her. Nessa could feel herself becoming something *else,* becoming something *other…*

The Rider had awoken an entity of unimaginable power, and that entity was awakening something in her, something that was rising to the surface, readying itself to be released into the world.

Nothing would ever be the same again if it did.

The chanting, hypnotising and strangely inciting, rose in a frightful crescendo, the words finally reaching Nessa over the roar of the fires and the howls of the winds. They were foreign, a language that few had ever heard of, and one that even less had uttered. It was old, perhaps even as ancient as the formless entity that filled the ruined square with its unspoken promises and sweet but terrible lies, with its insatiable hunger and inhuman lusts.

Images flashed through Nessa's mind, runes and

sigils, both elegant and sharp. They were peculiar, having no place in the common tongue, and yet there was a sense of familiarity about them. Nessa had seen them before; she was sure of that.

*When?*

*How?*

A memory surfaced, and Nessa eagerly reached for it, hopeful that it would help her in some way. But just like every other time, the promise of a memory was a fleeting one. As soon as she came close to catching it, it faded away to nothing as if it had never really been there, drifting through her fingers like smoke.

The formless entity drew away from Nessa, allowing itself to be pulled into the swirling winds, its attention going elsewhere. Nessa could feel it spinning and dancing around the square, claiming it. Without its gaze focused on her, Nessa drew in a ragged breath, only then realising that at some point she'd stopped breathing.

Hands clenched into tight fists, Nessa battled against the bonds keeping her arms locked against her sides, trying to break them apart. Maybe then, she might be able to free herself completely and make for an escape while the dragon and Rider were distracted with their spell weaving.

For a heartbeat or two, she was met with no success. She was very securely pinioned, and Nessa was soon panting with effort, beads of sweat rolling down her face, mixing with tears of frustration. The *thing* clawing beneath her skin paused; then, like a dragon arising from a long slumber, it came awake with a ferocity that shook the earth.

A scream tore from her throat, and her bonds disintegrated with a shower of sparks. Nessa fell to her knees just as the Rider finished his incantation with a mighty roar, his head falling back, his arms reaching up as if he could pluck the moon from the sky.

Magic pulsed and flashed, and the wind howled and blustered, sending ash and embers flying in a vicious burst. Flames flickered and danced, pushed sideways by the gale.

Then, like an eye of a storm passing overhead, everything abruptly fell still and silent. The fires, burning bright and fierce only a second ago, wilted, becoming small and inconsequential. Their light was weak and ruddy, and the ruined square was enveloped in a sinister gloom that not even the moon could impede.

Nessa stared, wide-eyed, as she sensed the formless entity drift around the Rider with ever-increasing fervour, its presence a dark, malevolent energy. It was gathering itself, readying itself for something. The incantation was finished, but by no means did that mean it was the end. No, it was just the beginning.

She staggered to her feet, her bones singing with pain and her muscles weak as the thing beneath her skin continued to move within her, consuming her. Claiming her.

With the fires subdued, Nessa saw a path of escape that had previously been closed to her. She went to run, to flee whilst she could, whilst all three beings, corporeal and otherwise, had their attention focused elsewhere.

Nessa only managed a couple of steps. The pain became unbearable. Acid surely flowed in her veins instead of blood, melting flesh and bone. Nessa couldn't move. She couldn't scream. Her body was frozen in agony.

Nessa was all but helpless to watch as the Rider

brought down his arms and pulled off his gauntlets, casting them carelessly aside. He didn't bat an eyelid as they landed on the bodies beneath his feet. From a golden scabbard at his hip, he drew a ceremonial dagger. Its blade and hilt were covered in glyphs and it shimmered with an inner light.

Without hesitation, the Rider ran the blade across his palm, slicing it open. Blood was quick to well, a stark line of liquid crimson. His black eyes, which were strangely unfocused and glazed over, showed no pain or discomfort. He shifted his grip on the dagger and repeated the action on his other hand.

Horrified and fascinated, Nessa watched as he calmly sheathed the dagger and held his arms by his sides, bleeding palms angled outwards. His eyes slid closed and his lips shaped soundless words, chanting again.

The formless entity danced with eagerness, with glee.

The *thing* cruelly residing under Nessa's skin stilled. Watching. Waiting.

The unsettling stillness over the ruined square became ominous. All at once, it felt as if a thousand eyes had turned their gaze upon it.

A shiver ran down Nessa's spine when she sensed similarities between those watchful eyes and the dark entity, a connection that surpassed human comprehension. They were one and the same, and yet profoundly different, a candle flame compared to a raging inferno.

The *thing* beneath Nessa's skin, empowered by the formless watchers, awoken and unchained by the chants and the swell of magic, stirred again. With a jolting punch to Nessa's core, it joined with her, uniting with her. It became one with her.

Instantly, the pain vanished. The clawing, burning sensation was gone, and the relief was profound. Nessa staggered back a step, her vision wavering. She raised her hands, pressing them against her chest, feeling the echoes of her heartbeat.

Nessa was changed.

Different.

Reborn.

Power, wild and untamed, flowed in her veins.

The Rider's eyes snapped open and locked onto her.

Nessa saw something in their black depths: surprise...and something else...something that made her stomach drop.

Without breaking his chant, the Rider's fingers twitched, like he wanted to reach for his dagger and stride forwards. Despite the glint in his eyes, he stayed as he was, else he risked his spell going awry.

Blood dripped from his fingertips, landing on the bodies beneath his feet. The formless entity stilled, coming to a stop by the Rider, hovering around him, in front of him. Then, with explosive strength and velocity, it shot outwards, upwards.

The entity claimed the ruined square, the destroyed town, as its own, consuming and devouring, taking everything on offer.

A darkness, profound and deep, settled over the square, a cloud of pain and despair. The moon and stars were blotted out, their gentle light smothered, and the surrounding fires burned black.

Little strange lights flickered into existence, ringing the ruined square, steadily rolling inwards, inching closer to the mound of bodies, leisurely climbing over them, lingering on them.

At first, Nessa thought that it was fire, slow burning and dim. But as it advanced over the bodies, flickering gently, she saw that it was something a lot more otherworldly. Whilst it moved and looked like fire, there was something that differentiated it. It reminded Nessa of a thin layer of mist, with curling tendrils and shifting patterns. There was no smoke, no crackle of flames, just an eerie, loaded silence as the unearthly fire-mist delicately kissed its way up the mound of bodies, caressing faces and twisted limbs instead of burning them.

Nessa was unable to tear her gaze away from the leading wave, watching as it reached the Rider's feet, swirling and climbing over the lower half of his legs. Hungry and curious, yet leaving him unharmed, his armour unscathed.

Another droplet of blood left his fingertip, and with a sizzle, it was swallowed by the fire-mist.

A shock-wave pulsed through the ruined square, blasting outwards with enough force to knock Nessa off her feet and to send more than a few surrounding walls tumbling down.

Stunned, ears ringing and the air kicked out of her, Nessa lay where she had fallen, struggling for breath, ash tickling her nose and sticking to her eyelashes.

Bright light pierced through the dimness, turning her eyelids red. Nessa groaned and pushed herself up on shaking arms, coughing out what felt like a lungful of soot. She squinted, half-blinded.

The mystic fire-mist blazed with hypnotic light, almost too bright to look at. It danced and skipped over the mound of bodies, flickering and pulsing, a silvery white like that of liquid starlight.

Crowding around the Rider, enveloping his lower half, thin tendrils snaked around his hands, searching, seeking. They found the bleeding wound on each palm, and like a striking snake, they shot into the wounds, pushing themselves deep into the Rider, filling his veins.

The Rider's back arched, and his head fell back, an agonised roar renting the air.

Nessa scrambled to her feet, wide-eyed and alarmed.

The mystic light swelled, the tendrils climbing up his arms, up over his waist and chest like vines, growing and converging, the lower parts thickening and merging together. It swallowed him in a writhing mass, bright and alive. His howl was drowned out as the light filled his mouth, as he swallowed it like a man half-starved, desperate and greedy.

Nessa couldn't tell if it was consuming him or if he was consuming it. Her eyes went to his dragon, a mountain of scaled muscle, and saw that the lights were twining over him too, a spider web of delicate lines that rested in the cleft between each scale.

Both the dragon and his Rider glowed. The light seeped into them, filling them, charging them. Energy crackled, and the air wavered and hummed. The Rider's magic, which was already unfeasibly strong, strengthened to a level that was unearthly.

Nessa, heart in her throat, was helpless to watch as the Rider drank in the light, taking all the energy it had to offer. It had so much to give him, so much more. Her eyes ran over the mound of bodies, at the flow of light that drifted over them, and came to realise something deeply unsettling.

The light, the mystic fire, wasn't just drifting over the bodies, summoned by the Rider and the dark entity, it *came* from the bodies. Whatever the Rider was doing, whatever magic he was wielding, Nessa somehow knew that he was drawing something from the bodies' lingering life forces, taking the raw magic that was life itself for some perverse reason.

Something brushed against her hand.

Nessa flinched and whipped her hand up, trying to shake loose whatever was tickling her knuckles. It clung, coiling gently around a finger like a vine, warm and light, and strangely alive. A current of energy shot through her Rider's Mark, and it tingled pleasantly, almost in recognition, in welcome.

Nessa froze, scared and uncertain.

Squeezing her eyes closed, Nessa hoped to find a moment of clarity in the chaos surrounding her. She found a little courage instead and managed to peer down at her hand, at the thing that was latched onto her, slipping under her arm warmer and curling around her wrist, prodding at her Rider's Mark. Even though a part of her instinctively knew what it was, it still came as a shock to see a thread of mystic fire coiled around her finger and hand.

It had branched away from the rest, a thin offshoot that trailed across the ground, snaking around holes and rubble. Its light was softer, gentler, compared to that of the blaze covering the mound of bodies. Somehow, it had escaped being drawn in by the Rider and his dragon, and for some reason, had chosen to approach her instead, like it had a mind—a will—of its own.

The wild, untamed power that had rushed through Nessa's veins only moments ago started to rise again. Something about it and the mystic fire called to each other, recognising a secret quality, a shared connection between them.

Fear slowly melted away, and curiosity arose. Hesitantly, Nessa toyed with the fine tendril of mystic fire, twining it around her fingers like it was a loose thread from a frayed hem, feeling it tightening around them, pressing into her skin. She lifted her hand, holding it before her eyes, watching as the tendril shifted with the movement, clutching at her, desperate to remain in contact. Little wisps drifted off, fluttering in the air as delicate and as fleeting as a butterfly.

A hunger came over Nessa, almost strong enough to double her over. Everything was forgotten as she wrapped her arms around her middle, gasping for breath. A primal pain gnawed at her innards, begging to be fed. Nessa looked down at the tendril of light fervently.

She'd experienced a taste of power. The raw magic that hid inside of her had seen to that.

Nessa wanted *more*.

The mystic fire would give it to her. It would sate the hunger. She knew it would.

The dark entity turned its gaze to her, quivering with anticipation, watching as Nessa's eyelids fluttered closed, as she tugged on her thread of liquid starlight, needing to draw it into her, just as the other Rider was.

Intangible hands brushed against her cheeks, claws caressing her throat. The entity started whispering in her ear, promising great things, terrible things. Everything she had ever wanted, all she could ever want, would be hers for the taking. All she needed to do was open a vein, spill some of her lifeblood, give herself over completely to…to…

Sharp talons scraped against her shoulders and

tangled in her hair, scratching and pulling. Wings battered her face in a frenzy, and shrill shrieks pierced her ears, too loud and too close.

With a strangled cry, Nessa's eyes snapped open, and the gnawing hunger faded away, vanishing as if it had never been. She felt as if she was waking from a dream, a nightmare. Finding herself suddenly back in the real world was jolting and terrifying.

Nessa stumbled back, blinded by hair and wings, swatting wildly at the raven. It was strong and relentless, deranged. She began to run, hoping to escape from it, one arm thrown across her eyes, protecting them from its sharp talons and jabbing beak. Nessa dashed towards what she prayed was a pathway between the rubble and collapsing buildings, and the fire. Since she didn't immediately trip and fall over, or run headlong into a burning wall, Nessa assumed that she was in luck and picked up speed, going as fast as she could.

The raven eased its assault on her, but by no means did it leave her alone, staying painfully close. Its presence was a threat, a warning, a driving force that kept her going with a promise of violence. Wingtips brushing against her cheeks and rough *caws!* were a constant reminder that never allowed her a moment of hesitation, or a chance to look back over her shoulder.

The raven didn't allow Nessa to give into the dark, alluring voice that called after her.

Nessa ran until the crunch of broken cobblestones and bricks gave way to the soft whisper of grass, and until the crackle and hiss of flames were nothing more than a terrible memory.

Nessa ran until the blue-eyed raven once again parted ways with her, and arms, warm and strong, wrapped around her, holding her close to a chest that shuddered with relieved sobs.

# Chapter 17

Nessa sat huddled against Aoife's side, shuddering, her arms wrapped around herself. She stared unblinkingly at the horizon, at the ruddy ember there, at the glowing remains of what used to be a bustling market town. The scent of smoke still clung to her, filling her nostrils.

"He's not coming," Hunter said, voice raw, pausing his pacing to clap Orm on the back.

Nessa blinked, eyes burning, and looked to where both of them stood nearby, little more than dark shapes in the chilled autumn night.

"He would have come by now," Hunter murmured.

Orm folded his arms across his chest, hugging himself. "He'll come. Just you wait. You'll see. It takes more than Dragon Fire to kill him."

Hunter opened his mouth, ready to argue, but quickly snapped it shut with a sigh. He could see the pain shining in Orm's eyes, bright in the moonlight.

*Is there any hope?* Nessa asked timidly. *Could Chaos have escaped the razing?*

*I fear not,* Aoife said gently, coiling her tail tighter around them as if she would create a barrier to protect Nessa from what had happened. *I have tried my hardest to find him, but I cannot sense his mind at all. He is lost to us.*

*Maybe it's just due to distance?*

*Distance has very little to do with it.*

*Well…perhaps he's simply shielding his mind?*

*It doesn't work like that, and you know it. Even when you were shielding your mind down there, I could still sense that you were alive. Although I couldn't talk to you or feel your emotions like I can now.*

*So what you're saying is…*

*There is little to no hope that Chaos is alive. If he was, whether he was shielding his mind or not, then I would know. I would easily sense one such as him. Anyway, it's been an hour since the Dragon Rider and his beast left. There is no need for Chaos to conceal himself now.*

Nessa shifted and pressed a cheek against Aoife's side, a deep sadness coming over her. *Poor Orm. Should we tell him?*

*A part of him already knows. He's just not ready to accept it yet.*

*Poor Orm,* Nessa repeated. *I'll admit I wasn't particularly fond of Chaos, but I never wanted him to die. Certainly not under such awful circumstances.*

*It's a fate that few deserve to meet. He was not one of them. The world has lost someone it couldn't afford to.*

*And Orm. He looks like he's about to shatter.* Even in the gloom of night, Nessa could see his shoulders slumping under the weight of his growing despair, his eyes glimmering with unshed tears. He had stood atop a crest for over an hour, unmoving, gazing at the stretch of land between them and what remained of Arncraft, searching for any sign of movement, for any hint of life.

*Chaos helped him when he was younger, when his powers first emerged. Orm looks up to him as a father figure rather than a mentor. While Chaos wasn't one to show emotion, I could tell that he loved Orm in his own unique way. I think Orm knew that too, although he never dared to bring it up.*

*So Orm's lost a father rather than a friend?*

*Yes.*

*Poor Orm.*

*Poor Orm,* Aoife concluded.

The mention of father figures made Nessa's mind turn to family in general, and she couldn't help but wonder about Orm's and Hunter's...and hers.

Orm was clearly lacking a meaningful relationship with his biological father, perhaps even lacking a father to start with. It was a dangerous and complicated world, and Nessa guessed that anything could have happened. But what about the rest of his family? Where was his mother? Did he have any siblings? Cousins? And what about Hunter? Where were his parents? Was he part of a large family, or was he all alone?

Nessa thought it was bad enough that she couldn't remember anything about friends she had supposedly known for years, but it was so profoundly wrong that she couldn't recall *anything* about her life, even her own family.

Nessa wondered where they were, *who* they were.

Nessa searched for anything that might be likened to a memory, a feeling, an image. Even a sense of recollection would do. But just as always when reaching for her past, she ran into a wall. Her memories were there, somewhere. She was just unable to access them.

Why that was, Nessa didn't know, the whys and the hows escaping her. The idea of someone tampering with her mind, hiding her memories, was raised. Chaos and Orm were under the impression that it was a permanent thing. However, the little creature from the forest brook implied that wasn't the case. Who was Nessa to believe? A strange little creature or the friends she couldn't remember?

Nessa sighed, overwhelmed by so many questions and emotions, and contemplated asking Aoife about *before*, as she liked to call it: *before* she had been taken by Margan, *before* she had lost access to her memories.

Hunter chose that moment to amble over, and Nessa had to abandon her contemplations, saving them for another time.

"Let me in," Hunter said, nudging Aoife's tail with the toe of a boot. "Otherwise I'll be forced to clamber over you."

*I think the word you're looking for is "please"*, Aoife murmured dryly. *Did you think of that?*

"I try to think as little as possible. I get myself in less trouble that way."

*Do you, now?*

"Maybe." He shrugged. "Sometimes it works."

Nessa found herself smirking.

"Come on, you giant lizard," Hunter huffed. "I would just like to nestle against you for some body warmth."

*Is that all I am to you? A breathing hot-water bottle?*

Hunter scowled. "Please, oh, wonderful, magnificent dragon, let me sit with you for a short reprieve from this bitter cold?"

*There, now,* Aoife moved her tail for him to pass, *was*

*that so hard?*

Hunter grumbled something under his breath as he settled beside Nessa, his shoulder bumping into hers as he shimmied to get comfortable, stretching out his long legs and crossing his ankles.

"That's better," Hunter sighed. "Now I can start to relax. I practically had a heart attack when we were separated. And when Aoife told me that you wanted me to go ahead without you, I nearly passed out."

*And called me a few choice names that I have yet to forgive you for,* Aoife added, curling her tail closer around herself, surrounding Nessa and Hunter in a ring of comforting warmth. *You were mean.*

"Mean!" Hunter exclaimed with mock outrage. "I was not mean."

*I'm still of a mind to eat you,* Aoife said, *such was the level of your meanness.*

"No eating Hunter," Nessa admonished her companions, "and no being mean to dragons."

"I wasn't mean," Hunter corrected, "I was panicked. I barely remember what I said."

*Oh,* Aoife said brightly. *There were insults to my intelligence, my species and my appearance. Not to mention a selection of words I'd rather not say in front of my Rider, lest she picks up some of your bad habits.*

Hunter squirmed. "Ah, yes. It's coming back to me now."

*Is it, now?* Aoife mused. *I'm waiting.*

"Waiting for what?"

*An apology.*

Hunter blinked owlishly. "And why, pray tell, are you waiting for an apology?"

Aoife grunted, and with a level of dignity only a

dragon could achieve, decided to ignore them both and rested her angular head on a front paw, closing her large eyes. Nessa and Hunter didn't let that fool them, though. While Aoife may appear to be resting, she was by no means unaware of what was going on around her, too riled up for sleep.

Hunter slouched a little more, his eyes half-lidded, and rested his shoulder against Nessa's. He sniffed and said, "You smell like a bonfire."

"Yeah, well, you don't smell any better."

Hunter looked her over, and Nessa knew what question was about to follow. He'd already asked it a dozen times in the last hour or so.

"So, you're sure you're not hurt?"

Nessa stifled a sigh, just. She knew he was concerned and frightened, they all were, but having to answer the same question over and over again was getting on her nerves. Nessa drew upon her last reserve of patience, not wanting to snap and say something regrettable, and very tolerantly said, "Yes, Hunter. I am sure I'm unhurt."

He still had the impudence to look unconvinced.

Nessa tried a different tactic and plucked at her top, forcing a smile. "Although I can't say that your tunic has escaped the ordeal unscathed." Just visible in the pale moonlight were little blackened spots, small holes where embers had burned through the linen.

"I noticed that," Hunter said with a hesitant grin. "You owe me a new one now."

"I suppose that would be the only polite course of action, wouldn't it?"

"Afraid so."

"Guess I'll have to get a job and get some money together."

"Or you could learn how to cheat at cards and join Orm on an excursion or two."

Nessa laughed, then clamped a hand over her mouth. It felt too soon for laughter, for joy. A town had been reduced to nothing more than piles of rubble and ash, and its inhabitants...not to mention Chaos...

A sob caught in Nessa's throat, and she turned, burying her head against Hunter's chest. His arms went around her, and he held her gently, a hand rubbing her back, trying to console her.

"There, there," he murmured. "It's alright."

"No," Nessa moaned, "it's not alright. None of what's happened is alright. All those people... It's my fault."

Hunter jolted. "Whatever makes you say that?"

Nessa shrugged.

"Come on. Tell me. Why do you think it's your fault? Have you hit your head? Gone mad?"

"I'm not mad."

"You sound a bit mad."

"Well..." Nessa searched for a witty response. "...I'm not," she finished lamely.

"Then tell me why you feel this way."

Nessa didn't want to explain herself, yet the words came spilling out of their own accord, a confession of sorts.

"It's my fault that we were there in the first place," she whispered. "If I hadn't wanted new clothes and a comfy bed in an inn, then we wouldn't have been there and Chaos wouldn't be..."

Hunter sucked in a breath. "We all decided to go to Arncraft. We all wanted to spend a night in comfort, under a solid roof with drinks and food and amusements aplenty." Nessa squeezed her eyes shut, trying to block out Hunter's words, but he continued without pause, his tone quickly going from mild to heated. "And I'll tell you that it wasn't a frivolous thing, getting new clothing. It was a necessity. You had to have new clothes, and that's that. Orm wanted to play a few games of cards and fleece some rich fops out of their not-so-hard-earned money. I wanted a soft mattress and a night where I'm not kicked by a bald giant. I also wanted to get some fresh supplies in the morning. Besides, it wasn't like Chaos protested an awful lot, now, did he?" Hunter tugged on a lock of Nessa's hair, making sure that she was listening. "We're all adults. It was a group decision to go to Arncraft rather than another town or village. None of us are to blame."

"Indeed," Orm said, his voice deep with grief. "It seems as if it were nothing more than a weird sequence of events, a series of tragic happenings. An unavoidable mistake. One that we were, perhaps, destined to make."

Nessa frowned, peering at him in the night-time gloom. "Are you implying that we were supposed to witness all of that?"

Orm shrugged. "Maybe, maybe not. I don't know. But it seems a little strange that we were there at the same time that King Kaenar decided to pay Arncraft a visit. Perhaps divine powers were in play, leading us unknowingly into the belly of the beast."

"Divine powers?" Hunter scoffed.

"The king!" Nessa's spine snapped straight, and she sat upright, leaving Hunter blinking in surprise as his arms fell from her. "The king?" she croaked. "Are you telling me that the Rider was the bloody king?"

Orm's brows rose. "Oh, you didn't know?"

"Of course I didn't know," Nessa hissed. "I have no bloody memories, remember?"

"Ah, yes. Now you mention it, I do remember."

Nessa looked at Hunter for validation, hoping that Orm was playing a peculiar game with her. "The king?"

"The king," Hunter confirmed with a nod of his head.

"But that would mean that I…"

"Ran straight into King Kaenar and his monster of a dragon?" Hunter finished for her. "Yep."

Horror ripped through Nessa's chest like a lightning strike, making the nape of her neck prickle and her heart skip a beat. "He looked right at me. He saw me. He smirked at me."

"And we should thank the Creator that he was too busy doing whatever the hell he was doing to chase after you."

"Do you think there's a chance he knows about me. As in he could tell that I was a Dragon Rider, or…or an Old Blood?"

Orm scratched his chin, his fingernails rasping against the bristles of stubble. "From what you told us, I would say not. I don't think you would be alive if he did."

Nessa fidgeted. *What she had told them…* She wondered if she should fill in the parts of her story that she had so far left out.

After escaping from the burning ruins of Arncraft and running into Hunter, it had been a whirlwind of nonstop questions as they retreated further from the town, and meeting up with Aoife and Orm was followed by even more questions. The four of them had stood on a rise for a time, not far from the foothills of the Cleā Mountains, watching as the town continued to burn, a ruddy ember on the horizon with black smoke belching into the sky, creating a dark stain that blotted out stars and smothered much of the moon's luminosity.

It had been a long while before the Rider and dragon had departed, flying leisurely away without any effort to extinguish the fires. Power had seeped from them, spilling over the land in a sickening wave, heavy and filled with sinister threat. It had been strong enough to even make Orm flinch and Hunter shift with unease as it rolled over them.

Only once the Rider and dragon disappeared from sight, their magic fading to nothing more than a bad taste in her mouth, did Nessa regale the others with her tale of escape. She told them how, after being separated from Hunter, she had seen a path through the fires and she'd taken it. She explained that, like so many of the town's inhabitants, she had unknowingly been channelled towards the square where the Rider and dragon awaited her. The flyovers may have seemed random at first, but they weren't. They were strategic, intentionally leaving small paths through the town. They had wanted as many people in that square as possible.

With her hands trembling, Nessa had told her companions how the Rider had stared at her, and how she had become frozen, unable to run. She'd been helpless and could do nothing but watch as the Rider had cut his palms and spilled his blood, summoning the wave of pure power from the mound of bodies, drawing it into himself.

It had been Orm's speculation that she had been released from her bonds by a lapse of concentration on the Rider's part, not that she had broken free by herself. Nessa hadn't corrected him. She had intentionally left out how she'd sensed the dark entity, how it had briefly awoken something in her, something that had shocked the Rider.

Nessa didn't want them to know that the power coming from the bodies had been drawn to her too, without her ever calling to it. Was she wrong in keeping that from them? Maybe. But Nessa found that the words needed to explain what happened, what it had felt like, evaded her. Not even Aoife knew, thanks to Nessa having kept her mind shielded during the encounter.

Hunter plucked at one of her arm warmers. "He couldn't know you're a Dragon Rider. Could he?" He looked to Orm.

Orm was unsure. "Since she's alive and the mark was covered, I think it's safe to say that her being a Rider is unknown to him. However, I worry that he might have been able to sense the *otherness* about her."

An image flashed in Nessa's mind's eye, his surprise when the *thing* inside of her had awoken. He'd sensed something alright, and it had shocked him.

Nessa opened her mouth, about to make her confession.

Orm began thinking aloud, cutting her off.

"Although saying that," he mused, "if he had even the slightest inkling that she was an Old Blood, then he would have ended her without hesitation. Perhaps her shielding her mind was a saving grace?"

*And something that I'm still not particularly happy about,* Aoife grumbled.

*I've said sorry,* Nessa whined. *Multiple times. I only did it to keep you safe from them.*

*Be that as it may, I don't appreciate being locked out of my Rider's mind during something like that. You scared me half to death.*

*But it may have kept us both alive and out of the king's clutches, so how about cutting me a little slack? I'm still getting used to this whole "bonded to a dragon" thing.*

Aoife sighed softly, a puff of smoke rising from her nostrils, thin and curling. *Shall we call a truce, then?*

Nessa settled back against Aoife's side, the dragon's warmth bleeding through her ruined top. *Indeed, we should. Truce.*

*Truce,* Aoife murmured. *For now.*

Nessa rolled her eyes and turned her attention back to Hunter and Orm, who seemed oblivious to her silent conversation.

"Well, since it's unlikely that the king knows Nessa is an Old Blood or a Dragon Rider," Hunter was saying, "we have to wonder why he was there in the first place."

"The rebels?" Not even Orm sounded convinced of that, and he was the one suggesting it.

"They're little more than a rumour. A network of lazy criminals" Hunter said. "Anyway, if they are real, then they hardly deserve to be called 'rebels'. From what I've heard, they do very little in the way of rebelling."

Nessa's curiosity got the better of her. "Then what do they do, if they don't rebel?"

Hunter shrugged. "Smuggling, mostly. Sometimes, if they're feeling gutsy, they might assassinate some lord or another, or rob them blind. They're hardly worth the king coming all this way to deal with them himself."

"If he wanted the Arncraft branch of rebels dealt with," Orm added, "then he would have simply sent out one of the other Riders instead."

"Anyway," Hunter said, "if he wanted to deal with so-called 'rebels', then he would have destroyed The Hidden City long ago. And let's not forget about the pirates that operate out of Emerence. If I were King Kaenar, they would be at the top of my little list of people to massacre."

"Ah, yes," Orm whispered wistfully. "The pirates. Oh, how I miss Rozalin."

"Rozalin?" Nessa whispered, intrigued by the faraway look in Orm's eyes.

"A flame-haired bitch of a woman," Hunter murmured. "Has a couple of ships under her command."

"She's a pirate?"

"Indeed she is, and a pretty fearsome one at that. Her disposition matches her hair, fiery and wild."

"And she's a hellcat in the bedroom too," Orm sighed happily. "I had claw marks on my back for a week after our, ah, rendezvous."

Hunter groaned, "You're an animal."

"So was she." Orm grinned smugly.

Nessa grimaced. "That's more information on Orm's antics than I ever wanted to know."

*I concur,* Aoife grumbled.

"So, getting back to the matter at hand," Nessa said, trying to steer the discussion away from Orm's past shenanigans. "If the king didn't go there because of me, or the rebels, then why was he there? There must be a reason."

"I'm sure there is," Orm agreed. "However, whatever it may be, it's escaping me at the moment."

"Perhaps it has something to do with whatever magic he used," Hunter suggested. "The power he summoned?"

"Maybe," Orm murmured, gazing up at the moon as if it might hold the answer. "Maybe."

Nessa wrapped her arms around herself as a chill crept over her. "And what, exactly, was the magic he used?"

Orm bit the inside of his cheek. "I don't know." He turned and looked at the ruddy ember on the horizon. "A part of me feels like we're better off not knowing."

# Chapter 18

None of them had much sleep that night, which was both a blessing and a curse. At most, they garnered a few hours of restless dozing; their eyes sliding closed just long enough for the nightmares to come calling. Sleep hadn't been their intention, but as it was, exhaustion wore them down in the end, putting an end to their dissections and speculations. They dozed where they had been conversing, sat in a small circle, Aoife curled loosely around them, her gemstone-esque body acting as a partial windbreak, protecting them from the worst of the autumn cold.

Time became a strange thing, a fickle thing. Seconds felt like hours and minutes were all too brief, gone in a blink of an eye. It was in this strange state of stretched timelessness that Nessa entered into an odd, dream-like haze.

The images were broken and jumbled, pale and faded as if she was looking through misted glass. Nessa saw herself walking in a forest at springtime, the trees' leaves fresh and green, casting dappled shade on the ruins she explored whilst being urged forwards by a cunning raven. Walls of pale stone were broken and crumbling, concealed beneath trailing fingers of ivy and honeysuckle. She saw herself in a dark, underground room, the floor covered in a whispering carpet of decay, walking over to a mirror of liquid mercury, the surface covered with eerie, flickering lights.

The dream-like visions showed her things too strange and outlandish to surely be real. Nessa saw roaring dragons, flames of blues, greens and purples spewing from their mouths as they flew over a battlefield on which armies of silver and gold were fighting each other. There were men with antlers...women with large cat eyes... The sky filled with clouds of arrows... A river of blood flowed down a hillside, a waterfall of gore... Screams filled her ears, a cacophony of noise that was muddled by the whispers of a creature unseen, offering tantalising titbits of secrets and truths, of promises and prophecies.

With those whispers echoing in her ears, all light seemed to fade. Shadows crowded around a mighty throne on which a man sat, a crown perched on his head and a golden torc resting around his neck. He toyed with it, his fingers rubbing over the fine woven threads, over the black diamonds and the dark, gleaming opals...

Nessa shot upright, pain lancing down her thigh from a rather sharp kick.

She scowled and turned, finding Hunter twitching in his troubled sleep, his eyelids fluttering wildly and his limbs spasming erratically, his muscles straining and flexing as he fought against devils only visible to him.

The tension slowly eased from her, and Nessa abandoned her intention of slapping Hunter for her rude awakening. She swiped away the sweat peppering her forehead and leaned back against Aoife, seeking warmth and companionship, and a bit more time before she'd have to deal with the troubles that daybreak would surely bring.

Pulling the blanket tighter around herself, shivering a little from the cold, Nessa squeezed her eyes closed, begging for a reprieve from dark thoughts and nightmares.

Hunter emitted a low moan, one that came from deep in his throat, primal and anguished.

Too tired to feel much sympathy, Nessa flung back her blanket, dodged another kick, and reached out a hand, intending to shake Hunter awake. She nearly jumped out of her skin when someone grabbed her wrist.

"I thought you were asleep," Nessa gasped.

Orm pulled himself out of the awkward sprawl he'd somehow got himself in, arched over Aoife's tail and rolled his head, loosening the stiff muscles in his neck and shoulders.

"Oddly enough," he murmured, releasing her wrist, "I wasn't. I just couldn't get comfortable."

"Mm, odd indeed." Nessa turned back to Hunter as he groaned again, his head lolling from side to side, sweat beading on his skin. "He's having a nightmare. Should we wake him?"

"Never wake a man from a nightmare," Orm advised. "It's bad luck. Anyway, he needs to face his devils. Otherwise, he'll never be free of them."

"And what devils is he facing?"

"Let's just say that wasn't the first massacre he's got

himself caught up in..."

༽◆༼

An odd smell drifted through the air. Nessa sniffed, trying to sleepily identify the offending scent, and pushed herself up on her elbows, uncurling from the ball she had slept uneasily in.

"Is that burning egg?" Hunter murmured, groggily rubbing his eyes.

"I think so."

Horror washed over Hunter's face, and he jumped to his feet. "Orm's cooking."

Nessa recalled Orm's prior attempt at scrambled egg and stood, grimacing, praying that their sense of smell was awry after the trauma of last night. Unfortunately, though, she caught sight of Orm just a few yards away, sat by a small fire, nursing a pan that spewed noxious smoke.

"I'm pretty sure I've mastered this whole cooking thing," Orm said with a wry grin, looking none the worse for wear. "Breakfast is nearly done."

"Breakfast, eh?" Hunter peered up at the bright, blue sky. "If you say so."

Orm waved a hand. "Breakfast. Brunch." He shrugged and prodded at the blackened jiggling mass in the pan with a spatula. "Lunch. Same difference."

Nessa glanced at Hunter, feeling a little panicked. "I thought we had no food supplies left."

"We didn't. We don't."

"Then where did the eggs come from?"

"When it comes to Orm, it's usually better for the questions to go unanswered."

"I don't think I can stomach nice food at the moment,

let alone something Orm's whipped up from...I don't even know where."

"Yeah...umm..." Hunter cast around, looking for a solution. "Maybe, when he turns his back to us, we can fling our plate-load into those bushes over there."

"That way," Nessa said, relieved at the plan, "he doesn't get his feelings hurt, and we don't have to eat whatever monstrosity he's cooked up."

Hunter grinned. "Everyone's as happy as can be. It's win-win."

Carefully stepping over the scaled tail encompassing them, mindful not to wake the sleeping dragon, Nessa and Hunter cautiously made their way over to Orm. Nessa fixed what she hoped was a cheery smile on her face and sat down next to him, murmuring a greeting as she eyed the *thing* in the frying pan.

Hunter plonked himself down opposite them and leaned forwards. "And what, my dear friend," he asked, jabbing their "breakfast" quickly with a finger, "is this monstrosity?"

Orm raised the spatula threateningly. "You know full well what it is."

"A delicious meal?"

"Exactly."

"It certainly looks interesting," Nessa added, "and smells..."

"Divine?" Orm finished.

"Um."

Hunter clapped his hands. "Well, as you said, you've mastered it today, so best dish it up so we can get on with the day and...and..."

"And what?"

"Yeah," Nessa said slowly, "what are we to do now?"

"Whatever do you mean?" Orm asked, somewhat confused, using the spatula to cut their meal into three pieces before scooping them onto plates, where each bit retained its shape with disturbing perfection. "Has something changed with our plans?"

Nessa and Hunter shared a loaded look.

"Well," Hunter said, hesitant, "after what happened last night and to…umm…Chaos—"

"Chaos," Orm cut in, voice suddenly thick, his Adam's apple bobbing up and down as he swallowed his simmering emotions, "would expect us to continue with the original plan. So that's what we're going to do. We're going to go to Ellor. We're going to figure out why the bloody king is calling back his cursed Dragon Riders, and we're also going to find out why he came here and razed an entire town. Then, when the time comes, I'm going to ensure that *King Kaenar* meets a very painful, very slow end for killing my friend."

With tears in his whiskey-coloured eyes, Orm picked up his plate and hurried away, disappearing into a cluster of trees, swiftly vanishing from sight.

Hunter released a pent-up breath. "Well…I really don't know what to say…"

"I don't think there's much to say," Nessa murmured.

"Mmm. Seems like Orm is of a mind for a wee bit of revenge."

"He was crying earlier," Nessa confessed. "Before sunrise."

"Oh?"

"You woke me," she peered at Hunter through her lashes, gauging his reaction, "when you were having a nightmare." He shrugged, appearing nonchalant, although Nessa saw a muscle tick in his jaw. "Anyway,

Orm was awake too, and we just kind of, well… He just started talking about Chaos, rambling on about how he was going to miss him and how he thought he would always have Chaos to turn to if he needed help of the magical persuasion. Aoife mentioned something last night about how Orm looked up to Chaos as a father figure, but I think that Chaos meant a lot more to Orm than just that."

Hunter cleared his throat. "Orm's never met his birth father, and since his mother is human, when he came into his powers, he hit a rather rough patch that she couldn't help him through. I think Chaos was the only one who could help, who did help, and because of that, I think Orm…" Hunter sighed. "Well, you get the picture. Now, quickly, fling the 'scrambled eggs' into those bushes over there before he comes back. I'm pretty sure mine's moving."

ಯ✦ಚ

Nessa ran a hand down the front of her long dress, smoothing out a couple of creases and checking that the lacing sat just right. With a twinge of sadness from knowing the fate of its seamstress, Nessa admired how well the dress fit, how fine the detailing was. Eliza's fate. With a sigh, Nessa slipped her feet back into her shoes, which fit a lot more comfortably without being squeezed over Hunter's chunky socks, and double checked that her arm warmers were covering her Rider's Mark and that they sat neatly over the dress' sleeves.

Bending over, Nessa picked up the bag which held a jumbled mixture of both hers and Hunter's clothing, and moved out from behind the coppice of young trees she had used as cover whilst changing.

Hunter and Orm were sat shoulder to shoulder, poring over a map and bickering about which route to take. They had changed into fresh clothing too, not that it made all that much of a difference. Both of them were dressed in their customary tunic and trous, favouring plainer, darker colours today. Nessa left them to it, seeing as she wouldn't be of much help, and went over to Aoife, who blinked sleepily at her.

*I see you've gone with the blue dress.*

*I'm in a blue dress kind of mood.*

*Oh, Nessie.* Aoife stretched out her long neck, touching the tip of her snout to the top of Nessa's head. It was a dragon's version of a comforting pat on the back, Nessa supposed. *Mourn for those who perished in Arncraft, but do not let sorrow consume you.*

Nessa strapped the clothing bag onto Aoife's back alongside the others, making a mental note to squirrel away Chaos' strange book later, before Hunter and Orm could stumble upon it.

The book held secrets. Nessa wanted to be the one to uncover them.

Patting Aoife's side, Nessa stepped back, her eyes running over the web of ropes holding three tents and bags of other things and supplies onto Aoife's back, checking that everything was secure.

*Thank you for the advice,* Nessa said. *Have you thought about sharing it with Orm? He seems to be on a warpath.*

Aoife turned and peered at Orm contemplatively. *Hmm. Hopefully, he'll calm down in a day or two?*

*Hopefully.*

*Maybe Hunter will talk some sense into him?*

Nessa snorted. *Hunter and sense? I don't think those two go together.*

*No, perhaps not. I suppose we'll just have to wait and see how this plays out. If worst comes to worst, I could always fly him somewhere remote and abandon him there for a little while. Just until he sees reason.*

*At least we have a backup plan.*

"Right, it appears that we are ready to go," Hunter said, jumping to his feet and rolling up the map. "Everyone's dressed. Aoife's all loaded up. And our course has been decided."

"Oh," Nessa raised her eyebrows, "and dare I ask what that entails?"

Hunter smirked. "More walking for a start."

Nessa groaned.

"We'll be making a slight detour south. There's a decent-sized village about six miles away. Orm managed to not only pocket his winnings last evening, but also managed to grab the other player's coins as they ran from the attack, so we're oddly well off at the moment, financially speaking. Hopefully, we'll be able to purchase a trio of horses."

"Horses?" Nessa was surprised. "I thought you weren't to be trusted when it came to horses?"

"Orm's changed his mind on the matter, provided I have nothing to do with them other than ride one to the capital."

"Ah."

"With horses," Orm said, hopping to his feet, "we'll be able to shave a day or two off our journey." He began walking away from them, heading over to a group of bushes. "I want to get to the capital in time for the gossiping to start."

Hunter frowned. "Then why are you going northward instead of south?"

"Because, my dear boy, I need a piss, and those bushes, northward they may be, look like a mighty fine place to have one."

"I don't know about you," he said to Nessa, scowling as Orm disappeared behind the bushes. "But that was a bit more information than I really wanted to know."

"Well, you did ask."

"Yeah, but he could have simply said that he was going to deal with some 'personal business'."

"Mm, well. At least he seems cheerier?"

Hunter grimaced. "While you were changing, he gave me a rundown of his plans once he has King Kaenar in his clutches. It's brightened his mood up considerably."

"Ah."

"There was mention of eye-gouging."

"Ew."

"With a spoon."

"A spoon?"

"Yep." Hunter looked a little too animated for Nessa's comfort. "Apparently, the bluntness would add to his suffering, and the shape of the spoon would make for a nice scooping action."

"He's put an alarming level of thought into that."

Hunter shrugged. "What can I say? Orm's had a meditative night."

"Oh dear."

"There's nothing like planning sweet revenge to warm the cockles of a man's heart."

Nessa raised a brow. "Oh, sounds like you're speaking from personal experience. Don't suppose that has something to do with what's between you and Margan, now, would it?"

"Ah," Hunter's eyes brightened. "Margan. Yes, I

suppose I am talking about him, in a way."

"And what, dare I ask, are you planning on doing to him?"

"Apparently, I'm going to be leaving him to stew for a bit longer while I make sure my childhood friend doesn't get himself hung, drawn and quartered for a failed drunken assassination attempt on the king."

*Both he and Orm are mad,* Nessa said with despair, *completely and utterly mad.*

*At least you know that, if you were to meet an unfortunate demise, then they would try to avenge you with a delightfully foolhardy plan.*

"Oi!" Orm bellowed, startling a few pigeons from the nearby trees. "Why the bloody bollocks are there bits of scrambled egg over here?"

༄ ♦ ༄

There was talk of going back into Arncraft with a slim hope of finding survivors, people who might be injured or trapped beneath the rubble. When Aoife flew over the smouldering ruins, they quickly realised that there was no point. No one could be trapped. There simply wasn't enough left of the buildings for that to happen. Hours of hungry fires had reduced homes and businesses alike to little more than piles of fuming ash, with a few blackened beams and the odd section of stone wall here and there.

Arncraft was nothing more than a dark stain on the earth.

*I can scent nothing but death here,* Aoife told Nessa and her companions from above Arncraft as they crossed through open meadowland, staying their course for Ellor.

*Is there no chance of survivors?* Nessa asked, watching Aoife's glittering form swoop down low over the ruins, stirring up clouds of ash and smoke in her wake.

*Anyone who's escaped the razing has scattered to the four winds. They didn't linger, and neither should you.*

*What makes you say that?*

*Something foul resides in the air, like that of a dark presence.*

*Could that be the thousands of unfortunate people who got roasted?*

*I fear not. There's nothing left of those poor souls other than bone and dust. But look at this...* Aoife shared an image through their bond, implanting it directly into Nessa's mind. It was brief, little more than a flash, but it was just enough for Nessa to see the town from a different perspective, from Aoife's perspective.

Viewed from above, Nessa could see something that wasn't obvious from the ground, something rather peculiar.

The way the fires had burned... The way the buildings had burned...

There had been more strategy behind how the town was set ablaze than simply herding people towards the Rider and his dragon. There had been another purpose behind the fires.

A very sinister purpose.

Nessa looked at the scorch marks through Aoife's eyes, committing the patterns, the arcane shapes, to memory.

*Is that a...pentagram...?*

# Chapter 19

Nessa ran a hand over the book's metal front cover, her fingers brushing over the delicate ridges and dips. Aoife's eyes were bright, focused on her face, watchful and ever so thoughtful. Nessa ignored the hum of Aoife's mind pressing against her own, half-tempted to throw up her walls of amethyst for a moment of peace. She didn't though, thinking that it would be a bit rude, especially after recent events.

Aoife was still displeased at being barred from Nessa's mind when she'd come face to face with the Dark Rider and his monster of a dragon, when Nessa had witnessed *King Kaenar* and his infamous dragon, Spite, using a villainous type of magic.

Even now, a shiver ran down Nessa's spine when she recalled how close she had been to him, the one who would kill her for simply being who and what she was. With savage clarity, she remembered the gleaming blackness of his eyes and how powerful his magic had been, syrupy and smothering, sinister and tainted. His strength was terrifying. Nessa couldn't understand how Hunter and Orm thought she would someday be his rival. Surely only a god would be his match?

Nessa was positive that she was no god.

Nessa turned the book over to inspect the peculiar lock holding the covers firmly closed. She was careful with where she put her fingers, not wanting to be pricked again. Nessa had enough cuts, scrapes and bruises as it was. She was unwilling to add another wound to her collection, even if it was a minuscule one.

*It's certainly a strange book,* Aoife said, lowering her head, bringing it down beside Nessa's for a closer look.

"I wonder why Chaos had it all wrapped up and hidden?"

*Maybe he didn't want nosy girls to go around stealing his stuff.*

"I had only planned on borrowing it," Nessa grumbled. "Borrow. Not steal. And it's not like I can give it back to him, now, is it?"

Aoife snorted. *You sounded so much like Hunter just then. It's a little alarming.*

"Well, I have apparently known him for years," Nessa sighed as she tried to pry the metal covers apart, "so something must have soaked in, even if I can't remember exactly what."

Aoife fell silent, and it took a moment or two for her to find her voice. *If you didn't steal it, then why don't you want Hunter or Orm to know about it?*

Nessa set the book down on her lap with a sigh. The pewter glinted with a golden hue in the dwindling sunlight. "I've already explained it as best I can."

*Ah, yes, your delightful explanation of "it called to me".*

"It did," Nessa argued. "It still does. Kind of."

*And how does a book, an inanimate object, call to someone?*

"I don't know," Nessa confessed. "I suppose it's nothing more than a sense that I was meant to find it. A feeling in here." She tapped her chest, her heart. "I'm meant to discover something about it. Something that's only meant for me."

*And me too, now.*

"Well, I could hardly keep it a secret from you since you caught me trying to hide it."

*Indeed. That should teach you a lesson about stealing and trying to hide things from a dragon.*

"You scared me half to death," Nessa said. "I thought you were asleep. And it's not stealing. I'm just borrowing it. Indefinitely."

*Uh huh. If you really believed that, then you wouldn't have acted so guilty when I caught you trying to hide it.*

Nessa glared. "As I said, you caught me by surprise."

*I had to catch you out. You were acting shifty as soon as Hunter and Orm left us here to go to the village.*

"Shifty?" Nessa mumbled in disbelief, turning her attention back to the book. "I was not acting shifty."

*Yes, you were. As soon as you thought I was fast asleep, you went straight for that book, just like a squirrel diving for a particularly nice nut.*

"What can I say? After being abandoned by Hunter and Orm whilst they went to get more supplies for our travels tomorrow, and believing that you were out of it, I quickly grew bored. I thought the book would offer some kind of entertainment until they returned."

*Barely ten minutes had passed.*

Nessa was about to argue, then paused. "Was it really only ten minutes?"

*I'm afraid so.* Amused, Aoife added, *Impatience makes time move slowly.*

Nessa frowned. "And whilst we're speaking of time, how much of it do we have before Hunter and Orm come back?"

*They've only been gone for an hour or so, and have only just reached the village. They have yet to get the supplies and the horses. They also have to walk back. I'd say they'll be at least a couple of hours.*

Nessa relaxed a little, knowing that she had plenty of time left to discover the book's secrets, and she grinned playfully. "Don't forget that Orm wanted to 'nip into a tavern to see if there's any gossip'."

*Ah, yes,* Aoife's eyes twinkled with humour, *he did seem determined to go to a tavern, didn't he?*

Nessa laughed, remembering Orm's long list of reasons—excuses—as they had set up camp for the evening, trying to sway a less than eager Hunter before they had set off for the village. Hunter had endured it with sardonic quips during the erection of the tents and the building of the fire, but Nessa was willing to bet that Orm would have worn him down during their walk.

"I love how his argument for listening to anything relating to Arncraft was the last in his list of reasons."

Aoife chuckled and nudged Nessa with her snout. *Scoot forward a bit and sit closer to the fire. You're starting to shiver.*

Nessa did as she was told, having discovered only an hour ago that it was futile to argue with a dragon. At best, as she had found out, you might be able to negotiate with them. *Might.* If they were in a giving mood. Having just had a quarrel with Aoife about why she had *borrowed* Chaos' book, why she had been trying to keep it hidden,

Nessa didn't have the energy levels for another bickering match.

She shuffled closer to the fire, trying to ignore how the crackle of flames and the dancing light made her feel sick to her stomach, reminding her all too much of the ravaging blazes of Arncraft. She tried to ignore it all, but that wasn't enough.

Frightfully forceful, the memories of last night came rushing back. It was as if Nessa was there all over again, reliving it all. The taste of ash filled her mouth, and the scent of black smoke enveloped her, smothering her. She wasn't sat in a small grove of old trees anymore. She was there, with him and his dragon, and... And...

Aoife nudged with her nose, almost pushing Nessa over, knocking her out of the vision with a jolt.

Nessa sucked in a shaky breath and pressed her palms against the cold ground, fighting a wave of dizziness.

*Oh, my little Rider,* Aoife said gently, watching Nessa as she struggled to regain her composure, *where did you go?*

*Somewhere I never want to go again.*

*It was only a flashback. I'm sure these things are natural after something so awful, especially so soon.*

*Maybe. Or maybe I'm scared of fire now.*

*My Rider, scared of fire?* Aoife snorted dismissively. *I think not.*

Nessa sat up straight and gazed at Aoife with uncertainty, her mind in turmoil.

*Come now,* Aoife said, *don't trouble yourself with fears and worries, not this evening. Remember, you only have a week to discover all the secrets that book has to offer before you're to come clean to Orm and Hunter about it.*

"Are you trying to distract me from my worries?"

*Yes. Is it working?*

"Perhaps."

Still stewing over the fact that she hadn't had much sway during negotiations, only managing to garner a week with the book before having to share it with Hunter and Orm, Nessa drew it closer to herself. "Gathering secrets from it within a week is going to be hard if I can't even get it open."

Aoife peered over her shoulder. *Tilt it this way so I can see that funny, little lock better.*

"Do you think that it might be broken?" Nessa asked. "The last time I was looking at it, something caught on my finger and drew blood, although I can't see what might have done that."

*It doesn't look broken to me.*

"Well, can you see a hidden catch or anything that might pop open? There's no sign of there ever being a keyhole."

*I have a feeling that a key would be too simple and easy.*

"Maybe a magic word would open it?"

*Like what? Please?*

Nessa glared. "I mean a spell or something, and you know it."

*Unlikely, in my opinion. If you look closely enough, the lock has that odd, little indentation, and in that little indentation is a tiny needle. I think that's what you pricked your finger on the last time you were nosing around.*

Nessa chose to ignore the use of the word "nosing", and instead examined the indentation closely, trying to spot the needle. She came to the conclusion that Aoife's eyesight was considerably better than hers, for she couldn't see anything that could draw blood.

"I'll take your word for it."

*Press a finger into it. See if that opens it.*

"What?" Nessa stared at Aoife, not sure if she had heard correctly.

*I'm working on a hunch here. Just do what I tell you to.*

"I'm not going to stab myself with a needle," Nessa muttered, reaching forwards and picking up a small twig from the ground. "I'll poke it with this instead."

Aoife gave a long-suffering sigh, but didn't comment as Nessa jabbed around at the little indentation with the twig.

Nessa was unsurprised when the book remained locked.

"Well," she muttered, throwing the twig away, casting it into the fire, "that didn't work."

*Obviously*, Aoife said dryly. *I told you to press your finger into the indentation, not a damn twig.*

"Bu—"

*Just do it.*

Huffing, Nessa placed her thumb into the shallow hollow, wincing as something fine and sharp jabbed into her skin. Even without lifting it, she knew that a bead of blood welled. Nessa could feel it seeping out through the minuscule cut, quickly filling the indentation that now seemed oddly suited for a thumb to rest in.

Her thumb throbbed dully, and Nessa peeled it back slowly. A delicate coating of blood glistened in the firelight, covering the pad. Grimacing, she wiped it clean on the grass. Dew was already starting to collect in preparation for tomorrow's sleepy morning, and it was blissfully cool, soothing away the sting.

Nessa stared at the lock.

Her blood, startlingly red, clung to the sides of the hollow and spread across it thinly.

Before Nessa's very eyes, it started to vanish, seeping into fissures so small they were barely visible to the human eye, a spider web of bloody threads. There was a gentle *click* and the metal covers sprang apart by a finger's breadth, the lock loosening its grip.

"Well," Nessa murmured, "I'll be damned."

*See,* Aoife said smugly. *I was right.*

"So you were."

*Maybe that will teach you to question my orders in the future.*

"Maybe." Nessa quirked a brow. "How did you know that blood opened it?"

*It was just a hunch.*

"But *blood,* of all things? *Blood?*"

*A bit old fashioned, I know,* Aoife said with a touch of distaste. *But that's how things were done in the olden days; vows and promises, oaths and pledges, were often written and sealed with blood.*

"But why would a book be opened with blood?"

*Once you open it, I think you come to understand.*

༄✦༄

The pages were old and soft, made from parchment and vellum. They'd been slowly collected over decades, perhaps centuries, bound between the book's metal covers as they'd been written and procured. Many were brown with age, mottled and creased, smudges lining the outer edges from where the pages had been turned countless times.

Nessa's fingers gently caressed the pages with a sense of wonder, with a measure of unease, carefully tracing the faded texts and illustrations. Once a stark black, they were now a pale grey, soft and delicate, deceptively elegant despite what they depicted.

There were so many things written and drawn on those pages, things that Nessa and Aoife looked at with trepidation. There were illustrations of strange plants and odd symbols, pentagrams featuring nine-pointed stars, and intricate sigils and seals. There were images of skulls and bones, some human, some animal, and others that were surely the fanciful imaginings of an artist. A very disturbed artist.

With a fingertip absently following the blurred lines of a grotesque creature she hoped wasn't real, Nessa asked, "What is this book?"

*It's a grimoire,* Aoife said breathlessly. *An old and powerful one, I'm willing to bet, because of its age.*

"A grimoire," Nessa murmured, turning another page. "A spellbook?"

*In a broad sense of the word, I suppose you could call it that. Anyone can buy a spellbook. A handful might even be able to get a few of the spells to work. But a grimoire,* Aoife's eyes twinkled with excitement, *is so much more than just a book of spells. It's an heirloom, passed down from generation to generation within a family of spell users. The things mentioned in this book will be unknown to all but those whose lineage it belongs to. Its secrets are for one family alone to know.*

"Secret spells, hey? How very intriguing."

*Not just spells, but knowledge too. The more knowledge you have, the more power you gain.*

"Oh, the whole 'knowledge is power' thing." Nessa tapped a drawing of a monster made of shadows and darkness. "And what power will I gain by knowing about that, whatever *that* is?"

*To avoid it.*

"Are you saying that's real?" Alarmed, Nessa looked

closer at the illustration, taking in the broken, jagged teeth, and the eyes that looked as if they burned with fire. "What is it?"

*I'd presume it's real,* Aoife said, *given that it has a name and what I presume are the means of summoning it.*

"Name?" Nessa queried, squinting at the long title written across the top of the page in an inelegant scrawl. "That's its name? How do you even pronounce that?"

*That's not important right now,* Aoife said, urging Nessa to turn the page. *See how passages have been scribbled out and rewritten, and how people have added their own notes and advice? This is a glimpse into a world which few can only dream of seeing.*

"And now we get to see all of it. You know, before sharing it with Hunter and Orm soon."

Girl and dragon gazed at each other.

*Given the rather unique position we've found ourselves in,* Aoife said slowly, carefully, *I think we should extend our allotted time alone with the book. We wouldn't want to rush into anything that might have adverse consequences.*

"No, we wouldn't want to rush," Nessa murmured in agreement. "And given the size of the book, it may take us quite some time to go through everything thoroughly. It has some heft to it."

*A fair bit of heft, by the look of things.*

"And given Orm's current eye-gouging mood towards a certain all-powerful king, we wouldn't want him to get his hands on a grimoire and start getting any more foolhardy ideas."

*We certainly wouldn't want that.*

"It's really for Orm's own safety that we should keep the grimoire a secret for a while longer."

Aoife and Nessa nodded in harmony, both of them

satisfied that they had argued their reasoning quite soundly, and felt marginally confident that keeping the grimoire to themselves wasn't a selfish move in the least. In fact, they felt that it was very *unselfish* of them, keeping a friend safe from his own homicidal tendencies.

*Anyway,* Aoife whispered in an afterthought, her eyes riveted on the grimoire, *they've kept things from you, so why shouldn't you keep something from them?*

Nessa frowned and went to turn to Aoife. *What do you mean by that?*

A loose page fluttered free from the book, captured in an autumn breeze. Nessa caught it before it had a chance to get far, and peered down at it, her question abruptly forgotten as curiosity crept up on her.

The page was, perhaps, judging by the state of it, from the oldest section of the grimoire, torn free from its bindings long ago. The paper was unusually thick, which was probably the only reason that it had survived the level of abuse it had endured. The edges were velvety soft, frayed almost, by centuries of people running their fingers over them, and the corners were rounded, the rips and tears created too long ago for them to still be crisp. Most of the text was faded beyond the point of legibility, especially in the low sunlight of encroaching dusk. What wasn't faded was concealed beneath a dark-reddish-brown stain that left much of the page badly wrinkled.

*What's written there?* Aoife asked. *Can you tell?*

Nessa held the ruined page as close to the fire as she dared, not wanting to accidentally set it alight as someone had clearly done in the past. The small singed hole in the top right-hand corner was evidence to that. Nessa's guess was that someone had held it too close to a candle flame once.

The flickering firelight helped her to see, but not by much.

"It's hard to tell, but I think it's a family tree."

*It must be the family to which the grimoire belonged.*

"Do you think so?" Nessa began flicking through the book, searching. "It was loose, so it could have come from anywhere."

*Maybe, maybe not. We'll see.*

It wasn't until they were at the back of the book did they find that a small section was missing; a few pages had gone astray. The binding was shredded, a few strands of thread hanging free from the yellowed glue, evidence that they had been torn from the book. A small sliver of one page still remained, the edge ripped jaggedly. Speckles of a brownish mark peppered the surface, similar to that on the family tree. Nessa brought the pages together, trying to match the torn edges. Whilst they didn't correspond perfectly, Nessa felt more confident that the family tree did belong in the grimoire and hadn't been added accidently.

"It looks like it probably came from this part," Nessa concluded, trying to smooth out some of the page's wrinkles.

*So it does.*

"I can just about make out the last couple of names."

*They'll be the last few generations, right?*

"Right."

Nessa's eyes scanned over the bottom of the page, where the text was more legible, the black ink fresher, more vivid, not quite drowned out by the stain. One name stood out to her, ringing loud and clear like a peal of a dainty bell.

*Ysandre.*

Mouthing the name silently, Nessa traced the letters with a fingertip, almost in reverence, like there was a mysterious tie connecting the two of them together.

Aoife's gaze was locked onto Nessa's finger, her violet eyes strangely bright.

*An unusual name, Ysandre,* Aoife mused.

"There's something about it," Nessa whispered.

*I know,* Aoife murmured, *I can feel it too. There's a strange form of familiarity about it, a hidden bond linking the three of us somehow.*

"But what kind of bond, I wonder?"

*One that we'll have to puzzle out later,* Aoife said with a sigh. *Hunter and Orm are nearing.*

Surprised that they were returning so soon, Nessa hastily flipped the grimoire shut and looked around, searching for a place to stash the book. It was only then that she noticed the sun had long since dropped beneath the horizon and that the woods around her were only illuminated by moon and firelight.

Nessa quickly came to realise that she and Aoife had been looking through the grimoire for hours without knowing it.

# Chapter 20

Nessa and the chestnut-coloured horse stared at each other with hesitation and uncertainty. Neither knew what to make of the other, or indeed, what to do next. The horse, which apparently went by the name Bryan, was saddled, his reins held by an expectant Orm. Eyeing the gap between the ground and the stirrup, Nessa tried to figure out how she could get onto the saddle without making a complete fool of herself.

"Are you sure I've ridden a horse before?" Nessa asked. "Because I'm having some serious doubts."

"Of course you've ridden a horse before," Orm laughed. "Why would we make up such a thing?"

Nessa shrugged. "I'm not sure about the reasons behind half the things you say or do."

"You've ridden before," Orm chuckled, taking another drag from his peculiarly flaky cigar, making the tip flare green.

Hunter, already perched on his horse's back, sitting with such ease that it was clear to Nessa that he was no stranger to riding, glared down at his friend with disapproval.

"You've ridden a horse before." Hunter turned to Nessa with a curiously tight smile. "It's just been a while, that's all. All you need to do is get on up there, and good, old Bryan will do all the hard work for you."

"Hard work?" Nessa scoffed. "I don't think poor, old Bryan here as done such a thing in years."

Bryan snorted lazily, as if in agreement.

Hunter waved a hand, batting away her words. "That means the old chap has plenty of energy saved up."

"Bryan looks like he's falling asleep," Nessa remarked.

"He isn't falling asleep. No, wait. Maybe he is." Hunter scowled at the horse. "Bloody animal. No wonder he was free when we bought the others."

Nessa's mouth fell open. "You got a *free* horse?"

"Indeedy we did," Orm said, grinning. "We were going to get a matching set," he nodded at his and Hunter's horses: two youthful geldings with glossy, black coats, "but when the seller offered us Bryan for free," he clapped a hand on Bryan's rump, almost waking him, "we couldn't resist."

"Huh."

"Now, come on, I'll give you a boost up." Orm handed Bryan's reins to Hunter. "Before the horse is completely out of it, again. It took a good ten minutes to wake Bryan up this morning."

"Yeah, Bryan and me both," Hunter grumbled under his breath, still displeased at being woken up at the crack of dawn that morning.

An over-energetic Orm was almost as bad as a grieving, murderous Orm.

Orm rolled his eyes and lured Nessa closer, reeling her in by curling his index finger.

Nessa groaned, sensing that there was no way of delaying the inevitable. It seemed that she was going to be in that saddle, whether she wanted to be or not. Best to get it over and done with, Nessa told herself, praying that she wouldn't do something embarrassing or stupid, like fall off, for example. Hunter and Orm, Aoife too, would never let her live that down. A Rider who couldn't ride... Nessa could hear the jokes already.

Orm placed his cigar between his lips, holding it steadily in the corner of his mouth, and tugged Nessa over to Bryan's side. "That," he said, taking her left hand and placing it on the saddle's pommel, his voice a little muffled, "goes there." He cupped his hands together and stooped down. "Now, put your left foot there, and I'll give you a boost up. Then we'll adjust the stirrups."

Nessa hesitantly did as instructed, and before she knew it, she was up in the air, barely able to swallow a surprised squeak.

Instinctively, Nessa swung her right leg over the horse's back and settled down awkwardly on the saddle, her dress' skirts tangling around her legs in an unladylike way. Orm, all business, went to work adjusting the stirrups, lengthening the leather straps that connected them to the saddle. After enquiring as to what they were called, Nessa learned that they were creatively called *stirrup leathers.*

"This feels most unnatural," Nessa said as Orm, humming to himself in approval, placed her feet into the stirrups and tugged her skirts so that the blue fabric was arranged around her legs in a more dignified way.

"Nonsense," Hunter gave her Bryan's reins, "you look perfectly at ease."

Orm snorted, at least decent enough to not laugh outright. Done with the saddle adjustments, he reached over and positioned the reins so that Nessa held them correctly.

"Relax Nessie," he advised as he swung himself up onto his horse with practised skill, "the trick is to relax."

"Relax," Nessa muttered. "I'm perfectly relaxed. Well, as relaxed as I can be given that I'm sat on a horse and have no idea what I'm doing."

*You're not remotely relaxed,* Aoife told her. *I can see that as clear as day even from all the way up here.*

Nessa turned her gaze upwards and spied Aoife flying overhead, circling them like a bird of prey, almost high enough to be mistaken for one at first glance. She frowned. *No, you can't.*

*Can too. Your back's as straight as a rod.*

*It is not.* It was, but Nessa wasn't going to admit that. She rolled her shoulders, trying to rid herself from the tension that held her firmly in its clutches, and shifted carefully so that she was sitting a bit more comfortably. The saddle wasn't nearly as padded as it looked.

*That's better,* Aoife told her.

*This isn't as easy as Hunter and Orm said it would be. I'm also a lot higher off the ground than I really want to be.*

*Just you wait until you're sat on my back, shooting through the clouds. Your perspective of heights will change drastically.*

Nessa watched as Aoife dived through one of a handful of puffy clouds dotting the topaz-blue sky, executing rolls and loops just for her own benefit. Nessa grimaced, not particularly thrilled at the notion of riding a dragon thousands of feet above the ground.

Clicking his tongue, Orm urged his horse onwards, beginning the day's journey. Hunter turned to Nessa, his brows raised.

"Are you ready for your first day of horse riding?"

"I guess."

༂✦༃

Bryan wasn't a fast horse. Neither was he particularly energetic. However, he was calm and steady, and of a peaceful disposition. He never faltered or argued, provided he was given a steady supply of treats and a good scratch behind the ears when he settled down for the night.

Days and miles slowly passed, and the city of Ellor drew ever closer. There was a quiet hum of nervousness and excitement between all of them, a buzz of energy that made it feel like they were marching into war.

After what Nessa had witnessed in Arncraft, she no longer felt any kind of hesitation at the idea of taking the king's life. Her only worry now was *how* she was going to do it.

The power King Kaenar wielded was terrifying. Nessa couldn't stop thinking about it, even though both Hunter and Orm told her not to dwell on the matter. There would be time for thinking about how they would defeat him later, they'd always say; now was the time she needed to listen and observe, to learn everything she could.

And learn Nessa did, absorbing every titbit of information offered to her. But still, no matter what she was taught about the Twelve Houses and the Dragon Riders, Nessa felt as if it wasn't enough, that memorising countless names and colours of current dragons was nothing more than a distraction. So, each night, when Hunter and Orm were fast asleep, Nessa would sneak out of her tent, join Aoife, and open the grimoire with a drop of her blood.

For as long as she could, Nessa would pore over those pages, trying to glean something useful from them, sometimes until the sky started to lighten. But the grimoire continued to keep its secrets to itself. Nessa's limited understanding of magic reduced the grimoire to little more than a book filled with mystery, eerie notes and drawings.

Often, during those stolen hours, Nessa would also try to awaken the *thing* residing deep within her, powerful but dormant. Just like with the grimoire, she wasn't met with much luck, having little to no success. A couple of times, Nessa thought she felt something stir, but that was the extent of it. Each time she reached for the sensation, the niggle of something there, it would fade away, disappearing to somewhere she couldn't quite reach. It was beyond frustrating, and only fuelled her sense of hopelessness, the feeling that she wasn't good enough for the tasks she would surely have to face.

Aoife was the only one who could ease Nessa's troubled mind, murmuring words of reassurance, telling her that it was only because she had yet to come of age. As soon as she turned eighteen, Aoife was confident that she'd come into her powers, becoming an Old Blood in "full".

For Nessa, her birthday couldn't come quick enough. With hungry longing, she eagerly awaited each day's end, sure that it brought her closer to the one when her veins would flood with magic. Nessa was convinced that the real tutelage would then begin in earnest and she'd master the arcane arts.

Perhaps, with the emergence of her magic, understanding would follow, and the grimoire might reveal something that would give Nessa the upper hand.

☼✦☾

It was three days of travelling before the land around them changed from something other than wild meadows and small groves.

They had been keeping to themselves during this part of the journey, avoiding other travellers as much as possible for as long as they could. This way, they delayed the inevitable of Aoife having to separate from them, which she would be forced to do once they neared the capital. There were no purple dragons under the king's command. If someone were to see Aoife and word got back to the king, there was no telling how he would react. His wrath would be unparalleled. There would be no way for them to escape from it.

Aoife kept to the air during the day, staying up in the clouds when there were some, or high enough for the gleam of her scales to appear blue or red rather than purple, depending on the angle of the sun. There were a couple of dragons with those colours that Aoife could be mistaken for at first glance.

At night, once they had found a safe place to camp, Aoife could join them for a short time, landing once the earth was swallowed in darkness, and taking off before the sun had the chance to brighten the sky.

The time Nessa and Aoife spent together dwindled to almost nothing as they drew ever closer to the capital as it became increasingly difficult for them to find places to camp that were safely tucked away from prying eyes.

Once they reached the western edge of Lake Nyma, which to Nessa seemed more like a sea, stretching far into the horizon in three directions, the number of villages grew that were established close to the lake's shores. With this, there came an increase in travellers passing by: a steady stream of traders and low-key merchants, plus a handful of people hoping to find a better life in Ellor.

They headed northeast around Lake Nyma rather than catching a ferry from one of the fishing ports. The fewer people who saw them, the better, just in case King Kaenar was looking for a girl matching Nessa's description, a girl who had somehow escaped from the razing of Arncraft and from under his very nose. They were taking no chances. The element of surprise, of them remaining unknown, was the only thing working in their favour.

Margan was also a threat, even if they hadn't seen or heard anything of him since he'd been called back to the capital. Still, there was no doubt that he'd ever forget about Nessa. He would want her back under his thumb. He needed to clear up the mess he had created before the king discovered his treachery. Whether Margan planned on coming after her himself or sending someone else to do it for him, they didn't know. They were hyper-vigilant, cautious.

There was too much at stake for them to make any kind of error.

☼✦☾

Autumn was rapidly giving way to winter.

On the fourth day of their travels, Nessa woke to the first hard frost of the season. The edge of the lake was ringed with ice, and the pebbled beach where they had spent the night glistened with a delicate dusting of crystals. A thick blanket of mist rolled in from the water, enveloping the shoreline in a mystical haze, lingering long after Aoife had flown off for the day and they had continued with their journey.

It was nearing midday when Nessa first caught sight of The Three Sisters, a trio of jagged mountains that jutted from the ground. They were in the distance, much of their forms concealed behind the silvery mist, the pale sunlight defused, giving everything a soft, ethereal edge. Nessa felt as if she was travelling through the outer reaches of a dream.

The mist painted The Three Sisters in pale grey, clinging hungrily to their bases, dampening their sharp outlines and making it seem like they were floating. Their peaks were shrouded in crisp, white snow, and they stood proudly over the surrounding land, watching over it.

Nessa urged Bryan onwards, knowing that tucked away at the base of those mountains, nestled between them and Lake Nyma, was Ellor.

৪০✦ଓ

Ellor, the city of gold, was named such because of the castle. It was fashioned from solid stone, carved from the mountainside, painstakingly chiselled over countless generations thousands of years ago. No seams or joins were to be found anywhere, not on the outside walls, nor in the turrets and corridors, the throne room and the great hall, and the hundreds of other rooms besides. The castle of Ellor was made from a single piece of black granite that was intersected with threads of pure gold.

In the evening sun, the castle practically glowed, sitting large and proud atop a rock outcrop that projected from the base of The Three Sisters, overlooking the city that sprawled beneath it, a city illuminated by a million street lamps.

Orm and Hunter, sat upon their handsome, black steeds, gazed at Ellor like it was theirs for the taking.

Nessa, though, had eyes solely for the castle.

Somewhere behind its beautiful facade was a king who dressed in fearsome armour, and a monstrous dragon whose scales glimmered like black diamonds, like the finest black opal.

Ellor, the city of gold, was where beauty and foul things were one and the same.

PART II

# CHAPTER 21

In the gloom of midnight, with the sound of their footsteps echoing softly around them, Nessa, Hunter and Orm slowly made their way along the riverside, keeping to the shadows as much as possible. Whilst there were no other souls wandering around that part of Ellor, the higher-class civilians preferring to stay off the streets at that time of night, locked safely behind their elegant mullion windows and hand-carved front doors, that didn't mean there weren't eyes on them. After so much hard work, and so much waiting, they were reluctant to make the foolish mistake of allowing someone to follow them, especially when things were about to get so much more interesting.

Orm paused under a tall, cast-iron street lamp, one of many that lined the street at regular intervals, and pulled a battered piece of parchment out from a pocket of his heavy winter tunic. For what felt like the hundredth time since they'd mysteriously received it a few days prior, Hunter and Orm once again pored over the crumpled note, trying to decipher the coded directions. Nessa turned her attention elsewhere with a sigh, her mind quickly wandering.

Although they had been in the capital for the best part of a month now, and Nessa had grown used to the unusual method employed in keeping the streets of the more well-to-do parts of the city lit, the lanterns still captured her fancy.

Nessa's eyes ran over the floral detailing on the lanterns' heavy bases and posts, over the shapes of climbing ivy that formed the ladder bars and the frog collars that held the lanterns aloft. The lanterns' glass was thick but clear, neatly framed in bright-copper edging. Instead of housing a flame, as conventional lanterns did, the street lamps of Ellor instead hosted a handful of ethereal mushrooms. They were pale and delicate, having a translucent quality to them, and they glowed ever so softly, chasing away most of the darkness along the walkways and streets of the High Quarter.

With a twinge of longing, Nessa wished that the three of them could afford to live there, just so she could see the terrarium lanterns light up each time the sun dipped behind the sea of rooftops. Looking at the rows of grand townhouses, even the smallest still being twice the size of their current lodgings, which was quite a substantial building in itself, Nessa thought that it was unlikely to happen anytime soon, no matter how much Orm won during his biweekly gambling expeditions. They were beautiful houses, all fine stonework and large windows, with a trio of steps leading up to the front doors and little matching gardens out front. They were the homes of lords and ladies who had their hair perfectly styled, and who wore silks and velvets in the latest fashions of the king's court. Their lives were completely separate from Nessa's. A world away.

For now, at least.

Nessa's gaze slid up to the castle that presided over the city like a glittering crown. It was too dark and too far away to make out much detail. The grand mansions and townhouses of the High Quarter stood between them, and the wide ledge of the mountain on which the castle was built hindered her sight. But that didn't matter, not really. Nessa had long since memorised every detail visible from the ground. She knew the castle, from the outside at least, off by heart. Nessa knew that the ledge it was sprawled across rose even the lowest of its many tiered gardens well above the highest rooftop of the High Quarter. She also knew how many halls and towers and spires it had, some of which were so tall that they had bridges spanning from one to the other, just so that people could get around the castle in a timely manner. It was beautiful, as beautiful as a castle could ever hope to be; it was almost beautiful enough for Nessa to overlook the danger lurking behind those fine, gold-threaded walls.

Despite the castle's fair visage, Nessa knew that monsters resided up there, human and creature alike. While it was a rare and often fleeting sight, she had seen dragons soaring overhead, scales glittering like the finest of gems. They were giant, older and more grown than Aoife, although not quite as immense as Spite, King Kaenar's dragon, who she hadn't seen since that fateful night in Arncraft. For that, Nessa was grateful, because, for short bursts of time, she was able to push aside her fear, forget the danger that was forever looming over her and just be a normal girl every now and again.

Right in that moment, though, Nessa wasn't a normal girl. In fact, at first glance, anyone would assume that she was a young boy. Her long hair was pinned up and concealed beneath a cap, the ends of a few locks artfully positioned so that they gave the appearance of a short, messy fringe. Her form was hidden by a loose, shapeless tunic that fell to just past her thighs, and baggy trous that were tucked into a pair of scuffed boots. A short cape rested around her shoulders, fighting off the chilled air that had been holding the promise of snow for the last few days, and her faithful arm warmers were in place, concealing her Rider's Mark.

Any longing Nessa felt to live in a grand house, on a street lit by glowing terrarium lanterns, faded as Hunter and Orm began to bicker. Rolling her eyes, Nessa stepped between them and peered at the coded message.

"What are you arguing about this time?" Nessa asked in exasperation.

"This," Orm flapped crumpled parchment in the air. "The bloody directions make no sense."

"And why is that?"

"Because the meeting point would be on the bridge, and I don't think I can see anyone there."

"Then maybe the meeting point is under the bridge?"

"Ha!" Hunter snorted triumphantly. "Told you so."

"I told you so?" Nessa cocked a brow. "Really? Don't be so immature."

"Yeah, Hunter," Orm chirped. "Don't be so immature."

Nessa slapped the two of them on the arm. "Behave, both of you. We don't have much time to dither around arguing. I suggest we look under the bridge first, and if no one is waiting for us down there, then we'll go onto the bridge and see if anyone's there."

The bridge was only a few hundred yards away, long and narrow, arching gracefully over the River Serpentine, which originated in the mountains and cut through the city, feeding into Lake Nyma.

"Why would anyone be waiting for us *under* the bridge?" Orm muttered, even as he followed after Nessa and Hunter as they started off.

Nessa grinned. "It wouldn't be a very secret meeting if it was out in the open, now, would it?"

Orm's eyebrows shot up with a sudden burst of understanding. "Ah," he murmured. "That makes a wee bit of sense, come to think of it."

"Glad you think so," Hunter muttered.

Nessa, although unable to stop herself from grinning, jabbed him in the side with an elbow.

Orm grumbled something under his breath.

"Relax," Hunter urged his friend. "We were invited. I doubt they'd leave us out to dry if we're a few minutes late."

"You don't know that for sure," Orm argued. "This is an amazing opportunity. If we miss this—"

"Then we'll be right where we were before we knew about this 'amazing opportunity', which, I would like to point out, we weren't even aware of a fortnight ago."

"I can't believe you two honestly think that being invited to join a lucrative gambling den is advantageous to our end goal," Nessa said. "I mean, you've called these people 'lazy criminals' on a number of occasions."

"Have not," Orm grumbled, plucking one of his peculiarly flaky cigars from his coat pocket. "I'm sure they're outstanding members of criminal society."

"Outstanding members of criminal society?" Nessa laughed. "I think you need to slow down on those cigars of yours."

"I've only had one today," Orm disputed, puffing on his cigar, making the tip glow green, "and besides, I'm getting into character. We wouldn't want them getting suspicious of us because I'm non-stoned, now, do we?"

"In my opinion," Hunter quipped, "you're never actually out of character anyway."

Orm glared half-heartedly. "Lies. Malicious lies."

The bridge and the Serpentine came before them, and Orm deflated a little as it became abundantly clear that no one was waiting on it, his broad shoulders sagging. The mushroom lamps highlighted nothing but an empty road and a stray black cat.

Hunter went over to the edge of the street and peered down at the sloping bank that led to the riverside and the underside of the bridge.

"Well," he murmured, "there's enough space down there for people to gather, I suppose. Just."

Nessa joined him, asking, "Can you see anyone down there?"

Hunter shook his head. "It's too dark, which I suppose is perfect for secret dealings and whatnot."

"Shall we go down there, then?"

Nessa and Hunter shared a look, concerned that the meeting was a trap of some kind.

With a long-suffering sigh, Hunter said, "I suppose so," and hopped off down the bank. Loose pebbles were kicked up as he skidded a couple of steps before he regained his balance and held out a hand for Nessa, helping her down onto the unsteady riverside. As Orm ambled over to join them, Nessa quickly checked that her hair was still tucked under her cap. Nerves were starting to creep up on her.

"I find myself wondering," Nessa mused quietly, tugging her cape tighter around her shoulders, "that if these people are such outstanding members of criminal society, then why am I in disguise?"

"I said that they're *probably* outstanding members of *criminal* society," Orm explained, "not society in general."

"Besides," Hunter interjected thoughtfully, "after what happened last week, it's probably best for you to go incognito from now on, for everyone's safety."

"That wasn't my fault," Nessa argued. "I had nothing to do with that whatsoever."

"I never said you did."

"I was just minding my own business," Nessa continued, "and all of a sudden this drunken man starts accusing me of causing bad luck and others got involved—"

"And then there was a giant punch-up," Orm recalled fondly. "I haven't been in a bar brawl like that in years."

"Men like him, men who spend more time on a ship far out at sea than on dry land, tend to get funny notions. They're a very superstitious lot," Hunter said, his tone low and placating. "When they feel like they're being struck by bad luck, they look for someone or something in the vicinity to blame."

"Which was me, clearly," Nessa grumbled, recalling the man's beady, little eyes landing on her from across the table.

The three of them had been at a small gathering, a party of sorts, to celebrate the coming of winter. It had been held in a small courtyard only a few streets away from where they were lodging. It had been a modest assembly, about twenty local men and a handful of women, some of the men's wives, most likely. A collection of tables and chairs had been dragged out from surrounding homes, and a couple of barrels of mead and ale had somehow been added to the mix. There had been drinking and card games, and a fair amount of gossiping. The gossiping was why Orm had insisted they went to the small gathering rather than one of the lavish street fairs that had popped up around the city. A few of the men had just returned from several months at sea, trading things along the northern coast. Orm wanted to know what, if anything, was happening over there.

Displeased by Orm forcing her to miss out on one of the street fairs to watch him spend another night gambling and blindly searching for titbits of information that *might* come in useful at some point in the future, Nessa had milled around, bored and cold. Like Hunter, she had kept an ear open for anything of interest, going from table to table, pretending to be watching a game or two. Nessa had come to stand by Orm's shoulder, watching as he won another round, as he usually did, seeing as he was nothing but a rather skilled cheat, and was listening to the men behind her as they talked about mysterious creatures and fell fogs.

They weren't the things that Nessa was meant to be listening to, but they were a lot more interesting than the drunken ramblings of the other men around, Orm included. The fanciful tales of thick mists appearing out of nowhere with strange creatures moving within them had kindled Nessa's imagination. While sipping on her tankard of mead, she had pictured them in her mind's eye, drawing up images of spectral men with majestic antlers and black shadows with eyes of mystic fire.

Wrapped up in her own mind, Nessa hadn't noticed that Orm had got carried away with both his drink and the game he was playing. Instead of throwing a round or two so people wouldn't get suspicious of his unnatural winning streak, Orm forgot. Rather than claim Orm was cheating, the man opposite him had cried bad luck and witchcraft.

Nessa had awoken from her daydream as the man shot to his feet, his beady eyes locked onto her, his finger pointed in accusation.

"Witch," he wailed. "Sorceress. You bring bad luck upon me!"

Nessa was taken aback. Never had she expected to hear such accusations.

What happened next was a bit of a blur, but Nessa recalled a lot of drunken shouting and quite a few flying fists. It was something she didn't care to experience again.

Coming back to the here and now, Nessa turned to Orm. "What happened that night was entirely your fault."

"It was not," he quickly denied, looking affronted.

"I wanted to go to the nice street fair," Nessa said, "but you wanted to listen to sailors' gossip. And did you listen to their gossip? Oh, no. Instead, you got drunk and forgot to throw the game, and I somehow got blamed for your rather fortuitous winning streak."

Orm began to chuckle. "Woah, Nessie. You should be more careful throwing all the blame around. Besides, you were the one staring vacantly into space."

"I was daydreaming."

"Oh, were you, now?" Orm smirked. "Look at who

wasn't paying attention to her surroundings, or listening to the gossiping like she was meant to."

"Rule number one," Hunter said over his shoulder as he led them under the bridge, "always be alert in unfamiliar surroundings, especially when there are strangers around."

"Ah, now you wade into this little debate," Nessa murmured. "I'll take the opportunity of reminding you about your stupid rule that I'm not allowed to be left alone, and must be accompanied by one, if not both, of you when out and about. Therefore, I also hold you accountable for that less than enjoyable excursion."

"And I stand firmly by that rule," Hunter replied, unapologetic. "We can't risk anything happening to you. Besides, those people might come in useful later on. You should make appearances around where they rub shoulders beforehand so they know and trust you."

"You want me to be trusted by some of the most untrustworthy people around?" Nessa grunted. "I think you've spent too much time listening to Orm's drunken ramblings."

"There's an insult in there somewhere," Orm said, blinking owlishly.

"You know, I'm not a child," Nessa continued. "I don't have to be babysat all the time. You can trust me not to do something stupid."

"Oh, I trust you," Hunter insisted, spinning in a circle, kicking up pebbles and grit from the riverside. "It's other people I worry about. And while we're talking about other people, there seems to be a lack of them waiting for us here."

Orm swore and once again consulted the piece of parchment. It was dark under the bridge. No light from the moon or the mushroom lamps was able to reach there, merely catching and glinting on the calm water on each side of the bridge. As Orm and Hunter pored over the coded directions once again, bickering as to whether they'd got the time and place wrong, Nessa reached out her mind.

*Should I tell them that we're a little early?* she enquired.

*And interrupt them arguing,* Aoife responded. *I think not. I find their quarrelling amusing.*

*That makes one of us, at least.*

With Aoife's presence hovering at the edge of her mind, enjoying the entertainment that was Hunter and Orm, Nessa took in her surroundings, wondering why, of all places, the directions had led them there.

The bridge was one of the largest in the city, wide enough to allow multiple carriages to pass side by side, and it was long, stretching over the great expanse of the Serpentine, which ran slow and steady beside her. Thanks to the tall arches, the underside of the bridge was high enough for them to stand without having to stoop, and there was a small pebble beach on which they waited, hidden and secret. The bridge concealed the little beach from prying eyes in nearly all directions, and there was nowhere for anyone to hide should someone approach from the street. Nowhere, that was, except for the storm drain that resided in the arch's wall to Nessa's right. Not that it really offered much in the way of a hiding spot or an escape route, seeing as it was set low to the ground, only coming up to knee height, and was securely barred, the rusted grate padlocked shut.

For a second, Nessa's mind went elsewhere, fogging over slightly, and she half-expected someone's head to pop up from behind the grate as they had…like in…at…

The memory was gone before it could properly form, just like they always were. The memories, for that's what she presumed they were, appeared reluctant to be remembered, only offering tantalising hints of things that were both alien and familiar.

Nessa blinked as the fog lifted and sighed, and then blinked again.

A shadow moved behind the grate, and to Nessa's bewilderment, a pale hand reached through the metal bars and began tinkering with the padlock.

Orm and Hunter spun around at the noise, both of them clutching a dagger, alert and ready to pounce.

"Put those blades away, lads," said a gruff voice. "They aren't needed. Not for the moment, at least."

Nessa frowned, knowing instantly who that voice belonged to and finding herself a little perplexed as to why their landlord was standing in a storm drain. She looked to Hunter and Orm for an answer, but they seemed just as flummoxed as she was.

"Jerome," Nessa hissed, "what in the Nine Devils are you doing here?"

"Come now, lass," Jerome snorted, "that should be obvious." The padlock clicked and the metal grate swung open without a sound. Surprising, given the level of rust on the hinges. "I've come to take the three of you to the den."

"*You*," Hunter all but sputtered. "*You're* the one who left the invite in Orm's room?"

"Indeedy I did, and at the boss' orders too."

Whilst most of Hunter's features were lost in the darkness, and though it was hard to tell, Nessa was pretty sure that he was scowling. "Bloody hell," Hunter growled, sheathing his dagger with an angry jerk.

"You've led us on a right royal run around. You know that, right? What kind of game are you playing with us, eh? Because it's not one we care to be a part of anymore."

"The games are for later, lad," Jerome chortled, "and mostly for Orm, considering you're shit at pretty much everything played down here. But the boss told me to extend the invite to Orm and his friends, and so I did, and here you are."

Hunter scoffed. "Do you honestly expect us, me in particular, to believe that you're part of a secret criminal network?"

"I don't much care what you do or don't believe," Jerome sighed. "But since you seem of a mind to think that I have, for some devil's reason, lured the three of you here under dark pretences, I'll ask you one simple thing: why would I be standing in a storm drain unless it was to take you somewhere that's best kept a secret?"

"I don't know, Jerome," Orm mumbled, taking a draw on his cigar, which was now little more than a nub, "you're a pretty strange man. I wouldn't put anything past you at this point. For all I know, you might have a storm-drain fetish."

"A storm-drain fetish?" Jerome wheezed. "Where in the Nine Devils do you come up with this kind of crap?"

"I don't know," Orm said airily. "It just comes to me."

"I wager your mother dropped you on your head a great many times when you were a young'un."

Orm nodded. "And almost drowned me on one occasion."

Nessa looked at him in alarm.

"She was young," Orm shrugged, "and has since assured me numerous times that it was an accident."

"Glad to hear it." Nessa turned back to the dark shape

that was Jerome. "It's not so much a question of *if* you're taking us somewhere secretive, but of *what* that secret place might be."

"You think I'm lying about the invite *and* the den?"

"No," Nessa said diplomatically.

"Yes," Orm and Hunter grunted simultaneously.

"Look at this from our point of view," Hunter murmured. "You lure us here with an invite to join an underground gambling network, a network that's operated by a bunch of smugglers, high-profile thieves and I don't even know what else. Now, this we're perfectly happy with. After all, these are our kinds of people. However, your alleged knowledge of supposed criminal networks raises the question of whether this 'den' you want to take us to is actually a den of fun and gambling or a cover for some other activity of a less favourable variety."

Jerome reluctantly asked, "A less favourable variety?"

"Indeed, you might have lured us here under the pretence of gambling, something Orm particularly enjoys, but you actually plan on taking us to our doom."

"Your doom?"

"Yeah. You might be intending to sell us into slavery or...or..."

"To a brothel," Orm helpfully supplied.

Nessa rolled her eyes in exasperation. This was not how she thought her night would go. *I can't tell which is worst: their bickering with each other or this ridiculous conversation.*

*Shh,* Aoife murmured. *I'm pretty sure this is the best thing I've heard all week.*

"A brothel? Slavery?" Jerome was incredulous. "What kind of ship do you think we're sailing here?"

Orm and Hunter shrugged.

"I've heard some particularly strange things in my day," Jerome muttered. "Especially of late, but this has to be one of the most bizarre." He shifted and turned to Nessa. At least, Nessa presumed he did, for it was hard to tell in the gloom. "You seem to be the voice of reason here," Jerome stated, "so I'm just gonna talk to you until these two buffoons realise how ridiculous they sound."

Nessa grinned. "That seems fair."

"You think I'm running an elaborate operation of luring people into slavery or selling them to brothels?"

"Not really."

"Oh?"

"Yeah, I reckon that if you were, then you'd have a far better house than your current one."

Jerome snorted, then burst into laughter, wheezing a little. "Good gosh, my dear girl. If I were a slaver, with the money they make, I sure as the Nine Devils wouldn't be standing in a bloody storm drain speaking to the likes of you."

Nessa chuckled. "No, I don't suppose you would be, would you?"

"And I sure as the Nine Devils wouldn't be running a guest house in the Stickworks either."

Nessa could hear the truth behind Jerome's words. He was no human trafficker. "Would anyone in that position?"

"No one but these two fools."

Orm turned to Hunter. "How very insulting."

"I know, right."

Nessa crouched down by the storm drain and peered into the endless darkness that stretched out behind Jerome. "It's rather grim, isn't it?" she said, with equal levels of intrigue and dismay. "And a storm drain makes for a very unusual entrance."

"Ah, lass. This is but one of several entrances to the den," Jerome explained. "The others being a fair bit more pleasant, I might add. Just around the corner, though, I have us a fair old lamp to light up the way. So don't you worry about the likes of rats and whatnot."

"You're not really selling this route to me, Jerome. I find myself forced to ask why we're to take it?"

"Well, see here, lass," Jerome said with good humour, "it's to keep the exact location of the den a secret. It's a bloody rabbit's warren down here, what with drains, sewers and many other tunnels, besides. It takes more than a handful of trips before you can ever hope of learning the way to the den. Once we're sure that you're trustworthy folks, you'll be allowed to use the front door."

"What are you saying?" Nessa asked, grinning playfully. "Do you not trust us? Don't you trust me?"

"Oh, lass," Jerome chuckled. "You don't get to my age without employing a bit of caution every now and again, especially with the opposite sex. You females are fickle and unpredictable. How do you think I lost my right eye?"

"You told me you lost it in a brawl."

"Aye, I did tell you that, didn't I?" Jerome confessed. "But that brawl only started because I was trying to impress a fine, wee lass."

"And did it work?" Hunter enquired, intrigued.

"Dunno, you tell me, lad. We'll be celebrating forty years of marriage in two months' time." Jerome stepped back from the storm drain. "Come now, let's get a move on. We don't have all night, and you need to win some coin. Your rent's due in a couple of days, and as much as I like the three of you, I like money a lot more."

Orm snorted. "You underestimate my skills, dear, old Jerome."

"Mmm, and I think you're overestimating yourself." Jerome gave Nessa a helping hand through the storm drain's narrow entrance. She scurried through and sat on the lip, her legs swinging as she blindly searched for the ground.

"Here," Jerome said, plucking Nessa from the entrance and setting her down onto damp earth. "Only a short drop. Though, considering how small you are, it might not seem like that, eh?"

The storm drain opened up onto a tunnel, which, whilst pitch black, Nessa could tell that it was larger than she had previously thought. The ceiling was high enough that even a bear of a man like Jerome was able to stand upright, just, and the sides were hidden in a darkness so disconcerting, so absolute, that Nessa couldn't perceive any difference between having her eyes open or shut.

With a hand on her arm, Jerome guided Nessa away from the drain's entrance, giving Hunter and Orm enough space to clamber through. Nessa's steps were small shuffles, hesitant. With her free arm, she reached out, feeling for the tunnel's wall, needing something solid to hold onto to steady her nerves.

Hunter slipped into the tunnel, landing in a puddle with a splash. He was quickly followed by Orm.

"Now, just to lock the grate," Jerome muttered as he patted himself, searching for the pocket where he had stashed the padlock, "and we can get on our way."

# Chapter 22

Given the less than enjoyable path they'd taken, led through dark and dank tunnels by an overly chatty Jerome, Nessa's expectations for the den were low. However, upon arrival, she found herself pleasantly surprised

Indeed, what with the low lighting and the lavish furnishings, the den looked like it belonged in one of the grand townhouses of the High Quarter.

The floor was covered in an array of lush carpets, and the walls played host to a vast collection of artworks, everything from fine oil paintings to old tapestries. The barrelled ceiling, supported by square columns, was illuminated by crystal chandeliers, the candles creating soft lighting. Most of the tables were arranged in the centre of the room, a ring of entertainment and activity, a zone fully dedicated to all manner of card and dice games, and anything else that could be bet on.

Hunter and Orm had already joined the rabble at the

tables, mingling and conversing with such ease and confidence that Nessa felt a stab of jealousy, wondering how they could turn complete strangers into friends so quickly and effortlessly.

Nessa sat on a plush armchair, her fingers absently stroking the blue, velvet upholstery, drawing faint images in the short pile. She watched Hunter chat with a couple of men who were around his age, possibly a couple of years older, identical twins with cropped, sandy-blond hair and muscular builds. They were dockworkers, from what Nessa had gleaned from eavesdropping every now and again, their faces rugged and tanned even in the winter from long hours outside. The three of them stood around a large, oval table with high sides. Nessa presumed that's where some form of rodent racing was held, judging by the cheering and jeering, and the occasional bout of swearing aimed at creatures unseen by her.

Her eyes went to Orm, who was sat a couple of tables down from Hunter, doing what he did best: drinking, smoking and gambling. By Nessa's estimation, they had been at the den for less than an hour, and he was already deep in his second glass of drink with a pile of coins in front of him. Nessa noted, with a faint hint of amusement, that there wasn't as many coins as there usually was, given the amount of time Orm had been working the game.

"Not doing quite as well as he usually does, is he?" Jerome observed as he slipped into the armchair opposite her. "The other cheats and scoundrels are giving him a run for his money, eh?"

"I suppose a game between equally skilled cheats makes for a pretty even game after all."

Jerome chuckled and placed a dainty glass of liquor on the low table between them, sliding it over to Nessa in invitation. "There, lass, try that. I know you prefer a hearty ale, but they don't serve that here."

Nessa plucked up the glass, peering curiously at the amber liquid contained within. "Oh, is a hearty ale too common for the likes of this fine establishment?"

"I don't know about that, but I do know that it's not strong enough to get the job done."

"Job?"

"Aye, getting them drunk faster." He nodded to the gaming tables. "That way, the boss stands to make more money and get an ear in for some good gossip. No one says things they shouldn't be saying like a drunk man, you get me?"

Nessa blinked, taken slightly aback. "I get you."

*It seems that particular idea isn't solely employed by Hunter and Orm,* Aoife murmured from her corner in Nessa's mind.

*And what could the owner of a secret gambling den want to hear, I wonder?*

*Look around you,* Aoife said, *there are people from all walks of life there, from gypsies to wealthy merchants. It's a bit of a strange gathering when you give it a bit of thought. Especially when you realise that there's no nobility there. You would have thought that there would be at least one or two nobles amongst them.*

Nessa, frowning, scanned the room quickly and realised that Aoife was correct. Whilst there was a large number of well-dressed individuals, clothed in finery like brocade doublets and velvet overcoats, they weren't anything more than wealthy merchants and businessmen, those who had struck luck, or maybe gold, and had risen through the ranks. The social hierarchy that dictated the everyday life in Ellor didn't seem to reach down to the den. No matter who you were or what you did for a living, everyone was one and the same around those tables.

Although, in all honesty, that only appeared to be so if you were male. Whilst women were present, there was only a handful of them, and they mostly kept to themselves, staying with their tight group of friends.

Slowly but surely, Nessa was coming to realise something unsettling about the role of women in society. Despite the fact that the vast majority played an active part in the community, running shops and owning their own businesses, they weren't always treated as equals. Nessa couldn't help but feel that they were second-class citizens. Their wants, their rights, seemed to come after those of the men in their lives. It didn't matter if those men were fathers, brothers or husbands, women had very little say in what went on in their lives, subjugated by laws and blasé attitudes. This unfair treatment, the subtle belief that women were somehow less than men, boded ill with Nessa. For some reason, she couldn't help but feel that there should be more for women than, at the end of the day, being little more than someone else's property.

Not to say that all men there treated women like objects. The vast majority of men that Nessa had come to know since arriving in Ellor were quite decent. At least, they were towards her. But these men, like Hunter, Orm and Jerome, were well travelled. They had spent a fair amount of time in the south, where things were a little different, more liberal, apparently. Nessa endeavoured to socialise with these men as much as possible. The subtle oppression she witnessed on a daily basis was more than a little unsettling for her. There was just something profoundly wrong with it all, but whatever it was exactly, Nessa couldn't quite put her finger on. It was a half-remembered memory, a hint that there was something *more* to it all...that there should be so much more for women, that there was so much more for them...

Turning towards Jerome, who was sipping from his glass tumbler, Nessa ran a considering eye over him, trying to see beyond the man who simply ran a guest house, a man who was almost as tall as Orm and who was a little soft around the middle. There were hidden depths to him that Nessa had never expected. When she had first met Jerome, she had found him to be an interesting character: chatty and filled with stories about his adventures from when he was younger. Some of his tales had sounded true, others, not so much. After tonight, though, she thought he was fascinating; Nessa's mind likened him to something close to a spy or secret agent, a key figure in an underground organisation that did... Well, Nessa wasn't quite sure what they did.

She thought back to what Hunter and Orm had said about the people down here, calling them a network of lazy criminals, which clearly wasn't a correct description, judging by the den's luxuries. Their activities were clearly profitable. There had been mentions of smuggling mostly, and on occasion, the assassination of someone noteworthy. Hunter and Orm also referred to them as rebels who did very little in the way of rebelling.

The questions of what they were rebelling against and what they hoped to gain from their secret ventures arose in her mind. Nessa guessed that it was her task to find out. It was, after all, why they were there in the first place.

Under the guise of socialising, drinking and gambling, they were there to glean whatever information they could.

"How's the drink, lass?" Jerome asked, knocking Nessa from her musings.

Nessa took a quick cursory sip of the liquid amber, and sweet fire coated her tongue. She coughed, swallowing it before she started to choke and spit in an undignified manner.

"What do I think?" she sputtered, setting down the cup of liquid flames. "I think you're trying to poison me."

"Na," Jerome laughed, "poison's a woman's weapon, and I sure ain't one of them."

Nessa smirked and nodded to his bushy beard. "I don't think anyone would ever make the mistake of thinking you were."

Running a hand through the salt and pepper frizz that covered the bottom half of his face, Jerome peered at Nessa with his one remaining eye. "Hmm, got more hair on my face than the top of my head these days."

"And yet you still have enough left for that ridiculous topknot."

Jerome scowled, making the leather patch over his right eye shift a little. For a brief moment, Nessa saw the corner of an old scar, pale and stretched. "I've had this topknot for nigh on twenty years. It's my signature hair style."

"Twenty years? I think it's about time for a change."

"I'd advise against insulting a man's topknot," Jerome snorted dismissively. "You risk hurting his feelings, and you never want to hurt a man's feelings."

"Oh?"

"Indeed," Jerome said with mirth, "we might start to

doubt our entire existence, and then who knows what might happen."

"You'll start sulking."

Jerome's head fell back as he roared with laughter, the creases around his eyes and mouth deepening. "Ah, lass. You are a rare gem."

Nessa tugged her cap nervously, uncomfortable under the handful of curious stares coming from men on the closer tables. "Shh, Jerome. I'm in disguise. You can't keep calling me 'lass' around here."

"Mmm, and what a disguise it is," Jerome hiccupped, trying to swallow his laughter. "You are very disguised. Eh, *laddie*."

Nessa rolled her eyes and muttered, "Time to change the subject, I think."

"Ooh, what to?"

"You and your boss."

"Ah."

"Yeah," Nessa slouched back in the armchair, getting comfortable, "I'm very intrigued."

"I bet you are."

"Is he here?" Nessa asked, scanning the room again, searching for someone who looked like they might be in charge.

"Maybe he is," Jerome said slyly, "maybe he isn't."

Nessa glared. "That's not a real answer."

"It's the best answer you're going to get," Jerome said, hiking a shoulder, "regarding who and where the boss is."

"Will I ever be allowed to know?"

"Dunno, almost everyone here doesn't know who he is."

"But you do?"

"Oh, aye," Jerome nodded. "I know him. I've known him since I was a young lad."

"That's a long time." Nessa's eyebrows shot up. "Are you friends, then? Business partners?"

Jerome shook his head vigorously, his salt and pepper topknot jiggling from side to side a little. "No. No. Nothing of the sort. I owe him a life debt, and this is just part of the payment. Over the years, though, I like to think he's grown to trust me. Well, as much as someone like him could trust anyone."

"How fascinating…"

"Aye, it would certainly be a tale to tell."

"But it's a tale you can't tell yet?"

"Not yet, lass. I'm not one for telling unfinished stories, even if I wasn't sworn to secrecy. No, even if I could, I wouldn't. I'm old, but I'm not that old. I reckon there's still a few chapters left to go before my story's done."

"I'm glad to hear it," Nessa murmured, watching as he downed the last mouthful of liquor from his tumbler. *Whisky*, she thought absently. "I've never been a fan of short stories."

"Me neither. Especially if it's in regards my own life's tale."

"I think all of us feel that way," Nessa speculated quietly. "Now, if you're not in a partnership with this mysterious boss, are you the manager of this delightful den?"

Jerome stared at her long and hard with his dark eye, the brown almost black as he considered what he could—should—divulge. Under that gaze, Nessa saw the secret side of Jerome, a man who was part of a criminal network, a man who was something more than a good-natured landlord dressed in plain clothing. For a second, Nessa's questions, her curiosity, faded away to nothing, replaced by a peculiar desire to disappear.

Nessa's breath caught in her throat, and her Rider's Mark tingled in warning. Aoife's mind crowded her own, tense and watchful. Aoife must have alerted Orm and Hunter, for they looked over in Nessa's direction, ready to rush to her aid, should they need too.

It seemed that their help wasn't required. Yet.

Jerome sighed and shrugged. "You have a natural curiosity, eh? Practically filled to the brim with questions. I suppose, given the less than ordinary circumstances, that's normal, maybe even expected."

Nessa released her pent-up breath, "I don't mean to pry."

"No need for any of that." Jerome waved away her apology with a flick of his wrist. "The fault lies with me. I've been in this line of work for too long. I tend to jump to conclusions and react on instinct, even though I'm partially retired now. So, you can relax and have your guard dogs stand down. It's all right. I know you're an inquisitive soul. There's no maliciousness to you at all. I have to be careful, though. Many people's questions tend to have less honourable intentions than simple curiosity."

"Is that so?" Nessa looked at Hunter and Orm, trying to give them a reassuring smile, but only managing a pained grimace.

Orm simply shook his head in despair and went straight back to his game. Hunter, although turning his back to the twins, kept glancing at her from the corner of his eye, periodically checking on her.

*I think that less invasive questions would be a wise move for now,* Aoife advised. *At least until you've established some kind of understanding with one another.*

*After knowing Jerome for a couple of weeks,* Nessa murmured, *I thought we had.*

*When he was simply Jerome, owner of the guest house, maybe. However, now he is Jerome, senior member of an underground criminal network that participates in dealings that aren't fully disclosed yet.*

*Don't you think we should find out what this network really does before we have anything more to do with it?*

*I fear that option is not open to us at the moment.*

There was no need for Nessa to voice her next question. Aoife knew what it was even as the thought formed, such was the nature of their ever-strengthening bond.

*This is a test,* Aoife explained, *a way of seeing how you behave when in unfamiliar territory, when you're in* their *territory. They want to know who you talk to, what you talk about, what questions you ask. And when you leave, I bet they'll have a way of keeping track of you, seeing if you tell anyone about this place.*

*So this is a vetting process,* Nessa said, *to see who they can trust?*

*That's what I think,* Aoife decided. *This is like a holding pen, keeping anyone who may be of use to them later on in an environment where they can make sure that potential recruits are trustworthy and able to keep secrets secret.*

*By that logic, the people running this operation must be under the impression that we might be of some use to them.*

*Most likely.*

*So, the question is what possible use could we be to them?*

*That, my little Rider, is the question that intrigues me the most tonight.*

"That used to be one of my main roles," Jerome was

saying, "to make sure our secrets were kept secret."

"Sounds interesting," Nessa murmured, more than a little engrossed with her and Aoife's thoughts.

"Not really," Jerome said, flagging down a server and signalling for another drink. "Most of the time it's just listening and keeping an eye on people. And since we're so careful with whom we invite before we even invite them, there's not much to do really. These days I mainly keep an eye open for new talent who might help us with furthering our ventures."

The server appeared, saving Nessa from having to give an immediate response. He swiftly deposited two glass tumblers on the table, and collected Jerome's empty one and her abandoned drink. With relief, Nessa saw that both of the drinks were whiskey. As Jerome thanked the server, she picked up a tumbler and took a tentative sip.

*For someone who's meant to keep the den's secrets secret,* Nessa mused, *he sure is mentioning a few of them.*

*Maybe it's another test of sorts,* Aoife said. *He throws out a few titbits of information and waits to see if anything comes back to him.*

*You reckon?*

*That, or he's just chatty.*

*Hmm.*

*Maybe you should throw out some of your own titbits and see what happens?*

*I thought you said no more questions.*

*So I did, but I wouldn't count these as questions per se. More like throwing out a line and seeing if anything nibbles.*

*And what should I do,* Nessa asked, *if something bites rather than nibbles, and if it has big, gnashy teeth?*

*Then I would recommend using the little knife you have hidden in your boot.*

Nessa sneaked a glance to her right boot, where the handle of the switchblade was digging into the flesh of her calf. Hunter had gifted it to her shortly after arriving in Ellor, saying that every respectable young lady should always have a concealed weapon upon their person. It was small, dainty; the hilt fitted perfectly in her palm, and the blade was only a few inches long, although razor sharp, making up for its diminutive size. It was a more feminine version of the knives both Hunter and Orm had hidden on them somewhere.

*Hark at you*, Nessa said with a touch of delight. *Giving me orders to uncover the inner workings of a criminal organisation, and instructing me to stab anyone if they get antsy.*

*I'm not telling you to go around stabbing people willy-nilly,* Aoife huffed, *just if they look like they're about to get a bit stabby themselves. Besides, I'm bored, and this has the potential of being reasonably interesting.*

*How can you be bored? Don't you have a cave to decorate?*

*There's only so much cave decorating a dragon can do in a day.*

*Ungrateful dragon. The three of us spent days collecting all those pillows and blankets, not to mention the small fortune it all cost. And dare I remind you of the effort taken in getting all of it to your little hidey spot? Did you have to choose the most difficult cave to reach? Wasn't there a more accessible one?*

*No,* Aoife sniffed, *there were no other satisfactory caves. I would know. I did try out almost twenty before settling on this one. The entrance is in the perfect position, and the size is just right.*

*If you say so.*
*I do.*
*Alright, then.*

*Now, hush up. Jerome is looking at you with a peculiar expression. I'm pretty sure he said something to you.*

*Oh crap. What? What did he say?*

*I don't know. I wasn't paying attention...* Aoife withdrew to the back of Nessa's mind, leaving her to flounder.

Nessa blinked owlishly, slowly coming back to herself. After having a debate with Aoife in her head, Nessa found her surroundings overwhelming, bombarding her with light and noise. It was disconcerting, almost painful.

It nearly always was. Sharing yourself with someone else, with someone you are so irretrievably bound to, was an otherworldly experience. It seemed that each time Nessa fell deep into herself, her mind merging with Aoife's, which was becoming ever more frequent as the bond between them strengthened, they became more one and the same. The world suddenly became infinite and silent, like they were floating in a pocket between space and time, where there was nothing but Nessa and her bonded partner, no one but her and Aoife.

"You there, lass?" a voice asked softly, breaking through the fog in her mind.

The den was filled with boisterous laughter and the bellowed calls of half-drunk men placing bets. The lighting, which before had been low and atmospheric, now seemed borderline blinding.

Forcing her eyes to focus, Nessa looked over and saw that Jerome was peering at her curiously, his eyebrow cocked in question.

"Pardon?"

Jerome shook his head, raising his glass to his lips. "You were in a different world just then, weren't you?"

"What can I say?" Nessa said with a tight smile. "I'm a

bit of a daydreamer."

"That you are."

"So, what were you saying?"

"Oh, nothing of importance." Jerome shrugged, his eye casually running over the den. "I just remarked that whisky seems to go down a lot better with you than the fire wine."

"Fire wine?" Nessa glanced down at the table, but the dainty glass was gone, cleared away by the server. "An apt name, I think."

"Yeah," Jerome chuckled. "It warms the cockles, no?"

Mumbling, "Not sure if the cockles were being warmed or burned," Nessa took another sip of whisky. It wasn't her favourite drink, but it would do, seeing as it was there. It was strong, settling in her stomach with a heated glow.

"And before the server came," Jerome continued, "I do believe I had started talking about sourcing potential new talent."

"Oh?" Nessa said, pretending to act surprised. *Throw out a line and see what you can catch,* she told herself. "Potential new talent? Judging by our invite here, you must have thought that we fit the bill in some way?"

Jerome inclined his head. "It wasn't just me who thought that thought. The others had to agree too before the three of you were invited."

"The others? There are other people who run places like this one?"

"Of course, there are," Jerome snorted. "What did you think, that this was the hub of our operations? That it's just me and the boss running things with a handful of happy helpers?"

"Umm…"

Jerome downed the rest of his whisky in one go, throat working as he swallowed. He swiped the back of his hand across his mouth, and set the empty tumbler heavily on the table.

*Oh dear, I think I've angered him again...*

*No,* Aoife murmured, *I think the drink is starting to hit him.*

"This is just one of many similar establishments," Jerome continued, signalling to the barman for another refill. "A little pebble on a rocky beach."

"That's very impressive," Nessa said hesitantly, taking a sip of her drink for some liquid courage.

She was in unfamiliar territory, and that made her increasingly nervous, although she tried her best to hide it. She prayed that she was pulling off her disguise successfully, that she wasn't making a fool of herself, that she wasn't being too obvious with the type of enquiries she was making.

Nessa was the listener in their little group, the one who was almost invisible and who hung around the fringes, observing and learning what she could as Hunter and Orm worked the scene, chatting and slipping in subtle questions here and there when the time was just right. Nessa didn't have the natural knack like they did. Before now, other than being a little rueful, she had been quite content with the role she played. However, that had changed, and Nessa wished that she had paid more attention to how they worked people so well.

"Oh, aye," Jerome agreed. "Me and the boss have built this network from nothing. Built it from the ground up. It's been hard work, dangerous, but it's paying off slowly." He paused as the server handed him another glass, whisking away the empty one faster than you could blink. Jerome had a mouthful before he continued. "We have people working in almost every trade imaginable, in almost every single town and city across all of the Twelve Kingdoms."

"That must have taken years," Nessa murmured, nudging him gently into continuing.

"Aye," Jerome nodded. "Perhaps eighteen years, almost nineteen."

Nessa found herself smiling. "That's longer than I've been alive."

"Is that so?" Jerome mused into his glass. "I suppose that's right, eh. What are you? About seventeen?"

"Thereabouts..." Nessa said, barely able to stifle a grimace. It was getting to be a bit of a sore spot for her, not knowing how old she was, when her birthday was.

Any day now could be her birthday, and Nessa wouldn't know it, not unless she came into her Old Blood powers at that precise moment. Each night she went to sleep, Nessa would faintly wonder if it would be the last time she'd be all but powerless. When the morning came, though, and she opened her eyes, Nessa knew instantly that she was the same, that nothing had changed.

The power that had briefly awoken in Arncraft had since remained dormant, coiled up somewhere deep inside her, unwilling to be found. The waiting and uncertainty were bordering on painful. Nessa wanted to do more than observe and listen, sifting through hours' worth of boring drivel in the hope of gleaning something useful.

That being said, a small sense of fear and uncertainty accompanied the longing for her powers, whatever they may be. Orm had mentioned some of the trouble he had got himself in during the first year of coming into his Old

Blood powers, and while they made for amusing stories, Nessa was not looking forwards to experiencing similar situations.

"...almost eighteen."

"Eighteen, eh?" Jerome grinned. "That's when all the fun starts."

So far, being seventeen hadn't been all that fun. Nessa wasn't holding out much hope that being a year older was going to be any better. Once Nessa came into her powers, *if* she ever came into them, they would have to go on the run again. Otherwise, they'll risk the king or one of his cronies sensing and coming after her.

"What do you mean by that?"

Jerome shrugged, his eye twinkling with memories. "Ah, it's just the right age to spread your wings and start exploring the world, seeing all that it has to offer." He winked. At least, Nessa thought it was a wink and not a blink. It was hard to tell since he only had one eye. "Maybe a nice boy will catch your interest, eh?"

"It's not the best time for romance right now."

"Oh, really?" Jerome chuckled and nodded to the tables. "It seems to me that others might be inclined to think otherwise."

Nessa followed the direction of his motion, her gaze swiftly falling on Hunter and Orm. "I don't think so," she croaked. "We're just friends."

"Just friends," Jerome mused knowingly. "I've heard that before. Many a time."

"And anyway," Nessa continued, pretending that he hadn't spoken, "even if it was the right time for romance, none of us are so inclined. We have other things on our minds."

"*Not so inclined?*" Jerome chortled. "Ha! I haven't

heard anything so daft for quite some time, lass. And I know some pretty daft people. It's pretty damn obvious that a certain someone is *so inclined,* as you put it. And by how red your cheeks are getting, I don't think I need to say who that certain someone is."

"I'm pretending that this conversation isn't happening," Nessa said, clapping a hand to a burning cheek. "I'm just warm. That's all. It's a tad bit hot in here."

"Make all the excuses you want, lass," Jerome smirked. "If that's what you want to do. But a word of caution, if I may?"

Feeling like Jerome was going to give his opinion no matter what, Nessa took another sip of her whisky.

"Time isn't something everyone has a lot of," Jerome said wisely, "and throwing out excuses is just wasting precious amounts of it. Make the most of what you have whilst you have it."

Nessa's eyebrows pulled together in a small frown, watching warily as Jerome's throat worked, swallowing some kind of emotion.

"You sound like you're speaking from experience?" she asked softly.

"Aye, it does sound like that, don't it?" Jerome looked away from her, his eye misting with tears. "When you get to my age, you'll have seen some things, experienced a few losses, but death always hits you hard, especially when it comes out of the blue."

"I...I take it you've recently lost someone close to you," Nessa murmured hesitantly, putting the pieces together.

"Aye, I did. A couple of people, actually. Close friends I've known since I was a wee lad."

"I'm so sorry."

"No sense in being sorry, lass," Jerome said gruffly. "It wasn't your doing. No, it was King Kaenar and his devil of a dragon."

Nessa stilled. Aoife's mind pressed against hers, listening intently.

"The...the king?"

"The very man himself, so I'm told. He left Ellor a handful of weeks ago, which is a rare occurrence these days, and flew westward."

*Arncraft,* Aoife whispered.

Jerome shuddered. "Don't even know why he did it. It makes no sense. In one fell swoop, he destroyed an entire town. My friends were incinerated in Dragon Fire, their entire families wiped out in a single night. It wasn't even one of our major bases, either."

Nessa didn't know what to say. He was talking about Arncraft. He had to be.

"It was only a small hub," Jerome continued absently, his gaze far away. "A place where goods were held until they were sold off or split into different shipments. There are other places he could have hit, more important ones."

"Perhaps it was an unfortunate coincidence?" Nessa said gently, feeling like she had to say something even as her thoughts went back to that fateful night. The ghostly echoes of screams filled her ears, and once again she could feel the heat of phantom flames against her skin. Nessa could remember the fires and the panic, the sheer terror, as King Kaenar and his black dragon flew overhead. She remembered the ruined square, the buildings crumbling and falling down around her, and the bodies... She could remember the bodies covering the ground, too many to count, heaped carelessly into a mound...a mound upon which King Kaenar and his dragon stood...

Nessa was trapped, held firm by the memory.

King Kaenar's eyes met hers, locking them together as the dark entity danced around them, filling the square with...

"What in the devil are they doing here?" Jerome sputtered, jumping to his feet. Nessa was knocked from her waking nightmare with a sudden jolt.

Startled, Nessa could do nothing but blink and stare after Jerome as he stumbled away from her, a little unsteady on his feet, his almost empty tumbler of whisky held by his fingertips. He hurried over to the far side of the room where a small group of men stood. Nessa's eyes ran over them, taking in their bedraggled appearances and the air of urgency that hovered around them.

Nessa frowned, watching as Jerome reached the group and started a hushed argument. *I wonder what that's all about?*

*Maybe he doesn't want riffraff like them using the front door,* Aoife sighed. *It looks like your intriguing conversation with him has come to a sudden end, and on that note, I find myself bored once more. I shall take this opportunity to catch some shuteye. Should anything interesting happen, feel free to wake me.*

*In all honesty, I hope nothing interesting does happen. Then we can swiftly call an end to this little venture, and I can snuggle into bed for a day or two.*

*Mmm.*

A man strode in behind the group, and Nessa was instantly transfixed. Spellbound. She hardly noticed Aoife's presence fading from her mind.

The man was a commanding force dressed in all

black, hooded and cloaked in such a way that he was little more than a shadow, unnoticed by almost everyone. His overcoat, long and dark, hung heavily over his shoulders, reaching to his ankles, concealing much of his form, leaving only his booted feet and his arms clearly visible. While he wasn't particularly close, Nessa could still make out the lines of well-defined muscles beneath the leather of his tunic's sleeves. Loosely wrapped around his broad shoulders was a hooded scarf, the edge pulled down low over his face.

Shifting in her chair, Nessa tried to catch a glimpse of the stranger's face, but the hood was too deep and the lighting was too dim. She could see nothing but faint outlines of his strong jaw. Her eyes darted to Hunter and Orm, wondering if they had noticed the new arrivals. Their attention, though, was focused solely on the game Orm was playing.

The hooded stranger turned to Jerome and said something, an order perhaps. Jerome gave a nod of his head and began ushering the others away, leading them through the den to a doorway on the opposite side of the room. The hooded stranger went to follow, taking a few steps, then paused.

As if he could sense eyes upon him, his head turned slowly, his gaze sweeping over the room. Nessa told herself to turn away, that she didn't want to be caught staring, but it was as if he could hear her thoughts. As soon as the impulse to look elsewhere entered her mind, his head snapped to the side.

Nessa was ensnared, instantly and completely.

The dimness of the room didn't matter, nor did the shadows of his hood. Eyes of the deepest blue captured hers, gleaming with an almost magical quality. Nessa's breath caught in her chest. Her Rider's Mark tingled with warmth, with eerie recognition.

"I know you," she whispered with surety.

# Chapter 23

With blood roaring in her ears, Nessa leaped to her feet, sweeping up her tumbler as the blue-eyed stranger strode through the den, following after Jerome and the other newcomers with single-minded purpose. Although on the other side of the room, people and pillars between them, Nessa never lost track of him, keeping him in her sights. There was something about the hooded stranger that called to her, powerful and strange, pulling her after him.

Nessa approached the bar, the guise of getting a refill her reason for being up and about.

The bar took up almost an entire wall of the den, and would have if not for an archway that stood in the corner, the archway the hooded stranger stalked through. Red drapes hung on either side of it, and a long corridor ran parallel to the room. Nessa knew that the corridor was dotted with a handful of doors, one of which led to the tunnel they'd used to enter the den.

The youthful bartender raised his dark brows as Nessa deposited her tumbler on the countertop, surprised that such a little thing could want another. Nevertheless, without a question asked, he took her glass and turned to the shelves behind him.

Nessa's fingers tapped impatiently on the counter, leaving faintly smudged fingerprints on the polished walnut as the bartender perused the shelves, searching the fine decanters and bottles displayed there. From the corner of her eye, Nessa watched the group as they headed down the hallway, swiftly disappearing from her line of sight. The blue-eyed stranger was a few steps behind them. For a second, Nessa thought—hoped—that he would pause, turn, and that their gazes would lock for another spellbinding moment.

Instead, without turning, without even the faintest hesitation, he followed after the others, shoulders tense and gloved hands balled into fists.

Nessa could see him no more, and she felt deflated at being ignored, dejected that she wasn't worth a backwards glance. Her heart twisted in her chest. She needed him to look at her. She needed those breathtaking eyes of his on her.

"There's not much down there," someone purred, their voice a honeyed drawl. "Nothing but a few storerooms and the restrooms."

Startled, Nessa turned.

A woman had sidled up beside her, waiting to be served. Her hair fell in ringlets to her shoulders, a deep brown that was only a shade away from being black, and her skin was a lovely caramel that made the green of her eyes sparkle.

"I wasn't interested," Nessa said quickly. "Just

curious."

The woman smiled, her red lips parting just a little to reveal bright, white teeth, and shrugged a slim shoulder. "I don't particularly care who or what you're staring after. Others might, though. This lot," she cast a nod over to the crowded room behind them, "are a bit of a strange bunch, always jumping to conclusions, always believing one superstition or another. Many of these folks have a 'stab first, ask questions never' kind of approach to life. But then, what can one expect from this eclectic group of criminals, am I right? You see, most of them come from the streets, grew up in poverty and such, pickpockets and cut-throats, whores and smugglers. They're survivors, not thinkers. Though, saying that, most of them aren't stupid, not really. Well, maybe Clive, but he's not involved in much, so it doesn't really matter, now, does it?"

The woman turned to Nessa, who stood stock-still, mouth slightly agape. The woman had barely paused for breath after one sentence before launching into the next.

Nessa, unable to form a cohesive response, settled for simply nodding.

The woman appeared satisfied with the wordless response and continued with her unsolicited nattering without waiting another second.

"I heard," she continued, a finger toying with a ringlet, "that this one time, a chap drank too much and became peculiar, staring at nothing, muttering about a girl with purple eyes and men with antlers, and many more strange things, besides. Some folks here didn't like that, stupid and superstitious as they are. A couple of them took him outside and…" she ran her finger across her throat, stretching out the ringlet. "Seeing as you were staring a wee bit, I thought I should give you a word of warning. The poor chap couldn't have been much older than you."

Nessa blinked and swallowed nervously. "I…um…thank you. I think."

"No worries." She winked. "We girls have to look out for one another, right? Otherwise, we'll never survive in this dog-eat-dog world. I like the disguise, by the way. It's a good idea. Although, once someone gets up close to you, it's easy to see through it. But I suppose, as with presents, it's the effort that counts."

"Umm."

The woman, whose age Nessa guesstimated as being in the early twenties, stuck out a hand. "I'm Sissy."

Nessa murmured a quick greeting, shaking Sissy's hand somewhat reluctantly.

There was something about Sissy that didn't sit well with Nessa. She couldn't put her finger on it, though, as it wasn't anything that stood out. Perhaps it was the things Sissy said, or the way she had sprung up out of nowhere. Maybe it wasn't even Sissy and was Nessa's own desire to follow after the mysterious stranger that made her want to leave the conversation. Whatever the reason, Nessa searched for a suitable excuse to make her escape.

The bartender returned, setting the refilled tumbler in front of her. Nessa fumbled for her coin pouch, eager to pay and be on her way.

"No need for that," the bartender said quickly. "It's on the house. Boss' order."

Nessa blinked, surprised, and abandoned her rummaging. "Oh, that's nice of him."

"And speaking of the boss," the bartender continued, his gaze sliding to Sissy, "I wager he'll be displeased to discover that you're here."

"On the contrary, Jem," Sissy said, grinning smugly, leaning forwards and resting her elbows on the countertop. "I'm here on official business. My mistress sent me to have words with certain people."

"Did she now?" Jem was less than impressed.

Sissy nodded, her ringlets bouncing. "Mmmhmm."

Nessa's eyes darted between the two of them, and seeing that they appeared to have momentarily forgotten her, she decided to take her leave, slipping away quietly.

With the chant of *just going to the restroom* repeating over and over in her head, should anyone ask what she was doing, Nessa approached the archway. With a sip of liquid courage, she turned into the hallway and promptly collided with something hard.

Her drink sloshed over the lip of her tumbler as she rebounded, stumbling back a step. Hands caught her upper arms, preventing her from falling to the floor in a humiliating heap. Realising that she had careened into someone, Nessa's cheeks burned with embarrassment. *So much for trying to go unnoticed…*

"There we go," the person murmured, releasing her and retreating to an arm's length away. "Wouldn't want to spill any more drink. Would be a terrible waste, no?"

"Well," Nessa said, trying to collect her jumbled thoughts to piece together a half-decent response, "it's a shame about the drops on the carpet."

"Ah, that's no more than a mouthful at the most." Nessa looked up from the dark splodges on the carpet into a pair of amused, hazel eyes. "I doubt it'll stain."

"That wasn't really what I was worried about…" Nessa's words dwindled away as she took him in, recognising him. He was in the group she was trying to covertly follow, the one who Jerome had rushed to, seeking an explanation. Nessa was willing to bet that he was in charge of the group or, at least, was in a position of some authority.

Her irritation at being caught was replaced by curiosity.

If Nessa's assumption was correct and he did hold a measure of influence there, then he was an intriguing choice, in her opinion, young and perhaps a little too conspicuous to be a part of a network of thieves and smugglers, and many other things, besides.

His black hair tumbled and curled to his shoulders, held back from his face by a faded, green bandanna. His red shirt was baggy and worn, missing the top few buttons and featuring a couple of badly sewn patches of mismatched fabrics. It was clinched at his waist by a wide belt that looked like it was a re-purposed, multicoloured scarf, tied in a loose knot with the twin tails hanging down to his knees. Striped trous, so voluminous that at first glance Nessa mistook them for a skirt, were tucked into a pair of scuffed boots. He was a riot of clashing colours. Nessa faintly realised that he was a gypsy.

There weren't many gypsies in the city, most of them preferring to head east during the winter months, where the climate was milder. A small number had chosen to stay, however. Nessa had seen their colourful caravans and tents from a distance. They were camped just outside the city, their dwellings sitting between the main road into Ellor and Lake Nyma, a colourful labyrinth of greens and golds, pinks and purples, blues and every other colour imaginable.

They mostly kept to themselves, to their own community, with only a few venturing into the city itself.

Nessa had seen a handful of gypsies every now and again, usually at the markets or spending an evening at a tavern, enjoying a drink or two. Until now, Nessa had never really had the opportunity to talk to one by herself. The few times she had found herself by one of their market stalls, Hunter and Orm always took over the conversing and haggling during the sales. They bought fabrics, mostly, to fill Aoife's snug cave-dwelling with comforts. Having seen it through Aoife's eyes, Nessa knew that a thick bed of pillows covered the floor, and that the rough sides were swathed in plush drapes, warding off the chill of the mountains. It was with a bit of mirth that Nessa realised that Aoife's cave was better decorated than her room at Jerome's guest house.

"What are your worries then?" the gypsy asked. "That you wouldn't get to enjoy your drink fully? Fear not, you still have plenty left, and you're only little, so I doubt you'll need much more. Otherwise, you won't be able to walk in a straight line."

"Considering that I ran into you just now," Nessa said, eyeing her drink like it was to blame, "maybe I don't even need this one."

The gypsy laughed and went to say something. Before any words could leave his lips, both Nessa and the gypsy were startled by a loud shriek.

"Heimaey!"

The gypsy—Heimaey—winced as he turned towards the source. Nessa didn't need to look to know who it was.

"Unholy hells," Heimaey muttered under his breath. "What is she doing here?"

Sissy swiftly descended upon them, a whirlwind of bouncing ringlets and twirling skirts. Nessa barely managed to step to the side before Sissy leaped into

Heimaey's less than eager arms, her own twining around his neck, elbows almost catching Nessa in the face. Heimaey staggered, taken by surprise, and his hands rose to Sissy's waist, trying earnestly to peel her off.

Nessa watched in bemusement as Heimaey was met with limited success. Contrary to her willowy figure, Sissy was a lot stronger than she appeared, and she clung to Heimaey like a limpet. Other than viciously shoving her away, something which Heimaey seemed reluctant to do, he was forced to put up with Sissy's attentions.

"I thought I told you," Heimaey growled in her ear, "that under no uncertain terms, were you to ever come here again."

"Come now, cousin," Sissy groaned. "Don't be like that."

"Why are you here?"

"My mistress sent me."

"I don't care if the Creator herself sent you," Heimaey said. "When I tell you that you're not welcome here, that means you're not to come here. It's really quite simple."

Nessa began to slowly edge away, sensing that an argument was about to ensue, abandoning her intentions of stalking after the blue-eyed stranger.

"But Heimaey," Sissy whined, "my mistress had a vision. She sent me here to tell you about it. She said that the gods of old are awakening, donning their antler crowns once again, their monsters lurking in the mists and shadows, called forth from their slumbers by she whose blood can command us all, the girl with the amethyst eyes—"

Heimaey jerked his head angrily, cutting Sissy off, and muttered something under his breath. Nessa frowned, the mention of antler crowns striking a chord. Trying to figure out why that was, and wanting to hear more, she paused, listening hungrily.

"I don't want to know," Heimaey hissed, his eyes flashing. "Not now. Not ever." His hands grasped Sissy's wrists firmly, and he pried himself free from her hold, taking a cautionary step back. "That woman is a snake, a liar and a fraud. I— *we*— don't want anything more to do with her. Or with you, to be honest. Not whilst she has you under her thumb."

Sissy pouted playfully, not at all fazed by Heimaey's words. "She's only trying to help."

"Yeah," Heimaey snorted. "Herself."

"You have it all wrong."

"I don't think so. She had her chance to prove her worth. She failed. We won't fall for her games and tricks a second time."

"They weren't tricks."

"No? What were they then?" Heimaey raised his brows. "Thinly veiled lies? Tall tales? A twisted version of a number of small truths?"

"Deciphering visions is a difficult thing to do," Sissy argued. "Sometimes things aren't always what they seem, or the images are blurred or jumbled."

Heimaey rolled his eyes. "Of course they are."

"Stubborn as ever, I see," Sissy sighed.

"You need to leave."

"Heimaey. Listen. Please."

"No." Heimaey folded his arms across his chest, looking both frustrated and weary. "I don't have time for this. Not today and certainly not while your loyalties lie with your *mistress*." He spat the word with disgust. "I've made myself clear on this: whilst you're sided with her, I want nothing to do with you."

"Fine," Sissy said stiffly. "Be that way. Reject our help if you wish. But I warn you, cousin. You will regret it. Change is coming to this land. If you are not ready for it, then you will be swept away, lost to the shifting tide of war."

"I'll take that under consideration." Heimaey nodded to the room behind her. "Now, if you would be so kind as to show yourself out, it would be most appreciated."

"Don't you want to escort me out?" Sissy asked with a playful smirk.

"Not particularly."

"But it's dark out, and the streets are no place for a lady to be walking around alone. Who knows what kind of souls might be skulking out there, or what their intentions might be."

"I'm sure you'll be fine," Heimaey said dryly, nonplussed by her plea. "Besides, if you were in any danger, I'm sure your skilled *mistress* would have seen it in a vision and warned you prior to sending you out to do her dirty work."

Sissy scowled and muttered, "It's not like that, you blind fool," and turned on her heel. Her gaze settled on Nessa with an almost fevered intensity.

Nessa blanched, immediately wishing that she had taken the opportunity to retreat when she could have. Unfortunately, she had missed her chance and was now acutely aware that she was an interloper in a conversation between two strangers. Nessa looked away, staring down at her drink as if it was the most interesting thing in the world, and wished that she had the power to vanish from sight.

"I'll leave you be," Sissy murmured in defeat. "At least until you see the sense in my mistress' warnings.

But first things first." She frowned. "Or maybe it's lastly? Anyhoo, whichever one it is, I was assigned another task that I must fulfil before I go."

Sissy plucked something from her skirt's pocket and placed it in Nessa's free hand, curling Nessa's fingers around it.

"My mistress," Sissy said in a conspiratorial whisper, leaning in close, her green eyes bright, "wishes for you to have this." Her hands were clamped around Nessa's fist, cupping it tightly, making the object dig into the flesh of her palm. "She says to keep it close to your heart and it will lead you to what you have lost."

Nessa could only blink in way of an answer, dismayed, all other responses forgotten. Over Sissy's shoulder, Nessa spied Heimaey shaking his head, his patience wearing thin, his fingers tapping against his biceps.

"Sissy," he warned, voice low and dangerous.

Sissy shot him a venomous glare, her back straightening, her jaw clenching as she bit back a sharp retort. Without another word, an explanation, she spun on her heel and stormed away. Nessa watched Sissy go with a pent-up breath, her fist still held out in front of her, the other clutching her tumbler, the whisky rippling as she trembled.

What Sissy said echoed in Nessa's head, and she had to wonder, could Sissy have been referring to her lost memories? If that were so, how did Sissy's mistress, whoever she was, know about that? No one, not even Jerome, was privy to that knowledge. Only Aoife, Hunter and Orm were. Chaos, of course, had known, but seeing as he had been slaughtered by the king, Nessa felt that it was safe to say that he wasn't the one spilling her secrets.

"What has she given you?" Heimaey asked quietly, softly, the anger leaching from him ever so slowly.

Sucking in a breath, trying to settle her rattled nerves, Nessa unfurled her fingers and peered at her palm. Heimaey stepped closer, inspecting the object in her outstretched hand with an air of suspicion.

Nessa's eyebrows pulled together in puzzlement "It's a brooch?"

"So it is," Heimaey murmured, his fingers neatly plucking at it, turning the brooch over so they could have a better look at it.

The brooch was small, dainty and made from silver. A bundle of fine, interwoven stems formed the main body of the piece, with a scattering of tiny leaves and flowers dotted throughout. Set into each of the flowers' carpels was a single gemstone that flashed a vivid blue as it caught the light.

"It's a brooch of forget-me-nots," Heimaey said. "If I'm correct."

"Forget-me-nots?"

Heimaey made a sound of confirmation. "A pretty weed that's commonly associated with aiding those who suffer memory loss…in certain arcane circles, of course."

"Of course," Nessa murmured, her thoughts running a million miles an hour. She closed her fingers around the brooch, hiding it from sight, more than a little tempted to cast it aside, unsettled behind its potential meaning. She didn't, though, deciding that it may be of some value. The craftsmanship was respectable: the gemstones neatly set, the tiny petals and leaves having a charming amount of detail. Perhaps she could sell it later?

The thought of having her own money, even if it was only a small amount, was a pleasant one.

So far, any money Nessa had was from Hunter and Orm and their gambling exploits. To start with, she had been happy with the arrangement, having someone else deal with the finances, earning and managing everything. Her feelings had quickly changed, however, and she slowly began to feel useless, little more than a burden, someone who wasn't pulling her weight. No matter how many times Nessa protested against her less than active role in their group, she was met with the same response: just because she wasn't sat at the tables with them didn't mean that she was doing anything less important.

Nessa was listening and learning, and not just during their night-time excursions. During the day, when she wasn't catching up on lost sleep, she was being educated in a vast number of things: self-defence, the history of Ellor and the Twelve Kingdoms, and the Twelve Houses and their Dragon Riders. Nessa memorised their names, the colour of their dragons, which House each Rider belonged to. It was important, Nessa knew that, but she just couldn't shake the feeling that no matter what she did, how much she did, it was never enough.

"Lost some memories, have we?"

Nessa shook herself. "No. Of course not. What makes you think that?"

Heimaey pursed his lips, quirked an eyebrow, and then shrugged. "No reason, I suppose. Sissy's puppet master must be back to her old games again."

"Sissy's mistress," Nessa mused, her thumb absently rubbing the brooch. "You don't seem to like her much."

Heimaey laughed a short, sharp bark. "Ha! What gave it away? No. No, I don't like Sissy's alleged friend at all."

"Obviously. But who is she?"

"Oh, just someone who runs a small shop in the

Barrel. She claims to be a powerful seer, blessed by the spirits. Weirdly enough, people actually buy into all that. She's nothing but a fraud, though, in my opinion. A hedge witch who's particularly good at drawing in and manipulating gullible fools."

"Ah. Alright."

"She seems to have lured my dear, stupid cousin into her service, against both mine and her parents' warnings."

"Well, sometimes people make bad decisions," Nessa said diplomatically.

"Yeah, and Sissy goes out of her way to make as many as possible."

Nessa grimaced. "Maybe this fraud isn't quite as much of a fraud as you think she is?" *Seeing as she somehow knew where I'd be in order for Sissy to give me the brooch, and let's not forget about its very pointed symbolism...*

"Be that as it may," Heimaey said. "She's still bad news and isn't someone you should get involved with."

"Who said I was planning on getting involved with her?"

"Just thought I'd warn you," He shrugged. "What Sissy said about finding what you had lost; it's just a vague line used to get you to start questioning things, things that only Sissy's mistress can answer. The problem is, there will be strings attached, and in the end, you'll only be left with more questions than answers."

"Warning duly noted."

Heimaey's eyes twinkled at her dry response. He went to say something, but the quiet sound of a door opening made him pause, his attention going elsewhere.

"I thought you had already left," a deep, resonating voice intoned from the shadows of a doorway, "yet here I find you, standing idly about and chatting to…"

The hooded stranger's gaze settled on Nessa. She was entrapped by the sheer intensity in those blue eyes of his. She was hypnotised, utterly and completely, by their dark-sapphire depths.

There was no escape.

There was no one else in the world but them, *nothing* but them.

For the first time in weeks, for the first time since Nessa had awoken in the woods, alone and frightened, all the fear and uncertainty faded away, replaced by a strange and profound sense of tranquillity, of belonging.

# Chapter 24

Orm held the brooch between his thumb and forefinger, angling it so that the pale sunlight, filtered through the iced-over windowpanes, made the silver twinkle and the blue gems flash.

"So, what's the verdict?" Nessa asked from where she was huddled, wrapped in several layers of blankets and sat on her sorry excuse for a bed, back pressed against the wall.

"Verdict?" Orm murmured, peering intently at the brooch.

"On the thing you have in your hand." Nessa shared an exasperated look with Hunter. She'd been awake for less than an hour and already she wanted to throw Orm out of the window. Hunter smirked and continued to fiddle around in the fireplace, feeding twigs and wood shavings to the sad flames that clung helplessly to the last slivers of blackened logs, trying to revive them.

Nessa couldn't help but think that it was a futile

endeavour. The only thing that would help the fire was a good cleaning, which hadn't happened once during the time they'd been lodging at Jerome's guest house. The metal grate was overflowing with ash. Any logs that were added would sink down into it by a couple of inches. Even as she thought about it, Nessa had absolutely no intention of cleaning it out anytime soon. Certainly not today. She wasn't in the right frame of mind for tedious tasks.

"Oh," Orm said brightly, "you want a verdict on this brooch."

"What else would I want a verdict on?"

Orm shrugged. "On why you're in such a grouchy mood?"

"I am not in a grouchy mood," Nessa scowled. "Even if I were, which I'm not, I think I'd know why without your input."

"Oh, I think everyone in the den knows why you'd be in a grouchy mood," Orm mused, fiddling with the brooch's clasp. "We all heard the sound of your skull hitting the floor when you fainted."

"Felt it, too," Hunter said with a sympathetic wince.

Embarrassment reared its ugly head again. How could she have fainted like that in front of so many people…? Especially her blue-eyed stranger… It was beyond mortifying, made worse when she recalled the reason behind the fainting. So busy staring at him, drowning in the sense of tranquillity and belonging, she had forgotten to breathe.

Glaring, Nessa muttered, "I thought I told you to stop bringing that up."

"You told us," Orm smirked, "but we just can't help ourselves. It was one hell of a bang. How's your noggin?"

Nessa prodded the bump on the back of her skull. It was swollen and tender to the touch, throbbing in time with her heartbeat. "Sore."

"Well, finish drinking the magical drink I whipped up for you," Orm told her. "It will make you feel better."

Orm had presented her a mug of noxious liquid upon her awakening. The potion was the colour of bile and tasted like it, too, in all honesty. Despite being abandoned quite some time ago, exiled to the nightstand beside the bed, steam still rose from the mug, drifting up in delicate swirls. Whatever magics Orm had poured into the potion were still going strong.

"I tried some," Nessa said. "It didn't work."

"You had two sips."

"It tastes like liquid death."

"It does not."

"Does too. Anyway, how would you know?"

"Oh, I've had my fair share of the stuff after sustaining a head wound or two," Orm said, reminiscing. "Falling out of trees. Falling off horses."

"Being hit over the head with a broom by a disgruntled father as he chases you out his daughter's bed," Hunter mumbled from his place by the fireplace.

Orm frowned, sifting through the memories of his misadventures, then grinned. "Ah, yes," he murmured, smiling coyly. "Isabelle. She was most definitely worth the concussion."

Hunter rolled his eyes. "I should hope so."

"Another one of your conquests, I gather?" Nessa said with indignation. It seemed that Orm had a talent for getting himself into trouble, causing mayhem wherever he went. "You're a real lady-killer. You know that, right?"

"Oh, Nessie," Orm gave her a wink. "I'm a lady-lover. Not a lady-killer." He turned and scowled at Hunter and his feeble attempts at stoking the fire. Orm clicked his fingers, and green sparks went flying from his fingertips, whizzing around the room in a hectic dance, darting this way and that. One shot over Hunter's shoulder, flashing erratically, and dashed into the fireplace.

Flames flared and roared, ferocious and bright. Hunter yelped and fell back, landing in an awkward sprawl on the floor.

"How many times," Hunter fumed, pushing himself up onto his elbows and flicking messy locks of hair out of his eyes, "have I told you to give me a bit of warning before you do something like that."

"Sixty-three times now, by my count." Orm turned his attention back to the brooch, peering closely at the tiny, blue gems, almost going cross-eyed. Then, abruptly, he cast the brooch away, flinging it onto the bed. Nessa frowned and snaked out a hand from her cocoon of blankets, scooping it up.

"I guess there's nothing special about it then," she murmured with a twinge of disappointment. "Nothing that might lead me to 'what I've lost' like Sissy said it would."

"Oh, I wouldn't say that," Orm said. "It's got a touch of magic about it. It might do something."

Hunter picked himself up from the floor and joined Nessa on the bed, settling down beside her, close enough for their shoulders to brush against each other with the slightest of movement.

"Something?" Hunter scoffed, squinting at the brooch as Nessa perched it on her knee.

"Yeah. Something."

"Like what?" A fragile kind of hope bloomed in Nessa's chest.

Orm shrugged. "I dunno."

Nessa sighed. Of course, when it came to Orm and magic, there was never a straight answer. "You don't know?"

"There's magic embedded in the gems," he explained, "but it's weak, barely there. Whatever the spell was designed to do, it won't be doing it with any kind of potency, that's for sure. I can barely detect the magic."

Nessa ran her fingers over the brooch for what felt like the hundredth time, the tiny ridges and dips of the gems and detailing almost ticklish against her fingertips.

"How can you sense it?" she asked, wondering, because she certainly couldn't. It wasn't like she was completely insensitive when it came to detecting things of magical origins, either. Such as her grimoire, which made her blood sing and her Rider's Mark tingle when she handled it, or the presence of the dark entity back in Arncraft.

"I can see it." Orm grimaced. "Kind of."

Nessa was impressed. "I wanna be able to do that."

"It's an easy thing to learn. There's a knack to it."

"A knack?"

"A knack," Orm confirmed, leaping onto the bed, making the wooden frame groan in protest, the slats straining under the combined weight of all three of them. "All you need to do is focus on it, let your mind relax, then unfocus."

"Are you serious?" Hunter said. "Focus and then unfocus? That's utter rubbish."

Nessa had to agree. She raised her eyebrows quizzically and looked at Orm, her doubt clear for him to see.

Orm rolled his eyes and reached out, forcing the brooch into her grip and positioning it in front of her face. "Look at it," he murmured, his voice dropping low, suddenly holding a hypnotising quality. "Focus on the details of the gems. See how they shine? See how they shimmer?"

"I'm looking," Nessa said, doing as Orm instructed even though it felt like he was working under the influence of alcohol. She was fairly sure she could smell it on his breath. It was faint, but it was there. Whether or not he was still tipsy from their time in the den, or if he'd had a glass or two since their return, was anyone's guess.

"I'm looking too," Hunter stage whispered from Nessa's left. "What do you reckon we'll see? The answer to life? How to get rich in a matter of hours? How to turn an enemy into a toad?"

While keeping one hand on Nessa's wrist, holding the brooch aloft, Orm reached around her with his other and gave Hunter a sharp cuff.

Hunter scowled and shifted out of reach, rubbing his head. "Just trying to make light of things, ensuring it remains all fun and stuff."

"Well, don't," Orm said. "Nessa is taking her first official step into learning about magic."

Nessa turned to him in surprise. "I am?"

"Yeah. Kind of. I suppose. Baby steps first, eh? Slow and steady wins the race, right?"

"If you say so." Nessa hadn't heard a word after the 'yeah' part, excitement coursing through her veins with a wild roar. She'd been waiting, longing for this since she'd learned that she was an Old Blood. Magic hid somewhere inside her, soon to be awoken. Nessa was sure of it, and she was impatient to learn what she could before that happened.

"Now," Orm continued, "as I was saying before Hunter decided to try and delight us with his wit, or lack thereof, focus on the gems. Look deep into them, see past their facets and peer into their core. That's where the magic lies."

"They're only small, Orm," Nessa said, staring at the tiny gems until she was on the brink of going cross-eyed. "There's not much for me to look at."

"Shhh. Let's have less talking and interruptions. And can you just do what I say without arguing? I'm the teacher here. I'm in charge."

There was no need to look to know that Hunter was smirking. Nessa could feel it and was helpless against murmuring a sarcastic, "Yes, master."

Hunter snorted, shoulders shaking as he bit back a laugh, and earned himself another cuff around the head. He'd underestimated how far Orm could reach.

"No more of that," Orm instructed. "Now, Nessie. Can you see how the light catches on the back of the stones, reflecting around inside?"

Nessa nodded. The gems were small, and although they were coloured, they held a strange translucency, allowing her to almost see the interior of the settings through them.

"Now, can you see how the light catches on the facets? Twinkling gently with even the slightest of movement?"

Another nod.

"Tell me about the difference between the two."

"Between the light on the surface and the light inside?"

"Yep."

Nessa frowned and tried to bring her hand closer, tugging against Orm's grip so that it would be easier for her to see the gems. Orm stopped her, though, his hold tightening on her wrist.

"Focus," he whispered. "You can do it like this. All you need to do is focus."

"Focus," Nessa muttered. "Easier said than done when it feels like you've got a herd of angry dwarves stomping around in your skull."

"I told you to drink your magic drink. If you had, you would be feeling better by now."

"If your magic drink was as magic as you say it is, then I wouldn't need to drink so much for it to work."

Orm looked contemplative. "I suppose it could be made more concentrated. It could be like a shot."

"If it's possible to make it more concentrated, then why haven't you done it yet?"

Orm shrugged, jostling her hand a little. "Never really thought about it. Now, back to the matter at hand, pun intended. Focus, Nessie. Focus with all your focusing might."

Blowing out a breath, Nessa blocked out the world around her, drowning out the sound of the crackling fire and Hunter's mumbled musings as to whether or not "herd" was the correct term employed when describing a number of dwarves. The room's walls, painted a pale yellow, faded from sight, as did the curtains and the matching rug.

Nessa's line of sight contracted until she could see nothing but the brooch. She felt like she was looking through a kaleidoscope, an ever-shifting sea of blue and silver...blue and silver...

"Now *unfocus*."

The words seemed to float through the air, as soft and intangible as the gentlest of summer breezes. They pushed at her kaleidoscope, making it twist and spin. Blue and silver...blue and silver...blue and silver.

Ever faster it went, the colours spiralling together until they were almost indistinguishable from one another, a bicoloured swirl of hypnotic quality.

Then, suddenly, it shattered into a million pieces like a pane of fragile glass.

Instantly, Nessa's vision cleared and sharpened, and she was back to staring at the brooch, held up a foot away from her face. She blinked, waking from the trance, and frowned.

"The brooch," she exclaimed. "It's glowing."

A gentle shimmer of golden light came from each of the little gems, soft and mystical.

Orm let go of her wrist, and Nessa brought the brooch closer, turning it this way and that, watching, marvelling as the light shifted and moved, refracting around inside the gems like they were prisms. The gems, though, weren't prisms. No, the halo-like glow came from within the gems themselves.

"What you're seeing there is magic," Orm said, his lips curling with a faint smile as he watched Nessa's growing fascination. "Energy in its purest form. A perfect, if somewhat weak, example of external magic."

Nessa looked at him. "External magic?"

"Oh, bollocks," Hunter groaned, head falling back against the wall. "This is going to be a long-winded discussion about something I can't join in with because I'm a boring, old, non-magical human."

"Shhh, little human," Orm said, grinning from ear to ear, his eyes twinkling with mischief. "You can still take part in the theory side of magical learning."

"You're making me feel very excluded and unappreciated."

"I appreciate you," Nessa said. "Sometimes. You know, when you're actually being helpful and not annoying the devil out of me."

"I am never annoying," Hunter said confidently. "I am charming. There is a difference. But, I thank you nonetheless for trying to make me feel better. I think."

"What else are friends for but to fill one another with a sense of value." Nessa's attention went back to the brooch, only to find that the glow had vanished. The brooch once again appeared to be nothing out of the ordinary. "Hey, the glow's gone!"

"No, the glow is still there," Orm told her. "You've just stopped seeing it, that's all. You let your concentration slip when you were talking to us."

"Oh."

"Anyway," he continued, looking at Hunter, "we don't have time for a long chitchat. We have work to do. People to meet. Plans to conjure."

Nessa raised her eyebrows. "Work? Plans?"

"Yeah," Hunter became oddly animated, sitting bolt upright, excitement pouring off him in waves. "Just before you fainted and caused a wee bit of commotion—"

Cheeks reddening, Nessa muttered, "Haven't I told you to stop mentioning that already?"

"...I was engaged in conversation with a delightful pair of lads."

"The identical twins? I remember."

Hunter nodded. "Bo and Luca. Don't ask me which is which. I doubt I'll ever figure it out. Anyway, they work in the warehouses down by the docks and are in need of a pair of extra hands. Being the kind and ever-helpful chap I am, I kindly offered mine and Orm's services for the day."

"I'm sure Orm is over the moon that you did so."

"I haven't done an honest day's work since…" Orm paused, having to give it some thought. "…Well, since ever."

"Then it's about time you did, my old friend," Hunter laughed. "However, I have the feeling that the work isn't all that honest, considering the type of people who are running the operation."

"So, what are you doing?" Nessa asked hesitantly, fearful that Hunter had also volunteered her services too.

"Dunno yet. The fun is in the mystery."

"Probably something boring and tedious," Orm grumbled. "And it's most likely hard work."

Nessa gave him a sympathetic pat on the shoulder. "It's okay, Orm. When you're finished for the day, you can tell me all about external magic and, ah…um…"

"Internal magic," Orm helpfully supplied.

"Yeah. You can tell me all about internal and external magic. Isn't that something to look forward to?"

"I s'pose. But I'm going to be drunk."

"I expect nothing else."

"Very, very drunk," Orm warned.

"Of course."

"But, in the meantime," Orm said, rising from the bed, making the wooden frame sigh with relief as his weight left it, "you can practice what I've just taught you. By the time Hunter and I return, I expect it to be second nature, doable in a blink of an eye."

"Wait, what?" Nessa looked to him and Hunter. "You're going now?"

They gave twin nods.

"And you expect me to stay here all day and wait until you come back?"

"Pretty much," Orm said.

Nessa looked out the window, measuring the time by the angle of the sun. "But it's only early in the morning. You could be gone for hours."

"Which gives you plenty of time to practice."

Gazing at Hunter beseechingly, Nessa said, "That isn't fair. This isn't fair."

"It's only for today," Hunter murmured, wincing a little at her growing displeasure. "Once we know that everything's safe, you'll be able to tag along with further excursions. Besides, it's not like you have to stay in your room all day. You can always join Jerome downstairs for a meal and share a drink or two. Maybe have a chitchat, find out some more useful titbits. From the sounds of things, you were getting somewhere with him at the den."

Nessa flung the brooch away. It landed on the sideboard with a clatter. Orm and Hunter flinched and stared at her with wide eyes.

"Ah, yes," she said through clenched teeth, "that delightful little chitchat with our landlord who has a darker side to him. You know, that was the first time since arriving in this damn city that I've heard anything remotely related to Arncraft. Don't you find that strange?"

"Well…" Hunter began.

"I thought one of the main reasons for coming here was to learn why the king attacked that town," Nessa snapped, her repressed irritation and anger bubbling and boiling to the surface. "And yet, all I've seen you two do is try and infiltrate an underground criminal network. Why, I keep asking myself, when there are so many more useful things we could be doing? For three weeks all you've had me do is memorise facts about the Twelve Houses. I know their history. I know who their current Riders are. I know which coats of arms belong to which House. I've learnt everything I can about their dragons: what colour they are, how old they are, their names and everything else there is to know. I know enough about them!"

"That's important information," Hunter insisted.

"But I need to know other things too," Nessa argued. "I need to be doing more than just going over the same stuff again and again. I should be learning everything there is to learn about the Old Bloods, about magic. *You* should have started teaching me that already," she told Orm. "Yet every time I try to bring it up, you just brush me off."

Orm looked guilty even as he sputtered a weak, "I do not."

"You do too. Just now, instead of explaining about internal and external magic, you declare that you're abandoning me for an unspecified period of time, running off on some fool's errand to help a bunch of people you've just met. You should be helping *me*." Nessa sniffled, fighting against the lump at the back of her throat. "You should be helping me. But all you're doing is keeping me in the dark, keeping things from me. I've tried to be patient through all of this," she waved a hand, indicating to her room and all that it represented to her.

"I've silently gone along with you as you've tried to further your agenda: gambling dens, pubs, parties. I've listened to the endless drunken rambling of men, trying to glean something of use, and I'm sick to death of it all. I'm sick to death of either being left alone here, or having to be escorted by one of you wherever I go, all because of some perceived threat. Now, I don't know about you, but I'm pretty damn sure that neither the king nor any of his cronies are running around the Stickworks looking for me." Nessa buried her head in her hands and allowed her loose hair to fall around her shoulders in a dark curtain. The lump at the back of her throat turned into sobs.

There was a moment of stunned silence. Hunter or Orm cleared their throat, Nessa didn't know who, and there was a quick, whispered conversation. The bed creaked as someone crawled across it, and Nessa held herself still, refusing to react as an arm wrapped around her shoulders.

"Alright," Hunter said softly, resting his cheek on the top of her head, "something else is going on here. What is it?"

"I just gave you a list of reasons," Nessa grumbled. "Do I have to repeat them?"

"No, but there's something else that was excluded from that extensive list."

Nessa shrugged. Her anger, as quickly as it had come, vanished, leaving her feeling deflated and forlorn. "It's nothing."

"Come on, Nessie. Tell us. Otherwise, we won't be able to sort the problem out."

"No." She sniffled. "I already feel stupid enough."

"Don't say that," Hunter murmured, nudging her shoulder with his. "We don't think you're stupid. A bit mental, yeah. As scary as the Nine Devils when you're angry, also, yeah. But certainly not stupid."

Nessa shifted and peered through her fingers, trying to gauge how sincere Hunter was. His amber eyes were earnest, filled with worry, and his brow was furrowed in consternation. She looked over at Orm, finding him standing by the window, staring down at the street several floors below, his attention far away, his eyes filled with a million thoughts, his arms crossed, his thumbs tapping nervously against his linen-clad biceps.

"We're your friends," Hunter said, sensing Nessa's hesitation. "We're on your side no matter what. You can tell us anything."

"I can't help but feel so useless, so incredibly unready," Nessa confessed in a whisper, letting her hands fall onto her lap, feeling oh-so vulnerable. "No matter how hard I try, I just can't shake the sense that something looms over us, something big and scary. Something that's rapidly approaching. Worse yet, I don't think I'm strong enough to face whatever it is. I'm incomplete. Don't you understand that? I have so many questions, so many missing pieces." She gazed into Hunter's wide eyes. "I want to remember. No, I *need* to remember. Who I am, what I am; these are things I should know, and yet I don't. Why can't I remember, Hunter? What happened to me?"

Hunter was shaken. His face paled and his lips parted in shock.

"I want my memories back," Nessa insisted gently. "Else I'm not really myself. If I'm not myself, then I'll never be able to fully trust anyone."

"You don't trust me?" Hunter looked like she had slapped him.

"I don't think I even trust myself."

# Chapter 25

Stunned by her own words, Nessa barely registered Hunter's arm slipping from her shoulders, or Orm grabbing the solitary chair that sat by the dressing table, which also acted as her makeshift desk, and setting it down in front of the bed.

"Right," Orm muttered, slouching back as much as he could in the little, old chair, making its joints let out a high-pitch screech of protest. "Right. Okay. Yeah. I think, since we're clearly having a candid moment between the three of us, I'll be forthright and say that I maybe haven't handled all of this in the best way."

Nessa looked at him, more than a little surprised. Hunter stared at his friend too, his eyebrows shooting up and disappearing into his mop of unbrushed hair.

"Handled what the wrong way?" Nessa croaked.

"This," Orm waved a hand at the window, at the crowd of buildings outside. "Coming here. Arncraft. You. I haven't forgotten about you, Nessie. I see I haven't done right by you so far, causing you distress." Orm pulled a flask out from his trous' pocket and unscrewed the cap, swiftly taking a hefty swig. His throat worked as he swallowed several mouthfuls.

Nessa turned to Hunter for an explanation, a bit of guidance, but he seemed just as perplexed as she was.

"You see, Nessie, after we found you, you were so scared and confused," Orm said, wiping the back of his hand across his mouth. "It was an easy decision to allow you time to re-adjust, to recover from your ordeal. I never thought I'd have to teach you about magic and what it means to be an Old Blood. I thought—expected—Chaos to be the one who would guide you into that world. But…ah…since he isn't here anymore, that responsibility has fallen to me. To be blunt, that terrifies me."

"Why'd that scare you?" Nessa asked. "You're pretty damn proficient with magic, in my opinion."

"Thanks, Nessie," Orm smiled sadly, "but truth be told, my skills aren't quite what they should be."

"But you can do all kinds of things. You can start fires, make disgusting, magical drinks, and conjure us awful scrambled egg from I-don't-even-know-where."

"Them and a handful of other things, too." Orm nodded. "But they're little more than parlour tricks compared to what Chaos could have taught you. I can talk your ears off when it comes to magic. However, when it comes to helping you *perform* it, I worry I'll be of little use. That's why a part of me thought that last night's rendezvous could be useful to us. Life-changing, in fact."

"Life-changing?" Nessa mused. "That sounds intriguing, doesn't it?" She glanced at Hunter, catching his slight nod whilst deep in thought. Nessa felt a smidgen of relief knowing that her spontaneous words hadn't driven an irretrievable wedge between them. Nessa would have never been able to forgive herself if she had damaged one of the few friendships she had, if she had hurt one of the handful of people who mattered to her the most.

"Life-changing?" Hunter muttered. "How so, my friend? Pray tell."

Orm shot Hunter a warning glare, then shrugged. "Perhaps 'game-changing' is a better way of phrasing it."

"What do you mean?" Nessa asked with a perturbed frown. Something had been conveyed in Orm's glare, a message solely for Hunter. It made the skin on the nape of her neck prickle with uncertainty.

"Think about it, Nessie," Orm said, his whisky-coloured eyes brightening, softening as he turned his gaze away from Hunter. "The three of us stand no chance of getting anywhere close to King Kaenar. We need help. Quite a lot of it too, I reckon."

"Like an army?"

Orm venomously shook his head. "No. No. Not an army. Definitely not an army. Many people have tried to take that monster of a man down with armies and rebellions and whatnot. It never ends well."

"They all tend to die," Hunter clarified, his tone oddly hollow.

Nessa grimaced. "Oh."

"No, we don't want to rally up an army," Orm continued, "that would take too much time and require more resources than we could ever hope of getting our grubby, little hands on. No, what we need is a small, select group of highly skilled people. Our best chance of success is keeping the element of surprise. We need to keep everything top secret. Keep it underground. Where better to scout out potential accomplices than places like the den?"

"Well," Nessa said hesitantly, thoughts—possibilities—whirling around in her head at a hundred miles an hour. "I suppose it kind of depends on what particular set of skills you're looking for…"

"Whoever's in charge has done all the hard work for us," Orm said, his eyes sparkling with excitement, one foot tapping away like a merry, little drum. "There's already a network in place, filled with all kinds of useful links and connections. They know all kinds of things, have access to places we could only dream of. Moreover, they have influence."

"It sounds like, out of all those reasons," Nessa mused, "influence is the most important one to you?"

Orm grinned. "Never underestimate how influence factors into things. A man can be as poor as dirt, but if he has charisma, a powerful presence, then he's as rich as he needs to be. There's many a man and woman who have risen through the ranks of society by doing little more than saying a few sweet things to just the right people."

"I'll have to take your word for it."

"A lot of dangerous work has already been done for us."

"How so?"

"First off, the network has been around for a number of years." Hunter was the one who said that, finally emerging from his glum mood.

"Around eighteen years, according to Jerome" Nessa remarked with a small smile, reminding them. On awakening from her faint, after finding herself tucked safely in her bed back at Jerome's guest house, Nessa had given them a debriefing of what she had learned during her short time at the den.

"Around eighteen years," Hunter agreed. "That lengthy period of operations means they have a secure and trusted system."

"Which is good?"

"Oh yeah," Hunter nodded enthusiastically. "It means there's no leaks. Everyone there has been vetted for us, and we know that they can keep their mouths shut. Another added perk is that they hold no esteem for the king. None of them are loyal to him or to his minions. It's as perfect, or as near to it, as we can hope for."

"Well..." Nessa searched for the right thing to say. *Was she meant to be encouraging? Approving?* "For putting a team together for a coup, that's all, ah, quite useful I suppose?"

"Besides," Orm said, "there's a small chance that someone from the network might be able to help you with your mental block."

"My memory loss?" Nessa shifted, muscles tensing. Anticipation and something else, something not too dissimilar to fear, snaked through her veins. "Is that...is that what's really wrong with me?"

"It's one possibility."

"A mental block," Nessa muttered, tasting the term. She cast her mind back to the forest, to just after she'd been found by Hunter and the others, and had overheard them talking about her. Hadn't Chaos mentioned something about a mental block? It all started to make sense: how the ghosts of memories would sometimes rise, only to be forced back down before she had a chance to grab a hold of them; how things would seem both familiar and foreign to her at the same time. "What does that really mean?"

"Simply put, it means that someone, a very skilled and powerful magic user—"

"Margan or Shadow," Hunter summarised darkly.

"…has, during your imprisonment, entered your mind and built, for a lack of a better way of describing it, a wall. This wall then locks away anything that the 'builder' wants hidden from the recipient of this manipulation. Anything from specific feelings to a memory, or…"

"Or all of my memories," Nessa finished. "But why all of them? Why not just one or two?"

Orm spread his hands. "I can't be completely sure. Maybe the mental block was done in a rush. Perhaps they didn't have time to pick and choose the things they wanted you to forget. Possibly, just possibly, a more sinister—"

"Orm," Hunter cut him off. "I don't think this is the best way to be explaining things. It's a rather sensitive subject."

Placing her hand on Hunter's arm, both in way of quieting him and showing that she appreciated his concerns, Nessa urged Orm to continue.

"A more sinister thought is, if they took away all of your memories, basically making you a blank slate, then you'd be easily manipulatable, more compliant in whatever plans they have for you."

"Considering that I'm here with you," Nessa croaked out, "I'm clearly not as compliant as they had hoped to make me." The thought of being made into a "blank slate" was too unnerving to even contemplate.

Orm laughed, a short and humourless bark. "Indeed. Who knows what they had in store for you if you hadn't escaped."

Nessa didn't want to think about that, finding the possibilities almost endless, and all of them unpleasant to say the least.

"So, if this wall was built in my mind," Nessa murmured thoughtfully, almost earnestly, "hiding away my memories, then does that mean they're still there? They haven't been erased. Is there a way of breaking down this mental block?"

"Well, yeah," Orm admitted after a heavy pause, his eyes darting between her and Hunter a couple of times. "Yeah. There is a way for the mental block to be broken. Before I say any more, though, I must urge you: don't get your hopes up."

*Too late for that*, Nessa thought. Her blood already thrummed with anticipation. Her heartbeat was loud and fast in her ears.

"The only way for the mental block to be broken is for the one who made it to take it down."

Nessa's heart skipped a beat and she bit her lip as the implications slowly sank in. A low hiss, that of a breath forced out through gritted teeth, made Nessa turn around in surprise. Hunter's face was flushed as he leaped up from the bed, jostling Nessa roughly in his haste. His hands were clenched into tight fists, and he looked like he was about it hit something, someone. Hunter's eyes, usually so bright and cheery, darkened dangerously as he fixed Orm with a glower, flashing with a rage rarely seen.

Orm met Hunter's stare unflinchingly, almost daring him to do something.

For a split second, Nessa thought Hunter was going to launch himself across the small room at Orm. Aoife must have thought the same thing too, for she shot awake, her alarm joining with Nessa's, their bond amplifying it.

A gasp left Nessa's lips, small and barely discernible, but seemingly enough to make Hunter pause.

Reluctantly, slowly, Hunter turned and he gazed down at Nessa, taking in her wide eyes and her fearful countenance, her small form huddled on her bed. Little by little, the anger began to leach out of him. His shoulders sagged in defeat.

"You," he pointed a finger at Orm with a quick, stabbing jab that reminded Nessa of a dagger being thrust into someone. "You are so full of it. You know that, right?"

Orm's eyebrows shot up and his mouth opened in preparation of a response, a defence. He was cut off by an angry wave of Hunter's hand, a slash through the air like a merciless knife.

"You are unbelievable," Hunter continued, his voice an unrecognisable growl, his body hunched like that of a wounded animal beneath his grey winter tunic. "This is so bloody unbelievable. After everything that's happened, after everything that's been said, you're still determined to go down this path? No. You know what? No more! I'm not being involved anymore. This is all on you now."

Hunter spun on his heel, stalking over to the door.

He paused, his hand on the doorknob, and cast an apologetic glance over his shoulder. "I'll catch you later, Nessie," he murmured, his tone softening just for her. "We'll go for a walk or something later, just you and me, and find a nice place for dinner?"

Nessa could do nothing more than nod, tongue-tied and unable to form any other kind of response.

Hunter offered her a brief, hesitant smile, which swiftly disappeared when his gaze shifted to Orm. "I'm off to the docks. I'll make up some excuse for you being late, but I wouldn't dally too long. Otherwise, you risk pissing off the twins and ruining everything even more." Slamming the door behind him with enough force to make the furniture in Nessa's room rattle, Hunter left.

Orm stared after him for a long moment, his eyes troubled, and swiped a hand over his face as if he could wipe away the weariness that settled over his strong features like a mask.

"He'll calm down," Orm sighed, his way of an explanation. "In a couple of hours, most likely. Definitely after lunch. Maybe. Hopefully. It's just the stress and the sleepless nights. He'll be back to his usual self in no time."

Finding her voice, Nessa croaked out a, "I bloody well hope so." Seeing Hunter being anything other than his usual happy-go-lucky self was unsettling. Questions arose, a dozen more to join the hundreds she already had. Aoife's consciousness once again retreated to the back of Nessa's mind, where she had been since Nessa had awoken from her fainting spell. She was watchful and alert, but barely noticeable, allowing Hunter and Orm to do all the fussing, the talking and, apparently, most of the fighting. Nessa could tell that Aoife was thinking about a great many things, but when Nessa reached out an enquiring thought, all she would get back was the sense of later.

"Soooo," Orm drew out the word, searching for something to say, anything to say. "I...ah...yeah. Not the best way to start the day by far, am I right?"

Nessa scowled and drooped, both mentally and physically exhausted, and leaned back against the wall, wishing that she could disappear into it. Hunter's words spun around in her head, angry and insistent, jumbling with Orm's.

"Is there really no other way of breaking the mental block?" Nessa murmured, dejected and lost. "You know, other than having the one who put it there take it down?"

Orm pursed his lips, and his eyes darted to the door. "I'm afraid not." He cleared his throat. "There's no easy way of telling you this, but your memories are most likely gone. They are probably never coming back. I know this might be hard to accept. However, you can't keep clinging onto a hope that's not there. It will only bring you misery and pain."

Nessa's gaze settled on the brooch, and she couldn't help but do exactly what he was warning her against. "But Sissy said..." Nessa's wistful attempt of keeping her fragile hope alive fractured with each shake of Orm's head. She bit her lip, trying to contain a sob.

"Heimaey's probably right," Orm told her gently. "Sissy's mistress is most likely little more than a fraud."

*But Sissy and the creature from the forest stream, the water sprite, both hinted...* "The brooch, though. It has magic. Surely that means Sissy's mistress has some—"

Orm sighed and reached out a hand, tapping the brooch with a finger. "The magic is weak. There's no way it would lead you anywhere, least of all to..." He frowned. "How did this Sissy put it? *'To what you've lost'*. It's a trick and nothing more. A particularly cruel trick, admittedly, and pretty damn distasteful, but there it is."

"But if it's just a trick, then why do it in the first place?" Nessa struggled not to cry, swallowing back sobs. She knew that if she started crying, then she wouldn't be able to stop. "What did—do—either of them hope to achieve?"

"Who knows." Orm hiked his shoulders. "Money? Power?"

Nessa grunted, her thoughts turning bitter.

Both Orm and Nessa fell into a frosted silence, looking at anything in the room but each other. Orm knew that Nessa was hurting. And hurt she did. Nessa sat bundled in her blankets, even though they weren't really needed since the fire was now warming the room nicely. Nessa watched listlessly as the frost on the windowpanes melted, fat droplets running down the surface, pooling on the narrow windowsill. A dark cloud of despair settled over her, a rolling thunderstorm of turmoil.

*Come see me*, Aoife murmured. It was the first thing she had said to Nessa all morning, and it seemed like a fine idea. Nessa decided then and there that she was uncaring of any consequences. She was going to see her dragon.

Nessa stood and crossed over to the door.

Holding it open, she gave Orm a pointed look, indicating that it was time for him to leave.

Orm paused mid-sentence. Whatever he was talking about—something about *Atheals*—was abruptly abandoned.

"Shoo," Nessa said when Orm made no move to leave. "I'm getting changed," Orm's eyebrows rose, surprised by her unusually firm tone, "then I'm going to see Aoife."

And that's exactly what Nessa did.

༅་♦་ཙྪ

Orm had offered very little in the way of a fight, nothing more than the obligatory "I don't think that's a good idea" and "could you perhaps wait until tomorrow?"

Nessa had stonewalled him, giving away no hint of what she was thinking, *feeling*... It seemed to have had the desired effect. Quicker than Nessa expected, Orm had left, muttering a few orders that were along the lines of "no dilly-dallying", "no going anywhere else but straight there and back" and "be back before it is dark".

Nessa had, so far, ignored two of those three requests, and as she cast her gaze upward, she knew that she was about to break the third.

The sun slipped down behind the tall buildings, and the shadows rapidly grew ever deeper and darker. Nessa knew that she should start making her way back to the guest house. It probably wasn't a wise decision to stay out past her curfew, especially so soon. After all, Nessa had only just won the right to be out and about by herself a few hours prior. Still, she couldn't bring herself to change her course, to turn around and make her way back to the guest house, to Hunter and Orm, and to all the problems that awaited her there.

Slowly traversing the streets of Ellor by herself for the first time was refreshing. The cobwebs in her mind were being swept away by the crisp breeze that was funnelled through the narrow streets. Nessa had finally found a sense of inner peace that had been absent since she had witnessed the king's razing of Arncraft. All evening long, she had done little else but wander and ponder about a great number of issues with a marginally clearer perspective.

There were a lot of them.

There were many, many things she had to think about, to process.

Over and over again, Nessa replayed what Orm had told her earlier, what she had learned from him. She tried desperately to make sense of it all, but it was all too much to deal with, especially when she added the argument she'd had with Aoife to the mix.

While Nessa was well aware that she'd have to make amends at some point, probably sooner rather than later, she wasn't quite ready to do so. It had taken her hours to calm down, and she was reluctant to reawaken the anger, the hurt, that had sprung to life during their fight. Having a dispute with a dragon in itself would be bad enough for anyone's psyche. Having a dispute with a dragon you are bonded to, both of your thoughts and feeling colliding together, was particularly unpleasant.

*Especially since it was about...*

Nessa shook her head, dislodging the upsetting thoughts. She turned her mind back to earlier that morning, focusing on what had happened after her outburst at Hunter and Orm.

*I don't even trust myself...*

Hunter couldn't have looked more shocked and, oddly enough, betrayed. Nessa had immediately wished that she'd kept her mouth shut. She never wanted to hurt Hunter or Orm. Not ever. In all honesty, Nessa had no idea where the anger had come from. The irritation, yes. That had been bubbling inside her for a short while. The anger, though... The anger felt different, sudden and fiery. Raw. It was as if it belonged to someone else.

The sun had finally set, the sky was now a beautiful shade of deep cobalt. A fine peppering of stars littered the heavens to the east, and to the west, the last lingering reaches of the sunset gripped onto the vaporous clouds that stretched across the horizon, turning their undersides a delicate pink, making them shimmer like pearls.

Nessa looked around, wondering where she was, and tried to catch sight of the castle. As the capital's main landmark, nestled high into the mountainside, easily seen from most places in the city, it acted as a compass, a guide around the endless warren of streets.

Unfortunately for her, though, Nessa couldn't spy it. The tall, stone buildings that lined either side of the narrow street on which she walked hindered her view.

Lanterns lit her way, casting circles of golden light at intervals down the street. They were, to Nessa's disappointment, simple oil lamps and not the ones found in the High Quarter, which illuminated the way with light cast by the delicate, glowing mushrooms they contained. Still, having some form of light was favourable to walking in the dark. It was just a shame that Nessa didn't get the opportunity to see the ethereal mushrooms again. She was awfully fond of them. Sometimes, it felt like she could spend hours staring at them without ever growing bored.

With nothing much of interest to distract her, Nessa didn't linger. She set off again, continuing her near-aimless wandering. In her opinion, she wasn't really breaking her curfew yet. Technically, it wasn't completely dark. It was only *almost* dark. By her guesstimate, she still had half an hour or so. If she picked up her pace, she might make it back to the guest house in time. Nessa couldn't have wandered too far from the Stickworks. She hadn't even reached the High Quarter.

By that reasoning, Nessa deduced that she must be in the Stickworks' neighbouring neighbourhood, the one sitting between it and the High Quarter. The buildings were built taller and stronger compared to the timber-framed buildings that dominated the Stickworks' architecture, made from more expensive materials such as brick and stone. They were, however, not quite as fine as those closer to the High Quarter, or as grand. Whilst built with more skill and organisation than those seen in the Stickworks, the buildings around Nessa were tall and narrow, and they were packed tightly together, making the roads and streets only marginally better than those that crisscrossed the Stickworks, just a little wider and not quite as filthy.

Having a vague idea of where she was, Nessa was sure that the guest house wasn't far. After all, she had only made it back from visiting Aoife a short while ago. She couldn't have wandered all too far. Most of her day had been consumed by the time taken to journey to and from Aoife's cave. Even on horseback, it wasn't a short or easy trek.

Bryan wasn't particularly fast, but the two of them had grown used to one another, and he did make the hike a lot more pleasant, and a touch quicker compared to Nessa being on foot. Bryan saved Nessa time, energy and her feet from a few blisters. In return, Bryan was often rewarded with his favourite things: a handful of oats and a good rub down.

Nessa felt a twinge of guilt when she thought about Bryan.

In her turmoil, Aoife's harsh words still echoing in her ears, Nessa felt like she had all but neglected him. Upon her return to the city, she'd deposited him in his stall, unsaddling him as swiftly as she could, and left him with little more than a pat on the head and a handful of hastily grabbed hay. Nessa had gone to Aoife under the assumption that she'd be a shoulder to lean on, an ally of sorts.

Nessa had assumed wrong.

Aoife had said, simply put and with a few choice words that shouldn't be repeated in polite company, that she and the others had Nessa's best interests at heart. Nessa wasn't quite so sure...

Turning right, Nessa strolled down an old alleyway, hoping that it would be a short cut back to one of the main roads. A layer of dirt partially covered the cobbled ground, and the buildings crowded in on both sides, almost looming over her. The lanterns were placed few and far between, and the wooden shutters on dwellings were pulled shut, little more than thin seams of light showing around the edges. It was gloomy and dark, and held an eerie sense of familiarity.

Nessa shook her head, trying to fling aside such silly notions. Nothing could be familiar to her. Her memories were gone. Everyone was telling her that. Chaos. Orm. Aoife. *Aoife...* The one who Nessa thought would be on her side no matter what, wanting her to find the answers to the questions that had plagued her for so long.

*Why are you so eager to remember?* Aoife's words lashed through Nessa's mind, still as savage and as wounding as they had been several hours ago. *What do you think the past holds for you?*

*Everything*, had been Nessa's response. *The past holds everything that makes me, me.*

*There's nothing but darkness and suffering. Don't you understand that? The scars on your wrists bear testament to that. Having a few happy memories won't lessen the pain... Nothing will. Save yourself the heartbreak and let the past stay where it is: buried.*

Nessa's hand automatically wrapped around her wrist, where, hidden beneath the cuff of her sleeve and her felted arm warmer, was a wide band of scarring. Nessa didn't need to see it to know that the skin was pink and glossy, sensitive and at times tender as it continued to heal. The exception was that of her Rider's Mark, which was now undamaged, healing faster and neater compared to the skin around it.

Nessa knew that her scars were glaring evidence that her imprisonment was less than pleasant, to put it nicely. Surely, though, whatever torments she must have suffered are worth remembering in the long run? The way Nessa saw it, it was six months of darkness versus an entire lifetime of light, of living, of family and friends, of excitement and experiences. These are the things Nessa longed for, the things she wanted to remember. Weren't they worth reliving everything for?

Nessa certainly thought so. The others, however, were of a different opinion.

A peculiar sensation fell over Nessa, settling around her shoulders like a cape made of spider webs and spectres. Her heart skipped a beat and a wave of dizziness coursed through her. Nessa stumbled before she caught herself against a wall, bruising a shoulder. Her vision wavered, blackness threatening to overwhelm her, and she blinked rapidly, like that would stop the world from fading away. In each fluttering moment, imprinted on the inside of her eyelids, was an image.

Faded and dark, it was little more than a ghost of an impression: a woman walking down the very street on which Nessa now stood, a small bundle carefully held in her arms.

Nessa came back to herself, the dizziness passing, her heart racing. The image dissolved, drifting away like a morning's mist. Once again, the sense of familiarity trickled down Nessa's spine, a memory was trying to claw itself to freedom, battling to break through the wall in her mind. The wall—which Nessa now knew to be a mental block—put in place to hide away all that made her *her*, to make her biddable to Margan's and Shadow's plans, seemed to not be working quite as they had hoped it would. Despite their intentions, their efforts, it had all backfired. Nessa wasn't feeling particularly compliant, not right now, not anymore.

Straightening, Nessa pushed off from the wall, the ghostly sound of far distant footsteps echoing in her ears, the image of the woman coming and going, reappearing and shifting like fine fingers of smoke. Nessa felt a spike of indecision, and she looked around as if the alleyway held the answers to what she should do.

All was still. The street was unusually empty save for Nessa and her unearthly vision. In the distance, she could hear the faint sound of laughter and voices, the clatter of doors opening and closing. The noise was carried on a breeze, channelled through the labyrinth of streets.

Nessa shivered as the cold air of evening seeped through her layers of clothing, brushing against her skin like phantom fingers. A light breeze stirred up her loose hair, blowing it around her shoulders in a tangled cloud. Nessa sighed and pushed it back, wincing as strands caught on the brooch that was pinned over her heart. Her fingertips brushed against the blue gems and silver, and Nessa's indecision was abruptly abandoned.

೩☯♦೧೩

Nessa chased after the vision, the closest thing to a memory she had, allowing it to lead her further into the maze of tall, stone buildings. The sky darkened and the lanterns' circles of light grew brighter, wider, showing the eerie mist that rolled across the ground in rippling waves. It had appeared out of nowhere, suddenly there in a blink of an eye, like it was rising from the cobblestones. Thick, white and heavy, it came up to Nessa's ankles.

She hurried along, the mist stirring in her wake. Thin tendrils curled under the hem of her skirt, coiling around the cuffs of her boots. For a brief moment, Nessa entertained the idea of the mist being alive, breathing in time with the night's calm rhythm.

That notion soon turned sinister as the mist continued to roll in, growing in depth and density. The light from the lanterns was smothered, defused, transformed into shallow pools of luminosity, little moons which hovered along the alley. Shadows lengthened and darkened, and the air suddenly held an unnatural quality, loaded with energy and danger.

A shiver of warning crawled up Nessa's spine. Her Rider's Mark tingled ominously.

Nessa paused under a lamp, her breaths coming fast and shallow, panicked. She cast around, searching the mist with wide eyes.

She didn't know what to expect, not really, but Nessa expected to see *something*: a figure standing in the distance; a monster lurking in a gloomy doorway, ready to pounce. Despite the distinct feeling of eyes watching her, hungry and intense, it appeared that Nessa was alone in that menacing alleyway. She could see that nothing—*no one*—was there with her.

With unease, Nessa continued down the alleyway, telling herself that everything was fine, that her imagination was playing tricks on her, turning something perfectly natural like mist into a menacing force. It was her imagination, Nessa insisted, that made her feel like she was being watched. It was definitely her imagination that conjured up the *clip-clop* echo of hoofed footsteps behind her and the softly spoken words that drifted through the chilled air like a siren's song, quiet and beguiling and ever-so-deadly.

Nessa rounded a corner and skidded to a stop. The pressure of imprisoned memories grew, building up against the wall in her mind, pushing against it like a dam that was threatening to burst.

A courtyard opened up before her, perfectly round and surrounded by tall walls. Mist swarmed around the edges, catching against the weathered stone and the small lanterns which dangled from brackets at head height. Great waves of mist rolled in from the alleyway behind Nessa, soft and cool as it brushed against her ankles, filling up the courtyard and flowing down into the pond-like feature that sat in the centre.

Nessa's eyes latched onto it.

The sense of déjà vu was nearly overwhelming.

All fears and uncertainties floated away as a haze settled over her. Nessa felt calm, detached even, almost like she was seeing everything through someone else's eyes.

Entering the courtyard, Nessa unhooked a nearby lantern from its wall bracket and used it to light her way through the ever-thickening mist. She approached the pond-like feature, the weight of the lantern straining her arm as she held it aloft; made from metal and with chunky glass panels, it was surprisingly heavy. The mist smothered the light, and little more than the lip of the feature was visible as she came to stand by it.

Nessa stared into the feature's impenetrable darkness,

unable to tell how far down it went. It could be a couple of feet or a hundred. Mist poured over the lip, streaming down like a spill of ivy tendrils. Over to the side, spiralling down into the darkness, was a staircase. Nessa moved over to it. Her borrowed lantern was only able to brighten the first few steps, but she saw that they were narrow and steep, and didn't seem to have any cracks or obvious signs of being loose. Nessa allowed the spectral memory to pull her forward. She allowed it to urge her down the staircase.

Nessa eyed the darkness that lay before her, beneath her, hesitating.

She swallowed her nerves and continued onward, downwards, heading into the void. As the darkness closed in around her, oppressive and consuming, Nessa couldn't help but feel like she was being swallowed by a giant creature unseen. Her lantern made a valiant effort against it, casting a protective ring around her. The deeper she went, though, the smaller that circle of light became.

It took a lifetime for Nessa to reach the bottom; at least, that's how it felt. It almost came as a surprise when her feet left the last step and she found herself standing in a large subterranean room.

"There's nothing here," Nessa told herself, her voice barely above a whisper. "It's empty."

Her words held nothing but the truth, for the only thing in the room was her. There was nothing else. No lanterns. No decorations. Nothing. Nothing to indicate it had ever been used for anything.

"This can't be right…"

Nessa had been so sure that something awaited her down there, something of significance, pulling her towards it. And yet, as she circled the edge of the room, searching for anything, a hint, a clue, despair settled upon her. Nessa began to doubt herself.

Maybe she had misread it all?

Maybe there was nothing awaiting her?

Maybe there never had been.

Was it a trick of her mind, a foolish hope that she might be able to remember a bit of her past, even if it was a sliver of an inconsequential moment in time? Anything would be better than nothing as far as Nessa was concerned.

Nessa was halfway around the room when the sense of familiarity left her, the ghost of a memory cruelly abandoning her. She staggered, catching up against the curved stone wall, the feeling of loss and emptiness almost too much to bear. The lantern dangled precariously from numb fingertips, banging against her knee, the flame flickering and dancing, the light skipping and jumping.

Following the shape of the stairs, Nessa turned her gaze upwards, knowing that she should start making her way back to the guest house before Orm and Hunter lost their minds to worry, wondering where she was. They'd get Aoife to contact her before long. Nessa couldn't face Aoife yet, not after their earlier argument, and definitely not after losing her grip on another hidden memory. There were too many emotions brewing between them, and there would be too many questions. It wouldn't end well.

The sky was a dark disk high above her, only a shade or two lighter than the darkness which swallowed much of the sunken room, clinging to the walls and the stairs like velvet drapes. She was loath to venture up there, unwilling to transverse through those lonely streets again.

A flicker of movement came from the top of the stairs. There and gone in a blink of an eye. Nessa frowned, taking a step forward. A bird, perhaps. Or, given the late hour, a rat.

Whatever it was, Nessa took it as a sign to go.

She went to cross over to the stairs but was brought up short. Something had snagged her woollen dress, ensnaring her. She twisted around, trying to free herself without ripping a hole, and noticed that her skirt had been caught on a rough edge of stone.

*How intriguing.*

There was an impression in the wall, shallow and inconspicuous, tall and fairly narrow. It was like something had been pressed into the wall, leaving behind an imprint that was no deeper than a finger's breadth. The stone brick on which Nessa had been caught formed the lip of the impression, a sharp line that fashioned a defined frame.

Unsnagging herself, Nessa turned and peered at the impression, her head cocked to the side.

"It's different," she whispered faintly, detached. Her hand rose, and her palm pressed flat against the centre of the impression, the stone cool and smooth to the touch. "There should be... Wasn't there a...?"

A soft sigh came from behind her. Then a quiet shuffle.

Fingers curled over Nessa's shoulder, heavy and biting, digging in under her collarbone, a thumb pressed into her scapula. Nessa was pinned in place.

"Wasn't there a...*what?*"

# Chapter 26

That voice.

*His* voice.

Deep and resonating, it invoked something in her, a mixture of emotions too rich and too complex for her to ever unravel.

Nessa froze, unable to move, almost unable to breathe. Her hand fell away from the wall as the grip on her shoulder tightened and she was spun around. Another hand clamped down, holding her, steadying her.

Capturing her.

Nessa knew who she'd be facing before her gaze swept over his features. Still, it came as a surprise when shockingly dark-blue eyes locked with hers.

If Nessa wasn't caught in his grip, then the weight of his stare alone would have held her immobile.

The mysterious stranger from the den had found her.

Nessa's eyes ran over his features, drinking him in, just as he was doing with her. She absorbed the smallest of details, like how long his eyelashes were and how his hair, thick and dark, fell around his face, framing his handsome features. Time meant nothing. It was suddenly a silly, trivial thing. There was nothing in the world but them. There was no gloomy, subterranean room. There was no eerie mist that slowly crept down the spiral stairs.

It was just her and *him*.

Tall and well built, muscular, he easily dwarfed Nessa. The top of her head barely reached his shoulder. Her stranger swallowed, his throat working, and Nessa's gaze lowered. She became transfixed. A torc rested around the base of his neck, sitting just above the collar of his black overcoat, twinkling in the dancing lantern light. It was made from fine silver wire that had been painstakingly woven together into an intricate pattern. On each end was a terminal that featured a large, gleaming gem which shimmered with mystic, blue light. It was beautiful. It was damning.

He was no ordinary man.

Nessa knew that from her hours poring over old tomes and diaries, listening to Orm's and Hunter's teachings. Only those from the Twelve Houses were permitted to wear torcs, and as Nessa gazed at the blue gems, she recalled that only a select few were allowed to wear bejewelled ones.

Nessa's blood turned to ice as the realisation dawned on her. This man, her mysterious stranger from the den, was a Dragon Rider.

*But which one?*

Nessa racked her brain, combing through everything she knew about the Houses and their Riders. Including King Kaenar, there were fourteen Dragon Riders, and the gems in their torcs were actually shell fragments they collected when their dragons' eggs hatched. Dragons' shells match the colour of their scales, and the colour of each dragon's Rider's eyes changes over time to also match their scales. Nessa had been unnerved when she'd learned that her chocolate-brown eyes would someday turn purple. This Rider's eyes, though, were a deep blue. There were only two Riders with blue dragons. One was Tolan of House Mægen. The other was...

Fear rushed through Nessa in a sickly wave as she put the pieces together. Tolan's dragon, she knew, was a light blue, a deceptively delicate shade not too dissimilar to apatite or sky-blue topaz. She'd seen Tolan and his dragon from afar a couple of times, flying together over the city in a show of power and strength, a reminder to the civilians of the Dragon Riders', and King Kaenar's, supremacy.

This Rider's eyes were too dark, though, and the gems in his torc were more like sapphire than apatite or topaz.

*If this isn't Tolan, then that means he's...*

"Who are you?" Nessa breathed. She needed to hear it aloud. The truth seemed too preposterous to believe otherwise.

Eyes as dark and as hard as the gemstone they resembled ran over Nessa's face, deep and fathomless. "You already know the answer to that," the Rider murmured. "Do you really need to be told it?"

Images of a room swathed in inky blackness and sinister forests arose. It was a struggle to keep her eyelids from fluttering closed. His voice washed over her, soft and caressing, strong and commanding, and oh-so familiar. His scent, sandalwood and something else, something rawer, primal perhaps, filled her with a strange range of emotions, encompassing everything from fear to longing, sadness to relief.

"Say it," he urged. "Say my name."

"Shadow." It was a gasp, barely detectable over the sound of her ragged breathing.

The wall met her back, hard and unyielding. He crowded her against it, boxing her in.

"Yes, my little wildcat," Shadow purred, his blue eyes gleaming. His breath caressed her cheek as he bent down, bringing his head level with hers. "I am he. Now, little wildcat, tell me this: was that a process of elimination or do you remember?"

"Remember?" Nessa whispered. It was hard to think straight with him so close, with him invading every one of her senses. "Remember *what*, exactly?"

"Me."

Nessa looked away. At least, she tried to. Shadow's hands left her shoulders, sliding up her neck and cupping her face. She had no option but to look at him. His eyes searched hers, seeking her secrets. Nessa was helpless against him, trapped and spellbound.

"Yes," she said against her will. "No." Nessa frowned. "I don't know."

Shadow pressed his thumbs into her jaw, mirrored on either side of her chin, and tilted her face up. The back of her head met the wall. His actions were gentle, and yet, there was no room for resistance. Nessa couldn't resist anyway. Her legs had turned to jelly, and her thoughts were a million miles away. Not a single fibre of Nessa's being wanted to be anywhere but there. There with him.

The space between them was practically nonexistent. Nessa could feel the soft brush of his breath on her brow. She could perceive the heat of his body seeping through her layers of clothing, warming her in ways she didn't want to understand.

Nessa wanted him closer.

She needed him closer.

With a clatter, the lantern she was holding fell to the ground, landing on its side. The flame sputtered and hissed in protest before resuming its hectic, little dance. Nessa's hands rose as if they had a mind of their own, slipping over his. Beneath her fingertips, she could feel calluses and fine scars on his knuckles and palms, evidence of his years of swordsmanship and combat.

"I can see it," Shadow whispered, his voice velvety and hypnotising, his lips inching ever closer to hers, "I can see. It's in your eyes. It's already happening. We don't have long now."

Nessa blinked as his words slowly filtered through the ever-growing haze in her mind. "What...what's already happening?"

"Shhh." Shadow closed his eyes, his brow furrowed in thought. "It's too soon. Things aren't in place yet." Absently, a thumb began caressing her cheek, stroking back and forth, back and forth, rough but also soft. Nessa wasn't sure if he was aware of what he was doing, of the effect he was having on her.

"Shadow?" Nessa swallowed, trying to gather her questions, her fragmented thoughts, into a cohesive bundle.

"Mmm?"

"Shadow," she tried again, finding it increasingly hard to concentrate. Her cheeks, under his touch, were growing painfully hot. It felt like fire was burning beneath her skin, flowing through her veins. "What...what are you talking about?"

"You're too strong for your own good," Shadow

murmured, his voice dropping into a low rumble. "The block was meant to give me more time, but I was too rushed. It didn't work how I had intended."

His words were a shock of cold water, jolting and painful. The haze clouding her mind vanished, and the fear and panic that she should have felt from the very start swooped down on her, grasping her with cruel talons.

Nessa tore herself free from Shadow, spinning away as he stumbled forwards a step, taken by surprise. His eyes snapped open, and he moved with inhuman speed. Shadow's arm whipped out in a blur, a hand wrapping around Nessa's wrist before she could make an escape.

"Where do you think you're going, little wildcat?" he asked, all softness gone from his tone. The intoxicating spell had broken utterly and completely for both of them. "I'm not finished with you yet."

Nessa twisted her wrist, trying to squirm out of his hold. His grip, though, was unyielding. No matter how hard Nessa yanked or struggled, it didn't loosen, not even a little bit.

"You," she gasped, disbelieving. "You're the one who put the mental block in my head? You're the one who took everything from me?"

"I didn't take," Shadow asserted with a scowl. "I gave. It was the best I could do given the circumstance."

"The circumstance," Nessa scoffed, fear gave way to anger. *How could he possibly think that? How would taking my memories, the things that help shape me into who I was, be a gift?* "And what circumstance would that be? The one where you and Margan kidnapped me? Or the one where the two of you locked me away in who-knows-where? I'd be happy to give you a few more possibilities, but I seem to be experiencing some memory problems. I'm sure you know all about that, seeing as you're the one who caused them."

A muscle ticked in Shadow's jaw as he stared down at her, his eyes darkening and becoming unreadable. His countenance became guarded. "Do you fear me?"

"Yes," Nessa said instantly. She then paused, a frown growing. The word tasted false on her tongue. "No. No, I don't think so."

Shadow tilted his head to the side, looking at Nessa from head to toe like she was an enigma, a puzzle he had yet to solve. Who was she, a girl not yet eighteen, compared to him and the things he had seen and experienced in the centuries he had weathered? Could anything really be a mystery to him?

Shadow's grip on her wrist loosened, and when Nessa made no move to flee, his hand fell away from her completely.

"No," Nessa murmured, growing surer of herself and what she felt towards him. "No, I don't fear you. Not as much as I know I should."

One dark eyebrow quirked up at her confession, and his gaze swept down, running over her layered, woollen dress before settling on her right forearm. Although her Rider's Mark was hidden beneath her arm warmer, concealed from his pointed gaze, it didn't seem to matter. He knew what she was hiding from all others. He had one of his own, after all. Nessa tried to catch a glimpse of his, but he quickly spied her furtive glance and shoved his sleeve down. Nessa didn't get the chance to catch a glimpse of it in the dancing lantern light.

"You really don't, do you?" Shadow mused. "You don't fear me."

Hearing him say it was merely a confirmation of sorts, and Nessa found herself having to look deep within herself to see if it was really true. Yes, she felt fear, she'd be a fool not to, but there was more to it. The fear she felt wasn't necessarily a fear *of* him. It was too complicated, too chaotic. If it were simple, if she simply feared him, hated him, then she wouldn't be experiencing the ever-shifting tide of emotions that raged inside her like storm waves breaking against a rocky shore. Whatever Nessa felt towards him was wild and messy and impossible to decipher.

"You should," Shadow said, his eyes dark and dangerous, almost black in the subdued light. "If you had any appreciation for self-preservation, you would."

"Why?" Nessa found herself asking. "You won't hurt me."

Shadow took a step forwards. "Will I not?"

"No." Nessa held herself still as he crowded her, the toes of his boots coming to brush against hers. She refused to be intimidated. There were a great many things shining in his beautiful dark eyes when she gazed into them, but the promise of pain was not one of them. Of that, Nessa was sure.

"And how could you possibly know that?" Shadow asked, voice soft, alluring. "A vision? A dream? Have you peeked inside my head, read my mind and seen my intentions?"

"A vision?" Laughter threatened to bubble up, catching in Nessa's throat. "No such thing, I'm afraid. And as for reading your mind, I wouldn't do that even if I could."

"Oh?"

"Too scared of what I might find in there."

Shadow's lips twitched, a corner quirking up just a little as he tried to suppress a grin. "A wise decision."

"Visions, though," Nessa mused, intrigued by the notion. "If I had that particular gift, it would save me a lot of trouble in the long run."

"Or cause a lot more problems for you in the short term," Shadow said bluntly.

His words, his tone, made Nessa pause. She tilted her head to the side and frowned at him. "You make it sound like me having visions is an actual possibility."

Shadow said nothing. He gave nothing away.

"Is it?" Nessa pressed, a desperate sense of urgency coming over her. "Is it possible?"

Shadow took a step back, slow, almost hesitant. Reluctant. A part of Nessa sensed that he wanted to leave, to flee. Something stopped him, though.

"It is." Nessa's eyes widened in shock. "I can have visions."

He gave an imperceptible nod.

"I can have visions," Nessa repeated, dumbstruck. "I can see the future?"

He twitched his head in an almost indiscernible shake.

"I—What?" Nessa's mind was racing. She didn't know whether to be jubilant or afraid. "I can't see the future?"

Shadow looked away from her, taking another slow step back, forcing himself to retreat before more secrets were revealed. Nessa followed him, matching him step for step. When no answer was forthcoming, she reached out and grabbed his hand. Shadow stilled, going rigid like he had been shocked. Nessa gazed at their joined hands, wondering why her skin tingled so pleasantly where it made contact with his.

"Careful, little wildcat," Shadow all but growled as he peeled his hand from hers. "You might end up losing one of your nine lives if you're not more cautious of where you put your paws."

Nessa heeded his warning, and her arm fell limp to her side as the growing sense of familiarity between them fled. Maybe she had imagined it all? "Can I, or can I not, see the future?"

Shadow's eyes ran over Nessa's face, dark and knowing, filled with secrets and truths. They took in her earnest gaze, lingering on her parted lips and flushed cheeks, absorbing the sight of the flyaway hair that drifted around her face. He seemed to wrestle with himself, weighing up his options, gauging her determination for finding the answer.

"The future." Shadow shrugged. "The past. The present. Soon time will mean almost nothing to you."

Nessa stumbled back a step.

*How can that be?*

*How is that possible?*

She shifted through every memory, every peculiar thought or feeling that she'd had since waking up in the woods all those weeks ago.

There was one particular moment that stood out.

She'd been walking with the others, journeying to Arncraft, and she had rested a hand upon a crumbling wall. Everything around her had changed, and yet it was strangely the same. The wall had reverted to what it had once been, and the trees were fewer and further between, smaller and younger. At the time, Nessa feared that she had momentarily lost her mind, but now, now she saw it for what it really was.

"You're telling the truth," Nessa whispered with

realisation, with wonder. "I've already seen the past once."

"The past?" Shadow gazed down at her with uncertainty. For a split second, Nessa thought she sensed a tingle coming through her Rider's Mark, an emotion that didn't belong to her. Something akin to dismay, possibly even alarm, invaded her being.

*Aoife?*

Scared that she had accidentally let her mental shield drop, Nessa hurriedly checked it. Instantly, she discovered that it was in perfect order. There wasn't a single hole or gap to be found, which meant that Aoife couldn't know who Nessa was with, or what she was doing. If Aoife wasn't behind the mysterious emotion, where did it originate from?

Nessa had no time to figure it out.

Shadow began pacing, his arms folded behind his back in consternation. "That should be impossible. I made it impossible."

"But you just said..." It slowly dawned on her, the pieces finally slotting together. "The mental block," Nessa gasped. "It doesn't just keep my memories locked away, but my powers too." She didn't need him to confirm it. She knew it was true. She could feel the echoes of rightness inside her, things clicking into place. "How could you? How could you do that to me?"

"You know why," Shadow said, voice devoid of guilt or apology. "You've figured it out all by yourself."

"If my powers are suppressed," Nessa muttered angrily, "then the king won't be able to sense me. He won't be able to find me."

Shadow dipped his head, a regal nod.

"But what about my memories?" Nessa demanded.

"Why did you take them from me? What reason was there for that?"

"Trust me. There were—are—many reasons."

"Trust you?" Nessa scowled. "I don't trust you. Not one bit."

"If you had some common sense, you would."

Nessa was outraged. "How dare you! First, you steal my memories and lock away my powers. Then you insult me. You have some bloody nerve, don't you?"

"And no shame," he agreed, darkly amused.

Nessa shook her head, trying to shake away the feeling that she was simply going in circles rather than getting any closer to the issue, treading around it rather than solving it. She was too tired, too torn, to make sense of anything. "It's late, and I can't deal with you, with this. So, unless you're going to kidnap me again, I'm done with this. I'm done with you. And, in all honesty, with today." Nessa turned to leave, taking a few steps towards the stairs.

Shadow had other plans, it seemed. He slid in front of her, as stealthily as a prowling cat, as unyielding as the oldest of mountains, barricading the way, blocking her retreat.

"You might be done with me," Shadow purred dangerously. "But I'm not done with you. Not yet. Not by far."

Nessa swallowed nervously, wishing that she hadn't mentioned kidnapping. It might have given him ideas. "What?" she grumbled, growing timid. Any prior confidence—fire—she'd had swiftly fled. "What do you want?"

Shadow tilted his head to the side, his raven hair shifting and brushing his shoulder. "What makes you think I want anything?"

"You wouldn't be here to start with if not. And you certainly wouldn't be stopping me from leaving if not for ulterior motives."

He smirked. "I'm stopping you from leaving? I'm the only reason why you're not running up those stairs for the safety of your lodgings?

Nessa folded her arms and eyed the stairs mulishly. The eerie mist rolled down them, ghostly and alive in the dancing lantern light. It only had a couple of steps left before it reached the ground. Already, seeking tendrils drifted out from the main body of the mist, curling and searching.

Shadow followed her stare, his shoulders tensing. "Actually," he said. "I think it would be pertinent for us to go our separate ways."

"What?" Nessa's eyebrows shot up. She couldn't have heard him right. "That's it? You're going. Just like that?" she didn't believe it. She couldn't believe it. Surely, she had heard him wrong?

"Just like that," Shadow confirmed. "The hour grows late, and the mist brings ominous tidings."

"Ominous tidings?"

His bearing, faintly amused only a moment ago, turned serious. "I found you this evening for a number of reasons. The foremost was to bring you a warning."

A spike of alarm shot down Nessa's spine. "A warning?"

"Easy now, little wildcat," Shadow murmured. "You're getting 'warning' confused with 'threat'."

"Am I?"

Shadow shrugged.

"Well, go on then," Nessa bit out, bracing herself for

what he could possibly say. It couldn't be anything good, threat or not. After all, he was an enemy Dragon Rider, a disciple of the dark king, a kidnapper and a user of powerful, mind-altering magic. "I'm listening."

Shadow leaned down, encroaching into her personal space. Nessa tensed, ready to back away. She found it too hard to think when he was close, too hard to concentrate. He conjured up too many feelings, all of them mixed and conflicting, confusing and unnerving, as his sapphire-blue eyes locked with hers.

His fingers twitched, and his hand began to rise; Nessa thought he was going to touch her again. With a disturbing level of disappointment, she saw him quickly shove his hands into the pockets of his black overcoat like he was trying to prevent himself from reaching out.

Nessa blinked and then scowled at herself, wondering why she feared his touch and longed for it in equal measure. It was near impossible to push aside her traitorous wants. Her gaze flicked upwards and was instantly ensnared by his. His eyes were tidal pools filled with heat and fervour.

"The night is a dangerous time," Shadow purred, "in a city such as this, especially for young girls. Things are stirring in the dark corners of this world. Creatures of old are awakening, nameless monsters that time has almost forgotten. The mist isn't what it seems. It hides and lies, little wildcat. And you, above all others, should be wary of it."

A chill crept over Nessa, running through her veins, turning her blood to ice. Goosebumps rose on her forearms, and she was forced to hug herself in an attempt to hide her trembling. *The things he said... The grim truths behind them...* Shadow's words, filled with forewarnings and sinister heralding, resonated through her core.

"Why me above all others?" she asked, her voice a hesitant squeak.

"Ah, now, if I wanted you to know the truth of that, I wouldn't have taken your memories away."

Nessa drew in a shocked breath, her spine snapping straight. *How does he have the nerve to be so brazen about such a thing, so matter-of-fact about it?* "Give them back," she demanded. "Give me back my memories."

Shadow shook his head, unapologetic. "No."

"Take down the mental block."

"It's there for your own good."

"I don't believe you. This is just another part of your and Margan's plan. A ploy to make me biddable and compliant with whatever the two of you are doing."

Anger flashed in his eyes, raw and powerful. The space between them, already minimal, vanished as he grabbed her by the upper arms and yanked her against him.

"Don't," Shadow growled down at her, breaths short and hurried, "think for one second that I am anything like Margan, or that I have any shared interests with him. He has his uses. That's as far as our partnership extends"

"Then why?" Nessa whispered. "Why do all of this? Why do any of it?"

Shadow's grip loosened, and his eyes lost a bit of their fire, although they were no less intense. "You'll see. One day, you'll understand everything I've done. It might not be tomorrow or any time soon. But I promise you, you will understand. You will see." He leaned down, his breath softly caressing Nessa's cheek as he shifted just a little, bringing his lips close to her ear. "Not everything is black and white, little wildcat. There are two sides to every story, if not more. Don't go jumping to conclusions before the end; otherwise, you might miss something very, very important."

# Chapter 27

Shadow's parting words still whispered through Nessa's head, haunting and perturbing, as she pushed open the front door of Jerome's guest house. The familiar noise and heat of the establishment rushed past her as she stepped over the threshold, escaping outside in a way that was almost like a greeting of homely spirits.

As the door settled into its frame once more, it nudged Nessa gently in the back, urging her forwards. A desk was positioned in the middle of the vestibule, and a young boy sat behind it, looking more than a little bored. The youngster was one of those employed by Jerome to keep an eye on the comings and goings of his boarders. There was a strict no-guests-without-bookings-allowed-upstairs rule. Only paying tenants were permitted, and their names were neatly logged in a ledger. If any guests had guests of their own, they'd have to entertain them downstairs in the common areas under penalty of a hefty fine and an urgent search for another place to lodge. Jerome wasn't a fan of freeloaders.

Nessa gave the boy a nod of greeting and looked around the vestibule, feeling like she was in a daydream, only half-awake. *Shadow...the revelations...* She felt an uneasy fluttering in her stomach... She'd been expecting an irate duo of babysitters to be in wait, ready to pounce as soon as she stepped through the door. The vestibule, though, was just as it usually was: the scent of tobacco smoke and murmured gossip from adjoining rooms lingered in the air, the small sconces filled the space with cosy light, and the old desk in the centre of the long room, half-blocking the way to the stairs behind it, minimising the chance of anyone sneaking past. There were two doors, one on either side, leading to the common rooms. The one to Nessa's left was for the public house, where food was served and drinks were procured. The one to the right was where the lounge was to be found, with its large inglenook fireplace and circles of soft armchairs and sofas.

Rather than trekking all the way upstairs to Hunter's and Orm's rooms, Nessa planned on checking the public house first. After all, it seemed like the most likely place to find them. They liked alcohol and food, especially at that time of evening. It's where they usually were. It's where she usually was, watching them play card games with a couple of other regulars, trying to figure out the games' rules with little success. The door to the lounge was shut, anyway, indicating that a private meeting was in operation. Whilst unusual, it wasn't entirely uncommon. Sometimes Jerome needed to conduct business talks with his suppliers. Since finding out about his double life, Nessa couldn't help but wonder if some of those meetings were about something other than the running of his guest house.

The public house was noisy and full. Large groups of people drank and laughed in the packed room, socialising and having hearty meals. Nessa scanned the closer tables, keeping an eye out for Orm's noticeable size and shaven head, listening for any hint of Hunter's cursing caused by his friend winding him up by doing or saying something annoying. Which happened quite often, in all honesty.

Neither of them was nearby. Nessa went to explore further into the room, intending to do a circuit before heading upstairs. The sound of a door opening made her pause. She looked over her shoulder, hoping to find Hunter and Orm coming through the front door. It stood to reason that they hadn't pounced on her because they hadn't been there in the first place.

*Are they out looking for me?*

"There you are, lass," Jerome said, standing half-hidden by the lounge's door. "The lads are in here, if ye be searching for them."

"They are?" Nessa went over to him, curious as to why they were involved with one of his private meetings.

"Yeah," Jerome said, his tone not quite as jolly as it usually was. His singular eye was grave as he gazed at her. "There was a bit of trouble down at the docks this eve—"

"Are they okay?" Nessa all but shrieked, alarm clogging her throat. "Were they hurt?"

"They're fine," Jerome quickly declared. "They're perfectly fine. Safe and sound. No harm done. Not so much as a bruise on their handsome bodies."

"You had me worried there for a second," Nessa

sighed, her shoulders sagging in relief. She rested a hand on her chest. Beneath her palm, she felt the heavy thump of her racing heart. It was like it was about to burst through her ribcage.

"Back at you, lass," Jerome chortled, his paw of a hand patting her on the shoulder. "Your eyes went so wide I thought they were about to pop right out of your noggin."

"That would have been gross."

"And very impractical." Jerome opened the door wider by a crack and ushered Nessa through. He swiftly followed her and closed it behind them. "I'll let the boys fill you in with all the happenings." Jerome nodded over to the back of the room, his sparse topknot bobbling with the movement. "They've been eager to see you since they got back." He paused as his attention was caught by someone near a window. "You go on ahead. I need to have some words with a certain scoundrel who's trying to hide behind that man over there, hoping I'm blind enough not to spot his worthless hide."

Nessa gazed after Jerome as he snaked his way through clusters of people, making his way over to the window where she spied the unlucky soul trying to hide between a rather hefty fellow and the curtain. The only shortcoming behind his otherwise highly sophisticated hiding spot was that he was wearing an obnoxiously bright-red doublet. The man he was trying to hide behind just wasn't hefty enough either.

After watching the ensuring confrontation just long enough to be amused, Nessa turned away and scanned the room. Hunter and Orm were in there somewhere.

The lounge was reasonably generous in size, long and low ceilinged, like many of the guest house's rooms. The lack of a bar or an adjoining kitchen allowed for wide circles of old armchairs and sofas. A large inglenook fireplace dominated much of the far wall with its flames roaring, which was always a guaranteed sight, throwing out dancing light that chased away the chill and gloom of encroaching winter. It was the perfect place to spend an evening, snuggled comfortably in one of the old armchairs, reading one of the many books that called the numerous floor-to-ceiling shelves home.

Spying Orm's distinct, shaven head on the other side of the room, Nessa started to make her away over to him. With what seemed like every chair occupied, every sofa overflowing, Nessa wormed around standing groups of men, none of whom seemed to be inclined to move out of her way. She didn't think she had ever seen the lounge this busy before, this jam-packed. There was no joy or revelry, though. The air was thick with tension, full of murmured arguments and discord.

*What happened at the docks?*

They were facing away from her, slouched in a two-seater, a shaven head leaning in close to a mop of messy, brown curls. At the sight of them, Nessa breathed a sigh of relief and flung herself forwards, wrapping her arms around Hunter's neck, uncaring that it was a little awkward and that the sofa's bony back dug into her ribcage.

Hunter jumped, surprised, then promptly relaxed when he realised who it was.

"Why," Hunter laughed, "hello to you too, little adventurer." He shifted, trying to turn around to face her. Nessa tightened her arms and rested her chin on the top of his head, holding him still.

"I'm so glad the two of you are alive," Nessa

murmured, her gaze swivelling to Orm, who had an eyebrow quirked and a glass raised to his lips, taking a sip.

"It appears that Jerome isn't particularly good at informing our late returner of today's events," Orm said, sounding faintly amused.

"So it seems," Hunter mused. "However, there's a silver lining: I get this kind of greeting."

"A silver lining for you, perhaps," Orm grumbled. "I don't get hug."

Nessa grinned. "Do you want a hug?"

"Can I save it for a rainy day?"

"If you want."

Orm shifted, sidling to the side, and patted the narrow gap between him and Hunter. "Come. Sit, little, late adventurer, and we'll fill you in with all the exciting things that have happened since we saw each other last."

"How could I resist such an enticing invitation?" Nessa clambered over the back of the sofa, settling down between them.

"I know." Orm winked. "We're irresistible."

"And modest."

Orm shrugged. "There's no sense denying the truth."

"So," Nessa said, attempting to get comfortable, jostling both of them a little. The sofa was intended for two people, not three. "Jerome mentioned something about *happenings*?"

"Ah. Yes. The happenings." Orm nodded thoughtfully. "And what happenings they are."

"Well," Nessa poked him in the arm with a smile. "Spill." Second only to Nessa's relief that they were safe and unharmed was her relief that they weren't angry about her earlier outburst or her late return.

"Oi, not so fast," Hunter interjected as Orm opened his mouth. "Where in the Nine Devils have you been?" He peered at Nessa, eyes bright. "It got dark over an hour ago."

*So much for thinking that I've got away scot-free...*

Nessa pursed her lips, hoping an acceptable excuse would arise. She didn't think that telling them she'd had a chance encounter with Shadow, their nemesis, would go down particularly well. Besides, Nessa was compelled to keep it a secret, reasoning with herself that she merely needed more time to contemplate all the things Shadow had said and done, to shift through all of her conflicted thoughts and emotions—emotions that only grew deeper and more complex as time went by.

Unbidden, the image of Shadow's eyes, dark and intense, flashed in her mind, kindling unfamiliar feelings.

"I...ah." Nessa cleared her throat. "I was exploring parts of the neighbour—"

"How strange," Orm's eyebrows rose in mock indignation. "I distinctly recall telling you to go to Aoife and then to come straight back?"

Nessa muttered a defensive "I was nearby the whole time." It wasn't strictly true, but what they didn't know wouldn't hurt them.

"Oh? So that's why, when it started to get dark, you rushed right back?"

"I was about to return," Nessa grumbled, the half-lie leaving her lips with relative ease. "But then I bumped into someone I recognised—" Hunter twitched beside her, a sudden spasm that sent his elbow knocking against hers, "...from the den," she continued slowly, gazing at him, curious.

"From the den" got Hunter to relax a touch, although

it looked like he had to force himself to do so. *How strange...*

"The den?" Hunter murmured, looking down at her with a mixture of uncertainty and surprise.

"Yep," Nessa confirmed, nodding as she surreptitiously tried to sneak a peek around the room. There were a few familiar faces, but most of the men were strangers to her. *Perfect*, Nessa decided, *this can work. There's less chance of tripping over the cover story with no-one around to catch me out.* "I ran into someone from the den. He recognised me. I recognised him. We started talking."

"Oh?" Hunter shared an astonished glance with Orm. "Well, that's good. It's really good that you're making friends from the den."

Nessa shrugged. "Yeah. I guess so. But I wouldn't say we're friends. I've only talked to him once."

"Technicalities. It will be nice for you to have someone else to talk with other than us or Jerome at the next meet up."

"Maybe." Nessa's thoughts shot back to the last meet up, as they called it, and Shadow. Would he be there the next time? Why had he even been there to start with?

Nessa couldn't help but frown, silently berating herself for not demanding an explanation from Shadow whilst she'd had the chance.

"So what was his name?" Hunter asked.

Nessa blinked owlishly. "I...uh...don't know."

Orm's glass was suspended in the air just before his lips, his intention of taking a slurp momentarily forgotten. "You don't know?"

Wishing that she had simply made up a name, Nessa nodded.

"You recognised him from the den, talked with him

for a good long while, and yet you don't know his name?"

"I'm good at remembering faces, not names. What was I meant to do, ask for it at the end? That would have been embarrassing."

"Yeah," Hunter mused. "That would be a bit awkward."

"Thanks," Nessa muttered dryly. "I'm glad you agree."

"You're welcome."

"Now," Nessa turned to Orm. "I've answered your questions. It's time for you to answer mine. What are these so-called happenings you and Jerome have mentioned?"

Orm finished his drink in one go, throwing back his head. "Ah, yes," he swiped his hand across his mouth, "the happenings. I suppose we can get into all of that if you want to."

"I want to."

"Fine then. But first things first. I need a refill, and you need a drink." Orm leaned forwards, reaching out for the rounded bottle that sat on the low table in front of their sofa. Snapping it up, he pulled free the cork and sloshed a measure of amber liquid into the glass tumbler. "That's for you," he handed Nessa the tumbler, "and this is for me." He patted the bottle fondly as he settled back.

Nessa peered at her drink, sniffing it tentatively. "Is this brandy?"

"Yep. Jerome brought out the good stuff once we got back. Drink as much as you can before he remembers that he should be charging."

"Um…" Nessa held out the tumbler to Hunter, "are you sure you don't want this?"

Hunter flicked a matching glass tumbler that was perched precariously on the arm of the sofa, half-full with caramel-coloured liquid. "Already have one."

"Okey-dokey." Nessa took a sip, feeling the smooth burn cruising down her throat, settling in her stomach, warming her from the inside. "We are all beveraged up, which is always crucial, so let's get down to business."

Orm blinked. "Business?"

"The happenings," Hunter supplied, shaking his head slowly in despair. "She wants to know about what happened earlier." He looked down at Nessa. "Orm's already had a bottle to himself. He'll be less than useful to us by the time he gets through that one."

"Is he ever useful?"

"Har-de-har, you two," Orm muttered, rolling his eyes, cradling the brandy bottle in the crook of his elbow like it was a treasured newborn. "Very funny."

"I thought so," Hunter sniggered. "Anyway, the happenings, as we seem to be calling them, have apparently happened a couple of times before. They just haven't been linked until now."

"Oh." *Intriguing prologue*, Nessa thought, "So the happenings have been happening for a while?"

Hunter nodded. "For a couple of months now. At first, it was all chalked up as a bit of misfortune, a handful of unfortunate accidents. However, after what we all saw this evening," he shivered, "the truth has come to light."

"And left us with a lot more questions than answers," Orm added.

"I know it's giving me very few answers and a lot of questions," Nessa said with bemusement. "You know, seeing as I wasn't there to see it."

Hunter blinked. "Oh yeah. I suppose I should start at

the beginning."

"That might be helpful."

"Well, Orm and I went down to the docks this morning, just as we were meant to, and met up with Bo and Luca, and a number of these other fine fellows." Hunter waved a hand to the crowded room. "Our work was simple, if a bit more boring than I was expecting. We were just loading up a ship that was bound for Vasindor."

"We weren't even loading it up with anything particularly interesting," Orm informed Nessa. "Just some concealed goods that were being smuggled out of the city."

Nessa smirked. "So the *mere* act of smuggling concealed goods on a ship isn't interesting enough for you?"

"I suppose it's alright." Orm shrugged. "But I was imagining something more cloak and dagger, something a lot more, you know, high stakes. Done under the cover of darkness, with lookouts and secret codewords and such. You know, not during the day right in front of everyone. Wasn't very exciting."

"What a shame."

"I know, right?" Orm shook his head. "Here I was, expecting so much more from a criminal organisation than simply putting rum into coloured wine bottles to avoid taxes."

"I think a bit more effort than that goes into it," Hunter said. "Besides, they do other things than just smuggle rum. But we're getting off subject."

Orm grumbled something under his breath and took a swig from his bottle, sulking.

"After we finished loading the ship," Hunter

continued, settling into storytelling mode, "it was just starting to get dark, and with the last bit of light, the ship set off. We were still on the docks, cleaning up crates and stuff, when this eerie mist appeared out of nowhere."

Nessa's heart skipped a beat. The cold touch of trepidation crept over her. To steady her growing nerves, she took a sip of brandy, hoping that it would warm her, soothe her.

"It rolled in so fast, so suddenly; it was like it rose from the waters themselves," Hunter was saying. "The ship was only a hundred or so yards out, but we could barely see it. Everything was fine one moment, quiet and peaceful. Then this otherworldly mist appeared and it was... It was..."

"There were *things* in that mist," Orm murmured, his gaze going distant, haunted. "I could feel them, sense them. Hear them. But I couldn't see them. They were there, and yet, somehow, they weren't." Orm stared at his lap, suddenly meditative and distant.

Hunter turned and leaned closer to Nessa, trying to avoid Orm hearing his next words. "As the mist rolled in, Orm got all jittery, started muttering and chanting strange shit. I don't even know what. Couldn't understand a word he said. Neither could a couple of guys who were standing nearby."

"Can't Orm tell you?" Nessa asked.

Hunter shook his head. "Every time I bring it up, he goes all odd. Kind of like how he is now: quiet and with that vague, faraway look in his eyes. Gives me the creeps."

"It is a bit creepy," Nessa agreed, peering at Orm from the corner of her eye. "It's like he's here, but not really."

"Mmm," Hunter picked up his glass tumbler, holding

it lightly by his fingertips, twirling it gently, watching as the brandy swirled, fetching up a little whirlpool. "Orm went all batshit crazy, saying that there were things in the mist. Then all this screaming started coming from the boat. Blood curdling screams. And... And sounds I can't even begin to describe. Inhuman sounds." His throat worked, his Adam's apple bobbing up and down as he tried to suppress a tide of emotions. Nessa tucked herself against his side, chilled to the bone. The roaring fire and the brandy did nothing to dispel the frosty grip of foreboding that wrapped around her heart, its clawed talons digging in.

"As quickly as the mist appeared," he murmured, "did it vanish, disappearing like it had never been. The boat was gone too. Nothing remained of it but a splintered mast and a handful of debris that bobbed on the water's surface."

"And the crew?" Nessa croaked, barely able to ask.

Wordlessly, Hunter shook his head.

"The screams..."

"The ship was close enough to the docks that even if it had run aground and sank, the crew could have easily swum ashore. But no one did. An entire crew. Gone. Just like that."

"What...what could have done something like that?"

Hunter shrugged. "Haven't got the faintest idea. It seems that no one does. Not really. Nothing that makes much sense."

"You said something about this happening before?"

"Yeah." Hunter peered over his shoulder, scanning the room. Nessa followed his gaze, her eyes locking onto Jerome standing in the far corner, surrounded by a circle of grim-faced men. "They're still going through the ledgers, letters and who knows what else, but they're slowly piecing everything together. At least, as much as they can at this point."

"So they've already uncovered something?"

"As much as we're able to tell, this has happened a few times before." Hunter met Nessa's shocked stare. "Mostly in the last couple of months."

"And they didn't notice anything until now? You're telling me that they haven't noticed entire ships disappearing?"

"They noticed," Hunter murmured, finding her astonishment amusing. "Of course they've noticed entire ships missing. More accurately, they've noticed their shipments not turning up."

"Oh."

"Whatever's happening isn't just limited to the smugglers' ships," Hunter said, his eyes brightening with speculation. "It's happened to a number of legitimate merchants, and even some well-known pirate ships."

"Not Orm's pirate lady friend, I hope."

"No such luck," Hunter sighed. "Maybe next time."

Nessa slapped him on his upper arm. "What a thing to say. Especially after what's happened."

"You chastise," Hunter sipped from his glass tumbler, "only because you haven't met her."

"Well, if pirate ships are on the mist's hit list," Nessa muttered, "then I may never get the chance."

"It's not just ships that the mist's interested in," Hunter mused. "So there's still a chance of her disappearing."

"What do you mean?"

"I mean, it's not just ships being targeted, but people too."

"People?"

Hunter nodded. "It's hard to come up with clear numbers. Ships are a little easier to keep track of, thanks to dock records and such. But even so, an exact number is still a tricky thing to pinpoint, what with some sinking due to incompetent crews or being stolen. People, as it turns out, are near on impossible to monitor. People vanish all the time without a trace."

"If that's the case," Nessa frowned, disturbed by the idea that the mist, or whatever lurked within it, was not only destroying ships, but stealing people too, "how do you know it's *not* just ships that are disappearing?"

"Because of *who* has disappeared."

Nessa sagged back against the tired sofa, knowing that Hunter was enjoying himself more than he really should be. He had a mystery to solve and a steady supply of alcohol. Nessa could tell that she was in for another long night filled with wild speculations and far-fetched stories.

*Sigh.*

༄ ♦ ༅

Listening with scepticism, Nessa waited for Hunter to finish with his narrative. As an eyewitness, Hunter knew without a doubt that something sinister had lurked within the mist, something evil and bloodthirsty. Nessa, though, couldn't help but be doubtful. At least, she was to start with. Yes, she'd been in the mist too. She had experienced the unsettling awareness of being followed, of being watched. But she hadn't vanished, hadn't disappeared alongside the mist as it had sunk into the ground, called back to whatever haunting abyss it had surely been summoned from.

Nevertheless, the idea of creatures moving unseen in the mist was chilling, especially if they were destroying ships and spiriting away unfortunate souls. Nessa didn't understand any of it, even as Hunter recounted accounts from traders. They were tales that were known to her; she had heard them all before. They were stories that involved eerie mists seen from afar, and of tall, antlered figures who lurked within. Nessa had been hearing such tales for weeks now, drunken ramblings from men who were less than reliable sources. Nessa had written them off as nothing more than made up fancies from fabulists. The stories had been interesting listening material during long nights whilst Hunter and Orm gambled and networked. Now, though, they held a threatening tone.

*Antlered men and ominous mists,* Nessa mused silently. *It's like something from a twisted bedtime story.*

The mist from earlier wasn't natural or normal, Nessa was sure of that. She could feel it in her bones. It had come and gone too fast. It had been too thick and concealing.

It had felt alive.

The more Hunter rambled on, the more places Nessa's mind went, jumping from one thought to another, dancing through a whole plethora of wild ideas. Her head was in a jumble, a chaotic mess. The pieces of the puzzle refused to go together.

Hunter muttered something about motive, his fingers tapping meditatively against his almost empty tumbler. Orm grumbled about how Chaos would know what was going on, about how he would say that the answer was staring them in the face.

*Chaos.*

Something clicked.

An answer arose.

"Old Bloods," Nessa gasped. "It has to have something to do with Old Bloods."

# Chapter 28

Orm was knocked out of his trauma-induced stupor, and faster than Nessa could have imagined, he shot upright, dragging her with him. She barely had time to grab Hunter, catching a fistful of his tunic, before she was being pulled through the room, up three flights of stairs, and unceremoniously shoved into her bedroom.

Shocked and out of breath, Nessa staggered over to her narrow bed, barely taking notice of the room's darkness. She settled down onto the edge of the mattress and realised that she was still clutching the front of Hunter's top.

"What," Hunter gasped as Nessa forced her fingers to uncurl, releasing him, "in the Nine Devils do you think you're doing?"

Orm sagged back against the door, the wood creaking under the strain, and clicked his fingers sharply. Green sparks whizzed around the little room, darting this way and that in a frenzied dance that was hard for the eye to follow. One by one they settled on the blackened wicks of the small number of candles that were scattered across the chest of draws and the nightstand. A singular spark shot into the fireplace that was still overflowing with ash.

Light bloomed, soft and warm, and tinged with green hues. It brushed against the cheery yellow walls and the exposed beams, chasing away the chill of winter nights and haunting stories. Nessa turned her gaze away from the fireplace, done with watching conjured flames, and looked at Orm, whose cheeks were a lively pink as he held a hand to his side, pressing against a stitch.

Orm blinked owlishly at Hunter, who stood in the middle of the room, hunched over and breathing deeply, trying to regain his breath after their mad dash upstairs.

"What am I doing? I'm lighting the room." Orm crossed over to the fireplace and threw in a couple of logs. Plumes of ash puffed outwards. "Why, do you want us to be in complete darkness? That's a bit strange, Hunter."

Glaring at Orm's back, Hunter muttered, "You know that's not what I was talking about."

"Obviously not."

"Why did you drag us up here like a demented demon?"

"Maybe because he *is* a demented demon?" Nessa's scowl went from focusing on Orm to eyeing the wet patch that streaked down the front of her skirts, seeping through the layers of cloth, making them stick uncomfortably to her thigh. She plucked at it mournfully. "I spilt my drink. I was beginning to enjoy that drink."

"I managed to keep a hold of mine." Hunter held up his glass and had to correct himself. "Well, some of it."

"Looks like there are a few more stains on the stairs." Nessa pouted. "I think it's time for Jerome to do a revamp."

"And what," Hunter smirked, "give up the illusion that he isn't a key figure in an underground smuggling ring and probably loaded?"

"I suppose he does have a certain image to uphold," Nessa mused. "Jerome the poor, one-eyed innkeeper. It might be seen as strange for someone in the Stickworks to have any kind of clean or newish furnishings."

"Oh, Nessa. We're in the Stickworks. You're lucky this place has glass windows. How many other places in this neighbourhood have you seen with glass windows? Windowpanes aren't cheap here in the capital."

Nessa had to admit that buildings with glass windowpanes were few and far between in the Stickworks. They were considered a luxury, something that many households chose to go without. People preferred to save their coin to move elsewhere, or to fill their empty bellies at the end of the day. The Stickworks was home to the lower class; it was a mere step or two above a slum. The buildings were ramshackle, built by inexperienced labourers over the decades, the layout ill-planned and crowded. The windows were small, and the walls were thin, constructed mainly from wattle and daub, with large, wooden beams keeping the buildings standing relatively upright. It was a place few wanted to live their lives in, yet many did, trapped there by the circumstance of birth.

"Forget about glass windowpanes," Orm muttered, striding over to the window and yanking the curtains shut, concealing their own glass panes. "They're not important right now."

Nessa watched Orm as he fidgeted nervously. "I think the people who don't have them during the winter would disagree."

Orm waved away Nessa's words with an agitated air and took a swig from his bottle. Of course, he had managed to keep a hold of it. Nothing could come between Orm and a decent drink, not even running from the room like a demented demon, as Hunter had so wonderfully put it.

"Downstairs," Orm said earnestly, his whisky-coloured eyes shining bright as they settled on Nessa, "you said something. Why, why did you say that?"

Nessa stared, more than a little alarmed by Orm's intensity. "What? What did I say?"

"Old Bloods," Hunter supplied quickly. "You said that it could be Old Bloods?"

Orm snapped his fingers and pointed to Hunter, nodding in consensus.

"Am I in trouble?" Nessa looked between them. "You're making me feel like I'm in trouble."

"You're not in trouble," Hunter soothed as he settled down beside her, the mattress dipping under the combined weight. "At least, I don't think you are."

"What makes you think Old Bloods have anything to do with what's happening?" Orm began pacing, which was a tedious thing to attempt in Nessa's snug little room. "Out of all the possible scenarios, why Old Bloods?"

"Well," Nessa said slowly, "there aren't that many possible scenarios. That's the one which makes the most sense."

Orm waved her on, his expression somewhere between reflection and alarm.

"Think about it," Nessa continued, trying to sort her jumbled hypothesis into cohesiveness. "Who—*what*— would be able to summon strange and mysterious mists out of nowhere? Who could have so much hatred for humans that they would destroy entire ships and actually have the strength to do so? And who, judging by the few eyewitness accounts, would stand like a man but also have large antlers?"

"Old Bloods," Hunter muttered, swallowing nervously.

Nessa shrugged. "They have means and motive, from the way I see it. After all, they have been hunted to near extinction under King Kaenar's rule. They have quite the excuse to be attacking anything they can get their hands on, especially anything to do with humans."

"Old Bloods clearly aren't quite as extinct as everyone thought they were," Hunter mused. "Considering that Chaos had gone undetected for so long, and let's not forget about Nessa here. There's also your father, Orm. You might not know who or where he is, but you know without a doubt that he's one of them. There may be more Old Bloods who have managed to hide and avoid detection."

*A lot more...*

"Maybe they've had enough of hiding," Nessa murmured. "Maybe some of them are taking a stand, fighting back in any way they can."

Orm looked troubled. "If it is an Old Blood, then why now? Why all of a sudden? Perhaps it's simply one of the king's games. Something to inspire fear, to keep the public in line."

"If it's the king doing all of this," Hunter mused. "If he's behind the mist and the vanishing people, then why attack his own forces? He's had two ships vanish in the last month, both of them disappearing soon after leaving Dayon."

"Why does the king do any of the things he does?" Orm stopped pacing. "Why is he calling back the other Dragon Riders? Why did he raze Arncraft to the ground? Why did he kill Chaos?"

Hunter opened his mouth, but there was no answer forthcoming. He couldn't come up with a reasonable explanation.

Orm did, though.

"He's a monster," Orm said quietly. "Monsters don't need reasons or excuses. He's the undisputed ruler of these lands. There's no one and nothing to stand in his way. He can do whatever he wants, whatever he fancies, and there will never be any consequences for him. If he wants to throw a lavish ball, then he'll throw a lavish ball. If he wants to burn a town to the ground, then he'll burn a town to the ground. It's as simple as that."

Hunter was subdued, his shoulders hunched. "Maybe an Old Blood has had enough. Maybe the tides are changing. Maybe the Old Bloods are playing a game of their own with the king."

"That's a lot of maybes, Hunter. An awful lot of them."

Nessa sighed. "Something's happening, though. Something big and unnatural." Her mind went back to Shadow and his warning. "We can't ignore this."

"No," Orm agreed. "We shouldn't ignore this. Nor can we." He took a shuddering breath and shook his head. "If only Chaos was here. He would know what's going on. He would be able to help."

Hunter stood and clapped a hand on Orm's shoulder.

"Don't fret about it, old chap. We'll figure it out. You know we will."

Mulishly, Orm nodded. "We'll go out tomorrow. We'll ask more specific questions and see if the answers reveal anything."

Hunter grinned. "There's the problem-solving spirit I know and love."

"Are we going to tell Jerome and his friends?" Nessa asked. "Give them a heads-up, you know? Try to stop something like this eve's *happenings* from happening again?"

"I'll think about it," Orm murmured.

Nessa's eyebrows shot up. She must have heard him wrong. "You'll think about it?"

"Yep. I'll give it a bit of thought."

"Isn't that," Nessa's gaze went to Hunter, searching for an ally, "I don't know, a little morally reprehensible?"

"Oooh, *reprehensible*," Orm chuckled. "Look who's using all the big words."

Nessa rolled her eyes and gave a long-suffering sigh. "If we have information that could save someone's life, most likely multiple people's lives, then shouldn't we share it?"

"If we had rock-solid information that could save people's lives, then yeah, we would share it," Hunter said slowly. "But so far, we only have an idea, a very plausible and somewhat chilling idea." He hastily added when he spied Nessa's growing scowl, "but an idea nonetheless."

"Even then," Orm added, "I'd still have to give it a bit thought. I don't want to divulge useful information needlessly if it hinders our cause."

"Orm," Nessa grumbled in warning. She wasn't sure she approved of or liked his train of thought.

"Nessie," Orm whinged, his eyes twinkling with brandy-induced intelligence. "Think about all of this," he waved a hand, indicating to her room and the building it was in. "It's easy to forget that Jerome is part of a much larger network. But he is. He's one of many in charge of and operating a kingdom-wide smuggling ring. He and those he works with aren't stupid or without means."

"And that prevents us from being helpful, decent human beings?" Nessa crossed her arms, glaring at Orm, her displeasure evident.

"Woah, little, angry Dragon Rider," Orm held up his hands in placating manner. "I have a moral code. I don't want any innocent person to come to harm under my watch. However, you shouldn't confuse the people downstairs as innocent people. Now, I like them as much as the next self-respecting, binge-drinking petty criminal, but I'm not going to go out of my way and run downstairs to give them a load of help without getting something for my—our—troubles first."

"These people trade in more than just goods," Hunter elaborated. "They also trade in information."

Nessa sucked in a breath. "So, what you're saying is, if we gather some solid evidence to support my Old Blood hypothesis, you want to trade that information for something else?"

Orm nodded. "An exchange of information. Maybe a favour."

"And then what?" she asked, feeling a kind of weariness that went beyond her years, a terrible tiredness that was slowly seeping into her bones. "What good is a favour in all of this? What good is a favour versus the king and all the people he has at his command? People and monsters and dragons. How is a *favour* going to help us compete against all of that? We're nothing compared to him."

"That's just what he wants you to think," Hunter murmured. "I'm sure the all-powerful king isn't actually all-powerful."

Nessa didn't agree. Once again, she was back in Arncraft, standing in the town's burning square with the king and his monster dragon. She'd seen the look in his dark eyes, the power and the surety born from five centuries of being the ruler of the Twelve Kingdoms. People had stood against him, entire armies, and he had crushed them with the barest of effort. Even other Dragon Riders, who should have been his equal, kneeled before him.

"You don't think that, do you?"

"It's a nice thought to have," Hunter said with a shrug of his shoulder. "You have to admit it. Let me have my nice thought."

"Fine," Nessa relented, pushing aside her doubts for now. "I'll let you have it. Just for a little bit."

Hunter gave her a playful wink. "Thank you, O Kind One."

Orm grunted, took a swig of his bottle, and crossed over to the door. He cracked it open and paused in the threshold.

"Get some rest, kids," he said over his shoulder. "It's been a long day, and tomorrow holds no promise of being any less taxing."

"Get some rest, kids?" Nessa repeated, a little bewildered. "That's it? You're off to bed?"

"Kids?" Hunter muttered, quietly outraged.

"Off to bed?" Orm laughed. "Off to bed? What a funny notion."

Nessa shook her head, waiting for him to finish having fun at her expense.

"Off to bed," Orm chortled, wiping a stray tear from the corner of his eye. "Ah, no. Alas, no. I'm going downstairs to see if the guys have uncovered anything else of interest, and to get me another one of these beauties." He held up the brandy bottle, shaking it, making the last mouthful slosh from side to side. Then, as sly as a snake, he slipped through the door, quietly closing it behind him.

"Kids," Hunter said, affronted, staring after Orm. "Did he seriously call us kids?"

"I do believe he did."

"The giant, arrogant turd."

Nessa snorted, dark thoughts of a dark king giving way to amusement. "Turd?"

"You heard me."

"Glad Orm didn't. You would have hurt his feelings."

"It would have been deserved for the 'kid' remark."

"Justifiable," Nessa agreed with mock seriousness. "After all, we are mature, sophisticated adults."

"Damn right we are," Hunter added, rejoining her on the bed, perching on the edge of the mattress. He was close enough for their arms to brush against each other's with the slightest movement. "We deserve nothing but the utmost respect."

"The utmost."

"And the occasional gift."

"Gifts?" Nessa grinned. "Aren't you being a little demanding? Respect *and* gifts?"

Cheeks turning pink, Hunter said, "I didn't necessarily say the gifts were for me."

"Then who would they be…" Nessa's question faded

away when Hunter pulled something from his pocket: a dainty parcel of neatly folded velvet.

With an unusual amount of shyness, Hunter slipped it into Nessa's hand, curling her fingers around it.

"I've...uh..." He cleared his throat nervously, his gaze lowered, fastened onto the square of mauve velvet, "...been meaning to have it done for a while now, but I couldn't find someone who...um...I felt would be able to keep everything under the table. Someone who wouldn't ask any unwanted questions."

Her fingers trembling with eagerness, with excitement, Nessa set the little pocket of soft velvet on her lap. Slowly, leisurely, she lifted back the corners, revealing the treasure inside. Nessa's breath caught in her throat when she realised what was nestled in the soft velvet.

A jewellery set, a necklace and a bangle, beautiful and delicate, slightly mismatched yet clearly meant to go together, was perfectly cushioned and sweetly presented.

With the lightest of touches, Nessa held up the necklace, the silver chain as fine as spider webs between her fingertips. She angled it so that the linked pendant charms caught in the merry candlelight, silver and gems twinkling.

There were three of them, joined together in a line by a tiny jump ring, a trio of deep-purple gems that seemed to have a soft inner light. They were framed in a decorative, silver bezel, the edges carefully rounded over to hold the smooth gems firmly in place. Rather than having a solid back, each of the settings had been embellished with an image carefully cut out to make a clear silhouette, the silver perfectly highlighted against the purple of the gems.

Nessa stared at the necklace, at the charms, at a loss for words. They were so beautiful, so delicate and unique.

"The castle is Ironguard," Hunter murmured, one fingertip gently tapping the first of the three charms; the castle charm reminded Nessa of a dark crown, tall and jagged. "The place where everything changed for us. And the mountains," the second charm, "are where the Hidden City is—was—and where we met up with Orm and Chaos. The dragon, of course, represents—"

"Aoife," Nessa breathed, running the pad of her thumb over the last of the trio of charms, the one that featured the silhouette of a dragon in flight.

"Aoife," Hunter confirmed with a shy smile. "I...ah...wanted to give you something with meaning. The more I thought about it, the more I felt that those three things, as of so far, hold the most... um...importance, I suppose. Significance."

Nessa's eyes jumped from charm to charm, the meaning behind each little image, from the sweep of dainty mountains to the cruel shape that was Ironguard, slowly sinking in.

"It's the best the silversmith could do," Hunter said, self-consciousness making him fill the void of awed silence with chitchat, "given how small the pieces are, and the timeframe I gave him. So they're not exactly the most detailed. But, you know..."

"Oh, Hunter," Nessa turned and wrapped her arms around his neck, pulling him close, "it's beautiful. You really shouldn't have. It must have cost a fortune."

"A small price to pay." Hunter murmured, his breath softly brushing against the shell of her ear as he relaxed into her embrace, propping his chin on her shoulder. An arm curled around Nessa's back, a hand resting lightly on the dip of her waist.

"Mmm, for what?" Nessa's eyes fluttered closed, her body melding against his. He was warmth and comfort, familiarity and friendship. He was her anchor, one of the few things that kept the coldness of loneliness at bay, a wall that blocked out the doubts and questions that would often plague her troubled mind.

"To see you smile."

Nessa pulled back, just enough for her to see his face, to see the mixture of emotions in his amber eyes, making them shine bright.

"There we go. My mission for today has been successful," Hunter said quietly. "I do believe I've successfully cheered you up."

"What makes you think I needed cheering up?"

Hunter's lips twitched as he struggled to hold back a grin. "Just a hunch."

"A hunch?"

"Yep. Pure guesswork."

"Impressive guessing."

"Thank you muchly."

Their eyes locked together, and there were so many things going through Nessa's head, so many thoughts and feelings. He was there for her, had been all along, no matter what obstacle stood in the way. Nessa's memories didn't extend back more than a month and a half, and yet she knew, without a doubt, that there was a deep understanding between them, a connection, something that was indistinguishable from friendship, and yet was so much more than just that...

A look that was akin to sadness, to longing, skittered across Hunter's face. Seemingly forcing himself to,

Hunter sat back, retreating. His hand lingered on Nessa's side a moment or two before withdrawing, slipping down onto the mattress beside him, a divider keeping a small gap between them. Hunter's gaze ran over Nessa's face and then focused on the velvet square on her lap.

"So, the necklace is a keeper," he coughed. "But what about the bracelet?"

Nessa frowned, dismayed to find herself already missing his proximity and warmth, even though he hadn't moved all that far away. She plucked up the bracelet in distraction.

Something about the design made a shiver run up her spine. She ran her fingers reverently over the fine silver wire that formed the rigid body of the torc bangle. It had been woven somehow, the pattern looking like it had been knitted. The candlelight made the threads twinkle and gleam in a mesmerising manner as Nessa held it up. A terminal featuring a small, dark-purple gem that perfectly matched those of the necklace finished off each end of the bangle.

Nessa brushed a thumb over the smooth dome of a cabochon, murmuring, "These are beautiful." She couldn't help but notice that their colour was the exact shade of Aoife's scales. "The style...hope you don't mind me saying this, but it reminds me of the neck torc's worn by the Dragon Riders."

Hunter grinned. "That's what I was aiming for."

"Really?" Nessa was stunned. "Why?"

"Well, you are a Dragon Rider. It's your right to wear a torc. It's a tradition. After a dragon hatches, some of the eggshell is saved and incorporated into the piece."

Nessa's eyes widened. "So these aren't just any gemstones, they're actually from Aoife's egg?"

"You saved a couple of pieces after she'd hatched," Hunter explained. "After you had been taken, I found them in your bag." He shrugged like it wasn't a big deal. "I've been keeping them safe. You can't have a neck torc at the moment because, you know, it may draw a bit of unwanted attention, what with the laws and the penalties."

"Ah, yes," Nessa murmured. "The laws and penalties. And what delightful laws and penalties they are."

"Yeah, those pesky rules." Hunter laughed. "I mean, why can't people from outside the Houses wear neck torcs? I think they make for a fine fashion statement."

"A fine fashion statement that could lead to a beheading."

Hunter grimaced. "I still feel like that's a bit of a harsh punishment for wearing a bit of jewellery."

"It's not the jewellery per se, but what it symbolises."

Nessa's eyes went to her makeshift desk, to the piles of books and notes that sat there. They were old books, their spines cracked and broken, their pages creased and stained. On those pages were hundreds of years' worth of history, bits and pieces that had been collected by a small group of people who had been forgotten by most.

It was from those books that Nessa learned much of what she knew about the Twelve Houses, their family histories and their past Dragon Riders. The information was, of course, supplemented by Hunter and Orm's knowledge. Which, if you asked Nessa, was often a little biased and over-exaggerated. The books, however, were more impartial, factual, a simple retelling of the history of the Twelve Houses up until a few decades ago.

Impartial to a certain degree.

It was a subtle thing, how the scholars slowly but

steadily put forth the notion that those belonging to the Houses were somehow better than the general populous, a step above everyone else. They never said it outright, and Nessa got a sense that it was grudgingly admitted, but it was there if you read between the lines.

"They're another way for the Dragon Riders to differentiate themselves from everyone else, a clear display that the Riders are more elite, more special."

"Considering they have dragons mystically bound to them," Hunter said, "I would have to agree with that, as much as I hate to."

"But it means so much more than that," Nessa insisted. "Because of the spell used to bind dragons and humans together, only a handful of people can ever dream of becoming a Dragon Rider. Instead, they fantasise about moving up in the world, finding their fortune and joining the upper class. They might even have aspirations of marrying into nobility. These are all achievable things, albeit incredibly hard. However, there is something, no matter how well they do in life, which they can never have."

"A torc?"

"Exactly. Not even other members of the Houses can wear them. They used to, back before King Kaenar came into power. But he swiftly changed that. The torcs, even though they are a piece of jewellery, are a clear display of how the Dragon Riders are a step above everyone else, even within the Twelve Houses. They're kind of like a crown."

"But they're not a crown."

"No, they're not," Nessa agreed. "And that's because only the king is allowed to wear a crown."

"Because he wants to show everyone else that he's a

tier above them, even his own Dragon Riders."

"You should read the books." She nodded to her makeshift desk. "You might become enlightened."

"I'm enlightened enough as it is," Hunter said, eyeing the books with a certain amount of distrust. "If I were to read all those many, many, really, really thick books, I fear I might become over enlightened. And trust me, we don't want that to happen."

"Don't we?"

Hunter shook his head. "No, we don't. I wouldn't be able to pull off the whole glowing thing."

"Glowing thing?" Nessa laughed. "That's not what enlightened means."

"I know that. Can't believe you actually thought I didn't, though. How foolish do you think I am?"

"Quite foolish."

Hunter shook his head, grinning like the fool he surely was. "Silly girl."

"Hey, I'm an enlightened, silly girl. Get your insults right. I've read those books through and through. I've even made notes."

Hunter grimaced. "You have far too much time on your hands. You need to get a better hobby. Perhaps you should take up knitting, or maybe watercolour painting?"

"I think I'll pass on those two options, thank you very much. I'm not a sixty-year-old widow."

"Hey, my mother paints *and* knits, I'll have you know. And she's nowhere close to being sixty." Hunter snapped his fingers, his eyes going bright. "I know. I know just what we need."

Nessa murmured a quiet, "Oh dear." *This can't be good.*

"We need to pick up on your combat lessons," Hunter continued, pretending not to hear her. "Start teaching you how to use weapons as well as your fists. That's a far better use of your time than just sitting in here reading boring, old books. If you ask me."

"No one had." Nessa blinked, then frowned in thought. "Pick up my combat lessons? As in continue from where we left off? Like we had actually started such a thing to begin with?"

Hunter waved a hand. "Of course we did, although you didn't appreciate it much. Nor were you particularly good at it."

Nessa scowled.

"Thinking about it," Hunter looked at her in a considering way, "we did only have a couple of lessons. It wasn't like you had much of a chance to improve."

"Combat lessons," Nessa muttered, a little fearful of what that might entail.

"Yeah," Hunter said, enthused. "We'll cover punching and kicking, and let's not forget about throws. Then we'll get you used to handling small blades before we move onto a bit of sword fighting."

"Sword fighting? You're not serious, are you?"

"I'm deadly serious." Hunter nudged her with his elbow. "This is going to happen whether you like it or not. Prepare yourself for bruises and aching muscles."

"But the bruises from Arncraft have only just gone," Nessa said morosely. "I rather like being unbruised."

"I'm sure you're a fast learner and will pick up the blocking techniques in no time. Besides, you're a Dragon Rider. Fighting and causing grievous bodily harm is in your blood."

Nessa thumped him on the arm.

"Ow." Hunter rubbed the throbbing spot. "See? That's what I'm talking about. You're already fulfilling your dark Dragon Rider destiny."

Nessa gazed down at the pieces of jewellery in her hand, her thumb rubbing gently over the smooth dome of one of the torc bangle's gems. A gem, Nessa had to remind herself, which was actually a fragment of dragon eggshell, an eggshell that had been shattered when her very own dragon had hatched for her. A dragon who, at that very moment in time, was angry at her.

Shoulder's slumping, Nessa sighed. She didn't feel like a strong and capable Dragon Rider right then.

Hunter misread the direction of Nessa's thoughts. "Aww, don't get all upset," he murmured hastily, his eyes going wide. "I was only playing around. I know you'd never go around maiming people willy-nilly. You are, without doubt, my favouritest Dragon Rider."

"I know you're only joking," Nessa said reassuringly, offering Hunter a small half-smile. "I'm not upset. Not at all."

"Really?" Hunter was dubious. "Because you're starting to look all depressed again."

Nessa played with the jewellery, her fingers toying with the gems and silver. "All this talk of Dragon Riders made me abruptly remember that Aoife and I had a falling out earlier. We don't seem to be on speaking terms at the moment."

"Ah, yes," Hunter nodded. "She did sound a bit flustered when she chatted with me and Orm at lunchtime. I do believe the words 'stubborn' and 'pigheaded' were used."

Nessa groaned.

"Plus a few other less-than-flattering terms."

"So I can imagine."

"You wanna tell me what the two of you were

bickering about? Aoife failed to give specifics."

"I don't want to discuss it," Nessa muttered, earlier hurt resurfacing. "However, I fear I'm going to have to if I want to put it behind us."

Hunter clapped her on the shoulder and rose unsteadily to his feet. The brandy was starting to take effect. "Build those bridges, little Dragon Rider. We can't have a Rider without a dragon, now, can we?"

Wordlessly, Nessa shook her head and watched as Hunter retreated from her room, shutting the door softly behind him. She gazed after him for a second, instantly missing the company. Without him, her room seemed to take on a sudden chill, feeling big and empty. Her gaze lowered and came to rest on the necklace that Hunter had commissioned specially for her. More accurately, her gaze came to rest on the silver silhouette of a dragon on one of the pendants.

Nessa tapped it thoughtfully with a thumb, resigning herself to the headache she was to receive once she lowered her mental shield. No one said that being bound to a dragon was an easy or pain-free experience.

Clutching the necklace and bangle tight, Nessa reached out to Aoife.

# Chapter 29

Perhaps divine intervention saw to Nessa being at the right place at just the right time. Perhaps it was mere chance. But in Nessa's opinion, that seemed less poetic, and certainly a lot less mystical.

She stood at the side of the street, staring at the shop front with mild disbelief, feeling like her eyes were playing tricks on her even as she watched Sissy push open the shop's door and step inside.

Out of all the places in the city, out of the one million people who lived there, and from the long list of shops that Nessa had been instructed to visit, what was the likelihood of her happening upon someone she knew?

Fancying the notion that fate was having a small role to play in what would otherwise be viewed as a coincidence, Nessa looked down at the small scrap of paper in her hand, eyes running over the messy lines of hastily scribbled names.

Orm had written them down that morning, bleary-eyed and hungover, and with a lot more enthusiasm and determination than he had any right to have. Over breakfast, he had compiled three lists of names, one for each of them to slowly work their way through. Orm had been a man on a mission, and he had been dead set on getting Nessa and Hunter to join him on it.

As they'd finished breakfast, Orm thrusted a list at Nessa and Hunter, tucking his own into the pocket of his woollen coat. They had stared at Orm with shared bemusement as he rattled off questions he wanted them to remember. They were to work through their lists, going to each place and seeking the answers to Orm's questions. Hunter had grumbled as they'd gone their separate ways, but Nessa hadn't minded, eager to enjoy her newfound freedoms. She saw it as an opportunity to explore parts of the city she had yet to discover.

So there Nessa was, a little after mid-afternoon, standing in the lazy sunlight, trying to absorb the meagre amount of warmth it offered. In her hand was her list, half the names crossed out, the paper creased and tattered from the number of times she'd folded and unfolded it over the last couple of hours. She peered at the next uncrossed name, checking and double-checking that she had the right place.

She did.

Working down her list, zigzagging through the city to each location, to each person, had somehow led to Nessa being in the Barrel.

The Barrel was an older part of the city, located on the opposite side of the city from the Stickworks, tucked between the High Quarter and Lake Nyma, backed up against the base of The Three Sisters. The honey-coloured, stone buildings were tall and narrow, the architecture an echo to that of the castle. Nessa guessed that it made sense, seeing as they had been built at roughly the same time centuries ago. Everything else in the city had come after King Kaenar's rise to power. The High Quarter, the Stickworks, even the docks as they were now, stood on the foundations of the old city. The Barrel and the castle were the only things to have survived the bloody siege that had devoured Ellor near on five hundred years ago, a siege that had ended in Dragon Fire and with a king who claimed the city for himself. Back then, the buildings had been homes, apartments for the middle class. Since the High Quarter had been built, they had been converted into boutique shops and cafes. Highborn ladies frequented them, enjoying the eclectic mix of things that were on offer, buying everything from little knickknacks to lavish ball gowns, from jewellery to fine furniture for their grand homes.

Surrounded by shops which sold things that were well beyond Nessa's means and by noblewomen who wore exquisite dresses of silk and satin, coats and capes made from the lushest velvets, Nessa felt a little out of place. Not that she was the only person of the lower class. There was a mixture of other people with different backgrounds. It was a small mixture to be sure, but a mixture nonetheless. At least she didn't stick out like a sore thumb.

There were the shopkeepers and their assistants, of course, who dressed as well as they could afford. Nobility didn't want to rub elbows with the riffraff after all. However, they still fell short when compared to the splendidness of the highborn. Their clothing was neat and simple, often plain, but it was the best their tight budgets would allow. The rent and taxes that came alongside running a business in the Barrel were steep. The landlords unforgiving. They tried to maintain the facade of having an affluent lifestyle, and it seemed to fool most. Nessa could see the truth of it, though. She saw the hope in a shopkeeper's eyes when it looked like there was a potential sale. She saw how their shoulders would droop if it fell through, or how their steps became lighter if it didn't.

Mixed in with the shopkeepers were the delivery boys, young lads who ran up and down the streets, dashing in and out of cramped alleyways, carrying baskets of fresh goods from the bakeries to the cafes, passing orders from shops to suppliers. None of them could have been older than ten or so, dressed in tidy, little, grey uniforms. That's how the highborn liked to see things, neat and orderly. To them, appearance was everything. They didn't want to see ruffians and dirty peasants during their shopping trips. They didn't want beggars and the homeless taking shelter in alcoves and doorways, pleading for coins, casting a grim mood over what they deemed to be "their side" of the city.

People who were viewed as less than pleasant were ushered from the Barrel and the High Quarter by the Watch, who ran small but regular patrols. Nessa kept as far away from them as possible. While there wasn't a warrant out for her arrest, as Margan and Shadow seemed to be keeping their knowledge of her existence to themselves, she wasn't taking any chances. Not when it came to the Watch.

She saw them around often, as they were a common sight in the city of Ellor, but mostly from afar. The Watch didn't have much interest in places like the Stickworks, only doing a cursory sweep through the winding streets every now and again, making sure that the riffraff was behaving and arresting those who weren't. Members of the Watch were easy to spot in any crowd, thanks to their black attire: chain-mail peeked out from under their surcoats, and the king's emblem, a rose surrounded by fierce flames, was embroidered over their hearts. Usually, there was a sword sheathed at their hip. On occasion, they carried a tall pike. Nessa noticed, during her hours there in the Barrel, that they kept a keen eye on anyone who wasn't highborn.

Nessa was grateful she'd taken the extra time that morning to dress in one of her nicer gowns and to do something with her hair other than sticking it in a messy braid. No, today Nessa's hair flowed in a shimmering cascade to just beyond her waist. Dainty twin braids held tresses back from her face, joined together at the back of her head by a silk ribbon. She had taken the pains of matching it to the colour of her dress, which was a deep burgundy. The neckline and skirt, which had additional gores to allow for soft pleating and a fuller shape, were edged in a contrasting trim of the most beautiful shade of blue Nessa had ever seen.

The dress was pretty, and perhaps her favourite out of the small collection of clothes she had accumulated since arriving in the city. That wasn't why she had chosen to wear it, though. The simple fact that it was one of the warmer dresses she owned was one reason; the other being that it was also the cleanest. Her warmest dress was currently strewn on her bedroom floor, a brandy stain running down the front of the skirts.

Nessa folded up her list and stowed it back in the spherical belt bag that hung from a chain around her waist. She made sure that the coin pouch was still safely nestled inside, and then shut it securely, making sure that the clasp was properly fastened. The bag's metal construction and the chain made it hard for pickpockets to, well, pickpocket her, but Nessa was still cautious. The young ones could be particularly crafty and nimble-fingered. Nessa wouldn't put it beyond them to somehow get past the clasp, even though it looked like a piece of artwork, what with the etched patterns and the hidden latch.

Nessa's gaze went back to the shop's window, trying to see inside. While the window was large, tall shelves and display cabinets stood across most of it, obscuring her view of inside. It was hard to tell, but Nessa was sure that she could see someone else alongside Sissy; two figures of a similar height were moving around, only just visible when they passed behind the gaps between display cases.

Telling herself that having someone present that she's met before would make things less awkward when it came to asking Orm's very specific, very weird questions, Nessa squared her shoulders and stepped forwards.

And almost crashed into someone.

A hand grabbed Nessa's elbow, yanking her back.

Startled, Nessa's eyes shot up, locking with a young woman's disdainful glare. She was, perhaps, a couple of years older than Nessa, her perfect features cold and aloof, her blond hair perfectly curled and styled. Her companion was similarly contemptuous and no less elegant, even though she was surely old enough to be the young woman's grandmother, her face deeply lined, her coiffured hair a stark white.

"Watch where you are walking," snapped the

younger of the two, her green eyes running over Nessa with distaste.

Nessa, too stunned to form any words, could only stare as a small voice from beside her elbow murmured a quick apology. The title of "Lady" might have been used.

The young woman, Lady Arrabella, as Nessa now knew her to be, gave a flourished twirl of her voluminous skirt and turned away, the green brocade of her gown glinting with metallic accents, and continued down the street. While Lady Arrabella spared Nessa no further attention, her companion couldn't resist a sharp glance back over her shoulder. Nessa could practically feel the woman's eyes running over her features, committing them to memory.

"You oughta to be careful when it comes to folk like them," someone beside her piped up timidly. "If someone of the likes of us bumps into them, they'd be likely to cry thief and call the Watch on us."

Nessa turned and found herself gazing down at a small, upturned face. The boy couldn't have been more than ten or so, by Nessa's estimate, petite and as delicate as a fairy, and as pretty as one too. Big, blue eyes dominated his face, peeking out from beneath a mop of dusky hair that hid most of his face, curling around his ears and cheekbones, coming to just shy of his little, pointed chin.

"Well," Nessa said, finally finding her voice. "In that case, I owe you a debt of gratitude."

"My elder brother accidentally bumped into a lord when he was late to his apprenticeship once," the boy continued. "And that's what happened to him."

"The Watch was called on him? Just for that?"

The boy nodded enthusiastically. "Oh, aye. The lord

said that he felt my brother's hand searching around in his pocket, so he demanded that the Watch punish him."

Nessa blinked, grim curiosity coming over her. "And did they?"

He gave another nod. "They took his hand."

In reflex, Nessa's hands clenched nervously. "They took his hand?"

"Right at the wrist."

Nessa grimaced. "How awful. How cruel."

The boy shrugged. "The wound was clean, and he's healed up quite nicely now. He says he's gonna save up some money and get a hook fitted. Look like one of 'em famous pirates from the stories fishermen tell."

"I'm glad to hear that he's keeping a positive outlook," Nessa croaked, more than a little disturbed. *To take a child's hand...*

"He did cry something fierce to start with." The boy frowned. "Although, truth be told, I'm pretty sure I would cry too. There was a lot of blood."

Feeling a touch faint at the image conjured, Nessa cleared her throat. "Well...ah...I suppose I owe you a lot more than gratitude since you potentially saved my hand."

The boy shook his head. "It was no hassle, miss. And I doubt they would have taken your hand in the first instant, what with you being a fine, young lass, and a pretty one to boot. Even if you had been labelled a pickpocket, you might have been able to get yourself out of trouble."

"That's a small comfort, I suppose."

"It's still best to keep a distance from the likes of them," the boy advised, his eyes big and earnest. "Just to be safe."

"Of course. I certainly will from now on." Nessa smiled gently. "Thank you..." her words dwindled away as she realised she didn't know the boy's name. "I'm sorry. I'm being rude. I haven't introduced myself." She held out her hand. "I'm Nessa."

The boy tentatively shook it. "Astrid."

Nessa paused. "Astrid?"

"Did I say, Astrid?" His cheeks flushed a vivid red. "I meant...ah...Astron. My name's Astron."

"Is it, now?" Nessa mused, torn between mortification and amusement, her eyes running over the child with a fresh sense of clarity. Astrid, as Nessa was now inclined to believe, wore her disguise well. At least, that's what Nessa told herself to minimise her embarrassment of mistaking a girl for a young boy.

The light-grey delivery boy uniform Astrid was wearing was baggy, the shirt hanging loosely from her slim shoulders, the trous shapeless. Whatever girlish shape Astrid might have had was further hidden beneath a waistcoat that was several sizes too big.

"Yes," Astrid squeaked. "Of course it is. Why would I lie about my own name?"

"I don't know." Nessa crossed her arms. "Why would a girl run around pretending to be a delivery boy?"

"Shh, don't say that so loudly." Astrid cast around, searching for any sign of eavesdroppers. "No one can find out. I'll lose the position if anyone does, and my family needs the money."

"Your secret's safe with me," Nessa said soothingly. "Girls aren't allowed to be delivery boys, I take it?"

"No," Astrid murmured. "We're not. And the boss is very strict about these things. If he were to find out, he'd tan my hide and my family would be blacklisted."

Nessa scowled. "What an unpleasant man. What does being a girl have to do with one's ability to run errands and deliver messages?"

"He says that girls are airheaded and unreliable, and are better suited to sewing dresses and raising children."

"I don't think I like the sound of this man very much."

"No one does, not really." Astrid shrugged. "But he pays the best, so it's worth all the hassle he dishes out. For the most part."

"Is that why you keep working for him?" Nessa couldn't help but ask. "Because he pays well?"

"Oh, technically *I* don't work for him. I'm just filling in for my brother, you see? The boss don't keep places for those who can't work. If you're sick, you need to find someone to fill in for you straight away. Otherwise, you find yourself out of work."

"I see," Nessa murmured, intrigued by the glimpse into this young girl's life. She was a little go-getter, someone who looked down on the rules placed upon her by society, promptly ignoring them if they went against her needs. It was a rebellion of sorts. A small, quiet rebellion, but perhaps it was all the more powerful because of that. "So you cut your hair and became your brother's replacement?"

"That's right." Astrid grinned a small, gap-toothed smile. Her left canine hadn't quite grown in completely yet.

"I'm impressed." Nessa toyed with a lock of her hair, twirling an end of a loose curl around her finger meditatively. "I don't think I would be able to do that. Is this a long-term thing or just until his hand—stump—heals?"

"Oh, this is just temporary, and I'm filling in for

another one of my brothers. He did something moronic on a dare and broke his ankle."

"*Ohh.* Your brothers don't seem to be having much luck at the moment."

"Pa says that he and Ma had so many boys 'cause the lot of them are as thick as mud. The Creator blessed them with a few extras just in case one or two of them did something stupid and got themselves killed."

"That's...ah...a very unique outlook on things. I guess you have quite a few brothers then?"

"Aye, nine of them. I'm the only girl."

"You're fairly outnumbered."

"I guess, but I can easily take them on in a fight if need be."

Nessa laughed. "With nine brothers, I imagine you'd have to."

"I'd never get any food if I couldn't," Astrid giggled. "They're worse than a plague of locusts when it comes to dinner time."

A sudden tightness was brought to Nessa's stomach at the mention of food, a small grumble that threatened to turn into a loud growl. It was a sudden reminder that the hour was growing ever later, and she was running out of time.

Astrid's eyes widened, misinterpreting Nessa's pause. "Oh, gosh, miss. I'm keeping you when I shouldn't be, what with my chatter and so on. I'm sorry. I'll stop bothering you now. That way you can get on with your business."

"You're not bothering me," Nessa was quick to say. "I've enjoyed our little chat. I feel like we're becoming friends."

"I don't have many friends," Astrid mumbled, her big

eyes bright with a lonely sort of hope.

"Well, you've got one now. Besides, I'm not really here on business, so don't feel like you're holding me up or anything. It's just a chore or two, a couple of questions a friend sent me out to ask a handful of people."

"You gonna see Mistress Pharawynn?" Astrid enquired, nodding to behind Nessa.

Nessa gazed over her shoulder, peering at the shop she'd seen Sissy disappear into. "Is that who runs that place?"

"Yep. She's one of the best spellcasters in the city, I've heard. Lots of ladies say so. Are you going to get your fortune read? 'Cause I've heard she's really good at seeing your future."

"That wasn't why I came," Nessa said absently, her mind buzzing with thoughts, with speculations. Was Mistress Pharawynn's "gifts" the reason why Orm had sent her there? Could Mistress Pharawynn be a half-blood like him? "But maybe I will, seeing as I'm here."

Astrid's eyes became misty, her gaze distant, dreamy. "Maybe she'll reveal that you'll catch the eye of a prince from a faraway land, that he'll marry you and you'll be a beautiful and kind princess, showered in gems and fine gowns, beloved by all."

"That's a nice thought. Somehow, though, I don't think that's in my future." *Instigating the overthrow of the king seems more likely... Or riding a dragon into a battle...* Nessa didn't often allow herself to think about whatever future she might have, but the few times she did, the image always faded from the merry ideal of friendship and exploring the four corners of the world to the darkness of war. That's what Nessa saw in her future. War, blood and death.

At times, that's all she saw.

Pushing away such disparaging thoughts, Nessa looked down at Astrid, forcing a small smile. "You could join me and see if she'll read your future if you want?"

"Oh, I couldn't do that, miss," Astrid said. "I'd rather keep the future in the future, so to speak. Keep my dreams alive for as long as possible. I do love the jewellery she makes, though. I could look in the window for hours if I had the time to spare."

"The time!" Astrid gasped, her back snapping ramrod straight. Nessa jumped, startled. "I've dilly-dallied again and lost track of the time. I'm sorry, miss, but I've got to dash. I need to get this message here," she waved a small piece of paper in the air, "to someone important. Else there will be a very displeased seamstress."

"Best be off then," Nessa said, her forced smile turning into one of genuine amusement. "I hear that displeased seamstresses are the worst."

Chuckling, Astrid added, "Especially when they're out of a specific fabric needed to finish a job."

"Especially then."

As fast as a whip, and with a joyful skip in her step, Astrid turned and darted away, disappearing into the light crowds of the Barrel, weaving between groups of people with expert ease. Nessa stared after her, hoping that she hadn't delayed the girl too much and got her into trouble. Nessa liked Astrid and their little talk. It had made for a pleasant distraction.

Nessa sighed. Distraction time had come to an end.

Turning to face the shop front, Nessa's eyes swept over the window and the honey-coloured stonework before settling on the front door. Squaring her shoulders and repeating the questions she was meant to ask, Nessa crossed the street, mindful not to accidentally bump into anyone. Astrid's words of warning still echoed in her ears. The door was painted a deep red, matching the sign that hung above it, announcing to passersby that this was the Græceling. Around the name was a scattering of intricate symbols painted with shimmering, gold paint.

Their shapes, the way they shimmered, made Nessa pause, her hand poised on the door handle. She peered up at them, wondering about their purpose, their meanings, at why some of them held an air of familiarity. When no answers, no memories, were forthcoming, Nessa made herself turn away, a slight frown born from a sense of ill-ease pulling her brows together.

*Time to gather more odd looks thanks to Orm's weird questions.*

A bell chimed daintily above Nessa's head as she pushed the door open, announcing her presence, and warmth enveloped her in a much-needed embrace.

"I'll be with you in just a moment," a cheery voice called. Sissy. Nessa gazed around but couldn't spy her amongst the maze of tall shelves and glass display cases. "Feel free to explore all the wonders we have, from beautiful gemstones to unique jewellery that's guaranteed to bring you whatever your heart desires."

Nessa peered over to where Sissy's voice came from, and locked onto a narrow archway at the very back of the shop, tucked away in the far corner, overlooked and half-hidden behind a cabinet. A heavy, golden drape was drawn across it, hiding whatever was beyond it. Nessa speculated that it was either a storeroom or where fortunes were read. Briefly, she wondered how it was done. *Were cards used? A crystal ball?*

Stepping further into the shop, Nessa's curiosity got

the better of her. The question she was meant to ask faded from her mind. She approached the wall of shelves to her right, her eyes sweeping over the array of gemstones and crystals arranged in little baskets and boxes. There was every size and colour imaginable, from clear quartz to the metallic iridescence of bismuth, from tiny beads to large geodes that were over a foot in height.

The next row of display cases called for her attention; delicate rings and bracelets were artfully arranged on miniature pillows, with rough gemstones clutched in the grip of tiny prongs and cabochons cushioned in decorative bezels. Earrings and necklaces, too, were hung on and draped over wooden busts and metal stands, the silver, copper and gold twinkling in a seductive manner.

The shop lured Nessa in, the sight of garnet-studded bangles, opal pendants and tanzanite charms, and many more things besides enthralling her. The shelves and cases were a riot of colour, filled with a wealth of jewellery featuring every kind of semi-precious and precious jewel known to man. Light flooded in through the window, catching and reflecting off polished metal and faceted stones, mixing with the soft illumination from the glowing mushrooms which were dotted throughout the shop, little clusters that were nestled within rounded bell jars, growing from pale moss. They ensured that there were no shadows, no dark corners that might subdue the lustre of the jewellery collections.

There was a whisper of fabric, and Nessa turned towards the source.

Sissy came through the archway, the velvet drape sweeping across the floor with a soft sigh. A burst of surprisingly cool air rushed out before it swept shut, and Nessa caught a glimpse of the space beyond it. While she saw it for no more than a split second, unable to see little else but vague shapes in the dimness, she knew that it was no storeroom. The air held a faint charge, an energy that rolled and churned within the room like an invisible thunderstorm.

Nessa didn't have time to wonder about it, to grow unnerved or alarmed before a whirlwind of twirled skirts and flying hair descended upon her.

"Holy spirits!" Sissy all but shrieked in Nessa's ear as she wrapped her arms around her, pulling her into a hug that Nessa hadn't seen coming. Taken by surprise, Nessa froze, her arms hanging rigid by her sides. Everything she'd planned on saying fled, fleeing much like Nessa wanted to.

"I can't believe it's you! Here! In person! Right now!" Sissy leaned back, her hands moving to Nessa's shoulders, holding her at arm's length. "She said you'd come, and here you are. She's *soooo* gifted. We're *so* lucky she's willing to take us under her wing."

"Sissy," Nessa croaked awkwardly, taken aback by Sissy's ferocious cheer. "You look, ah, well."

Sissy nodded, smiling wide, teeth shockingly white against caramel skin. "I am well. I'm very well. And look at you. You're in far better condition than you were the other night, now dressed like the girl you are and not falling unconscious. How nice. How very nice."

"Yes, I'm dressed like a girl." It took a fair amount of effort for Nessa not to roll her eyes, or to cringe at the reminder of her fainting. *How many people had noticed?* Nessa inwardly groaned. *And when would people stop bringing it up?*

"That's good." Sissy patted her shoulder, and to Nessa's relief, took a step back. "I'm glad. My mistress, or should I say *our* mistress," she winked, "doesn't like people being anything other than their true selves."

"*Our* mistress?" Nessa blinked, feeling like she had somehow entered into a strange dream. "I'm not here looking for a job or whatever. A friend sent me to ask some questions. This is, like," she did some mental calculations, "the twentieth place I've been to today."

Sissy's eyes twinkled like the gems that surrounded her, shinning with amusement and secrets. She giggled. "Come, meet Mistress Pharawynn. She'll explain what she can for you. After all, she has been preparing for this moment for so long. For months and months."

Nessa could offer no resistance as Sissy took one of her hands and began leading her away, overwhelmed and a little stunned by Sissy's enthusiasm. She had forgotten how insistent Sissy could be. "Months?" Nessa latched onto that, unable to let it go.

*Months?*

"Oh, yes. She had a vision about you six or so months ago. She's been anticipating your arrival ever since. Our mistress is most gifted, although she is most modest about it all, if you ask me."

"I'll take your word for it," Nessa mumbled as Sissy tugged her through the curtained archway with a surprising amount of strength.

The room beyond was dark. The shutters were closed. Thin slivers of light from around the edges were the only source of illumination. There were no candles or lamps, and yet the air was alive, warm and filled with the strange charge that Nessa had felt only a minute ago. Her eyes struggled to adjust to the gloom, and she couldn't identify what might be causing it. Sissy didn't seem to notice the air's charge, or if she did, she gave away no indication. Maybe it didn't affect her like it did Nessa.

Having been swiftly led around the dark shape of a table in the middle of the room, Nessa was taken over to the looming hole that was another arched doorway. With a click of a lock, Sissy pulled open the wooden door, and the gentle glow of candlelight came spilling through, faint and beckoning.

Nessa pulled Sissy to a stop in the threshold.

She had found where the charge was coming from.

The landing was small, no bigger than the average closet, but the stairs leading down from it were long and steep, burrowing deep beneath the shop before turning a corner and disappearing from sight. Soft candlelight emanated from the very bottom, bouncing off the stairs' smooth tops and catching on the walls' pitted sides.

Energy filled the air, climbing the staircase in rolling waves, brushing against Nessa's face with spectral fingers, threading through her long hair. Nessa shivered, both in fear and excitement. Orm's and Heimaey's words about Sissy's mistress, about how she was little more than a fraud, a weak spellcaster at best, echoed in her mind.

How wrong they were.

The charge in the air was magic. Residual magic. And it was strong.

If the person downstairs was Mistress Pharawynn, if she was the one to whom the magics belonged, then Nessa had no doubt about her being a powerful spellcaster. Perhaps one of the most powerful.

# Chapter 30

With the candlelight calling to her, and the magic beckoning with promises and truths, Nessa trailed behind Sissy as she led them down the stairs. They were forced into a single file. The staircase's walls crowded in on both sides, the corners of the stone bricks sharp and catching where the mortar had crumbled away over time, leaving deep grooves and pointed ridges.

The static crackle of the energy, of the magic, grew as Nessa rounded the corner, turning into a low hum that reverberated through the marrow of her bones. Warmth bloomed in Nessa's chest, an awakening of some kind, and she placed a hand over the spot, rubbing it. The tips of her fingers encountered something unexpected, brushing against something cold and hard. Nessa looked down, mildly surprised to find her brooch pinned over her heart, the silver and blue gems twinkling delicately in the soft candlelight. She had taken the time earlier that morning to remove it from her other dress, but had pretty much forgotten about it until now. The brooch was swiftly forgotten again as Sissy hopped off the last step with a merry, little skip, and Nessa found herself standing at the bottom of the stairs.

Nessa hesitated, her eyes sweeping around the underground room with a sense of amazement, and perhaps a little bit of trepidation. She felt as if she were balancing on the edge of a blade. One wrong step and there would be no turning back.

The room was big, larger than Nessa had expected, even though a part of her had known that it was going to be of considerable size. After all, she had gone down quite a few stairs. Still, Nessa marvelled at the vaulted ceiling, soaring high overhead, supported by a series of narrow pillars edged with swirls of fine masonry, twining around them and fanning out across the ceiling. It was like they were playing the roles of trees, the pillars acting as the trunks, tall and unbending, and the patterns on the ceiling mimicking branches outstretched.

The walls were covered in a thin shell of plaster, the tops stained a pale yellow in places and riddled with holes and cracks. The lower halves might have been in a better condition, but Nessa couldn't tell because most of them were hidden from sight, concealed behind a wide collection of artefacts, apparatuses and many things besides.

There were bookshelves and chests, boxes and bottles, benches and tables. There were books and scrolls everywhere, filling the shelves until they threatened to collapse under the weight. They were scattered over tabletops and stacked in corners. There were surely libraries less well stocked.

A long table over to the side of the room held an arrangement of peculiar vials and bottles of all shapes and sizes, some sitting in little stands, others propped on tripods, small oil lamps placed beneath them, making the colourful potions within bubble and froth. Steam drifted up into a complex spider web of tubing that hung above the table.

Nessa could have happily spent all day staring at everything in the cellar, investigating the curious sights of bones and jars filled with feathers, at the near-endless array of tiny, glass pots filled to the brim with loose crystals and gemstones.

Movement in the middle of the room drew Nessa's attention away from the sights.

A woman stood, rising from a crouch beside a worktop, the heels of her palms pressed into the small of her back, making it click quietly as she arched her spine. She turned around, facing them. Instantly her gaze locked onto Nessa. Her eyes, deep-set and troubled, flat but also oddly bright, were a strange flinty grey.

Nessa felt their stare like a punch. It knocked the air right out of her. She looked away, unable to meet the woman's gaze for longer than a second, looking at everything but those bewitching eyes. Nessa took in the silver threads peppering thick, dark hair that was styled in an elaborate mess of fine braids and curled tresses that merged together into a wild bun atop her head. A few fine tendrils escaped here and there, framing wide cheekbones and a square jaw. Nessa studied the large earrings hanging from the woman's earlobes, almost brushing her shoulders, and the creepy necklace that was draped around her neck. Composed of a chain and a bar of curled wire from which a peculiar mixture of things dangled, it rested low on the woman's chest. There were thin, quartz wands and collections of gemstone beads threaded into the necklace's trailing strands. In the centre of the arrangement were a long, white bone and a dainty skull of a songbird.

Something about the necklace was eerie, unnerving. A shiver crawled up Nessa's spine.

"Finally. You have come," the woman said, her voice low and gravelly. "At last, I may welcome you." She dipped down into a shallow curtsy, her dark skirts pooling on the floor, her beguiling gaze lowering. "Greetings, Nessa, Rider of Aoife. I am Pharawynn, and I am at your service."

༶꧁✦꧂༶

Nessa gasped, her eyes widening. Instinctively, her hand wrapped around her wrist, making sure that her Rider's Mark was hidden beneath her arm warmer, just as it always was. Such was her alarm, Nessa barely remembered to slam up her mental barriers before Aoife sensed her fear.

"How…how do you know that?" Nessa stumbled back, her heel bumping against the rise of the last step, threatening to trip her over. "You can't know that."

"I see and know a great many things, my young Rider," Pharawynn purred, rising from her curtsy. "It is a part of my gift."

"Your gift?"

"I have the gift of foresight. Alongside a few other things. Other talents." Pharawynn smiled gently, motherly, trying to put Nessa's fears at ease. It didn't work. Nessa felt that the smile held a sinister edge and that her words held nothing but thinly veiled threats.

"Long have I sensed that our paths were destined to cross. I swear to you, Nessa, Rider of Aoife, so long as you are under my tutelage, your secret shall remain just that, a secret. You have nothing to fear. I promise you that."

Nessa's foot blindly searched for the top of the step, ready to make a mad dash for escape. *This doesn't bode well...* She kept her gaze locked onto Pharawynn, weighing up the truth in her words.

"How long?" Nessa croaked. "How long have you known about me and...and Aoife?"

"For many, many years," Pharawynn said, her voice dropping low in remembrance, seeing a time and place far beyond the vaulted cellar. "Ever since I was a little girl, I could tell that something awaited me, something great and important. Change is destined to come to this world. It's been foretold by those with far stronger powers than mine, for a lot longer than I have been alive. But I knew. I knew that I had a role to play in bringing it about. My visions regarding this were vague, cloudy, little more than tantalising glimpses of what I needed to do. But I know what needs to be done. Oh, yes. I know."

"But what does any of that have to do with me?" Nessa interrupted, fighting against the enthralling sound of Pharawynn's honeyed voice. It was warm and soothing, alluring. It made Nessa want to step further into the room, to listen to whatever else she had to say.

Pharawynn frowned, the faint creases on her brow deepening. "All my life, I've tried to ready myself as best I could for what was to come." Her hand rose to her necklace, her fingers toying with the dainty bird skull, stroking it as if it were a live pet. "But with the visions so vague, it wasn't easy. Still, I did the best I could with what I had. I studied a great many subjects and learnt all I could. Then, one day, everything suddenly clicked, it all suddenly made sense. The fog that had concealed the details of my visions finally lifted." She sighed happily. "It was all because of you."

"Me?" Nessa squeaked, pausing her efforts of trying to creep up the stairs. She was well and truly ensnared by Pharawynn's narrative. "Have we met before?" There was something about her, something that echoed a likeness of recognition, of a memory.

A corner of Pharawynn's lips quirked up in the smallest of smiles. "*Met* would be stretching it a little."

"Then…"

"I saw you once, and you me," Pharawynn said, a hungry kind of energy in her voice. "Our eyes locked, and I knew what I had been waiting for. I understood. It was you."

"Me," Nessa repeated, unnerved. "Why would you be waiting for me all these years?" Her suspicions grew. "That is, if what you say is true."

"Why not you?" Pharawynn laughed. "Out of everyone in the known world, why not you? Of course, it would be you. There is no one else it could be."

Sissy startled to giggle nervously, but hastily stopped when Nessa fixed her with a frosty scowl. She looked down at her shoes, the tips of which were just peeking out from beneath her skirts, like a pair of mice peering out from their little hidey-holes.

"Start speaking sense," Nessa muttered, ill at ease, confusion and fear crowding her mind. "Or I won't listen any longer. Whatever *preparations* you've done will surely go to waste."

The brightness left Pharawynn's eyes, and her

countenance became a touch more serious. Her shoulders tensed beneath her dark dress, and her hand clenched around the bird skull. "I see you have a bit of a backbone hidden somewhere under that fine gown and all that pretty hair."

"Don't sound so surprised."

"But I am. Pleasantly so. Clearly appearances are deceiving. That will work in our favour."

"Our favour?" Nessa scoffed. "You make it sound like we'll be having further dealings after today."

Pharawynn appeared unconcerned. "Oh, but we will."

"Because you've seen it?"

A shrug of a shoulder. Neither confirmation nor denial.

"Be that as it may," Nessa said, nonplussed and feeling like she was being led around in circles. Useless, infuriating circles. "I've heard on good authority that you're little more than a fraud," *one whose lair thrummed with power and whose gaze felt as if it could see straight through someone's soul,* "who does simple spells and tricks people into thinking she's more than what she really is."

There was an indrawn breath. Nessa turned and saw that Sissy was staring at Pharawynn with worry etched into her features, like she expected her mistress to say something, to do something, in anger. For a second, Nessa panicked. Had she gone too far? Said too much? Would she now suffer for it? Sissy certainly appeared to think so.

*Maybe it had been a mistake coming here?*

Nessa resumed backing up, needing to escape, managing to make it onto the bottom step as the energy in the room crackled and swelled. Paper rustled, and the candles flickered and dimmed as if an unseen force was smothering them, sucking the oxygen out of the air.

"I see Heimaey has given you a somewhat tainted view about me," Pharawynn said, her eyes darting to Sissy, the tension slowly leeching from her shoulders. The energy in the room stilled, calming. The crackling energy fading. Gone. In the blink of an eye, the candles' flames once again danced brightly.

"I'm capable of forming my own opinions," Nessa retorted. "And I've heard things from other people too. Not just from Heimaey."

Pharawynn's brows rose, fine creases on her forehead deepening. "Oh really? How curious. I hadn't realised I was becoming a source of gossip."

"You're not," Nessa muttered. "Not really."

"Tell me," Pharawynn said, looking Nessa over with a considering eye. Nessa paused in her retreat, the toes of one foot poised on the next step. "What is your opinion of me?"

Nessa shrugged, hoping to appear nonchalant, like she wasn't completely disturbed by what she had just seen, by what she had just felt in the air around her.

"Fate has drawn her here," Sissy cried, jolting Nessa out of her line of thought, out of her memory of Arncraft. "Fate and the brooch you gifted her. You truly are the finest sorceress of our age. That too, must be why she is here, because she senses that…"

Pharawynn waved a hand as if she was brushing away an annoying gnat. Sissy drew back like she had been slapped, snapping her mouth shut, her teeth clicking sharply together, cutting off whatever else she was going to say. Nessa stared between the two women, wide-eyed and alarmed.

"Shush, my little cinnamon bun," Pharawynn

crooned. "What have I said about speaking when you're not being spoken to?"

Sissy mumbled something with her lips sealed shut.

Looking bored, Pharawynn flicked her hand.

Whatever hold placed on Sissy was lifted. She gasped, her lips shaping a startled 'O' as she gazed at Pharawynn with wounded wonder.

"Now," Pharawynn said, her attention returning to Nessa. "Pray tell, what is your view of me and my work? I am most curious."

Nessa licked her lips, finding them dry and sore. She had bitten them almost to the point of drawing blood. "I'm not sure it will be to your liking."

"But I wish to know nonetheless."

It felt like a challenge, a dare, and Nessa took Pharawynn up on it, barely taking the time to think things through. Anger made her bold, and what she had witnessed Pharawynn do to Sissy made her blood boil.

"Fine then," Nessa snapped, hopping off the steps and crossing over to the older woman, her hands balled into fists, her heart thumping heavily in her chest. Pharawynn was taller than her by a few inches, but Nessa didn't let that intimidate her. She stopped perilously close to Pharawynn, glaring up at her.

"To start with, I thought that you were misunderstood, judged harshly by those who called you a fraud. But you're not a fraud. Not at all. You're a bully. A trickster. You're someone who plays a part, a role which they want others to see, all the while concealing who and what you really are. I'm beginning to see the truth. I'm beginning to see you."

Nessa's voice dropped into a low whisper, her words intended for Pharawynn only. Her mind had gone elsewhere, uncaring of the world around her, of Pharawynn's shocked expression and the beings she could sense all around her, unseen yet felt, curious little things that darted through the air, dancing in time with the candle flames, the beat of Nessa's racing heart, alive and different. Special.

"You're not a weak spellcaster. I know. I can feel the power in this room. It's brushing against my skin, soft and gentle. Also strong and unyielding. It's a force unto its own, but one you somehow have the strength to control. Contrary to your strength, though, you keep it hidden. Secret. Cloistered down here. You use it in your jewellery, for reasons I'm not yet sure of. Just a small amount, of course, barely detectable to other magic users. I find myself wondering why you'd do that? What's your motivation? My friend says that whatever magic you put in here," Nessa tapped the brooch pinned over her heart, "wouldn't do anything. I think you lure people in with a drop of your magic, enticing them with the promise of giving them something they believe they need, and then get them hooked. You prey on the weak, making them dependent on something they believe only you can give them."

There was a moment of stunned silence. Nessa had even shocked herself.

She drew in a shuddering breath, anticipating the candles to sputter and dim ominously, for the energy in the room to turn heavy and sinister. In Pharawynn's flint-coloured eyes, Nessa saw a great many things.

Still, it came as a surprise to her when Pharawynn threw back her head and a mighty laugh burst forth. Nessa flinched, and then frowned in confusion as Sissy began chuckling with a nervous level of enthusiasm.

"Oh, my dear girl," Pharawynn chortled, half-heartedly trying to calm her laughter, the pad of her thumb wiping away a tear from the corner of her eye. "You really are a treasure."

"I..." Nessa blinked owlishly. "What?" She didn't understand. It felt as if she had just passed a test of some kind.

Pharawynn smiled softly, her eyes crinkling. Her hand came up, the backs of her fingers brushing over Nessa's cheek like she had to double-check that the girl standing before her was real, making sure that she wasn't an apparition, a figment of her imagination. "You truly are wonderful."

"You're not angry?" Nessa asked, voice timid and shaky.

"Why would I be angry?" Pharawynn mused. "I asked for your view. You merely gave it. I would like to point out, though, that you only had a few things right. The rest," she shrugged, "are a little off. But that will all be rectified soon enough, I'm sure."

Nessa eyed her suspiciously. "Which parts do I have wrong?"

Pharawynn winked and took a step back. "You'll figure it out in time, no doubt. You're a smart girl, when you put your mind into it." She crossed over to the far corner of the room, and with her fear slowly fading, Nessa trailed after her.

"Isn't she just awe-inspiring?" Sissy whispered, practically skipping beside Nessa, her wild curls bouncing around her shoulders. "I wish I had the power she has in just her pinkie finger alone. I'd be happy with that."

"She certainly inspires something," Nessa grumbled.

"But I'm not sure it's awe."

Pharawynn began pottering around in the corner that played host to a scattering of old armchairs that had piles of books and loose papers covering their seats, and an array of mismatched tables, all of which, bar one, were covered in all manner of tools and equipment, with pieces of half-finished jewellery scattered about. It was a workstation of sorts, a zone where Pharawynn set stones, polished fine metals and made her preparations. Large candelabras flooded the corner with light and warmth. If it wasn't for the strange illustrations and sketches that lined the walls, Nessa thought that it could have made for a nice, little studio nook.

"Come. Come," Pharawynn said, her hands fluttering excitedly in front of her, motioning to a settee nestled behind one of the tables, the only bit of seating that could actually be used for its intended purpose. "Make yourself comfortable. The tea has steeped to perfection, and the nibbles are ready to be nibbled."

Nessa approached the settee, watching wearily as Pharawynn plucked up a clear glass teapot from one of the crowded tables, loose leaves and coloured petals swirling around inside. It was perched atop a matching stand, a little candle tucked beneath, keeping the tea warm. Pharawynn placed the teapot on a tray that was laden with cakes and pastries and carried it over to a solitary cleared spot on a table beside the settee.

"Nibbles?" Nessa enquired quietly, eyeing the food on the tray.

"I knew you'd be hungry when you arrived," Pharawynn explained, relaxing down into the settee's cushions. "So I sent Sissy out to get you something to eat. One cannot learn if one is not concentrating. One cannot concentrate if one has an empty stomach."

"That's, ah...quite the selection," Nessa murmured, moving over to the opposite end of the settee.

"I didn't know what you like," Sissy said animatedly, standing by Pharawynn's shoulder. "So I got the yummiest things the bakery had to offer. We have iced buns, cherry-filled buns, cinnamon buns—although I confess that I kind of got one of those for me—and there's a collection of different-flavoured muffins and doughnuts. If you're not one for sweet things, then I got a couple of mini pies and a handful of pasties."

Sissy rattled on, giving a detailed inventory of what was on the tray, and the thought process behind why she had chosen them. Nessa peered at Pharawynn, expecting her to snap and force Sissy's mouth shut with a wave of her hand, but she seemed quite happy to let Sissy continue, content to pour two glasses of tea. Passing one to Nessa, Pharawynn nodded to the spot beside her, indicating for Nessa to sit.

Nessa held the dainty cup between the tips of her fingers, hardly daring to apply any pressure. Like the teapot and its stand, the glass was light and delicate, and frightfully thin. Small petals drifted around like tiny fish in a tank, their lovely, deep-pink colour slowly staining the heated liquid. Nessa peered at the petals, wondering what plant they came from, and perched on the edge of the settee, leaving enough room for Sissy, should she ever stop talking and join them.

Sissy was a talker, and a lot of what she had to say held absolutely no relevance or importance. Nessa put it down to a bubbly personality and a small dose of nerves. Still, she would much rather be sat next to Sissy than Pharawynn.

The hope of having someone between her and Pharawynn was a false one, Nessa realised. Pharawynn had poured only two glasses of tea, and neither of them had found their way into Sissy's hand. Nessa also remembered that the shop upstairs was still open for business. Sissy had either forgotten to lock the door before taking Nessa down into the cellar or was just oblivious to the fact that a whole plethora of gems and jewellery were completely vulnerable upstairs. Glass display cases offered very little in the way of a barrier against a fist and a thief.

"Sissy, my little cinnamon bun," Pharawynn murmured softly, like she was speaking to a young child she didn't want to upset, gently cutting off whatever else Sissy could possibly have to say about mixing cake batter. "I think it's time our Dragon Rider and I have some privacy. We have things to discuss that aren't for your ears."

Sissy blinked her big, green eyes, taken slightly aback. "Oh. Right. Of course. I'm so sorry. I was getting carried away again. I didn't plan to. I'll go back upstairs then, shall I?"

"That would be wonderful," Pharawynn smiled, resting a hand on Sissy's arm.

Sissy gazed down at Pharawynn's hand, at the spot of contact, in reverence, like it was the best, most precious gift in the world. Even though Sissy must have been a couple of years older than her, Nessa couldn't help but think that she had a sense of naivety about her, a childlike sweetness. "Baroness Milan will be arriving shortly, along with her entourage. Be extra diligent with them today. The youngest is facing an arranged marriage, and the Baroness' husband is falling out of favour in court because of certain nocturnal activities."

Snickering at the last part, Sissy nodded. "I'll try and point them towards the 'heart desires' and the 'peace of mind' sections. I'm sure something will call to them."

"Excellent, my little cinnamon bun." Pharawynn patted her arm. "I knew you'd have a knack for this kind of business. You are a natural."

Sissy beamed at the praise, then grabbed one of the buns that were her namesake and darted away, swiftly disappearing upstairs.

Nessa found herself alone with Pharawynn.

She sipped her tea, wishing that she had the courage to get up and leave, or better yet, had never set foot in the damn shop in the first place.

*Damn Orm and his damn questions.*

Pretending to be oblivious to the pair of eyes trained onto the side of her face, Nessa searched for an escape, a polite way of leaving. There was none to be found. She had been backed into a corner, and she hadn't noticed until it was too late. Somehow Pharawynn knew that she was a Dragon Rider. It hadn't been a lucky guess, a wild stab in the dark. No one knew what Aoife's name was, not even Shadow or Margan. No one outside of Nessa's tiny circle of friends, which was basically Hunter and Orm, knew Aoife's name. Chaos had known, of course, but seeing as he wasn't alive anymore…

"You have doubts." Pharawynn's deep voice resonated through Nessa, soothing, alluring. Powerful. "About a great many things."

"Of course I have doubts," Nessa murmured automatically. "How could I not?" The way Nessa saw it, she could march out of there and hope that Pharawynn didn't reveal her secret or deal with Pharawynn in a way that ensured she'd never be able to.

"And conflict," Pharawynn continued. "So much conflict and turmoil in one so young. It has only grown since I last laid eyes on you. You already feel the expectations of others upon your shoulders, don't you?"

Nessa didn't respond. Pharawynn's words echoed with a dreaded measure of truth.

"I had expected much of your inner turmoil to be gone. In fact, I confess that I'm surprised it hasn't, all things considered."

Starting to feel like a wounded animal that wanted nothing more than to be left to lick their wounds in peace, Nessa perched her tea on the arm of the settee and turned to face Pharawynn.

"I'm no fool. You can't trick me into revealing any more of my secrets. I think you know enough."

Pharawynn's brows rose. "My dear, you think me trying to trick you? Why in the blessed spirit of the Atheals would I do such a thing?"

Nessa shrugged. "You're the fortune teller; you tell me. Although I'm fairly sure that ulterior motives are involved."

"Ulterior motives?" Pharawynn let out a bark of laughter. "My dear, little Rider, I want to help you."

Nessa shook her head, not believing her. "Why would I need your help?"

"Because I'm the only one who can help."

# Chapter 31

"No," Nessa said with confidence. "No, you're not the only one that can help me. I have my friends. They'll help me. They *are* helping me."

"Perhaps." Pharawynn shrugged. "Perhaps not."

"What do you mean by that?"

"I'm sure they are helping you as much as they can."

Nessa bristled. "You make it sound like they're holding back."

"I'm not saying that, strictly speaking. However, I do know that they aren't able to help you in the way you need them to. Whether they are doing it on purpose or not is up to you to decide."

"And what can you possibly help me with that my friends can't. Or won't?" Nessa asked, pushing aside the niggling doubts that resided at the back of her head, quiet but constant companions.

"Well," Pharawynn was calculating, "first off, I can help you regain your memories."

Those words were a bucket of ice-cold water, a punch to the gut. Nessa barely contained a flinch. She plucked up her glass and slurped her tea, trying to hide her shock, her hopeful despair. The tea was sweet and warm, soothing. Thin threads of vapour filled her nose with the delicate scent of flowers and clarity. It was spring in a glass, revitalising and uplifting.

"My memories," Nessa repeated, a note of bitterness creeping into her voice. "Weren't you meant to already have helped with that? Sissy gave this brooch to me," she tapped it with a finger, "saying that I would regain what I had lost. As far as I'm aware, my memories are the only thing I've lost. As of right now, they're still lost."

"Therefore, you think that the brooch hasn't worked?"

"Therefore, I *know* the brooch hasn't worked."

"I suppose you wouldn't believe me if I told you that the brooch has completed the task I assigned it?"

Nessa scowled. "You'd have to make a compelling argument considering that my memories are still gone, and there's no inkling of them returning."

"And yet here you are," Pharawynn remarked knowingly. "The brooch has led you true."

"It didn't lead me here," Nessa said sharply, a little disturbed by what Pharawynn was insinuating. "My friend Orm led me here. Orm, coincidently, is the one who told me that whatever spell you placed within the brooch's gems is far too weak to have an effect on anything. I don't need you or your magical jewellery to help me with anything. I have Orm. He's a—" *Half-blood,* Nessa almost blurted out. *He has the legacy of the Old Bloods running through his veins.* That information would be dangerous in the wrong hands. Pharawynn's hands. "Orm's a magic user. He will teach me."

"Will he now?"

"You don't believe he will?"

"Oh, I'm sure he would if he could. I fear that what you need to learn is well beyond his capabilities of teaching."

Nessa had seen Orm use magic on numerous occasions. He was gifted, skilled. He could teach her easily. He was just unsure of where to start. "I don't understand what you mean by that." Nessa muttered.

"Do you not?" Pharawynn chuckled. She peered at Nessa and swiftly straightened from her lazy slouch, her eyes going wide. "You don't. You really don't. My goodness gracious, how can that be? Has he not told you?"

Misgivings grew in the pit of Nessa's stomach, heavy and cumbersome, borderline painful. "Told me what?" *What has he been keeping from me?*

Pharawynn appeared genuinely shocked. "I cannot believe that he has kept such a thing from you. Especially when you are so close to coming of age. I can sense that it is nearing, even with the block upon your powers."

"Kept what from me?" Nessa asked, an undercurrent of panic lacing her words. "And what about the block upon my powers?"

Pharawynn sagged back into the corner of the settee, half-turned towards Nessa. There was a look of pity in her eyes, pity and a touch of startled consideration. "I don't believe it," she muttered into her glass cup just before she downed her drink in one smooth gulp. "I can't believe it."

"What," Nessa bit out, teeth clenched together, attempting to contain a scream of frustration, of despair. "You can't believe what? Tell me." Something about

Pharawynn, something about her little half-truths, set Nessa on edge.

"I will," Pharawynn hastily promised, picking up the teapot and refilling her glass. "I will. I'll explain it all, as best as I'm able to. There's an awful lot that I have to cover, though, and I'll have to start from the very beginning."

"The very beginning?"

"Mmm-hmm," Pharawynn sipped her tea, then motioned for Nessa to do the same. "Drink your drink. It has calming properties. It will help you keep a level head while I start right from the beginning."

Nessa gazed down at her glass, peering at the scattering of petals that had now settled at the bottom. She wondered if a spell had been placed over it, similar to what Orm had done with that noxious concoction he'd tried to force her to drink. Since they were discussing magic like it wasn't an extraordinary thing, Nessa let her mind slip for a second, just as Orm had taught her to. *One couldn't be too careful.* It was with mild surprise that Nessa discovered her tea was just that: tea. There was nothing special or magical about it.

"There's no magic in this," Nessa blurted.

Pharawynn tipped her head. "You'll find that a great many plants contain medicinal properties that are on similar levels to some lesser spells."

Nessa looked at her tea with a newfound sense of respect. "Why waste your energy on performing a spell when you can get a plant to do all the work for you?"

"Exactly. You catch on quick. I like that. I do hate having to repeat myself ever so much."

"As do I," Nessa murmured, taking a sip of the tea before it grew cold. "So I'll ask this only once more. Tell me everything."

༄✦༄

"I presume you know a little of how King Kaenar rose to power?" Pharawynn asked, handing Nessa a small plate that was laden with surgery treats.

"Hunter and Orm have told me what they know," Nessa murmured. "Plus, I've read a couple of history books."

"*Pff,*" Pharawynn waved a hand. "History books. History is written by those who have conquered, my dear girl, not by those who were defeated. It's a warped version of what happened, no doubt. But alas, there is no helping it. Though their numbers are small, there are a few alive today who were there when Kaenar emerged from the dark mists, triumphant and unbeatable. They keep the truth alive."

*Dark mists...* Nessa frowned. "Already that's a different description."

"See what I mean? So much of the truth has been shrouded by secrets and lies, hidden away by a king who wanted to bury what really transpired five hundred years ago."

"What does he want buried?"

Pharawynn shrugged. "Who can be sure? There must be a reason behind such a long-standing subterfuge. A pretty good one, no doubt."

Nessa smirked. "And I suppose that out of all the people in the world, you're the only one who knows anything close to the truth?"

"Sadly, I can claim no such knowledge. I did, however, have an acquaintance who was there, all those years ago. He didn't speak of it much. In fact, truth be told, he didn't speak about much in general. He wasn't one who liked to rub shoulders with people like me. He was a firm believer that anyone who wasn't an Old Blood wasn't worth his time."

"He kind of reminds me of someone I know." *Used to know,* Nessa corrected herself.

"Anyway," Pharawynn continued, nibbling on a pastry. "During one of his better moods, he grew curious about some of my wares. Our conversation turned towards spirits and summoning. He gave me a tantalising glimpse into what happened long, long ago."

"And you, being a curious soul, decided to do some research?"

"And said research is still ongoing."

"But I'm guessing you had a few more tantalising glimpses along the way?"

"Something of the kind. In my research, I kept noticing a simple reference. It was unassuming, barely more than a couple of words here and there. But slowly, I began to realise that the stories we're told when we're young are false. Pivotal bits are missing."

"Like what?" Nessa asked eagerly, leaning forwards, hoping, praying, that this was her chance to uncover if the king had a secret weakness, one that he had tried to hide for centuries. Would she be able to untangle the dark web that was his rule, his power, and prevent what happened at Arncraft from ever happening again?

"Tell me what you know about the king's conquest," Pharawynn instructed.

Nessa racked her brain, a small crease derived from concentration forming between her eyebrows as they pulled together. "Only that an army came from the west, invading the lands and decimating the ranks of all the

Riders there at the time. The army was unbeatable, and yet, just as they were about to defeat the Riders, they left. Never to be seen again. From the destruction, a new Rider rose, a Rider who made use of the chaos and the weakened ranks of his fellow Dragon Riders. He took the crown for his own and has ruled the Twelve Kingdoms ever since."

"Nicely recited," Pharawynn said, nodding approvingly.

"Are you saying that's wrong?" Nessa wondered, sure that she had summarised everything correctly. "Or did I miss something out?"

"It's not *all* wrong, but it's not exactly right."

"Oh?"

Pharawynn licked her lips, contemplative. "Most tell it just as you did. A few, though, mention something else: an eerie mist that appeared and disappeared alongside the invading army."

"An eerie mist?" Nessa whispered. A cold shiver crawled over her skin like the fine skitter of spider legs. The sound of cloven feet upon the cobbled street echoed in her head, and once again it felt as if unseen eyes were upon her.

"Just so," Pharawynn murmured, her gaze far away. "It's mentioned in a couple of old journals I happened across, although they lacked much in the way of detail. When I discovered this, and when I thought back to when I was younger, I could faintly recall others mentioning it in passing."

"And what," Nessa cleared her throat, finding it suddenly dry despite sipping her cooling tea, "is the importance of this mist?"

"I'm not quite sure yet," Pharawynn admitted. "You

have to understand, I only came across my knowledgeable acquaintance six or seven months ago. Maybe eight… So I haven't had a great amount of time to investigate the handful of leads I've gathered. Though, saying that, I do have a strong hunch that the mist was somehow connected to the mysterious army."

"Really?"

"I find it too coincidental that this 'mist' appeared and disappeared the same time as the army did. An army that not only bested the Dragon Riders in their golden age, but also the Old Bloods, creatures that were born of magic."

"The Old Bloods were involved in the war?" Nessa had heard no mention of them. If she hadn't met one herself—one and a half if you included Orm—then she would have easily believed that Old Bloods were nothing more than a myth or fable.

A myth or fable, that's what they had been relegated to throughout the majority of the population. They had become little more than characters in stories parents told their children at night. They told legends of winged men and fanged woman, beings who breached the line between human and creature.

"Of course they were," Pharawynn sounded surprised. "This is their world too. Why wouldn't they defend it? They were, after all, as powerful as a dragon and its Rider, if not more."

A part of Nessa was still trapped in her memory of Arncraft's last moments, the tide of flame and darkness about to engulf it, and she couldn't help but recall how powerful the king had been. "What kind of army could withstand the combined strength of the Old Bloods and the Dragon Riders?"

"Nothing human, that's for sure." Pharawynn finished her pastry and licked the tips of her fingers, savouring the fine, sugary coating. "The impression I'm getting is that the army wasn't of this realm. They came and went with the mist. Like it was a door, an opening to elsewhere. A place that only those creatures could go."

"What makes you think that?"

"There are no mentions of them arriving or leaving by any other method. No boats, no other vessels. They came and went like they were a part of the mist itself."

"That's an alarming thought."

"It's certainly an unsettling one."

"But how does any of this tie in with Orm and the block on my powers?" Nessa nibbled her iced bun, hoping that, by having something in her stomach, it would stop rolling with nerves.

"Ah. Yes." Pharawynn's eyes brightened. "Intriguing as the mist-shrouded army is, that's probably something better discussed another day, eh?"

"Possibly."

As nice as the iced bun was, it was doing nothing more than feeding her unease, making her feel sick. Nessa set it aside, deciding to stick with her tea. At least that helped a little with her troubled thoughts, helping to put them into some kind of order.

"Since we've got this far, I going to presume that you know about the time after King Kaenar ascended the throne, when there were a few years of turmoil as a handful of Houses fought against him and his corrupted followers."

Nessa nodded. "But the rebellion ended when King Kaenar destroyed House Fæger."

"Indeed. House Fæger was at the helm of the fight

against the king. He knew that, without them, the fight would be easier to quash. He hunted them down, sparing no one. No man, woman or child who had so much as a drop of House Fæger blood in their veins was left alive."

"That must have been so awful," Nessa murmured softly, hardly able to bare imagining what that family must have endured. It must have been horrific, years of war and anarchy, bloodshed and pain, and then to be betrayed by someone you had fought side by side with, a fellow member of a House and Dragon Rider. To see your children slaughtered by someone who had once been your friend...

"Mmm. Soon after House Fæger was snuffed out, the other Houses quickly fell into line. Any surviving Dragon Riders either swore fealty to Kaenar or were executed and replaced."

"Even with fealty," Nessa mused, "the king's first band of loyal Riders didn't last longer than a generation."

"Read that in one of your books, did you?" Pharawynn chuckled darkly. "Yes. King Kaenar hasn't lived this long by being unsuspicious. Those first few Riders who joined him had already broken the vows they'd taken upon initially joining the Dragon Riders. Who's to say they wouldn't break the vows they'd sworn to him? History claims they met their ends due to accidents and warfare. But we know history can be manipulated, eh?"

"I guess history would have to be manipulated. It would be hard to get loyal followers if they feared they'd be murdered if they set as much as a toe out of line."

"Those poor, traitorous bastards." Pharawynn shook her head in mock shame. "In any event, they got what they deserved, if you ask me. The world has no place for oath breakers, especially not ones who abuse their powers. Anyhow, they were swiftly replaced by Riders more readily controlled, and the king began his new campaign. He sent out his minions, ordering them to find Old Bloods. He put out rewards for anyone who either killed or helped aid the capture of an Old Blood and dealt out extreme punishments on anyone who was found harbouring one." Pharawynn sighed. "It was with surprising swiftness that humanity turned against the Old Bloods. Hunting them, slaughtering them without pause or mercy. Old Bloods met their ends or became very adept at keeping to the shadows, hiding in the corners of the world or in plain sight, disguised, forced to pretend that they were something other than who they were."

"At least there are some who survived," Nessa murmured, a deep, aching sadness filling her bones, her soul. "At least they're not gone completely."

"Oh, they'll never be gone," Pharawynn said with quiet confidence. "Not really. Their legacy will continue. You and your friend Orm are living proof of that."

Nessa's eyebrows rose. "We are?"

"Of course you are," Pharawynn laughed boisterously, wiping away tears of mirth with the pad of her thumb. "Oh, my sweet, little Rider. You yourself are an Old Blood, a full-blooded one at that. I do believe your friend Orm is a halfling?"

Nessa gave a reluctant nod, little more than a slight dip of her chin.

"Well, there you have it. The world has a couple more Old Bloods than previously assumed. Maybe times are changing. Maybe others will emerge from their secret places, shrug off their disguises. Maybe the king's campaign against your kind hasn't been as successful as previously believed."

"My kind," Nessa said, disheartened. "I don't feel like I'm one of them. Every time I look in a mirror, or see my reflection, all that stares back is a girl. A very human, very average girl. If I didn't have the Rider's Mark wrapped around my wrist and hand, then I'd think that I've lost my mind."

"Being an Old Blood is more than having fangs and pointed ears…"

"Or wings," Nessa added.

"Or wings. Or tails. Or fur in weird places."

Nessa's eyes widened. "Fur in weird places?"

"When I was your age, I may have had a brief liaison with a handsome beast of a man." Pharawynn frowned. "Turned out he was a bit more animalistic than I had anticipated. I don't just mean passion-wise either."

Nessa didn't know how she felt about that revelation, but there was a mixture of gross fascination and a certain level of disgust. She wasn't sure if she wanted more details or to forget that Pharawynn had disclosed such a thing to her.

"If…ah…" Nessa searched for a way to steer the conversation away from such a personal subject "… if there's more to being an Old Blood than physical attributes, what else is there?"

"Oh, I don't really know." Pharawynn flicked a hand like that revelation wasn't a ground-shaking one for Nessa.

Nessa turned towards the older woman, dismayed. "You don't know?"

Pharawynn rolled her flint-coloured eyes, "There's more to being an Old Blood, no doubt. But seeing as I'm not one of them, I'm not exactly privy to their secrets."

"Their secrets?"

"Creatures who are being hunted to extinction don't live long by telling everyone about every little thing about them, now, do they?"

Nessa begrudgingly saw the sense in that. "No, I suppose they wouldn't."

"Seeing as you're an Old Blood, maybe you should take that idea under consideration."

"It's not like I'm running around shouting that for everyone to hear," Nessa said with a scowl, her fingers fiddling with the hem of her arm warmer.

"I'm just saying that you should be careful, that's all."

"I am being careful. I can't help it if people like you know, can I?"

Pharawynn grinned. "No, I suppose there is very little you can do about that. At least, right now."

"But I'll be able to?"

"Of course. How else do you think other Old Bloods remain secret?"

Nessa bit her lip with nervous thought. "Magic?"

"Yes!" Pharawynn almost jumped up with joy, shaking the settee. "Magic. You are a creature of magic. Think of all the possible things you'll be able to do in just a short while. Think of what you might even be able to do now."

"But I can't do anything. The mental bl—"

"The mental block," Pharawynn cut her off. "Yes, yes. That is a trifle annoying, but there are ways around it."

Nessa's voice sounded small, even to her own ears. "There are?"

"Of course."

Nessa was completely baffled, and it must have

shown on her face for Pharawynn sighed and muttered a low "Blimey, even Sissy knows more about magic than you". She reached for the teapot and topped up her little glass. Then, taking a measured sip, Pharawynn shifted and crossed her legs, one knee over the other. She arranged her long skirts and sat with her foot bouncing with contemplative energy.

"When an Old Blood comes of age," Pharawynn began, "it's viewed as a transformation. Their power bursts forth with great ferocity, like a moon turning into a sun. It changes them, inside and out."

Nessa clung to every word, hoping that it would be happening to her soon, hoping that she would be transformed into something more than just a girl, a hollow girl with no memories and no powers.

"When this happens, their power is raw and untamed, and often hard to contain until they've learnt how to reel it in, how to control it. Of course, this is a somewhat hazardous time for them."

"Nice way of phrasing it."

Pharawynn cast Nessa an amused grin. "Naturally, in the last five hundred years, they've come up with ways of protecting themselves, should their power pose a risk. Usually, they're able to control it pretty quickly. You know, the threat of the king or one of his Riders slaughtering them is a pretty good motivator. However, in rare circumstances, the strength of their magic is too much for them to rein in quickly, so they are forced to lock away their magics."

Nessa's brows pulled together. "Lock away their magic? How is such a thing possible?"

"With a mental block," Pharawynn answered simply. "It's like a wall within your mind, built between the planes of conscious and subconscious thought. This only works when the magic is new, the user young. Depending on who builds the wall and their skill, it's still a tricky thing to do successfully. There are a number of other things to take into consideration."

"Such as?"

Pharawynn shrugged a shoulder. "The strength of the so-called wall builder and their knowledge of these things are greatly important. But they also need to be aware of how strong the recipient is; otherwise, the mental block can be too weak and lead to a flare out, which is incredibly dangerous. Time is also a factor. Sometimes, an Old Blood's transformative 'coming of age' is a slow process, their power emerging over months, sometimes even years, showing itself in brief, sudden bursts that gradually increase in strength. Then bam—" Pharawynn slapped her hands together, making Nessa jump, "they burst forth for all to see."

"How will it be for me?" Nessa wondered, racking her brain for any kind of memory, any kind of hint or clue. Had her powers already started to show themselves and she simply couldn't remember? Was that why Shadow had placed a mental block upon her, to stop them from being detected? *Was he...was he trying to protect me?* But why would he do that? And why had he also squirrelled away her memories? "Am I undergoing a slow 'coming of age process', or is it just going to happen all at once?"

"It's hard for me to say, my dear Rider. I have only had the privilege of meeting but a handful of Old Bloods in my life."

Nessa had her doubts. Lies could be so easily mixed with truths to form an indecipherable concoction. "If that's true, then you seem to know an awful lot about them."

"What can I say?" Pharawynn winked. "I've done my research. Besides, all magic users must be cautious. It's not just Old Bloods who face the king's wrath. Strong magicians and sorcerers have met the same tragic fate after being mistaken for an Old Blood. You have to remember that the king's men aren't inclined to ask questions. There are never any trials or official executions. Those are only reserved for people accused of hiding or aiding a suspected Old Blood. Even then, the trials are short and only for show. It's a form of self-preservation, us spellcasters knowing about the Old Bloods and their powers. It helps to keep us safe. Magic users need to stick together during hard times, even if they don't like it or they don't want to. Some of the older generations of Old Bloods may despise mere mortals like me, but that doesn't always stop them from creating little half-breeds every now and again."

"Like Orm."

"Just like Orm," Pharawynn agreed with a snap of her fingers. "And Orm, just like so many halflings, was one of those who experienced a wee bit of trouble when he came of age."

"Really?" *Orm?* Nessa was so surprised she could've been knocked over with a feather. "But he's used magic around me. I've seen him do things. He's in perfect control over his powers."

"Oh, my sweet, little Dragon Rider," Pharawynn turned to Nessa and patted her on the knee in what Nessa assumed was intended to be a comforting gesture. However, it came across as a little patronising in Nessa's opinion.

Pharawynn was older than Nessa, over twice her age,

and she wore it with grace. But with age came knowledge, and knowledge was power. Right then, magic notwithstanding, Pharawynn had all the power when it came to the two of them. She was more than happy to wield that power like a sharpened blade.

"Orm's only in control of what little magic he has left because of his mental block."

# Chapter 32

*Orm? Mental block?*

Shock. Nessa tried to conceal it.

Judging by the cunning gleam that leaped in Pharawynn's flinty eyes, she failed. Her not knowing about Orm's mental block had revealed something to Pharawynn. It was confirmation. Of what, Nessa wasn't sure. She couldn't read people as well as Pharawynn could. Before she deciphered what the gleam might have meant, it vanished.

Nessa sipped her tea in way of a distraction, finding that it was nearing the undrinkable stage of being lukewarm. She swallowed a mouthful, nearly emptying the little glass, and grimaced. There were few things worse than being mid-sip and discovering that your hot beverage was cold, forcing you to either swallow the offending liquid or spit it out. The latter choice was poorly suited for when company was around.

Pharawynn moved, reaching for the teapot, her intent

of refilling Nessa's glass clear.

"If Orm has one of these blocks," Nessa rushed to say, not wanting any more tea. Unease and nerves made her stomach clench uncomfortably, painfully. The thought of eating or drinking was a sickening one. "Then how can he use magic?"

Pharawynn paused, her hand outreached. "What do you mean, my dear?"

"Well, I thought the whole point of these blocks was to stop someone's magic from being used."

"Oh!" Pharawynn looked surprised. "That's what you thought?"

Nessa shrugged.

"My dear girl, there's so much more to it than just that. Magic isn't as blunt as bricks and mortar within the mind. It is fluid, flowing, as intangible as mist and as strong as a raging river."

"And regarding a mental block, that means?"

Pharawynn sighed, her intention of refilling Nessa's glass long forgotten. Her hand settled on her lap, fingers tapping against her thigh. "Sometimes walls aren't always continuous, solid. Often there are windows and even doorways."

"And cracks," Nessa murmured, more to herself than to Pharawynn.

Pharawynn, though, heard her. "Just as in the real world, the things in our minds are subject to change based on outside forces."

Nessa slowly put the pieces together. "So, what you're saying is, Orm can still use magic because there's a doorway in his mental block, his wall?"

"Orm came into his powers a handful of years ago," Pharawynn told her. "They came on him suddenly and with great ferocity. He was helpless in controlling them. Almost immediately they were strong enough to be detected from afar. Which, as you can imagine, was incredibly dangerous for him, and to those close to him. Orm was luckier than most. He caught the attention of an Old Blood, one who was benevolent enough to take Orm under his wing."

*Chaos,* Nessa realised. *It's quite possible that Orm was literally taken under his wing...* Nessa barely stifled a snicker at the image that came to mind. There was a very long list of words to describe Chaos, and benevolent wasn't anywhere near the top of it.

"Before King Kaenar or any of his loyal followers could track Orm, and therefore him, down, the Old Blood tried to teach him how to get a hold of his powers, how to tame them just enough so that they wouldn't be found. I imagine the Old Blood had hoped to mentor Orm. After all, having someone with the power Orm had, loyal and in your debt, would be a great asset. Besides, the knowledge that elders hold needs to be passed down at some point. Lest it fades away to nothing, lost to the world."

"But the taming was unsuccessful?" Nessa asked, hungry to hear more about her friend, eager to know more about him and his magic.

"Your assumption is correct. Orm's magic was as wild and untameable as the fire he can so easily conjure, for fire is his innate gift."

"Innate gift?" Nessa interrupted.

"That's a discussion for another time," Pharawynn said easily, like there would be another time, like Nessa would be returning soon. "But right now, I want you to understand what a mental block is and what it can do."

"Oh," Nessa mumbled. "Alright."

"As it happened, control was beyond Orm's reach. The only option for him, other than a date with the butcher's block, was to have a mental block put into place. However, due to his strength, a solid wall couldn't be built. It would be too dangerous."

"Why is that?"

"Because it could lead to a flare out," Pharawynn tutored, her gaze filled with knowledge and sly smugness. "The power would build up behind the block, not unlike a dam. At some point, the power's going to build up to a point where the mental block fractures, cracks under the pressure. Magic, even stronger than it was to begin with, will be released uncontrollably, flaring out into the world like a supernova."

"Which is why it's called a flare out," Nessa murmured thoughtfully, absently picking at the detailing of her sleeve's hem, a touch disturbed to learn that there was a darker side to being an Old Blood than she had imagined. It was bad enough that the king and his leagues of loyal followers would have her head just for being born, not to mention that she was also a rogue Dragon Rider. To suddenly learn that her magic, should it ever decide to show itself, could have such dangers also attached to it was a little frightening. Nessa felt as if she was facing not just one battle, but many. It was like she was being attacked from all fronts. Nessa didn't know where to start, or what to do.

"Flare outs are very rare," Pharawynn continued, oblivious to Nessa's train of thought. "I guess they only happen, oh, once or twice every century. There's a very limited number of magic users these days. But flare outs are deadly."

Nessa stared. "Deadly?"

"Of course they're deadly. Flesh and bone aren't built to withstand such power. When a flare out happens, there's naught but a charred hole in the ground where the unfortunate sod used to be."

Nessa's mouth fell open, and she was unable to form any other response but a small, shocked squeak. Pharawynn paid her no mind, seemingly engrossed in her own narrative.

"When I was little," Pharawynn said softly, lost in a memory, "I would listen to the great tales my mother and grandmother told me about the Old Bloods, about their legendary magic and their extraordinary feats. Then I learned about all this nasty business with the flare outs and the king's intent on wiping out certain fractions of Old Bloods, and I decided that I was perfectly happy being just as I was."

"Lucky you," Nessa muttered, feeling rather disenchanted.

Pharawynn shook herself, freeing herself from her reminiscing. "Due to his circumstances, your poor Orm had a mental block built within the confines of his mind, locking away his magics. For the most part." Pharawynn gave Nessa a knowing wink, like they were sharing secrets. Nessa supposed that they were, kind of. "Because of the risk of his powerful magic building up, leading to one of those dreadful flare outs, his mentor allowed a small—how should I phrase it?—vent? A little window?"

Nessa grimaced, not all that interested in the correct terminology. "An escape-hatch type of thing?"

Pharawynn pursed her lips, mulling it over. "Well, however we describe it, it prevents a flare out. Orm can access a small amount of his magics. Not enough to be detected, but just enough to prevent the magic from building up to dangerous levels."

"Which is why Orm can still do the odd bits and bobs every now and again," Nessa concluded.

"Indeed," Pharawynn sighed. "It must be hard knowing that you could be so much more, that you could do so much more."

Nessa was quiet, wondering why Orm had kept so much from her. Not only did he have personal experience with mental blocks, but he knew so much more about Old Bloods. *Why had he never mentioned any of this? Why did he never explain?* Nessa couldn't help but feel let down, perhaps even a touch betrayed. She had a right to know about the dangers that came with magic, with blocks and flare outs. Yet there hadn't been even the slightest hint of Orm revealing any of it to her. Embarrassment must have played a part in why he hadn't disclosed his secret, his state, but that was no excuse as to why he hadn't shared anything else with her. There was no excuse for that. None whatsoever. Was that why he wasn't teaching her? Why he was always stalling when it came to learning about magic? He wouldn't be able to stall forever, making one excuse or the other. Sooner or later he'd run out of them. Then what? Would he tell the truth?

Would it matter?

Would it be too late by then?

"Be all as it may," Pharawynn patted Nessa's hand, pulling her away from her inner turmoil, "I can't help Orm. His magic is too wild to control. But I may be able to help you."

"Can you take away the block?" Nessa asked, her voice plaintive even to her own ears. "Can you give me back my memories?"

"I am but a sorceress," Pharawynn said. "The power I wield is vastly different from yours and the one who put that block in your mind." Pharawynn rose from the settee, moving to stand over Nessa. "But I swear upon the Atheals that I will do all that I can to aid you in this matter. I will help you if you so wish it."

Pharawynn extended a hand, and Nessa gazed at it. She felt as if destiny was looming over her just as this strange, powerful woman was. If she took the offered hand, if she shook it, then something would happen, something she would never be able to turn her back on…

Nessa hesitated for a heartbeat, but the promise of help, of aid, was too good a lure.

"Just one thing," Nessa murmured as she slipped her hand into Pharawynn's, setting in motion the wheel of destiny. "What's an Atheal?"

Pharawynn's bright, flinty eyes filled with despair as she gazed down at Nessa, at the small girl nestled into the corner of the old settee, a girl clothed in a pretty dress with big eyes and an innocent heart, a girl promised to the world long ago.

"Bloody hell," Pharawynn muttered, eyes sliding closed as she steeled herself for what was to come. "What have I just got myself into?"

༄✦༄

"The Atheals," Pharawynn began, crossing over to the wall of overflowing bookshelves, "are the ninety-nine divine spirits who govern the arcane arts. They are the powers sorcerers like me call upon for our magics." She prowled the shelves, her fingers tapping the spines of books as she perused them, her eyes running over gilded titles.

Nessa left the comfort of the settee, intrigued, following after Pharawynn as she moved further across the wide room. She reached the older woman just as Pharawynn made a sound of discovery, long, beringed fingers plucking a large tattered book from its hiding place on the crowded shelf. The spine was mostly gone; nothing more remained of it but a few loose threads and thin strips of fabric that looked like they wouldn't last much longer. With the spine lacking structural integrity, someone had punctured crude holes into the front and back covers, threading a length of dark ribbon through them, lacing the book together.

Holding the tome to her chest with one arm, Pharawynn reached out with the other, forearm swiping across a nearby desk, pushing aside a vast collection of glass bottles and jars. They clinked together as a space was cleared on the desk, threatening to break, to topple over the edge and shatter on the hard floor. Nessa hastened over, catching those that tottered perilously on the lip of the desk, carefully shoving them back before she found herself picking up a bucket load of broken glass. Pharawynn didn't strike her as someone who would clean up after themselves, and it seemed unfair for Sissy to have to do so.

The tattered book thumped down onto the desk, making a few of the remaining bottles bounce and rattle, and Pharawynn flicked it open with a snap of her wrist. Pages rustled as they were swiftly turned, sounding like fallen leaves caught in a breeze, tumbling along a cobbled street, crisp and whispery.

Nessa peered at the book from over Pharawynn's hunched shoulders, catching brief glimpses of strange illustrations and symbols as the pages were turned at high speed.

Further through the book she went, reaching the middle before finding what she sought.

Sprawled across the twin pages was a complex pentagram illustrated in ink that was once black but had long since faded to a pale grey due to age and generations of caressing fingers. The star had nine points, and interlacing lines made not only the pentagram's form, but also filled its body in an intricate, multifaceted web. Miniscule inscriptions in two different styles of hand writing filled every available space between the lines, hectic and strange. Each point of the star ended in a small circle with something that was between a signature and an intricate glyph in the centre.

*A seal,* Nessa realised with a shock. She'd come across similar things in her grimoire, perhaps even this exact image, although she couldn't be sure since she hadn't paid all that much attention to them. The minute text was like a foreign language to her, pretty much impossible to make sense of even when surrounded by the knowledge of generations of powerful spellcasters. Nessa was beginning to wish that she'd spent longer trying to decipher it, trying to understand it. At least then, she wouldn't be coming to this completely blind, like she was now.

As Nessa gazed down at the book, at the seals and the tiny writing, she couldn't help but feel like she had jumped into a river, one with unknown depths and a very fast current that was more than willing to sweep her away.

"The Atheals are split into two groups," Pharawynn murmured, taking a step to the side, allowing Nessa to sidle closer, one of her fingers slowly tracing the pentagram, pausing to tap at each seal when she came upon one. "Here we have the nine high lords: the Weaver of Speech, the Commander of Hearts, the Summoner of the Nameless." Pharawynn's finger did a circuit around the pentagram, and she listed the rest of the seals' titles. Once finished with that task, her finger slid inside the pentagram, tracing over the multitude of crisscrossing lines and the dainty writings. "Here we have the lesser dæmons who serve under the high lords. Don't make the mistake of thinking that just because they're referred to as *lesser* and serve under the high lords that they are inferior. See how the lines intersect?"

Nessa nodded, watching as Pharawynn's finger caressed the lines slowly, the rough gemstones in her rings twinkling in a hypnotising manner.

"Everything is connected," Pharawynn murmured, her voice deep and syrupy. "One spirit is connected with the other. That one is connected with the next…and so on…and so on. The spirits are united. They are separate."

"That sounds a bit riddley," Nessa said.

"Less of a riddle," Pharawynn said with a small smile, "and more like a web."

"Oh?"

"Think of it like this," her finger traced one specific line from a seal to where it intersected with others. "A spirit may look like it is completely independent, but at some point, its path will meet with another's. A lone thread of a spider web may be enough to capture its prey, but in order for the spider to know its prey is there, all the threads must work together to carry the vibrations to it. It's a similar principle when it comes to summoning and spellcasting. You may think that you only need to call upon one spirit when, in fact, you may need to call upon several. You see, their powers are all intertwined, they overlap."

Nessa frowned. Her head was starting to hurt. "If that's the case, then why would you call upon a specific spirit in the first place?"

"Their powers are intertwined, not exactly the same." Pharawynn tapped a couple of seals. "Each spirit has, shall we say, an area of expertise, a particular niche in which they work best. A handful deal with matters of the heart, others with matters of the mind."

"And so on," Nessa murmured, starting to understand some of what Pharawynn was teaching, bits and pieces coming together. It was a relief to finally be learning something. For so long, Nessa had felt like she was in the dark, stranded and alone. Now a weight was beginning to lift from her shoulders, and she could start the battle against the gathering darkness that seemed to surround her, slowly but steadily gaining strength. Nessa knew that she had so much more to learn, a great deal, but everyone had to start somewhere. At least she was making a start. The distrust she felt towards Pharawynn was fading with each revelation, with each discovery.

"With time," Pharawynn said, "you will come to understand the role each spirit has to play when you're casting and summoning. You'll have to carefully choose which one is the best fit for the spell you're doing, or if calling on just a single one is enough. You'll learn how to envision the outcome of the spell and what's required to achieve it. Spirits are fickle things, often coy and troublesome. Do something wrong or incorrect and they won't hesitate to turn on you and cause no end of mischief."

"They seem difficult to work with," Nessa muttered,

troubled.

Pharawynn shrugged. "Magic is a tricky business, whether you rely on external forces or internal ones."

"External? Internal?" *Hadn't Orm mentioned those in passing before?*

"When it comes to magic users, to witches, sorcerers and the like," Pharawynn began, "people commonly employ those terms to differentiate between the two types of magic sources. External magic refers to people like me, people who have to rely on external forces in order for our magics to work, such as spirits, incantations, even herbs and potions. Then there's internal magic. This is the type of magic you process. Old Bloods... their halfling counterparts... Dragon Riders... this is their type of magic. This is *your* type of magic," Pharawynn added pointedly. "The power, the magic, comes from *within* you. You don't have to rely on herbs or spirits to accomplish your desires. You can simply *will* whatever you want into fruition. Take your friend Orm, for example. If he wants a flame to appear in the palm of his hand, all he has to do is imagine that flame, draw on a little of his magic, and it shall appear just as he wills it to be."

"And it's as simple as that?"

"It can be, I presume. I'm a sorceress. My gifts are vastly different from yours and your friend's. From where I stand, though, it doesn't matter what kind of magic user you are, there's always pros and cons."

"And what are the cons of my type of magic?" Nessa asked, curious. To her, it seemed that if someone could simply make fire appear just by willing it, then they were pretty damn lucky.

"Oh, I imagine there are very few drawbacks for your

kind, other than attracting unwanted attention from a certain group of people, and the risk of flare outs. You are stronger than any user of external magic. You are able to do a whole range of things the likes of me can only dream of. I suppose the only real drawbacks you face are things that relate to the strength of your powers."

"Like flare outs and such?"

Pharawynn shook her head. "Not necessarily. Flare outs are more of a hazard. I mean that the only limits regarding the use of internal magic come down to the user's strength, both mentally and physically, and how much power they have in the first place. No one is the same. Not even twins. Yes, some may look identical, but there's always something that sets them apart. The way they walk. The way they talk. Even the way they think. The smallest of things can impact on how magic is used and how it reacts."

Nessa absorbed Pharawynn's teachings, for there were a great many things she needed to process and think on later, and looked down at herself. "Physical strength plays a part?" She had put on weight since arriving in Ellor. Hunter and Orm had seen to that. Jerome, too, was partial to slipping her a slice of cake every now and again. Her ribs had stopped sticking out, and she wasn't painfully thin anymore, but she still looked like a heavy gust of wind could knock her over.

"Only a bit," Pharawynn laughed, catching Nessa's meaning. "But don't worry about that. It's a common misconception amongst magic users that the saying 'strong of body, strong of mind' is literal."

"And it's not?"

"It's not quite as literal as people think. A healthy body is better equipped to deal with the after-effects, so having a strong body is fairly important—after all, mortal flesh wasn't meant to withstand the rush of magic. However, seeing as you're one hundred per cent Old Blood, I don't think you need to worry about that too much. For people with a less prestigious lineage, though, they aren't quite as lucky as you and often take a more cautious approach. Generally speaking, the healthier the body, the healthier the mind." Pharawynn tapped her temple. "You don't see many invalids with all their faculties in working order, now, do you?"

Nessa didn't think she was in a position to say, considering that she didn't remember anything from more than a couple of months back, and had yet to come across any "invalids".

"Strong of body, strong of mind has a measure of truth to it," Pharawynn continued. "However, it's worth noting that it's also possible for someone to be incredibly strong-bodied, but very weak-minded."

"What happens to them?"

Pharawynn shrugged. "Their power will eat at them, consuming them. Ultimately, there will be nothing left of them in the end."

"Oh."

"That's why I'm perfectly happy with simply being a sorceress. It may be considered a downside having to rely on external power sources to work one's magic, but I like to think of it as an opportunity to broaden one's horizons and discover new things."

"Well, that's always good."

"No matter how old you are, I find that there's always something new to be learnt. Provided you're willing to learn it, of course. Often there's a sense of laziness amongst some magic users. They're only willing to learn one specific thing, specialising in only one area. This is clear foolishness. Why only conjure fire when you could also control water?"

"Why indeed?"

"It's just narrow mindedness."

"The narrowest."

"I'm glad to see that your friends haven't installed such notions in your head yet," Pharawynn murmured, bejewelled fingers toying with a stray thread of the book's binding. "It would be a dreadful shame if they were to keep you from reaching your full potential." She grimaced. "Any more than they already have."

Nessa bristled. "They haven't been keeping me from my potential. They just haven't been…"

"Been what?"

"…able to help as much as I want them to."

"I think the phrase you should be using is 'willing' rather than 'able'. Your friends aren't *willing* to help as much as you want them to."

"Orm might not have been particularly forthcoming in regards to *his* magic block," Nessa argued defensively. "But it's not like he has any malicious intent as to why he kept that information to himself. And I doubt Hunter knows all that much about magic in order to help me. For all you know, he might not even be aware of the limits that Orm's had placed upon him."

Pharawynn pursed her lips, and Nessa could see the growing number of rebuttals in the woman's deep eyes. Pharawynn wanted to fight against her beliefs, her opinions. She wanted to argue. For reasons unknown, the older woman decided to keep her thoughts to herself. Perhaps she knew something that Nessa wasn't yet ready to hear. Maybe she didn't want to risk breaking the fragile truce that was slowly forming between them.

"I'll let you figure out your friends' roles in all of this," Pharawynn said simply. "After all, you know them better than I."

A sharp retort was contained behind Nessa's clenched teeth. Just. What went on between her and her friends was none of Pharawynn's business. Of course, Nessa knew her friends better than she did; after all, they were *her* friends. Who else would know them better?

The cruel sense of uncertainty enveloped Nessa. Who else *did* know them better than her? Probably quite a few people, in all honesty. Both Hunter and Orm have said that they've known her for years, and yet Nessa couldn't remember any of that. Nessa was suddenly forced to ask herself how well she actually did know them? Her working memory barely extended beyond arriving in Ellor. In that regard, Nessa didn't really know them much more than she did Jerome or the others who worked at the guest house.

"I do know them," Nessa muttered, more to reassure herself than to convince Pharawynn.

Pharawynn dipped her head in silent acknowledgement and resumed turning pages. Rather than continuing to the back of the book, Pharawynn returned to near the start. "External magic is the most common form of magic found these days. You don't have to look too hard to come across a witch or a conjurer, or even a fairly skilled sorcerer."

Nessa let out a small sigh of relief at the change of subject. She had enough doubts of her own as it was. She didn't need anyone adding to them, sowing seeds that were more than eager to grow. Nessa crossed her arms, warding away the lingering touch of mistrust, and rested a hip against the edge of the table. Her gaze darted between the book and Pharawynn, intrigued as to where all of this was leading, as to what she might learn next.

"But most are lazy and don't boast a wide array of skill sets," Nessa finished, knowing, by now, what Pharawynn was going to say.

Pharawynn smirked. "They allow their perceived magical limitations to become real limitations."

"Is that so?"

"You see, when it comes down to the core differences between internal and external magic, it generally boils down to strength and speed, if you set aside the power's source for a second." Pharawynn held up a finger, anticipating the tide of questions that were poised on the tip of Nessa's tongue. "Now, strength is a rather roundabout thing, as you may have picked up on. Speed, however, always leads to interesting debates between magic users."

"I bet it does."

"Don't turn your nose up at the notion. You'll soon discover that it's quite important when you start casting your own spells. Magic can't be rushed, my little Dragon Rider. That's when mistakes are made. If you ever make a mistake with magic, there's a good chance that you won't be making another."

"Because you'll have learnt your lesson the first time?"

"Because you'll be dead."

"Ah." *Delightful.*

"The moral of the story is to not rush into things beyond your understanding."

"And what a good moral it is."

Pharawynn snorted, faintly amused. "As I was saying.

In many cases, external magic users are at a disadvantage when it comes to speed. After all, in order for our spells and conjurings to work, we have to first call upon the spirits, brew our little potions and recite words of power. This can, of course, take some time. However, there are ways around this."

"That's fortunate, then."

"Indeed." Pharawynn laid a hand on one of the book's old pages, the handwritten text ornate but faded. "Do you know what this book is?"

Nessa peered at it, searching for a title, a clue. "Umm?"

"It's a grimoire," Pharawynn said, her voice holding a touch of reverence, of wonderment. "A textbook of magic."

Nessa felt a jolt of surprise. *Another grimoire?* Aoife had told her that such books were rare, kept within families of powerful magic users. She gazed upon the tattered book with new insight, dismayed to find that it looked so different from Chaos' grimoire.

"It's been passed down through countless generations of my family," Pharawynn murmured, not noticing Nessa's astonishment, her awe. "Being carefully curated by the hands it falls into, by the hands of my ancestors. On these pages, written by my kin, are the teachings of how we learnt to call upon the Atheals, how we learnt to command them to carry out our wills. This here holds the instructions on how to create mystical objects like talismans and amulets, and how to imbue objects with spells. Each grimoire is unique, the content within specially orchestrated to take advantage of the spellcaster's strength and minimise their weaknesses. Because, as I may have said already, magic varies from person to person. Each family of spellcasters has certain magic attributes that they want to utilise, to nurture and grow."

"I guess that if you have a unique gift," Nessa mused, "then you'd want to make the most of it."

"Just so, my dear girl. Just so." Pharawynn caressed the page, her fingertips gently brushing the calligraphy in the bottom right-hand corner. Nessa thought that it may have been a name, a signature, but the loops and swirls made it unreadable to her.

"Not many grimoires exist anymore," Pharawynn continued in a low murmur. "Not that there were all that many to begin with." Her eyes met Nessa's, their flinty depths filled with flecks of sadness and loss. "After all, few people know how to read and write, even today. I can't imagine how illiterate people were a couple of centuries ago. The few families whose blood was filled with enough magic to warrant a grimoire were fearful of getting caught up in the king's Old Blood purge, so they destroyed their priceless treasures."

Nessa cleared her throat. "But some survived? Not all of them were destroyed?" She knew that there was at least one other surviving grimoire out there: the one that was safely hidden away in her room on the other side of the city, a beautiful and rare grimoire with silver covers and a hunger for her blood that she chose to satisfy. That was her small sacrifice for a glimpse into a world denied to most, a world filled with secrets and mystery, with sigils and fickle spirits.

"Some, I suppose," Pharawynn said. "It would make sense that others survived if this one did."

"But you don't know how many?"

With a shrug of a shoulder, Pharawynn said,

"Grimoires are kept secret, only shared between those in the family. Outsiders rarely glimpse one. Most don't even know of their existence in the first place. After all, anyone who does know about a grimoire would also know how valuable they are on the black market. Other magic users would happily pay an arm and a leg for one of these." Pharawynn gave her grimoire another loving caress.

"And yet you've shown me?" Nessa said quietly, wondering at the motives behind that decision, especially since grimoires were considered so valuable, so secret and precious.

"So I have."

"Why?"

"Why not?"

Nessa opened her mouth but no answer was forthcoming.

"You don't seem like someone who would run around telling anyone and everyone that I have a grimoire." Pharawynn grinned. "Nor do you look like someone who would steal from me. Besides, it would be pointless in keeping it from you. Most of the lessons I'll be teaching you will be coming from it."

"But how can I learn magic when I can't access mine? Unlike Orm, I don't have a window or doorway. Is there a spell that can take away the block?"

Pharawynn tapped the book thoughtfully. "There might be something."

*Might*. Nessa's shoulders sagged with the heavy weight of disappointment. There was nothing on those tattered pages that would *definitely* help her. "This seems rather pointless then."

"Do not be disheartened, my little Dragon Rider. I have promised to aid you however I can. I do not break my promises. I will free you from the wall in your mind. You can count on that. Just because this book may not contain the answer—after all, my family is one filled with summoners and sorcerers, and blocks are commonly reserved for users of internal magic—doesn't mean that the answer isn't around here somewhere." Pharawynn's voice dropped down into a conspiratorial whisper and she winked. "I don't know if you've noticed, but I have a very large collection of rare books."

Nessa's eyes ran over the bookshelves brimming with tomes, scrolls and quite a few stacks of loose papers. It was a library, a museum, that specialised in the secret and the powerful. "If the answer is amongst all of that, then why are you showing me your grimoire?"

"Why?" Pharawynn's eyebrows rose. "Why? Because there's nothing better to guide you into the world of calling upon the spirits and channeling their powers."

༄༅༄

Nessa's mouth fell open. "Spirits? You want me to learn how to call upon spirits and use them?"

"Did I not make that clear to begin with?"

"No," Nessa said quickly, frowning a little. "Yes. I don't know. I thought it was more along the lines of theory and study, not, like...actually summoning something."

Pharawynn let out a long-suffering sigh. "Do you not want to learn?"

"I'm not sure. Can I?"

Pharawynn looked puzzled. "Can you what?"

"Summon spirits?"

Nessa jumped, wide-eyed as Pharawynn fetched up against the edge of the table, roaring with laughter, making it shake, the glass bottles chinking together. Tears streamed down her face as she spread her hands wide on the desk, gasping for breath. Nessa's back straightened and she scowled, torn between demanding an explanation as to what was so damn funny and simply storming out of there.

Nessa's indecision gave Pharawynn just enough time to wipe her cheeks clean of tears and suck in a calming breath.

"No, no. Don't go," Pharawynn hiccupped, flinging out an arm, catching Nessa before she had the chance to leave. "It's just that I forget about how naive you are when it comes to magic, and then you say something like that."

Nessa's scowl deepened. "I don't think my so-called naivety warrants such a response."

"Oh, when you get to my age and have seen the things I've seen, you'll take your kicks wherever you can find them."

Nessa remained unimpressed.

Pharawynn sighed and pushed herself upright. "Fine. Fine. You don't see the funny side right now, but you will in the future."

"One can only hope."

Chuckling, Pharawynn shook her head. "Of course you can call upon the spirits," she explained. "All you need to do is learn how. It's well within your powers."

"But my powers are blocked," Nessa said, confused. "So how can that be?"

"Your magic is blocked, caged away. But it's still there. A spark of magic still flows through your veins."

"And that spark will help me summon spirits?"

"See, this is what I was talking about. The

inexperience within our community is truly staggering sometimes." Pharawynn waved a hand at her. "And you're a fine example of this wee problem."

"I'm starting to feel insulted."

"Bah, don't be insulted. Simple ignorance can be easily remedied."

Eyebrows rising, Nessa muttered. "Great. I'm naive and ignorant. Anything else you'd like to add?"

"Easily offended?"

Nessa frowned, trying hard not to be, well, offended.

"As I was saying," Pharawynn continued. "The ignorance within our community, I'm forced to say, largely comes from your kind, the users of internal magic."

"Is that so?"

"If you ask me, yes, that is so. They assume that just because they're an internal magic user, then that's all they can use."

"But that's not so?"

"You are an Old Blood," Pharawynn said with wonderment. "You belong to a group of beings that have lived on these lands long before mortals reached these shores. You belong to a species that's tied to everything in this world. Surely then, that would mean you also have access to the Atheals? Give it a bit of thought. If someone who relies on external powers can call upon the spirits, upon the Atheals, then why can't someone who has internal magic, a magic that's thought of as far more formidable, do the same?"

Nessa swallowed nervously. "Are you saying that Old Bloods, users of internal magic, can also practice external magic?"

Pharawynn grinned. "Want to learn about the arcane

arts, my dear girl?"

# PART III
# Chapter 33

The day had begun like any other of that week, with Orm and Hunter going down to the docks to help shift concealed contraband. They felt like they were sticking a big, fat middle finger up at the establishment by doing such things. Nessa felt like they were playing with fire and that they wanted to get burned. They liked the taste of danger, dabbling in a trade that could easily end with their necks in a noose. There was no fun to be had with clean, honest work, it seemed, and work it was. They weren't paid much, but the need for them to gamble and cheat to fund their stay in Ellor was gone. Not to say that they had stopped. No, they still found an excuse to go out for a game or two, either for a friendly match between mates or to listen to the latest round of gossip. Most often, it was a mixture thereof. Nessa had discovered that dockworkers gossiped worse than old women.

Hunter and Orm had been working with Heimaey and his, as Nessa liked to think of them, minions, Bo and Luca. The five of them got on like peas in a pod, mischievous and often up to no good even when they were on their best behaviour. Together, they would coordinate the unloading and reloading of ships that came from and went to Vasindor, the next largest port town on the shores of Lake Nyma, and ready the latest arrivals of contraband for redistribution. Some of it stayed in Ellor whilst a large portion made its way north.

It appeared that Jerome and his mysterious partners, not to mention his nameless and faceless employer, operated on a kingdom-wide scale. They had contacts in almost every major city and town, ranging from lords and ladies, right down to the criminal underbelly of society, thieves and beggars. They had eyes and ears everywhere. Nessa saw the sense in employing from all walks of life. After all, who better to listen to the latest behind-the-scenes goings-on than the unassuming beggar who was sat beneath an open window? Who would know more about the latest court intrigues than a noble hoping to gain a foothold in the dark and seductive world of espionage and sedition?

Nessa had joined Hunter and Orm for a while that day, seeing the inner workings of the smugglers' operation and then swiftly distancing herself, allowing them to have their daytime activities while she had hers...

She had been spending every available minute with Pharawynn, learning about the Atheals, spellcasting and summoning. Orm and Hunter didn't know about this. She knew that they would disapprove. So, each morning, Nessa would wait until they had left for the docks and then slip out of the guest house with a gaggle of other guests, careful to make sure that neither Jerome nor anyone who worked for him noticed her escape. With her sly breakout completed and a cover story cleverly concocted should her absence be discovered, Nessa would make her way to Pharawynn's for the day.

It was easy for Nessa to keep Hunter and Orm in the dark about her daily exploits. She was always careful to return to the guest house before them. With Aoife, though, it was a little harder, although by no small means impossible. Whilst a part of Nessa liked to think that she had grown more skilled at controlling what she did or didn't share through their bond, she couldn't help but feel that luck played a significant role. Or was it fate? Whichever one it might be, Nessa was so profoundly grateful that Aoife was experiencing a sudden growth spurt. All Aoife had been doing for the past week was sleeping or hunting, the latter of which, apparently, needed full concentration and the former requiring, under no uncertain terms, no interruptions of any kind. When they did reach out to one another, it was during the quiet hours of early dawn and late evening, when all was still and calm around them. Nessa could easily keep the conversation away from any incriminating line of enquiry.

To start with, Nessa had felt the weight of her covert liaisons with Pharawynn bearing down on her shoulders, an oppressive burden of guilt and dishonesty. It had quickly faded, though, as the secrets of the arcane arts started to be revealed to her. Pharawynn had shown Nessa a glimpse into a world beyond her imagining. Before Nessa knew it, it was swallowing her whole.

A few days into her tutelage, Nessa was allowed to

summon a spirit for the very first time, calling upon it to carry out her will, to infuse a drop of magic into a dainty gemstone ring. Afterwards, Nessa had brimmed with pride, happy beyond belief. She had done it. She had used magic! On her way back to the guest house, the light around her rapidly giving way to night, Nessa had done little else but twiddle the ring around her finger, admiring the twinkle of the gem in the street lamps, marvelling at the gleam of magic that shone from within, the magic that *she* had put in it.

Aoife had contacted her, sleepy and mildly irritated by having to relay Orm's message, and informed her that he and the others were on their way to the den. They were in need of a drink after a long day of "tactical work". Instead of wondering what that could mean, Nessa decided to join them, such was her good mood. So, she met up with the gang a short distance from the den, their paths fortuitously crossing.

Together, they had made their way along the riverside, a merry group filled with chatter and laugher. Nessa spent most of their journey talking to Heimaey, getting to know him. His humour and narrative skills, regaling her with tales of the gang's antics over the last week, were highly entertaining. Nessa saw why Hunter got along with him, Bo and Luca so well: they were spiritual clones.

As they turned down an unfamiliar street, heading away from the river, Hunter, with much glee, informed Nessa that they were now permitted to use the front door to the den. They had proven themselves over the last week, and that was their reward. Nessa wondered why she was allowed to go with them, considering she had done nothing to aid the organisation in any way.

Her wonderings fell on deaf ears as her companions, her friends, came to a stop. *Have we reached it already? Why are they so quiet?* She peered at them, her eyes going from face to face. A shiver of warning crawled up Nessa's spine as she saw the blood drain from their cheeks, as their merry smiles faded away.

With trepidation, Nessa followed their fearful stares.

A stone's throw away was a small T-junction, a street from the left intersecting with the one they were on. On each corner stood a lamppost, tall and ornate, the ethereal mushrooms encased behind glass panes, throwing out rings of ghostly light in the gloom of night.

Light which caught in the fine tendrils of mist that crept along the ground.

Nessa bit her lip. Those eerie tendrils of mist reached across the cobbled street like spectral vines, searching and seeking.

There was a muttered curse when a hand wrapped around Nessa's wrist, tugging her up against a side. Nessa looked, finding that it was Hunter who held her to him, with one arm wrapped tightly, protectively, around her shoulders.

"This is how it happened before," he whispered. "With the ship."

Nessa had needed no explanation. She knew what the mist concealed, for the same night that Hunter had witnessed a ship being swallowed, she too had found herself engulfed by its shadowed depths. Just like that night, a strange charge grew around them. It was like the air was coming alive.

Hunter's grip tightened and he tensed. Nessa held her breath. They weren't alone. Her blood sang with the need to run, to flee.

"I don't know about you lot," one of the twins muttered. "But I'm getting a bad feeling about this."

"Not just you," the other twin breathed. "I'm having the exact same feeling."

"Glad to hear it. Not."

The unearthly mist flowed further into the street, growing denser and higher, rolling forwards in a churning wave. Tendrils snaked out, wrapping around the lamps, pulling the body of mist up, up and over the lanterns, engulfing them, smothering them. The light dimmed.

Nessa shifted uneasily, a movement that was mirrored by the others.

"I don't think we should linger," she murmured, the words hard to say, fear making them stick in her throat.

Hunter nodded; his gaze fixed upon the swelling wall of what was now mist as it rolled into the junction. "I like your line of thought."

Heimaey swivelled on his heel, and one of the twins had followed suit. They both stopped dead.

"Ah, guys," Heimaey said with a curse, "leaving might be a bit harder than first thought."

Nessa looked over her shoulder. Her heart skipped a beat.

The street behind them was blocked. Another wall of mist stood there, solid and foreboding. The mist had surrounded them on both sides, spilling from unsuspecting alleys, trapping them. It rolled towards them like waves whipped up in a storm, violent and angry, ready and willing to destroy everything in its path. Right then, standing in its path, were Nessa and her companions.

It was coming for them.

There was something about the mist that was different to what Nessa had walked through before. She could sense a hunger about it, a feral need that was a driving force behind it. Darkness, one that Nessa had experienced when the world around her had been falling to ruin by dragon fire, lurked within.

The mist swirled around them, circling them, a shifting cyclone of chaos. Nessa stood in the eye of a hurricane. It swallowed the walls of the elegant townhouses, engulfing the uniform gardens that sat in front of them. It drowned the light which seeped through the gaps between closed shutters, and it devoured the moon and stars.

The street was plunged into darkness.

Hunter's hand tightened painfully around Nessa's wrist, and she pressed herself closer against his side, wrapping an arm around his waist, hiding as much as she could.

There was no echo of footsteps, the sensation of being watched. Things had changed this time.

With a chorus of muttered swearwords and the whisper of daggers leaving sheaths, the guys in the group crowded together. Nessa somehow found herself pushed into the centre of their circle, their backs boxing her in. Nessa decided that this was probably the best place to be, and the safest. There was nothing better than an armed ring of protection around you when under attack by forces unseen.

Orm clapped his hands, the sound sharp and more than a little unexpected. Green sparks flew from his fingertips, whizzing around wildly before settling on the ground. They hissed and flared, spreading out in a ring, looping around the group, burning tall and bright, the tips of the green flames coming to stand near shoulder height. The fierce fire crackled with energy, with power, and filtered through the mist, forming a sphere of illumination that almost reached the townhouses that stood on either side of them. Nessa hoped that the fire would scare away whatever lurked in the gathering dark.

It was a fleeting hope.

The mist swelled and pushed against the ring of fire, devouring the outreaching light and leaving them standing in a tight bubble of illumination that was growing ever smaller and subdued.

Nessa's gaze went to Orm's face, and she was alarmed to see that rivulets of sweat ran down the side of it. His eyes were squeezed shut in concentration, with strain, and his out-thrown arm trembled. Nessa knew that Orm wouldn't be able to hold the ring of fire for much longer. The force of the mist was too strong, too unrelenting.

"We have to do something," Nessa whispered, clutching at Hunter. "Orm can't hold it back anymore."

"I'm open to any suggestions?"

"Ah."

"Heimaey?" Hunter's eyes darted to the man beside him. "Any ideas you want to throw into our already overwhelming mix?"

"Other than wishing Orm could magic us out of here?" Heimaey muttererd. "Then, unfortunately, no. I am all out of ideas."

"Unhelpful."

"Yeah."

"As much as I'm loving the chitchat," one of the twins muttered from behind Nessa. "There's something out there. I saw something move."

Hunter tensed, almost going to turn around.

Somehow, he managed to resist the urge. He couldn't risk giving his back to anything that might be lurking outside their bubble of light and protection. They needed to keep a tight formation.

"What can you see, Nessie?" Hunter breathed. "What's out there?"

Nessa slowly pivoted, being his eyes and ears.

"Nothing…"

Nessa squinted into the gloom, peering over a twin's shoulder, wishing that Orm's fire penetrated further into the darkness and mist, illuminating more than just a few yards at most. Nessa also wished that it didn't burn with tinges of green, for it made what were already deeply disturbing circumstances all the more alarming, catching eerily on waves and wisps of mist as it danced around them.

"No…wait…there's something…"

A shape moved in the shadows, keeping just out of reach of the flame's light, staying at a distance where it was near impossible to tell what it was exactly. Nessa couldn't see any details, but she knew that it wasn't human. Its hulking mass was too large, too hunched over. She was pretty sure that it was walking on all fours like a dog. She hoped that it was a dog. Just a big, feral dog. The guys would be able to handle a dog.

"It's an animal of some kind," Nessa murmured.

Hunter raised his brows. "A friendly one?"

"Umm…"

A low growl sounded out, deep and ominous. Nessa could feel its vibrations deep in her bones. A threat rippled through the air.

"I'm going to take that as a no."

The creature began to circle them slowly, prowling in

the gloom, its steps silent, its movements holding an almost liquid fluidity. It was unnatural. The notion of it being an animal made of mortal flesh and bone was abandoned.

"Orm?" Nessa said, her tone bordering on hysterical. "What might that thing be?"

"Off the top of my head," Orm groaned, a little breathless, exhausted. The act of keeping his flames burning high was taking its toll. "I would have to say that it's nothing good."

"How informative."

"I aim to help."

Nessa's next question was replaced by a strangled scream.

The creature...monster...whatever it was charged at them, taking leaping bounds out of the shadows, out of the cover of mist. It was a huge being of darkness and maliciousness.

Orm sensed what came at them, and whilst the others could do nothing more than blink in shock, or give a started yelp, he flung up both of his arms. With a mighty roar, the ring of fire rose in mimicry, bellowing and crackling to well above their heads, strong and proud.

The creature hit the flames, rebounding off them as if they were a solid barrier, an actual wall. A shockwave reverberated through the air, strong enough to make all of them flinch as they felt the echoes of it in their bones. The creature hissed and growled, angered at being denied its prey, and stalked around the edge of the fire, searching for any sign of weakness, slinking low to the ground. The mist, heavy and thick, swirled around it, tendrils wrapping around long limbs and a growling snout like loving hands, caressing this being of darkness and nightmares.

"I can't keep this up for much longer," Orm warned, his voice hoarse from the strain he was under, the flames as heavy as bricks.

"Don't tell that thing that," Hunter barked, panicked. "It might give up if it doesn't know."

*Urgh, what's all this ruckus?* A groggy, irritated voice groaned at the back of Nessa's mind. *I told you and the boys that I wanted no interruptions while I sleep. Yet here you are, practically pouring a rainbow of emotions down the bloody bond.*

*Well, if you'd bothered to check the rainbow of emotions,* Nessa snapped. *Then you'd realise that the boys and I are about to become monster food.*

*Oh, don't be so pedantic.*

Nessa shared an image of the scene with Aoife: the alarmed, fearful faces of her companions, the wild ring of green fire, the stalking shadow that lurked just beyond it. Nessa was not in the mood to argue with an overtired dragon. There was no time even if she had been.

*Oh...* Aoife sprang into alertness, her mind connecting with Nessa's in such haste that it was almost overwhelming. *Oh dear... Oh my...*

*Thus the cause of the emotional rainbow...*

Aoife's irritation was swallowed by a chilling sense of doom. That sense of doom became Nessa's as it flowed through their bond. Her knees went weak and she slid down to the ground, Hunter's grip on her wrist loosening. The creature came to a stop in front of them. The wall of fire was the only thing standing between them. A low growl sounded out, one filled with threat and cruel intent. It spoke of ripped flesh and snapped bone. It was a promise solely for Nessa.

Her eyes snapped up.

Through the gap between Hunter and Orm's legs, through the dancing flames, Nessa's gaze locked with that of the creature. From the depths of darkness and shadow, eyes began to glow like smouldering coals, a deep and terrible red.

*Devil,* Aoife whispered. *Demon.*

The creature crouched low, mist wrapping around it.

The growl grew louder, deeper.

The air quivered.

Orm's legs trembled.

Green flames wavered.

The creature pounced.

It launched itself at their wall of protection, and the wall was no more. The flames darkened and splintered apart as the creature shot through them, and small balls of fire were scattered throughout the street. They burned weakly in the mist's oppressive gloom, little mystical candles here and there.

The creature barrelled into the group, knocking them asunder, throwing them to the ground.

Nessa landed on her back, the breath knocked out of her, her head slamming against the cobbled street.

Her ears rang like church bells. Her breaths were whispery gasps.

She groaned and rolled onto her side. Someone was nearby, swaying on their knees as they struggled to get to their feet. Hunter perhaps, or maybe Heimaey? It was too dark for her to tell. The mist swarmed around them. Without the barrier of mystical fire to keep it at bay, the mist had claimed their bubble of former safety as its own. There was no sanctuary. There was no safety.

Nessa pushed herself up onto shaking arms and

knees. Aoife's encouragements, her orders, were strong in Nessa's ears. Her vision wavered. The world spun. Nessa sucked in a deep breath, trying to push back the rising wave of nausea, and peered into the gloom. Amongst the heavy waves of mist and the tiny spheres of burning light, she perceived the shapes of the others. Some were close, others not so. It was near impossible to tell who was who.

What Nessa did know, though, was that the creature had vanished.

Nessa scrambled to her feet, fear making her strong. Her nausea and trembles were forgotten. *Can you see it?* Nessa asked. *Has it gone?*

*It won't be gone until it's tasted blood,* Aoife told her. *It's been summoned. It won't leave until it's had its sacrifice, a payment of sorts.*

*How do you know that?* Nessa scrambled over to the person closest to her, half-tripping over herself in her haste. She recognised the individual as Orm as she dropped down beside him, bruising her knees on the cobbles. He was sprawled out on his back, his eyes closed and his face peppered with sweat.

*It was mentioned somewhere in the grimoire.*

*I don't remember reading that.*

*That's because you barely gave that section a second glance.*

*Oh dear.*

Nessa laid a hand on Orm's shoulder, shaking him, trying to rouse him. They didn't have much time before the monster returned. Nessa's eyes searched the street, looking for any sign of sinister shadows in the gloom and for any sign of Hunter.

The mist was thick, dense. Nessa could only make out hazy shapes in its silvery haze. Scattered throughout the street, barely discernible in the shallow light, the others were either standing or on their knees, unsteady and in shock. Orm was the only one unconscious. He must have expended too much energy with his magics. His body was unable to bear the effort taken to battle against the dark forces.

*Wake Orm,* Aoife instructed, her tone hard and urgent, *grab Hunter and get your skinny arse out of there. Right now!*

*But what about the others? What about Heimaey and the twins?*

*Not to sound completely heartless, but leave them.*

*That sounds completely heartless.*

*You barely know them. Sometimes you have to accept that you can't save everyone. Help Hunter and Orm, and hope that the others can defend themselves.*

*Ah...*

Orm groaned. Whatever else Nessa was going to say vanished. She leaned over him, shaking his shoulders until his head lolled from side to side. Blindly, he swatted at her, moaning something that sounded like "duck auf". His face held a sickly pallor, but Nessa couldn't be sure if that was just because of the balls of lingering fire—ghost lamps in the mist—that were tinged green with the residue of his magic.

Orm's eyelids flickered open as a charge in the air grew, heavy and static. Alive. Nessa had felt it a couple of times before. She knew that something was coming.

There was no warning. No stirring of air or footsteps. Something grabbed the back of Nessa's dress, hurling her upright, lifting her off the ground. Her dress' collar dug into her throat, cutting off her air, choking her. Nessa scratched frantically at her neck, at her dress, fingers scrabbling to alleviate the pressure. Her legs kicked out wildly, searching for purchase, for relief.

Whoever, whatever, held Nessa tossed her aside with little effort, like she was nothing. For a heart-stopping moment, she was airborne; then she landed on the ground with a sickening *thud*, momentum sending her rolling until she fetched up against a wall. Gasping for breath, one hand wrapped around her bruised throat, Nessa pushed herself upright, sitting with her back pressed against stone bricks, her body singing with pain and terror.

A shadow detached itself from the gloom, black and sinister, its red eyes alight with a malicious gleam. It prowled towards Nessa, joints moving with inhuman fluidity, its four legs long and thin, three-toed paws tipped with vicious-looking talons. A low growl erupted from its long, dog-like snout, its lips pulling back to reveal multiple rows of razor-sharp teeth. The creature stalked over to her, pausing frightfully close, one of its forelegs almost brushing against her out-stretched foot.

Nessa cringed as the creature bent down, lowering its lupine head, sniffing at the toe of her boot.

*Don't move,* Aoife instructed tightly, voice fearful and pained. *Don't. Move.*

Nessa didn't have to be told twice. She didn't need to be told at all. Her body was frozen. She was stuck in place, unable to twitch a muscle.

*Don't even breathe. It doesn't see with its eyes. Not like you and I do, at least.*

Nessa didn't believe it. The idea was ludicrous. What would have eyes that couldn't see? As the creature grew ever closer, scenting her knee, a foreleg coming to rest on either side of her legs, Nessa realised that Aoife might be right. The creature's eyes, Nessa saw, were nothing but deep pits devoid of anything but a glowing vapour that swirled around deep inside its body.

That wasn't the most alarming thing about the creature's anatomy. Not by far.

It was a thing built of nightmares and darkness, a monster constructed from people's worst fears.

Its form shifted and rippled as it moved, parts of it vanishing and reappearing in a blink of an eye. That's how it moved with such strange, soundless grace, Nessa came to understand. It wasn't so much walking but rearranging its limbs in the illusion of motion. It could shape itself at will, not bound by the constraints of flesh and bone. It was like Frankenstein's monster, a thing that had the features of several different beasts merged into one. Some were identifiable, others not.

An upturned snout sniffed her foot, her knee. Leaning forwards, it sniffed at Nessa's cheek. Nessa trembled as hot breaths fluttered across her face. *Puff...puff...puff...* She half-expected the monster to lunge at her throat, needle-like teeth ripping and tearing.

Nessa held her breath, and through the bond, she felt Aoife doing the same; she felt Aoife's despair at not being able to get there quickly enough. No matter how fast she flew, Aoife wouldn't be able to cover the amount of distance from her hideaway in The Three Sisters and get to Nessa before...before...

In this despair, alongside the gnawing frustration, something changed between them. Their bond, it grew and strengthened, the cord tying their souls to one another's thickening and contracting. They were bound more tightly than ever before. Beneath her arm warmer, hidden from sight, Nessa's Rider's Mark shimmered with a purple sheen, and far in the mountains, the breast of a young dragon began to shine, scales twinkling like stars.

Together as one, their hearts beat in a synchronised dance.

Surety and power flooded through Nessa's veins. Her senses became heightened: her vision sharp and clear, and her hearing acute, sensitive to even the smallest of sounds. And her mind...her mind was altered, expanding to new heights and depths, growing in ways that didn't seem possible. It became unfathomable; her mind playing host to an abundance of ancient knowledge passed down through the memories of generations. Nessa's consciousness had expanded beyond the confines of her mind, merging with Aoife's in a way that was dizzying and euphoric.

Two bodies, one soul.

One mind.

One will.

Nessa breathed out, her pent-up breath released as calmness settled over her. She raised her arm, holding out her hand, and time slowed down.

Nessa saw everything in a different light. It was like a purple filter had settled over her eyes. The sense of urgency had gone, as had her fear. Nessa no longer sat cowering before the monster of nightmares. She pressed the palm of her hand against its snout, shadows and dark mist shifting to form a strange imitation of skin beneath her fingers. It snorted as a shiver crawled over its body, and for a split second, Nessa saw something beneath its darkness: a different being, an entity born of moonlight. There was another side to the monster, one of benevolence and life. It had been hidden, buried by a deep and profound loathing, an ancient hatred. Its light was smothered.

Her glimpse within the monster vanished as a rolling wave of rage and a burst of pain flowed through her palm, cruising up her arm. The monster reared back, an unearthly howl sounding from its maws. The connection, the brief understanding between them, was severed.

Nessa clamped her hands over her ears, her eardrums screaming, threatening to burst. Heimaey stood over the monster, standing between it and her, pressing something against its forehead. So enraptured with the creature's other side, Nessa hadn't noticed him emerge from the mist.

It was a battle of wills between Heimaey and the shadow monster. The latter was trying to break away, writhing in agony; the former was struggling to keep whatever he held against the monster in place, matching it step for step as it retreated. Heimaey backed the monster into the middle of the mist-shrouded street, the last of the lingering balls of green flames doing little to illuminate their struggling forms. The monster's howl dwindled into a pitiful whine and it collapsed, its long legs buckling.

"Orm?" Heimaey called, crouched over the creature. "If you have any fire left in you, now might be a nice time to summon it."

Two shapes ambled out of the gloom, moving to stand beside Heimaey. Orm's arm was thrown around Hunter's shoulder, and Hunter seemed to be supporting much of his weight. Nessa noticed that even in the gloom, Orm appeared drawn and pale, his eyes open but unfocused. He was mumbling, lips shaping words that Nessa couldn't hear over the monster's gasping moans, and he raised a hand. Clutched in his fist was a dagger, the sharp edge glinting with spectral fire.

Nessa sat forwards, a shout rising in her throat, but she was too late. The blade was driven down with purpose, sinking deep into the monster's rippling flesh. She wouldn't get to see its other side again.

"Back to the Void with you," Hunter hissed. "Devil."

One second the monster was there. The next, it was simply gone like it had never been. But it had. It had been there and it had been alive, and now...now it was gone, and Nessa felt its loss deep in her bones. And what a terrible loss it was. A light had been extinguished that eve. A star lost forever.

The mist churned and swelled around the group, swirling wildly. It darkened and blotted out the faint light of Orm's lingering fireballs. There was a yell, a shout, as the all-consuming darkness fell upon the street. It was pitch black. It was a frightful void. There was a whisper, a sigh in the air, and then a wind came, hard and fast, roaring with brutal intensity. Nessa hunkered down against the wall, her spine grinding against the stone, and squeezed her eyes shut as her hair whipped against her face.

Like the monster, the mist was there one second and gone the next.

Stillness settled over the street, a peaceful silence.

Soft light bloomed, caressing Nessa's eyelids with a gentle kind of hope. She was hesitant to open her eyes, not quite believing that it was over, fearful that it was just an illusion, something born from wishful thinking. At Aoife's urging, Nessa peered through tangles of dark hair.

Heimaey and the others were crouched low, still hunkering down from the wind that was now gone. All except Orm, who was sat on the ground looking like he had been dropped. He made no move to stand as the others rose uncertainly to their feet, and Nessa was likewise inclined to stay as she was too. The surety, the inner calm that had filled her veins with power and strength, had left her, slipping away. The bond between Nessa and Aoife reverted to how it had been before, the deepness lightening, lifting. The withdrawal of such power left Nessa shaking and feeling weak and diminished, and a little faint.

*What was all that about?*

*I...* Aoife was at a loss for words. *I'm not quite sure, but I think that we somehow joined together. I think I gave you a bit of myself. My strength became yours for a moment.*

*So that's what it's like to be a dragon?* Nessa mused, bewildered. *No wonder you like to lord over us how superior you are compared to mere mortals. I know I would.*

*Careful there, my little Rider,* Aoife warned, although Nessa could tell that she was faintly amused. *I may take offence, and you won't like me when I'm offended.*

*Oh, will I not?* Nessa chuckled to herself. She swiped back her wild hair and saw that her hand trembled. Humour fled. *What happened and why? I don't understand how. I just can't wrap my head around it.*

*I can only speculate at this point, but I believe it's an instinct of ours, built into the bond to keep one another safe if we are apart, a safety mechanism if one of us is in great danger. I presume that, since you were in great peril, the bond snapped our souls together so that you were able to access a measure of my power and strength. That way you would stand a better chance of defending yourself.*

*Is it likely to happen again?*

*Since we've unlocked the ability, I'd imagine that we would find it easier to re-establish it at will.*

*How handy.*

*We won't be doing it left, right and centre. It's probably something best saved for emergencies. Besides, you had better not get yourself into a situation where it's required again if you know what's good for you.*

*Bah humbug.*

Bo and Luca joined the little gang, and together they made a loose circle around the spot where the monster had vanished, a ring of young, bedraggled men with wild, windswept hair and rumpled tunics. One of the twins tilted his head, considering, and stepped forwards, jumping a couple of times before inspecting the cobbles beneath his feet like he didn't quite believe they were solid. It was a good thing they were, otherwise he'd be joining the monster wherever it had been sent.

"Nice trick," the other twin said appraisingly, watching his twin's antics with a quirked brow before turning to Orm. "What's with the fire and the knife of fire," he then waved a hand at Heimaey, "and whatever you did."

Heimaey grinned and held up his hand. Loosely twined around his fingers was a length of rawhide. A small pendant, a talisman of sorts, dangled from the end. Nessa could just about make out the details from where she sat, the round, coin-like shape glinting silver in the street's light.

"That's a sigil," she said, unable to stop herself.

Heimaey looked at it fondly. "Old lady Nag gave it to me a few months ago. Said it would save my hide."

"Well, it certainly did that," a twin said dryly. Nessa thought that the words came from Luca, who was generally the more sensible one. Generally. Not always. "And then some."

"It's a seal," Orm added, peering curiously at the pendant from where he sat. "To be more precise, it's for Heīm, the Harbinger of Darkness. It's his personal one, if I'm correct."

"Heīm," Nessa mused. "He's one of the Atheals, isn't he? One of the nine high lords."

"Indeed he is," Orm turned to her, his tired eyes suddenly bright with interest. A healthy amount of colour was already returning to his naturally golden skin. "How do you know that?"

Conscious of the five pairs of eyes on her, and a dragon sitting in the back of her mind, Nessa just about managed to form a coherent response. "I...ah...read it in a book." *And Pharawynn's talked about them a lot,* she continued silently to herself, needing to confess her secrets in one way or another. Otherwise, they would build up inside of her, and she would be lost in them, lost in a maze of deceptions and lies.

"A book?" Orm asked, contemplative.

Nessa nodded. Aoife didn't say anything, probably assuming that she was alluding to their secret grimoire.

"Huh."

"Well," Hunter laughed, "maybe we should read more, then."

Orm smirked. "Maybe."

Nessa thought that was unlikely to happen any time soon.

"Talking about *maybes*," Luca said, looking at Heimaey. "Maybe you should apologise to old lady Nag. You know, for calling her a superstitious, old hag when she was looking out for you."

"Let's not get too hasty there, my good fellow." Heimaey slipped the leather cord over his head, the pendant settling against his chest, the silver bright against his dark clothing. "What happened could have been nothing more than pure coincidence."

"Yeah," Bo chuckled, pausing his attempts to follow the monster into the void. "That totally looked coincidental."

Heimaey shrugged. "I'm not admitting that the old hag was right without irrefutable proof."

"Don't suppose my input would sway you?" Orm asked, grinning. "Because she was right."

"That would be a firm no," Heimaey said as he tucked the pendant beneath his woollen shirt. "But your input might be nice when I start educating your little friend there in the fine art of self-defence." His next words were aimed at Nessa. "If there's ever a devil like that standing over you again, please employ another tactic rather than trying to pet the damn thing."

"Pet it?" Nessa all but spluttered. "I wasn't trying to *pet* it."

"It looked like you were."

"But I...ah..." In hindsight, Nessa supposed that it may have looked like that from where he was standing. "I guess that's what it might have appeared as."

"Ah-ha!" Heimaey was triumphant.

"That's not what I was actually doing, though."

"Did what you were doing involve stabbing the devil?"

"Well...no."

"Did it involve scaring the bugger away?"

"Uh...probably not."

"So, essentially, you were doing little more than giving it a pat on the head?"

*Give up,* Aoife advised. *I don't think you're going to win this battle.*

Nessa sighed and shrugged, neither agreeing nor disagreeing. It was pointless arguing over something not even Nessa was sure about. While she'd had no intention of petting the monster like it was a damn cat, she'd also had very little intention of actually harming it, especially after seeing what was hidden beneath the warped shadows and darkness.

"You see," Heimaey said to no one in particular, "this is the problem with girls. They're all sunshine and rainbows and 'oh, let's see the good in everyone and everything'. No. Stop doing that. There ain't no happy endings and magic wishes in the real world. No, there's monsters built of shadows and mystic mists and who knows what bloody else. Is there a way to solve these wee problems, I hear you ask, dear female friend?"

*I like him,* Aoife murmured. *He amuses me greatly. I take back what I said about leaving him to fend for himself. Should there ever be a time where he needs saving, you should most definitely save him.*

Nessa rolled her eyes. Over Heimaey's shoulder, she spied Hunter starting to grin. He, like Aoife, was enjoying Heimaey's little tirade.

"Oh, I'm so glad you asked, my wee, female friend," Heimaey continued. "I've found that the best policy is to stab first and ask questions later. That's always a winner when it comes to beasties."

Hunter's grin grew.

Nessa scowled. "I'm not sure—"

"I shall help teach you," Heimaey announced grandly, "in the fine arts of maiming and wounding."

Hunter's grin became a full-blown smile, complete with a devious twinkle in his amber eyes.

# Chapter 34

*Whoosh.*

Nessa barely ducked in time as the stick swung overhead, missing her scalp by the barest of margins, making flyaway strands of hair flutter in its wake. The brief amount of joy she felt at such an achievement was quickly knocked out of her, quite literally, when a booted foot connected heavily with her side.

She grunted, the air forced from her lungs, and fell to her knees, her arms instinctively wrapping around her waist.

"Up," the hazel-eyed fiend barked, twirling the stick by his side like it was a sword and not half of an old broom handle. "Fight me."

"Kind of hard…to…" *Gasp.* "When I can't…" *Gasp.* "Bloody well breathe."

The fiend smirked. "And yet, you can still offer up your lovely, little quips." He looked over to where a handful of darkly dressed men loitered at the side of the courtyard, perched on a row of empty barrels, onlookers who watched with an array of amusement and sympathetic winces. "I just don't know what I'm meant to be doing at this point."

"You're meant to be teaching her how to fight," Orm supplied helpfully, his voice a little muffled by the cigar he had propped in the corner of his mouth. "You don't seem to be very good at it."

Heimaey sighed and looked down at his stick, which was salvaged and modified to resemble something akin to a training sword, like it was to blame. Nessa, too, glared at it from where she was kneeling on the dirty ground, slowly regaining the ability to breathe, her ribs aching dully. She hated the thing with a passion. It was the source of the many bruises that covered her from head to toe. A natural-born fighter Nessa was not. This had been learned fairly quickly upon her foray into the realm of swords, punches, kicks and all manner of other painful activities.

"You missed the blow to the head," Heimaey informed Nessa, "but you didn't see the kick coming at all."

"Really?" Nessa muttered dryly, managing to pick herself up off the ground, tucking a few wisps of hair behind her ears. No matter how tightly she braided it, strands were always escaping, sticking to her cheeks and getting in her mouth. "I wasn't aware that I had just been kicked. Thanks for telling me."

"You're welcome."

Nessa glowered as laughter rolled across the courtyard. She whirled around, hands on hips. "What's so funny?"

Bo or Luca, whichever blonde-haired identical twin it was, shrugged a muscled shoulder. "You have so much sarcasm for one so small."

"Yeah," Luca or Bo agreed. "She's, like, sixty per cent sarcasm, thirty per cent rage and ten per cent bruises."

"And one hundred per cent angry cuteness," Hunter added sweetly, sensing that the thirty per cent rage was about to make an appearance.

"You'd be grumpy too," Nessa grumbled, rubbing her aching side, "if you were covered in as many bruises as I am."

*I think you've added another one to your collection,* Aoife notified Nessa oh-so helpfully. There was no attempt at masking her amusement. Nessa could feel it pouring through their bond.

Somehow, she managed to stop herself from snapping a sharp retort. Perhaps Luca/Bo was onto something…

*You know,* Nessa mumbled, *you could support me more. I'm struggling a bit.*

*A bit?* Aoife chortled.

*That's not supportive at all.*

*You don't want support. You want me to help you cheat.*

*It wouldn't necessarily count as cheating,* Nessa mused. *More like utilising our unique connection.*

*It's cheating.*

*Using it to its full potential?*

*Cheating.*

Nessa sighed. Sometimes it was pointless to argue with a dragon. *Can't you give me a bit of a warning? Point out what they're going to do so that I have a second to form a reaction?*

*That's cheating.*

*It's a pre-emptive strike.*

*You want me to tell you what they're planning so that you look like you don't suck so much.*

*I'm merely suggesting that we use our bond as any other Rider and dragon would. You know, sharing our strengths and weaknesses so that we are united, mind, body and soul.*

*Oh, my little Rider. You can try and put much reason behind this, but you're not going to sway me. There are times when you're going to have to rely on yourself. You need to be able to handle yourself in a fight without my aid. I would have thought that the events of the other night would have taught you that.*

Nessa flinched as the memories laid siege on her mind, frightful and potent. That night was happening all over again. She was forced to relive it.

There was a sharp jab to Nessa's side, bringing her back to the here and now.

"Less daydreaming," Heimaey ordered, "and more paying attention." He had poked her in her ribs with his training sword.

Nessa blinked away the memory of that night, the catalyst to how she had wound up in Jerome's courtyard, facing a fiend armed with a training sword, being whacked repeatedly—with an audience, no less. Nessa was beginning to think that she needed to redefine her definition of friendship so that it didn't include forms of physical abuse hidden under the guise of "self-defence lessons".

"It doesn't matter how much I pay attention," Nessa sighed. "We're just going to have to admit that I'm useless at this kind of thing."

"Maybe," Heimaey said, tilting his head to the side, thoughtful, black ringlets slipping over his shoulder. He wasn't one to sugar-coat things. "But I think you're improving a wee bit. A teeny-tiny bit. But hey, it's improvement nonetheless. I suppose." He grimaced. "Well, you almost have ducking and dodging covered."

Nessa glared, her hand still pressed against her still aching ribs. "Almost."

Heimaey shrugged. "Except for the kick at the end, you went for a good three minutes without me landing a blow. That's marginally better."

"You're not very good at making me feel better," Nessa said. "You do realise that, right?"

"I'm not here to make you feel better." He smiled sweetly. "That's something best left to your chap over there." Heimaey flicked his hand at Hunter.

Nessa scowled.

"I'm sure he's more than willing to cheer you up in any way he can."

Heimaey's murmured tone was a touch too suggestive for Nessa's liking. "Stop that."

He quirked a brow. "But he's over there, all bright-eyed and bushy-tailed, just waiting for an opportunity to come over and save your day."

Nessa resisted gazing over in Hunter's direction, refusing to give Heimaey the satisfaction of confirming whatever he thought he knew. Sometimes there was no point in trying to talk sense into certain people once they had a particular notion in their head, no matter how silly it might be.

"You're being stupid," Nessa said. "And that kick was mean and underhanded."

"That kick was the next obvious move, and you should have seen it coming from a mile away."

*I saw it,* Aoife traitorously told Nessa. *From miles and miles away.*

Nessa ignored her and the following echo of Aoife's chuckle. "How am I meant to see your kicks when you're wearing that...*thing?*"

Heimaey followed her gaze and plucked at his rather eclectic ensemble. "Thing? What thing are you referring to?"

"You know full well that those trousers are ridiculous."

"They're baggy."

"Too baggy."

"A man's legwear can never be too baggy," Heimaey argued. "They accommodate movement and have plenty of breathing room."

"They're so ridiculously baggy that you might as well be wearing a skirt."

Their audience laughed.

"You might be onto something there, Nessie," Bo chortled, his blue eyes bright with mirth. "He probably *is* wearing a skirt. The bugger just sewed up the bottom hem so we wouldn't see his unmentionables when he's arsing about."

"I'll have you know that these were a gift from my father," Heimaey said, plucking at the faded fabric that had once featured colourful stripes, the greens, pinks and purples only just visible. "He swore by these things. Came across them during his travels in the east. Reckons they're the reason my kin over there have so many children."

"Really?" Luca grimaced. "I would have thought that they're women repellents."

"Nonsense," Heimaey huffed, adjusting the waistband of his trousers, tightening the bow of a collection of silk scarves that acted as a rather decorative belt. "How else do you explain the fact that I have sixteen siblings?" Heimaey smirked at Nessa's dumbfounded expression and mouthed, "Breathing room."

"I'm going to go with the fact that he's a serial adulterer," Luca said. Bo nodded in agreement. "That's how his clan of curly-haired miscreants came about."

"Miscreants," Heimaey laughed. "What a great word. One day, I and the others shall rise up and take over the world. Just you wait and see. It's all part of a grand plan. There'll be stunningly handsome, green-eyed, black-haired beauties everywhere."

"And now we know how the world will come to an end." Luca shook his head. "Who would have thought that we'd succumb to a tide of beautiful idiots. What a grim way to go."

"Tragic," his brother agreed.

Heimaey twirled his training sword, his lips twitching with barely contained laughter. "You think me beautiful? My, my, Luca. I never pegged you as one who had such thoughts about me. I'm most flattered."

Luca looked unimpressed. "I merely meant that sometimes you look pretty enough to be mistaken as a girl."

"Yeah," Orm spoke up as he drew on his cigar, the tip glowing green. "When we were first introduced, it took me a couple of seconds to puzzle it out. It's those cheekbones of yours."

Bo and Luca howled. Nessa snickered. To be fair, Heimaey did have lovely cheekbones.

"It's all the hair," Hunter added, tears streaking down his face, shoulders shaking with laughter. "And the baggy clothes. No one can tell exactly what's going on."

"I'm finding this banter just proves that you're

jealous," Heimaey said, tugging at the ringlets that trailed over his shoulder in a messy cascade, barely held in check by a dark-blue bandanna. "Your envy is distracting and unhelpful."

"It's a great improvement to the previous activity," Nessa murmured, eyeing the practice sword in his hand, watching as he twirled it around and around by his side. "In my opinion."

"That lot can barely tell the difference between me and a girl," Heimaey informed her, "which means that they may occasionally mistake you for a boy. How does that make you feel?"

"I think we've established that it's *you* they get confused about, pretty boy," Nessa said breezily. "Not me."

"Wouldn't be so sure if I were you," Heimaey shot back, nodding to her outfit. "Dressed like that."

"Dressed like what?" Nessa looked down at herself, at her dark trous that were tucked into her black boots and at her loose, linen tunic. "In some trous and a top?"

"Exactly. Who knows what their feeble minds might mistake you for?"

"Someone who's dressed in a practical manner for an unpleasant and somewhat torturous 'training' exercise?"

"Ahh. There it is," Heimaey sighed, a mischievous gleam leaping into his eyes, bright and promising trouble. "The sass has returned. Which means..." He lifted his training sword, the point coming to rest on Nessa's chest, just over her heart.

Nessa groaned. "No. No more. I have enough bruises as it is. I don't want any more."

"Collect your practice sword, and let's resume," Heimaey ordered without mercy.

Nessa turned and searched for it reluctantly. Her training sword was on the other side of the courtyard, laying on the ground where it had landed after being launched from Nessa's grip by a particularly complex and painful parry.

"You're heartless," she told him. "You do know that, right?"

Heimaey grinned.

"Can't we just do some stretches?" Nessa implored, making no move to retrieve the wooden sword.

Heimaey shook his head.

"How about some sit-ups?"

He gave another shake.

"Push-ups?" They weren't one of her favourite exercises, but they were preferable to being whacked with a modified stick.

"Training sword," he said simply, pointing to it with his. "Then get into position."

"Hasn't everyone had their fill of watching me fail for today?" Nessa gazed at her audience, searching for an ally. "Obviously not," she muttered, turning back to Heimaey. They were all heartless, she decided, judging by the varying levels of anticipation and amusement on their faces.

"Come on, Nessie," Orm said encouragingly. "You'll catch on soon. Just like with horse riding. You learnt that fast enough."

Nessa frowned, uncertain. "The horse riding?" She could have sworn that they had told her she'd done it before. She just couldn't remember...

Hunter leaped off the barrel he had been perched on and jogged over to her, scooping up her discarded training sword as he went. Before Nessa could blink, he was at her side, thrusting the wooden handle into her hand, which reflexively grasped it. Nessa tried to look past him, wanting to tell Orm that he was mistaken, but Hunter was in the way.

"Come on," Hunter said. "Two teachers are better than one. You'll be kicking people's arses in no time."

"More interested in kicking your arse right now," Nessa muttered, her thoughts conflicted. Had it merely been a slip of Orm's tongue? Him getting confused about certain things? He did get things mixed up occasionally.

Or was it something else?

Nessa reached out to Aoife, needing a voice of reason to tell her that she was just being silly, that she was paranoid. She needed Aoife to tell her that Orm wasn't lying to her, that he hadn't been lying about things, especially small things like her having ridden horses before. If he could lie so easily about something so small, so trivial, then what else was he capable of? And if Orm was lying, did that mean Hunter was to?

Nessa discovered that Aoife had silently retreated, and Nessa got the sense that she didn't want to be disturbed. Perhaps Aoife was in sudden need of a nap? It was a little strange that Aoife had gone without saying something first, though, issuing a warning or some kind of threat.

Hunter laughed and nudged Nessa with an elbow. "If you ever want that to happen, then you had better start practising more."

"Can't I practise more tomorrow?"

"No," both Heimaey and Hunter said.

Nessa looked at them, a sense of doom settling in her stomach. One fiend was bad enough, but two? She wasn't sure she'd be able to cope. They got on like two peas in a pod. Sometimes Nessa couldn't help but speculate that they might be long lost brothers.

"Now," Hunter instructed, "get into position, and I'll help guide you through the next steps. Heimaey will go easy on you to start with."

Nessa glared at him, wondering at what her chances were of getting a few hits in before Hunter could defend himself.

"Ah-ha," Heimaey murmured smugly to her, his hazel eyes bright. "Here's Hunter to save the day." He gave her a knowing wink.

Save the day indeed.

If that was true, Nessa thought, then why did it feel like Hunter was merely trying to distract her from something?

# Chapter 35

Standing in the shadows of the alley, Nessa nervously bit her thumbnail as she gazed at either end of the street. To her right was Jerome's guest house, just in sight and with light streaming through the windows, streaking across the ground. Dark shapes of people moving around inside could be seen, and a couple of people loitered outside the door, waiting for friends to arrive, or just getting a breath of fresh air. That was what Nessa claimed to be doing. *Getting a breath of fresh air.* She was merely taking a breather from the overwhelming noise of drunken men and the eye-watering levels of smoke that spewed from pipes and cigars.

Hunter and Orm were somewhere inside, most likely milling around the bar waiting for their tankards to be refilled. They were in a good mood this evening. Probably due to another successful day at work, selling and distributing tax-free whisky. Who would have thought that doing something illegal would bring those two so much joy? As it was, Nessa couldn't share in their triumph. Not then. Not today. She had too much on her mind.

A mixture of guilt and excitement swirled around inside her. On one hand, Nessa felt like she was deceiving her friends, lying to them with every word that came out of her mouth. On the other, she felt that she had no choice. Not anymore. She was tired of waiting, tired of having to rely on other people, people whose trustworthiness she was constantly questioning. Were their intentions pure? Would they keep their promises to her? The unease that always sat in the pit of her stomach had grown too much. She could remain idle no longer. Orm and Hunter, even Pharawynn, constantly stepped around the issues at hand, keeping her in the dark no matter how she phrased her questions or how many times she asked them. They'd skirt around the issues, always finding another subject to talk about, another excuse to delay things. There was always another distraction lined up.

No more.

Nessa was taking things into her own hands. Finally. Whatever was being hidden from her, kept from her, was going to be uncovered. There would be no more secrets or lies. The truth would come out, and all would be revealed. There would be no more shared glances between Hunter and Orm, or furtive whispers between them. There would be no more of Aoife retreating when the subject of her forgotten memories surfaced or if Nessa dared suggest that something was being kept from her. Pharawynn said that she wasn't ready. Nessa felt differently. There couldn't be that much of a difference between calling upon one of the lesser dæmons and one of the high lords. Nessa had learned enough by now, surely? She knew what she needed to do, what needed to be done. What was the point of waiting any longer?

So there Nessa was, standing in the mouth of an alley, nervous in taking the first step in regaining her memories and discovering who she really was. Nessa just wished she wouldn't have to wait too much longer. It was bitterly cold outside, and her dress did little to ward it away. The sky was clear, no clouds strayed in front of the bright stars or the full moon, and the air held the frigidness of impending frost.

She shifted from foot to foot, trying to get the circulation back into her toes, and peered down the gloomy street once again.

"Come on," Nessa muttered impatiently, her breath a white haze in front of her face. It reminded her of the sinister mist that would often appear on nights such as this. "Where are you?"

"I'm right here, miss," a small voice squeaked from behind her. "Just like I said I would be."

Nessa jumped and clamped a hand over her mouth to muffle her squeal of shock. "Astrid!" she gasped, spinning around to face the small figure standing in the gloom. "What in the Nine Devils do you think you're doing?"

The girl smiled. "Sneaking."

"Well, don't sneak around me. Near enough scared me half to death." Nessa's heart still thundered in her chest, and her breathing was a little ragged even as she tried to calm herself.

"That wasn't my intention, miss." Astrid smirked. "Although it's nice to know that I'm able to sneak up on someone such as you."

"Someone like me?"

"A sorcerer," Astrid said in a hushed whisper, although there was no one nearby to overhear.

"A sorcerer?" Nessa laughed. "What makes you think I'm a sorcerer?"

"Well, since you're a lady an' all, I suppose the correct term would be a 'sorceress'." Astrid's little nose scrunched up in thought. "I reckon you're a sorceress because of several curious things."

Nessa was intrigued. A part of her rather enjoyed being mistaken for a sorceress. "Oh?"

"Yeah," Astrid said, getting excited over the prospect of being right. "You see, I know that you work with Mistress Pharawynn. Not in the shop like her other assistant, but downstairs where all the magic happens. Seeing as I've just been down there, I know that that's no normal shop basement. Then there's the things you had me steal."

"Borrow," Nessa corrected quickly. "I had you borrow them. When I'm finished with them, I fully intend on returning them. Preferably before Pharawynn notices."

"Then there's the things you had me *borrow*," Astrid amended, amused. "Ain't no normal person interested in that stuff unless they can actually do something with it."

"Maybe I'm just a curious soul who wanted a closer look at them without Pharawynn's discerning gaze upon me?"

"Perhaps," Astrid's eyes were bright in the moonlight, wide and knowing. "But if that was true, then why send me?"

"Why indeed?"

"Because you don't want the mistress to trace things back to you, should she notice."

"Mmm." Nessa was surprised, pleasantly so, at Astrid's keen mind. She had known that the girl was smart. After all, that's why she had given the task to her, but she was only just beginning to realise how astute the young girl really was.

"And then there's this." Astrid held up her hand. Twinkling just as bright as its owner's eyes, as bright as the watchful stars above, was a fine gemstone ring. Nessa recognised it immediately. It had been hers to start with, something that had marked an important milestone for her: her first summoning, when she had called upon a spirit to infuse the tiniest amount of magic within the gem. Nessa had gifted it to Astrid the day after being attacked in the mist by the shadow monster. That was the day when Nessa had started to question Pharawynn's true motives for helping her.

"What about it?" Nessa asked, struggling to keep the smile from her face.

"Whenever I wear it, I seem to gain a smidgen of extra luck."

"Extra luck?"

Astrid nodded, her short hair bouncing around her small face. "I take pride in the fact that I'm a little bit lucky anyway. What with being born a girl and being papa's favourite, and with being able to fill in for my brother without anyone noticing. You know, things like that."

"Right."

"Ever since you gave me this ring, though, I've had a bit more luck. I haven't had a chance to test it out fully, what with being busy with work and the tasks you give me, but I've noticed that I've been extra lucky." Astrid frowned delicately. "At least, I think it can be called luck, for that seems to fit best."

"Luck seems to be as good a term as any," Nessa murmured thoughtfully, impressed. The magic residing inside the ring was indeed luck, but only a drop, little more than a hint. Its effects should have been subtle, hardly noticeable. Astrid shouldn't have been able to perceive a change in herself whilst wearing the ring. The magic required for that was beyond the ring's capability. Only a bead of magic could be infused in such a small gem.

Nessa felt a touch of frustration bubble up. If only she knew more about magic, then she would surely have the answer as to whether or not the ring was acting as it should. Even with a tutor, there were gaps in her knowledge.

"I've always been swift on my feet," Astrid continued, oblivious to Nessa's turmoil. "But lately it seems that even if I'm running late on an errand, I still get there in plenty of time. And yesterday, I fell over when I was playing with my brother. Both of us swear that we heard my wrist snap. Once the shock wore off, though, it was perfectly fine. Not even bruised"

"How very fortunate," Nessa murmured, watching with disturbed bemusement as Astrid held up the wrist in question, rolling it in demonstration to show that it was, in fact, perfectly fine. *The ring shouldn't be able to prevent that sort of trauma.*

"Oh, and when I was in Mistress Pharawynn's place, the ring worked its luck once again."

Nessa didn't like the sound of that. "Please tell me nothing bad happened."

"Of course nothing bad happened," Astrid laughed, holding up and wiggling the digit that played host to the ring. "Extra luck, remember."

Nessa managed to stop herself from sighing in exasperation. Just.

"Of course," she murmured.

"Anyway, it went down like this," Astrid continued. "I waited until it was past dark and got into the shop perfectly, just as you said I would, 'cause the spare key was where you said it would be, and no one was about. At least that's what I thought."

Nessa closed her eyes in despair.

"Anyway, I found the pendant you asked for. Which, I would just like to add, wasn't very easy 'cause most of them all kinda looked the same to me. Then I made my way downstairs to the basement."

"Uh-huh."

"It was all dark, and I thought that no one was down there. You know, 'cause there were only a couple of lamps alight and everything was really quiet. Plus, it's fairly late."

"Mmm-hmm."

"Well, after being taken aback by all the things down there, I set about collecting all the pieces on that list you gave me. I crept around all stealthy like, 'cause I was kinda feeling all secretive and spy-like. I was also kinda enjoying myself."

"Okay."

"I got everything on that list fairly quickly. The most important thing was the only thing left to find."

"The book?" Nessa bit her lip. Of course, Pharawynn would hide the book somewhere. After all, that's what she did at the end of Nessa's lessons. Once Nessa had finished studying a particular passage, Pharawynn would quickly snatch it from her, tucking it away somewhere secret when she thought Nessa wasn't looking. It was always in a different place, but Nessa had noticed where she had put it a couple of times and had made a note of it. Most often the book was somewhere obvious, hidden in plain sight, tucked between others on the shelves or sat on a table with things strategically placed on and around it, camouflaging it.

"The book," Astrid confirmed. "I looked everywhere you told me to, but there was no sign of it. I was about to give up when the ring worked its magic again. I heard something that made me pause."

"And what was that?"

"A little snore."

Nessa blinked, wondering if Astrid was just fooling around, messing with her. "A snore?"

"Yeah, you know, it's when someone's asleep and they—"

"I know what a snore is," Nessa said. Hunter and Orm had educated her well on the subject of human foghorns. "It's just that if you heard someone snoring, then that means…"

"That someone was there?" Astrid chuckled. "Oh yeah. None other than Mistress Pharawynn herself."

"What in the Nine Devils was she doing down there?" Nessa questioned, incredulous, her stomach lurching. "She has an apartment above the shop."

Astrid shrugged. "Probably reading, by the looks of things. At least, she was reading before she fell asleep. I'd overlooked her because she was in the far corner, curled up on a settee that was facing away from most of the room. Anyway, I had a quick peek to make sure that she was completely out of it—which she was. And lo and behold, she had the book right there in her arms."

"Oh dear."

"Fear not, miss." Astrid said, mistaking Nessa's growing sense of dread for worry of a failed mission. "I got all the bits you wanted. Although it wasn't the easiest of extractions."

"Oh no." Nessa groaned. "Please tell me that you didn't take the whole book. The entire point was that she didn't notice anything misplaced or missing."

"I didn't take the whole book," Astrid muttered, her youthful tone caught between indignation and amusement.

"But?"

"But knowing that she was there, that she could wake any moment, I kinda didn't so much copy the pages like you asked but rather just ripped them out."

Nessa winced. "Ripped them out?"

Astrid scuffed her boot against the ground. "Yeah."

"Ah."

"In all honesty, the book was in a terrible state. A couple more ripped pages are hardly likely to be noticed anytime soon."

With a shuddering breath, Nessa said, "I expect you're right." The book was old and tattered, she reasoned with herself. Unless Pharawynn wanted those specific pages, another loose or missing page would be easily overlooked.

"Other than that, did everything else go smoothly?" Nessa asked, forcing herself to relax.

"Yep. Once I got everything on your list, I left. I even locked the door behind me and put the spare key back in its little hidey-hole."

"Excellent." Nessa smiled. "You didn't take anything else when you were there, did you? A ring or a brooch for your troubles?"

"No, miss. I'd never do that." Astrid was sincere. "I leave the stealing to my second brother. He can't keep his hands off other people's stuff. Drives papa crazy. Papa's given up trying to beat some common decency into him, often saying 'no sense, no feeling'. That must be true 'cause when papa did tan my brother's hide, he didn't so much as flinch."

"Oh." *Ahh...*

"I did have a quick look around the shop," Astrid confessed. "Not the second room. That kinda gave me the heebie-jeebies, what with the carved skulls, the talismans and the tarot cards. But I did have a quick peek at the pretty jewellery. I just had to, you know? All those twinkling gems. They just lure you in. I just had to look. I didn't touch, though. I don't want there to be any more reason for Mistress Pharawynn to curse me if she were ever to find out that I was there."

"She won't find out about you," Nessa assured her. "Not with your newfound stealth skills."

Astrid grinned.

Nessa slipped a hand into the pocket of her dress and fished around for the small coins that had gathered in a corner, and handed them over to the eagerly awaiting girl.

"It's not much," Nessa said. "But it's all I have at the moment..."

"Worry not, miss," Astrid rushed to say, her clever fingers curling around the shiny disks. "I don't do it for the money. I told you that. And I mean it."

"Then why do it?" Nessa asked quietly. "Why do any of it for me?"

"Well..." Astrid frowned. "Well, I guess there's a

couple of reasons."

"Oh?"

"First off, I guess I just want to. It's fun and kinda exciting. And…and I feel like I'm making a difference somehow. I know I might not be. Even if I were, I imagine that it would only be a teeny-tiny amount. But…but that's kinda how I feel about all of this. I feel like I matter and that I'm making a difference. I really like that feeling."

"You are making a difference," Nessa told her softly. "At least, you are to me."

"That there is another reason," Astrid gave Nessa a small, shy smile. "I like you, miss. I know that might sound silly and be a wee bit strange considering that I only met you a couple of weeks ago, but I really like you. You're pretty and kind and thoughtful. You don't treat me like I'm just a little girl."

Nessa looked at Astrid, at her mop of roughly cut hair that half-hid her delicate features, at the boyish hand-me-downs she wore when not in her courier's uniform. "You don't like being treated like a little girl?"

Astrid shrugged a skinny shoulder. "Being a girl is fine, I suppose. I'm okay with being a girl. I just don't like the limitations placed upon me by society. I want to have the choice of being something more than just a wife and a mother. I want to make my own way in the world if I want to, without a man having to be involved. I don't want to be a childless widow before I can own property or such. I want to be able to choose."

Nessa placed a hand on Astrid's shoulder. "I'm sure you're not as limited as you think. There are successful women out there, women who own their own businesses and manage their own land."

"Yeah, but how many of them inherited those things only when there were no male heirs to be found? How many of those businesses revolve around feminine things like sewing and such?"

Nessa sighed, knowing that what Astrid spoke of was the bitterest of truths. Women seldom made their own way in the world without a fight. Whilst possible, it was rare and hard, and their paths were paved with difficulties and disapproval.

"I'm not even supposed to be a courier, for goodness sake," Astrid continued, "just because I'm a girl. But I've proven that I'm capable of delivering letters as well as any boy."

"Perfectly capable."

"Surely that implies that I'm good at other things too."

"I'd imagine so."

"So, isn't it unfair that I may never be given the chance to find that out all 'cause of some stupid rules?"

"It's very unfair," Nessa agreed. "Maybe things will change, though, and you'll be free to do whatever you want. After all, there has to be a first for everything. Who's to say that you won't be the one to pave the way? You don't strike me as someone who obeys the rules. You're someone who makes new ones."

Astrid nodded eagerly. "I do like to do my own kinda thing. And I'm very good at ordering people about. I've found that out recently."

Nessa grew amused as she spied a mischievous glint enter Astrid's eyes. "Oh really?"

"Yep," Astrid smirked. "My elder brother, Rox, tried to take over leadership of the gang the other day. I swiftly corrected him in the errors of his conniving ways."

Nessa laughed. "Poor Rox." She had met him once last

week. Rox was older than Astrid by a little less than a year and looked like he could have been her twin, all fine-featured and thin, looking younger and more innocent than he had any right to.

"He brooded for a couple of hours, but I swiftly got him to fall back into line."

"I bet you did."

"The others now fear and respect me. That pleases me greatly."

"The others?" Nessa murmured with a measure of pity. Astrid was a force to be reckoned with. "Be gentle with them. They are but men."

Astrid pulled a face. "I'll be gentle as long as they know that I'm in charge."

"I'm sure there's no doubt about that now."

"There better not be. I ain't running no charity. If they want to remain in the Wildcats, then they better show some respect and do what they're told."

Nessa's eyebrows rose. "The Wildcats?"

"That's our name," Astrid said excitedly, going from a young girl to a strict leader in a blink of an eye. "We are small and fierce. We're the Wildcats. We decided that we needed a name a few days ago after we gained a few new recruits. Makes it easier to know who works for who. Ya know?"

"I'm not sure how I feel about you running a street gang," Nessa said slowly, all kinds of scenarios running through her head and none of them good. "It sounds a bit dangerous and…uh…unsavoury."

"Don't worry, miss," Astrid battered Nessa's concerns away with a wave of her hand. "It's not like we're dealing with the Guild of Thieves or the Alliance of Assassins."

"Alliance of Assassins…?"

"We simply deal with the exchange of information," Astrid said calmly. "If someone happens to pay for that information, we don't turn it down. We're running a legitimate business with no real main base. At the moment, the profits are quite small, but Alex says that, considering we've only been running for a fortnight, things are sure to improve. He's still housebound whilst his ankle heals, so he's taken over the role of being our accountant. He's good at counting and stuff. Besides, it's not like he's going anywhere soon, even though he's got quite good at hopping."

"Your brother Alex?" Nessa murmured, finding it hard to keep track of all of them. "Isn't Rox the one in the gang. Err, the Wildcats?"

"Oh, he is, too. But seeing as he only has one hand, he found the paperwork a little bit fiddly, so Alex took over. Rox is out and about, digging around for anything of interest in the streets. He knows lots of people, and if he don't know them, he certainly knows about them."

"Ah. So this is developing into a family business then?"

Astrid grinned. "Figured I'd make the most out of having so many brothers."

"You've wrangled all of them into joining?" Astrid had a lot of brothers, and Nessa struggled to keep track of the handful Astrid had already told her about. She couldn't handle having to learn more.

"Not all of them. Just most of them. Plus a few of their friends." A calculating expression settled on Astrid's face. "We have a nice, little network."

"I'll take your word on it," Nessa murmured, absently wondering why Astrid had the notion that social constraints were holding her back. It sounded to Nessa like she was in charge of a rapidly growing organisation. "Speaking of the others, have they heard anything of interest?"

"Nothing much in the last couple of days," Astrid said. "The report is being written up. I'll have it delivered tomorrow if you want? But it seems to have been quite boring the past few days."

"No sightings of any creepy mist?"

"Nothing major. A couple of people have claimed they've seen mist from afar, at the end of streets and such, but it was only at ankle height. So I'm guessing that we're safe from any devils larger than a rat for the time being."

"Can't say that I'm particularly fond of rats."

"I prefer rats to people-eating devils."

"We don't know for sure that the people disappearing are being eaten by them."

Astrid quirked a brow, unimpressed. "People venture into the mist and are never seen again. Whether they are eaten or vanish is just a technicality in my opinion. I'd rather not have either happen to me or anyone I care about."

"I take it that a list of disappearances is still being collected?" Nessa grimaced. This was what Astrid's little gang had been formed for, to gather information on the mist and those who had been swallowed by it. A little over a week ago, Nessa had been attacked by a shadow monster, a spirit of light gone dark. A little over a week ago, Nessa had, by chance, run into Astrid once again. Astrid's growing gang had already uncovered a string of disappearances that Hunter and Orm's friends had so far missed; they were people who were easily overlooked: beggars, thieves and petty criminals. The ones who had no friends, no family. The invisibles. Easy pickings for the foul things that lurked in the darkness and the mist.

One day, the man who lived in a shallow alcove in a lonely alley was there; the next, he was gone, his meagre worldly belongings left behind. The same went for the little girl who sat by the waterfront week after week, waiting for a father who had long since abandoned her to return, hardly daring to move in case she missed him. In what seemed like a blink of an eye, she was gone, like she had been nothing more than a ghost to start with.

They were the kind of people who others refused to make eye contact with, with whom they would never interact. They were the people about which others might faintly wonder "why is there a pile of blankets and an old backpack sat unattended in that alcove?" or "wasn't there a little girl who used to wait over there in that spot for hours on end?" Any concern, any arising thoughts would disappear with a shrug and a turned back. And that was the end of that. It was like those missing people had barely existed at all.

"We have a list," Astrid said, "but it's a tricky thing to sift through and identify who might have been taken by the devil mist and those who have simply met their end on the point of a criminal's blade."

"Tricky indeed."

"We're mostly working with descriptions rather than names," Astrid sighed. "It's not easy."

"No, I suppose it's not." Nessa placed a hand on Astrid's shoulder. "But keep up the good work. It's beyond valuable to me."

"It's no problem, miss. It gives us something to do when we're bored. And with most of my brothers out of the house, it means that there's usually more dinner left for me. And speaking of dinner..." Astrid shrugged, and a bag slipped free from her shoulder. Astrid handed a heavy satchel over to Nessa. "I best be heading home. Otherwise, I'll be getting naught but scraps."

"It's quite late for dinner," Nessa remarked, gazing up at the moon, noting how high it was in the sky.

"Pa works funny hours in the smithy," Astrid explained. "Ma tends to revolve meals around his shifts."

"Ah."

"Good luck with that," Astrid nodded at the bag clutched to Nessa's chest, "I'll see you soon." She turned on her heel and began to amble away.

"Safe travels."

Nessa went to leave, but paused in the mouth of the alley, casting a searching look behind her. A question was poised on the tip of her tongue. Astrid was nothing more than a dark shape in the near distance.

"The Wildcats?" Nessa asked, her voice echoing down the narrow passageway. "Where did you come up with that name?"

Astrid slowed but didn't stop. The call for dinner was too strong. "I had a dream the other night. Something to do with you and a man, a bird and a cat. It just seemed...right. Ya know? It just clicked. Seemed as good a name as any."

Nessa stood still; her lips parted even though she could find no words. Silently, she watched as Astrid disappeared into the shadowed gloom of the night, unable to shake the feeling that fate was in play.

*You and a man.*

*A bird and a cat...*

# Chapter 36

Sitting cross-legged on her narrow bed, Nessa surveyed her hard work. Admiring it. Her gaze darted from the pages of her book down to the floor, making sure that the twin summoning circles were identical, double-checking that she had laid everything out correctly. If even the slightest line was in the wrong place, too thick or too thin, there was no telling what could happen. If Nessa had to guess, though, it wouldn't result in anything good or particularly pleasant. Pharawynn had yet to regale her with any pleasant stories revolving around spells gone awry. Horrifying ones, yes. There had been plenty of those. Chilling ones, too. But never a tale with a happy ending.

Nessa shook her head, sending such thoughts away. She needed a clear head, a focused mind. As Pharawynn often said, *negative thoughts lend themselves to negative actions.* Negative actions could spell death.

Death.

*Nah, it will be fine...*

Nessa envisioned a successful outcome as she continued to check the summoning circle, making sure that the nine-pointed star was painted in perfect proportion, that the seals adorning each point were drawn correctly. It was slow work, tedious. The personal seals of the nine high lords, leaders of the Atheals, were tricky and complex, similar to each other yet filled with subtle differences, a shorter line here, a curled dash there. If Nessa had more time to learn, she was sure that she would know exactly what each sigil meant and what they stood for. At the moment, she figured that they were like signatures, ones which could channel specific powers. Whilst the exact method of how they worked was beyond Nessa's understanding, she knew that they *did* work. Even as she had drawn them with her stick of chalk, she had felt the seals' strength, their power. Each time she had completed one, a rush of energy went through her, a deep and ancient force.

It was exhilarating.

It was terrifying.

Nessa wanted to know more about the Atheals. She needed to know more about the Atheals. But Pharawynn's teachings had made her wary of them, and more than a little fearful.

They were once akin to gods, worshipped and prayed to by lesser beings in a time long before humans roamed the land. A time when the mountains were young and the sun had only just flickered into existence. They were powerful and wild, and as unpredictable as the winds and seas. And, if you were inclined to believe the stories Pharawynn told, they were the creators, the architects of all living things.

They breathed life into the creatures of the sky and the sea, the beasts of the forests and the land. They breathed life into the very earth they walked upon with each step, shrouded in mystery and mists. The Atheals were not of this world. They belonged to a realm inaccessible to mortal flesh, a place between worlds. In their many absences, the concept of time was created, and the forests grew, the rivers swelled and the creatures became unruly.

The land needed to be governed, protected against itself and its untamed nature, and so the Old Bloods came into being, created in the Atheals' own image, containing a touch of their powers. The Atheals divided their powers and themselves into nine groups; each high lord presided over a specific faction of power with their lesser dæmons serving under them, their own powers echoing those of the high lord they were bound to.

The division of the Atheals wasn't nearly as clean-cut as Nessa had hoped for when she'd started learning about it. The lines between each high lord were blurred, overlapping. It made calling upon them a difficult and dangerous process.

Spirits are fickle things, Pharawynn would often say, toying with her necklace, stroking the bones like they had the power to calm her, to soothe her, and there are always two sides to a spirit, much like the two faces of a coin. There was great light to them, but there was also a terrible darkness. They were powerful and immortal, and while they were not susceptible to the changes of time, the world they frequented was.

Humans arrived and with them came change. Forests were cut down. Rivers were tamed with weirs and dams. Towns and cities were built. The spirits didn't mind the castles and the bridges. They didn't mind the swathes of land that were cleared for crops and roads. Not to start with. What they did mind, though, was the dwindling belief in the Atheals, in them and their powers. Gone were the days of unrivalled worship and wildness, of praise and honour. Gone were the sacrifices and tributes.

There was a conflict of beliefs between humans and the Old Bloods, a battle of will. The humans won, for the most part. The principle that the world was made by the Creator spread, growing and taking root like a voracious weed. Slowly but surely, the Atheals were relegated to little more than a faint memory of a long-ago time, the Nine Devils of the old ways.

The Atheals withdrew from the land, their hold over it weakening, dwindling. It was only because of a handful of people, Old Bloods and external users of magic, sorcerers and summoners like Pharawynn, that old ways still clung to life. Just. Whilst the Atheals may not be in the forefront of most peoples' minds, or even known to most, that didn't necessarily mean that they had left the land entirely.

They were there when the seasons changed, when the tide rolled in and out, when the sun rose and set. Just because they no longer took their physical forms didn't mean that they had stopped existing. As Pharawynn often said, how else can one explain the power felt during summonings and spellcastings if not for the Atheals? No one ever felt so much as an inkling when calling upon the mighty Creator.

Pharawynn always talked about the Creator with scorn, taking every opportunity to point out that they were unsuccessful in stamping out the ways of old, even after thousands of years. Superstitions were still rife within the gypsy and seafaring communities. Stories were still told around hearths and at bedtimes. The legends lingered. People like Pharawynn were determined to keep the beliefs in the Atheals alive however they could, either by charming customers with secretly enchanted jewellery or converting non-believers, giving them a glimpse into the shadowed world of the arcane arts.

After all, it had worked with Nessa.

Nessa shifted on the bed, tucking the loose pages ripped from Pharawynn's grimoire into the back of her own, and turned to the section she had dog-eared. It had taken her days of careful reading before she had come across a spell that fitted perfectly with Pharawynn's, complementing it. For all of the time spent on her study and tutorage, she hadn't uncovered a singular spell that would do what she desired. That would have been just too easy, wouldn't it? Eager to get the ball rolling, Nessa decided to embrace the true spirit of spellcasting and do a bit of careful experimentation.

Such things were frequently done. The grimoires were evidence of that. They chronicled the evolution of spells throughout generations, tweaked and improved slowly over time. If others had done it, could do it, then why not Nessa? She'd found two spells, each one focusing on a single key outcome, half of what Nessa hoped to achieve. Combined, surely the two halves will make a whole.

Past and present was the theme of one of the spells. The other's theme was healing of the mind. Together, Nessa hoped they'd give her some control over her mental block. She deduced, from the notes in her own grimoire, that they would work together in harmony and give her back her memories. And perhaps, if she was really lucky, allow her access to a small measure of her powers. That's all Nessa wanted, her memories and a glimpse of what her powers might be.

Content as she could be that the summoning circle was at its best, Nessa rose from the bed, careful of where she trod. The complex shape of the summoning circle took up all of her room's floor space. The last thing she wanted to do was smudge a line and have to start all over again. She didn't have time for that.

Tiptoeing to the window, Nessa pushed it open, shivering as the winter air rushed in, crisp and oh-so cold. She stood there for a heartbeat, gazing up at the moon she'd had to wait for. Heavy and full, it hovered just above the city's skyline. A forest of roofs and chimneys were shown as silvery-grey silhouettes, and Nessa knew that if she was to lean out of the window and crane her neck, she'd be able to catch a glimpse of the castle in the near distance, nestled into the side of the mountains, gleaming with darkness and gold.

She didn't search for it, because if she did, then she wouldn't be able to stop herself from thinking about King Kaenar and his Riders, namely Margan and Shadow. Nessa knew she shouldn't think about them. She couldn't think about them. There were just too many emotions, too much conflict and blackness, and those were the worst things she could dwell on when casting a spell of light and new beginnings, of healing and growth. She shoved away the negative thoughts, telling herself that everything would become clearer once she regained her memories. She would be able to draw her own, unclouded conclusions. She would remember and she would know.

Nessa reached out and plucked the mug of rainwater from the windowsill and moved around the summoning circle, pouring a small amount into the little bowls that were positioned above each seal. She didn't have much, having collected it during the brief rainfall on the previous day. There was only enough to cover the bottom of the bowls. It was meant as a tribute, an acknowledgement that she appreciated the works of Grið, the Seeker of Secrets, for it was he who would aid with the mysteries shrouding her memories. It was he who created new beginnings from past things, and rain was a representation of that. Rain was something that had been around since the dawn of the Atheals' awakening and was, therefore, something from the past, but it was also tied to new beginnings, to new starts. It washes away stagnancies from the air, encouraging flora to grow, to bloom, and sustains each generation so that the next can be welcomed.

With one tribute done, Nessa busied herself with the next.

She set aside the now empty mug and pulled out a small box from the bag Astrid had handed her. She set it down on the edge of the bed and flipped back the lid. Inside, nestled together, was a collection of stumpy candles, three sets of three different colours. Fire was Nessa's tribute to Fæle, the Player of Passions. It was he who would help her heal and grow, he who would help her discover herself and her powers.

Hopefully.

Nessa positioned the first group of candles equal distances away from each other, along the outer line of the summoning circle. Then, she carefully arranged the other two sets between them, creating a ring of alternating coloured candles: white to promote open-mindedness, green for healing and growth and silver for vision and clarity. Nessa didn't light them prematurely, although the added illumination would have been nice. She was currently working by nothing more than moonlight and the glow of a single small oil lantern. She hadn't lit the fire, nor had she dared to light any other candles in fear of them affecting the spell somehow. Not even the lantern was burning at its brightest; the little knob was turned down to the lowest setting. She also didn't want anyone to think that she was awake and disturb her.

Standing, Nessa admired her handiwork.

"Almost done," she told herself. "Just one last thing."

Crossing over to her makeshift desk, Nessa ran her fingers over her small collection of jewellery. She owned nothing more than a necklace and bangle, both gifted to her by Hunter, and a pair of gemstone rings like the one she had given to Astrid. Like that one, these too were made under Pharawynn's guidance, the gems infused with a tiny measure of magic.

Slipping the rings onto her fingers, Nessa waited a heartbeat to see if she could perceive a change like Astrid could. Nothing happened, at least not that Nessa could notice, and she was the one who had put a drop of magic in the gems. She knew that there was magic in them. Nessa briefly wondered if Astrid had just made a lucky guess, or perhaps, was simply more susceptible to the effects.

Such pondering would have to be entertained later.

*Perhaps with the return of my memories, I'll know the answer?*

That thought made Nessa smile. There was no telling what she might know, what she might find hidden behind the mental block. It was an exciting prospect.

Determination flourished, blooming in her chest, and she placed the torc bangle around her wrist, touching the purple gems with fondness. To most, they would be mistaken as simple gemstones, but she knew. She knew what they were. The truth was staring her in the face. Alone in the sanctuary of her room, she was allowed to be arm-warmer free. Her Rider's Mark was visible, peeking out from beneath the cuff of her dress' sleeve. The torc's gems—remnants of Aoife's egg—rested against it, shimmering even in the low light.

Nessa's fingers lingered on the bangle, a small smile curling the corners of her lips up. It was something that incorporated two of her most beloved things: Aoife and Hunter. The only thing that could have made it even more special to her was if Orm had been involved in its creation. Nessa knew that he hadn't been. She was pretty sure that he had no idea that it even existed, let alone that Hunter had designed it. Nessa could only imagine the things Orm would say if he knew, the innuendos and crass suggestions.

Still smiling, Nessa reached out, her fingers grazing the necklace that had been gifted alongside the torc bangle and brushing over the charms, over the shape of Ironguard, of a dragon in flight and the Hidden City's mountains. She'd love to add more moments to the necklace, other charms to commemorate important events.

*And I will. Just as soon as I can remember them...*

As much as Nessa wanted to wear it, she didn't, settling for simply arranging it, making sure that it sat neatly. Instead, Nessa picked up the talisman that Astrid had commandeered from Pharawynn's collection. It wasn't something from the storefront, a pretty pendant of polished silver and twinkling gems. No, it was from Pharawynn's darker collection, the one that was tucked away in the backroom, hidden from the fine ladies with a delicate disposition by a heavy drape. Only Nessa and a select few knew what was inside that room.

She saw it each time she came and went from Pharawynn's basement.

It was a room always shrouded in shadows, the shutters pulled closed and candles rarely lit. It was dedicated to palm readings and divinations, and the occasional theatrical conjuring. Pharawynn took select groups of people in there every now and again, rich folk who paid for a good show or those who were soon to be converted to the old ways. Sometimes there would be a visit from another spellcaster, a sorcerer who sought Pharawynn's guidance or help.

The room's walls were lined with shelves overflowing with books and figurines, candles and jars that were filled with an assortment of creepy things. There were skulls, human and animal, painted and engraved with runes and glyphs, and boxes which contained rings, lockets and talismans that were covered in sigils and seals of power.

Nessa slipped the borrowed talisman over her head, wearing it like a pendant, a *lamen* of protection. The chain was cool on her neck, the metal disk heavy on the spot over her heart.

Sucking in a deep breath, trying to steady her growing nerves, Nessa picked up the lantern and removed the glass cover, exposing the dancing flame. Setting the cover on the desk, she moved around to the summoning circle, lighting each candle carefully, slowly, murmuring the blessed words as she went. They were a prayer of sorts, one filled with promise and question.

It was a prologue for the spell that was to follow.

With the candles lit, small flames dancing on stubby wicks, Nessa blew out the lantern. Whilst it hadn't been all that bright, there had been something that had seemingly made its light reach further, touching the now darkened corners of Nessa's bedroom. The candles' illumination appeared more contained, subdued; their rings of light were soft and cast down solely onto the floor. They made the white lines of the chalk appear stark against the dark wood of the floor; they made the seals and sigils seem to glow with their own luminance. It was like nothing else existed in the room, nothing but the summoning circle and the moon perfectly framed in the window.

Nessa stepped into the centre of the summoning circle, sitting down cross-legged in the area that was free of chalk markings. Typically, the object that was being bespelled, infused with the power of the Atheals, was positioned there. That was how Nessa had made her rings, placing them in the centre of a summoning circle that was not too dissimilar to the one she now sat in. Seeing as she was the one being bespelled, she simply took the rings' place.

The spirit—or spirits—that were called upon would be summoned by their seals, their powers answering the call if they felt inclined to share their otherworldly magics. The Atheals themselves wouldn't make an appearance, not in full. That was reserved purely for conjurings, and no one was mad enough to conjure one of the high lords. They were too powerful to be controlled, to be contained by a summoning circle. If one simply called upon one of the Atheals like Nessa intended to, she would only receive a token of its presence, little more than a wisp of its essence. In some instances, depending on the strength of the spell, the Atheals may decide to send one of their subordinates to answer the call, a lower spirit which worked beneath the Atheals, acting as an extension of them, carrying out their will. This, of course, only happened if the calling was answered at all. If you didn't give them enough of a tribute, or draw the seals quite right, nothing would happen.

Nessa's spell was a big one, a tricky one. Whilst the principles were the same as those she had practised with the rings, infusing them with a smidgen of magic, this was on a different scale entirely. Nessa wouldn't be working with one of the lesser dæmons. No, she was about to call upon not one, but two of the high lords, and instead of their power going into a ring or a pendant, it was going to go deep into her, changing her.

Fixing her.

From the deep pocket of her skirt, Nessa pulled out a piece of parchment, one edge frayed from where she had crudely ripped it from one of her notebooks; her handwriting was wobbly and a little smudged from where she had been folding and unfolding it. She'd written the words of the summoning on that crumpled piece of parchment, taking the body of the spell from the pages of the grimoires and rewriting it so that it was easier to read. The texts in the grimoires were old and faded, written by hand in something that was in-between calligraphy and a messy scrawl. Nessa had found them incredibly hard to decipher or read easily. The last thing she wanted to do was trip over some of the words merely because she couldn't read them.

Nessa set the paper on her knee, one hand stroking the surface, smoothing out the worst of the creases. The shadowed light from the moon and the candles only just touched the scripture, barely illuminating the words. It didn't matter too much. Not really. Nessa was sure that some part of her must have memorised them by now. After all, she had gone over them enough times. The notes were there as guidance, Nessa supposed. They were a comfort blanket of sorts.

She gave one last look around the summoning circle, double-checking for the hundredth time that everything was as it should be, and sucked in a deep breath, steeling her resolve.

Nessa pushed aside her doubts and hesitations.

It was now or never.

Gazing up at the moon, one hand reaching for the lamen, Nessa began the spell.

# Chapter 37

It was a slow build. A steady build. But as Nessa's confidence grew, as her low chant gathered momentum, so did the energy in the air. It swelled, filling the room, heavy and static like an oncoming thunderstorm, rolling in from the window, flowing down the chimney flue, rising through the floorboards.

Magic brushed against Nessa's face, phantom fingers twisting and twining her hair, stroking, toying.

Alive.

Playful.

Nessa's chant, the spell, spilled from her lips like a haunting song from a long-forgotten time. The words were not of the common tongue. They were the lingering memory of the old ways, a remnant, a language of power. A language first spoken by the Old Bloods, taught to them by the spirits before they became known as the Atheals. The words were primal, raw, tasting strange on the tongue. They conjured up images in Nessa's head, images of roaring bonfires and wild people adorned in animistic masks and headdresses dancing in ecstasy, in feral abandonment. The echo of deep drum beats reverberated through the air, through her, and Nessa swayed in time with them, her chant taking her somewhere beyond her room, somewhere else.

She was transported. Transcended.

Nessa's eyes closed.

Nessa sang.

Nessa cast her spell.

The candles' soft light became fierce, turning the insides of Nessa's eyelids red and orange, yellow and gold. Heat buffeted her in waves, blowing hair across her face, tickling her ears, her nose. The floorboards, once wooden and hard, became earth and leaf litter, soft and welcoming, whispering and secretive just like the wind that carried the rhythmic sound of stomping feet, the heavy breathing of dancing bodies. The wind spoke to her just as the trees did, just as the stars and the rivers did.

They chanted alongside her, copying her words, singing them with her.

The energy grew.

The tempo increased.

Phantom fingers morphed into real ones, into talons and claws, into the sharp tips of wings and tails. Caressing. Stroking. Pressing against her. Testing. Trying. Curious.

*Would she bleed?* the beings wondered.

*Would she cry?* the creatures purred.

*Would she stop?* the entities sighed.

*Or would she die?*

Nessa squeezed her eyes tighter shut, battling against the beguiling whispers that urged her to open them, to look and join the dance, the wildness. She clutched at the lamen, the raised edges of the protection sigil digging into the palm of her hand. It gave her just enough discomfort to focus on, and focus she did. She focused on the ridges that dug into her palm and the border of the pendant that stabbed into the soft flesh of her fingers as they clenched into a tight fist around it. Nessa focused and cast her spell, singing it over and over again, faster and faster. If she stopped, if she opened her eyes and gave into the whispered promises, the alluring caresses, Nessa knew that she would be lost forever, her soul left to wander in the wildness of Void for all eternity.

The coolness of mist drifted around her, soothing her heated skin, softening the burn of the air's crackling energy, dulling the pain that pierced her chest.

Nessa gasped, and her hand spasmed around the lamen. A sharp point hovered over her heart, a claw or perhaps something more barbaric. She didn't know. It pressed into her, cutting her, slowly slicing through fabric and skin. She continued her song with quiet desperation, making it sound more like a plea than the powerful incantation it was meant to be.

Wetness ran down her chest, warm and sticky. Her nose filled with the scent of salt and copper. Nessa felt weak, scared. Her heart fluttered away like the wings of an earnest hummingbird beneath that cruel, biting point.

Nessa wanted to turn back.

Nessa wanted to stop.

This was different. Too different.

It was too late to stop, to turn back. The payment had been taken. It had been sealed in blood, just as her grimoire said it would be.

The drumming, the dancing, faded into the

background, muted, hushed. The caressing claws and the toying talons lingered for a second, hungry for the feel of her skin, and then withdrew. They didn't go far. They were still drawn to her, reluctant to leave, compelled to hover near, watching, waiting, breathless as their masters approached.

It was working.

The spell was working.

Nessa battled through the pain.

She battled through the misgivings, the fear.

Nessa redoubled her efforts, strengthening her resolve. It was hard. It was a challenge. Somehow, she managed to push everything to the back of her mind, building a wall around the pain, the distress, a wall that was startlingly similar to the one that was keeping Aoife from sensing what she was doing, from sensing what she was feeling.

Nessa focused on unlocking her past, her memories, her powers. She focused on nothing but that. There was no pain, no fear or uncertainty. There was only the path to becoming whole.

Mist wrapped around her, just as her song did, her words of power, her spell of strength and change. They twined together, binding, coiling around one another like snakes, constricting, wrestling.

Something happened.

Something changed.

Nessa was thrown back, her head smacking against wooden floorboards, against the earthen ground. She was in two different places at once. Her body and soul divided, separated. It was strange. It was painful. Nessa's back arched in agony. Her incantation came to an abrupt end as a soundless scream ripped from her throat. That didn't matter. Not now. The spell had done all that it needed to.

The Atheals had heard her call and they had answered.

The candles were snuffed out.

The moon was hidden by a deep, silent darkness. A darkness that consumed all.

There was nothing in the world but her and an ancient energy, a magic as old as time. It made the air hum and vibrate, and Nessa's Rider's Mark tingled in warning before it began to itch and burn like it was coming alive, like there was something beneath her skin that wanted to rip free from its prison of blood and bone, clawing and biting for escape.

The sensation grew and spread, slowly working its way up her arm, making her veins squirm beneath her skin like worms, like enraged snakes. It crept across her shoulders and down her other arm, seeping into her chest, her heart. Something was taking over her, changing her. Nessa could feel herself becoming something *else*, becoming something other...something *more*.

There was an awakening in her, one that Nessa had experienced before.

A gust of wind battered Nessa's writhing form, blowing her hair across her face, strands sticking to the tears that she hadn't realised flowed over her cheeks, down her temples. The wind brought with it forces unseen, forces to be reckoned with. Nessa blinked open her eyes and stared, disorientated and confused. She could sense them all around her, beings of great and terrible power.

Nessa had an idea of what she would be calling upon, but now that it was here, now that *they* were here, she began to doubt herself. They flowed around her, filling the void of darkness with a power so strong that it was tangible. It was overwhelming. When she had called upon one of them to bless a ring or such, their power had felt unimaginable, but she was coming to realise that was nothing but a small drop in an unfathomable ocean. It was nothing compared to now, nothing but a tiny, minuscule peek at what they could do, what they were.

It was terrifying.

It was electrifying.

The magic in the blackened void was akin to a fierce storm that bore down on her, filled with wild chaos, lightning and thunder. Nessa didn't know what was up and what was down. Was she floating? Sinking? She couldn't tell. She wasn't even sure if her eyes were open or closed.

Words reached her ears, whispered and hushed, filled with an endless echo. Nessa couldn't quite make out what was said, but it struck a chord with her. The *thing* that clawed beneath her skin paused, listening, waiting.

Soothed.

Tamed.

The beings, creatures of pure energy and magic, swirled around her, murmuring those strange words; they were invisible to her, but were surrounding her, touching her, holding her, learning all that there was to her. The *thing* inside Nessa paused in its efforts of seeking freedom, and hovered patiently in her veins, letting itself be carried throughout Nessa's body by her racing heart.

Then it reached the wound on her chest and it seeped out alongside the droplets of blood.

The beings stilled.

A thousand eyes turned to her, to the wound.

Nessa tried to raise her head, tried to look down at herself, wanting, *needing* to see what had captured so many beings' attention. They were drawn closer to her, jostling and pushing, filling the void with crackling energy and fevered mumblings. Nessa couldn't move. She was stuck, trapped in a prison that was her own body. Her fingers refused to twitch. Her toes refused to wiggle.

Nessa began to panic, to struggle in any way she could, which, seeing as she couldn't move, didn't amount to much. A grim kind of fear grew inside her, one that spoke of her spell having gone terribly astray. Was she lost to the Void, her soul ripped from her body? Was it to wander for all eternity, lost and alone?

Was she dead?

Instead of taking a payment of blood, like her grimoire had said they would, what if the Atheals had taken her life? Had she made a mistake with the summoning circle? Did she say the incantation wrong? Nessa had so very little experience when it came to calling upon spirits. Anything could go wrong, and she wouldn't know what.

Nessa wanted to rewind time to when she didn't know about the Atheals, summoning, and mental blocks. Nessa just wanted to wake up and forget about everything magic related.

She just wanted it to be a bad dream.

But it wasn't a dream.

She couldn't wake up from it.

The fevered mumblings jumbled together in a chaotic mess, and the wind blew with fierce gusts. Nessa decided that if she had died, then this was surely the Void, the place akin to a Hell for magic users.

*Dead...?*

Terror swept through her like a tsunami. Nessa's mind turned to Aoife. Could she tell that something had happened to Nessa? That something was happening? Was she okay?

Dead... It can't be true... If Nessa was dead, then that would mean Aoife...

A silence settled over the abyss.

The winds stopped blowing. The voices stopped speaking. It was like everything had taken a deep breath and a step back. The beings no longer touched her, caressed her, toyed with her. They abandoned her, leaving her where she lay, watching from afar as light slowly bloomed, forming a ring around her, soft and gentle like starlight, a bubble of hazy illumination. Nessa felt as if she had been swallowed by a moon.

She blinked and frowned, bringing a hand up to rub her bewildered eyes. With a gasp, she sat up like shot. *Oh, blessed movement!* She was no longer trapped in her own body.

The relief was short lived.

"Oh no," Nessa whispered as she looked all around the alien landscape, her voice faint, overwhelmed by the roar of blood in her ears, the panicked thud of her heartbeat. "I really am dead. I messed up that spell. I've messed up something fierce."

Nessa's shoulders sagged, and she slumped, sad. Defeated. She brought her knees up to her chest and rested her forehead on them, the fabric of her skirt warm and soft on her skin. Her face was streaked with tears, and she sniffled, a sob rising into her throat.

*It's strange*, Nessa mused, her brows pulling together, her tears ticklish on her cheeks and jaw. *I'm pretty sure I'm dead, and yet...and yet my chest hurts...* Was it possible to still be in pain when you weren't alive? Nessa thought that it was very unfair if that was so. Very, very unfair.

Shifting, Nessa peered down at herself.

In the ghostly light, she could just about see the ever-growing bib of blood on her chest, the red coloured almost back by the hazy illumination. Keeping one arm wrapped around her knees, Nessa plucked at her dress with the other, grimacing as the fine, woollen cloth peeled away from her skin unpleasantly, the cooling blood sticky and repulsive. Her dress was ruined, and not just by the blood. A long slash cut clean through the spot over her heart, the fabric parting to frame the mess that was her chest.

The wound wasn't big, only a couple of inches, but it was deep, opening flesh and scraping bone. It was nauseating to look at. Nessa couldn't withstand more than a quick glance. *Is it possible to faint in the afterlife?* Judging by the dizziness that washed over her, Nessa was willing to go with a yes—yes, it was possible to faint in the afterlife. *How bloody unfair is that?*

Nessa released the front of her dress, groaning in disgust as cooled blood and tacky fabric slapped against her skin, unpleasant and making the wound sing with dull pain.

"I wonder where Aoife is," Nessa wondered aloud, her voice whispery and faint, smothered by the mist that crawled around her. "She must be here...unless...unless dragons go somewhere else..."

Sat on the ground, on a bed of silvery roots, Nessa looked around her, searching for a hint of purple amongst the pale light. If Aoife was near, it would be easy to spot her. After all, everything around Nessa was colourless. A purple dragon would stick out like a sore thumb. That didn't stop Nessa from gazing at the forest of trees, though, their trunks slim and tall, their bare branches graceful and far-reaching, making a perfect canopy. They formed a web above Nessa, just as their roots did beneath her. She couldn't help but feel like she was sat in a great hall with vaulted ceilings and high columns. A cathedral.

The trees shone just like the mushrooms that illuminated the High Quarter during the dark hours and those that brightened the front room of Pharawynn's shop. They were filled with ethereal light, making the world around Nessa glow with soft luminance. It was a calm light, gentle. Something about it eased a part of Nessa, soothing something within her. The clawing beneath her skin was gone, replaced by a flood of peaceful warmth. It felt as if a part of her was being welcomed home.

*What a disparaging thought, to belong in the Void...*

The trees were beautiful, Nessa had to admit, but in a strange, haunting way. They were ghostly, their inner light making them take on a slight translucency. Nessa wanted to have a closer look at them, wondering if their smooth bark was soft like the mushrooms they reminded her of, or if they were rough, real and made from living wood. Despite her curiosity, Nessa didn't move from where she sat. Getting closer to a tree meant getting closer to the beings that lurked behind the trunks.

Silent but curious, they peered around tree limbs when they thought Nessa wasn't looking. There was no way for her to tell how many of them there were, nor exactly *what* they were. Though humanoid, they weren't human. The antlers and wings she saw from the corner of her eye bore testament to that. What they were exactly, she couldn't tell. She couldn't see more of them than the barest of glimpses; she wasn't permitted to see any more of them than that. As soon as Nessa lifted her head or turned to look, they would vanish in a puff of silver smoke, reappearing somewhere else at the edge of her vision. It was like a mystical game of cat and mouse, and Nessa couldn't shake the feeling that she was the mouse.

Nessa wondered if they were lost souls like her, dead souls who were left to wander the Void, or if they were something else entirely.

*Are they creatures born of the Void sent to punish and torment me?*

Nessa's bottom lip quivered, and she pressed her head against her knees, her dark hair falling around her in a tangled mess, a curtain that offered her the illusion of privacy.

"It's okay," she told herself. "It will be okay."

She almost believed herself.

Almost.

There was a rush of wind, a whisper of movement, and the hum of awed whispers from the spectral spectators filled the air. Nessa could only presume that Aoife had finally found her, joining her there in that ghostly world. Instead of joy at their reunion, all Nessa could feel was shame and sadness. She couldn't bring herself to look up, to face her bonded partner, and admit to her terrible, terrible mistake.

There was a sigh, soft, quiet. It was the sound of resignation, of contemplation. A gentle ring of golden light enveloped Nessa as something moved to stand over her. A weight settled on her shoulder.

A hand.

It wasn't Aoife.

Nessa stilled, hardly able to breathe as an energy, ancient and powerful, washed over her. Tranquillity flooded her veins, a peace so deep and profound that she had surely only ever lived half a life filled with illogical longing and misplaced fears until then.

She lifted her head slowly.

Her gaze met with that of another's.

Nessa blinked.

She stared.

A man of golden beauty leaned over her, tall and graceful, hair long and flowing, held back by a glimmering circlet. Tresses as pale as the fluff of dandelion seeds drifted around sharp cheekbones and a fine jaw, stirred up by a light breeze that seemed to only reach him. Light spilled like rays of springtime sun from his skin, subdued enough for Nessa to look at him, but bright enough that she was only able to make out all but the barest of details. *Were his eyes amber or bronze? His complexion honey or ivory? His hair white or silver?* It was like she forgot him even as she drank in the sight of him and his aureate robes.

His hand left Nessa's shoulder, and gentle fingers twined around hers, pulling her hand free from its death grip around her knees. She was coaxed up, his touch giving her legs the strength they needed to stand. Nessa knew that if it were anyone else, somewhere else, she would be demanding answers, asking the millions of questions that bogged her mind. With him, though, she was tongue-tied, unable to do anything more than gaze up at him, transfixed. Bespelled.

Nessa felt the weight of his eyes on her, brushing over her features like a caress of a butterfly's wings. He smiled, and Nessa found herself searching for a hint of fangs or something like that. She was sure that he was an Old Blood. What else would explain the golden light and the unearthly beauty? He was no mortal man. He was something *else*.

Thoughts, speculations, fled as his hand rose, the back of his fingers soft and warm as they trailed over the line of her jaw, the edge of her cheekbone. His eyes locked with hers, searching inside her, learning all that there was to her. His hand drifted down, settling on the lamen that rested beside the bloody wound on her chest.

With long fingers, he turned it this way and that, the raised edges of the protection sigil catching in the golden light, catching in *his* light. The lamen was coated in her blood, the sticky substance slowly drying and turning almost black. His thumb brushed over the lamen's surface, and with a flare of light, the sigil changed before Nessa's very eyes. The surface shifted like water, like liquid mercury. The sigil morphed into another, one that was growing ever more familiar to her...

Warm metal settled back against her chest as the man vanquished his hold, his work done. The side caught on the edge of the wound, rekindling the forgotten burn of pain. Nessa hissed reflectively, unable to stop herself. The man's gaze latched onto the line of slashed fabric and gaping flesh. Nessa couldn't tell what emotion shone in the man's bright eyes. Was it confusion? Bewilderment? Disbelief?

He frowned, pale golden eyebrows pulling neatly together. His gaze became intense.

Angry.

Displeased.

Nessa's heart missed a beat. She became scared. She

feared him. She was frightened of what he might do, what he was capable of doing. Not to her, necessarily. There was something about him, something which told Nessa that she was safe from the darker side of him. No, Nessa feared the revenge he would wage against others, on the ones who had harmed her.

And what a terrible revenge it could be...would be...

"It's fine," Nessa lied, her words quiet, unsure, little more than the faintest of whispers. "It doesn't hurt. Not even a little bit."

His frown smoothed as one eyebrow quirked upwards. He saw through her as clearly as glass. Anger turned to amusement.

"I wasn't even aware that it was there until—"

With his golden gaze fixed upon Nessa's wound, skin glowing with godly light, it began to itch and tingle. Nessa could feel her flesh knitting together, healing with incredible speed. In a blink of an eye, the pain was gone. The wound was gone. Nessa knew that there would be no scar, no mark. Still, it came as a surprise when she looked down and found her skin unblemished. There wasn't even a bruise, not the slightest of flaws. If not for the bib of congealed blood and the slashed fabric, Nessa would have said that it had never been.

Awed, Nessa rested a hand on the spot, blinking rapidly in astonishment and wonder.

"Th—thank you."

The man's eyes were kind, and a small, perfect smile graced his features. His hands rose and cupped Nessa's face gently as he leaned down, pressing his lips to her forehead in the softest of kisses.

Nessa's eyes fluttered shut as she drank in the feeling of him being so close. The feel of his hands. The lightness of his lips. She drank in the intoxicating power as it wrapped around her.

She felt so warm and safe with him.

So loved and cherished.

A sudden wave of dizziness made all of that flee. The warmth, the golden light, abandoned her. Darkness rolled in, bringing with it a chill that seeped deep into Nessa's bones. The man's lips left her forehead. His hands fell from her face.

Nessa was suddenly alone. Lost.

She spun in the darkness, searching. Confused. Gone were the man and his light. Gone were the glowing trees and the spectral spectators.

Nessa tripped.

Nessa fell.

༄ ♦ ༄

She was in her room, sprawled on her back on the floor. She stared up at the moonlit ceiling, blinking slowly, confused. *Why am I down here?* She wondered. Her mind was empty of answers, void of everything but the heavy pounding of a thunderous headache. She reached up to rub her eyes, but something on her fingers made her pause. They were peppered with a dark, sticky substance.

"Is that..." Nessa frowned. "Is this blood?"

Hers?

Was she bleeding?

The spell. The wound. In a rush, it all came flooding back. *The place of glowing trees and...and...and someone golden. Someone beautiful.* She tried to conjure the image of his face, but all she could find was...

Nessa shot upright with a gasp, her hands going to her chest, to the ripped fabric of her dress, to the bib of cold blood that no longer had a source.

"Impossible," she whispered, looking around herself for an explanation. *A dream surely?* That place, the man her mind refused to remember in full, the details were vague, hazy. It had to have been a very real, very strange dream. What happened shouldn't have.

The summoning circle surrounding her was unchanged, a ring of dim chalk lines, of glyphs and seals. They hadn't been smudged or marred, not even when she had fallen back. Nessa shifted into a more comfortable position in its centre, drawing her knees up to her chest. All was as it had been before she had started her spellcasting, all except for the candles. They were evidence that something had happened, that time had come and gone. Now reduced to little more than puddles of hardened wax, the wicks had long since burned out.

*How long have I been unconscious?* Nessa questioned. *How long was I there, in the land of spectral beings and light?*

Nessa's hand drifted to the lamen, holding it up to the moonlight, marvelling at how it had been changed, at how one sigil had been transformed into another that was more runic and familiar to her.

*But why? Why was it familiar? Where had she seen it before?* A headache had started a constant pounding in her head, strong enough to make her eyes water. It was like someone was banging on a wall.

Nessa swore.

The lamen slipped from her numb fingers, abruptly forgotten. It felt like someone was banging on a wall because, well, someone was. That someone was a large, purple dragon, and the wall was one built from willpower and amethyst, a wall that Nessa had constructed before starting the spellcasting that night. She hadn't wanted Aoife to sense what she was up to. So far, all the other times she had built a barrier to keep Aoife out of her mind, she had been met with success and no suspicion. This time, though, she had been found out.

Nessa didn't know what to do.

Aoife was going to be angry. Very, very angry.

Nessa's indecision, her uncertainty, gave Aoife the foothold she needed to break through Nessa's amethyst wall, and a tide of inhuman rage coursed through Nessa.

# Chapter 38

*WHAT IN THE BLOODY HELL ARE YOU DOING?!* Aoife roared, her presence swamping Nessa's mind, filling it with a dragon's worth of rage and distress. If Nessa hadn't been so overwhelmed, she might have laughed at the notion of a dragon being used as a measurement in such a way. As it was, Nessa felt no urge to laugh or even giggle. There wasn't even a hint of a giggle. It was probably for the best, because if Aoife sensed that Nessa was feeling anything other than absolute terror at being screamed at telepathically by a dragon... Well, Nessa dreaded to think of how Aoife might react. There was no telling what an enraged dragon might do.

And Aoife was pretty damn enraged, if Nessa did say so herself.

*DO YOU HAVE ANY BLOODY IDEA OF HOW LONG I'VE BEEN TRYING TO REACH YOU, ONLY TO FIND THAT YOU HAD WALLED ME OUT?! YOU, MY OWN*

*DAMN RIDER, HAD BLOCKED ME OUT!*
*EXPLAIN YOURSELF!*

Nessa knew that Aoife wasn't there physically, but she still couldn't hold back a flinch. A part of her half-expected a blow, a slap or something else equally unpleasant. Never before had Nessa felt such boiling emotions pouring from Aoife. Sure, they had bickered and argued, such as anyone bound together would. This, though, was something new. Something Nessa wasn't prepared for in the slightest.

*Uh—*

*I WAS BEGINNING TO WORRY! DID YOU KNOW THAT? OR DO YOU NOT CARE?*

*I...* Nessa couldn't form a coherent response quick enough.

*A BIT OF PRIVACY EVERY NOW AND AGAIN, I CAN UNDERSTAND,* Aoife bellowed. *BUT TO LOCK ME OUT COMPLETELY, IGNORING MY CALLS FOR SO LONG, THAT'S NOT RIGHT! NOR IS IT NECESSARY! UNLESS...UNLESS YOU WERE DOING SOMETHING YOU DIDN'T WANT ME TO KNOW ABOUT!*

*That's not true.* Nessa winced, knowing that her words were weak and lacked any conviction. *I just needed a bit of time to myself.*

*WHILST YOU DID SOMETHING YOU KNEW I WOULDN'T APPROVE OF!*

*Please stop yelling,* Nessa begged. *You're giving me a migraine.*

Aoife growled. *Tell me what you were doing.*

*Nothing.*

*You can't lie to me, not when our minds are connected. I can sense everything you're feeling. I know that your heart is beating a million miles an hour, that you're panicked and not just a little scared. I also know that none of this is caused by me catching you out, so why don't you save us a lot of time and effort in trying to circle the issue and just tell me.*

Nessa hesitated, torn between telling the truth, even though she knew it would only anger Aoife further, and trying to concoct a believable lie. She had told so many by now that it was faintly surprising she wasn't a professional yet.

*Come on,* Aoife urged, tone sickly sweet. *Tell me.*

Nessa should have seen the warning in those four words, but she was too engrossed in thinking up a cover story. She didn't want to lie, not really, and certainly not to Aoife. Not anymore. A half-lie would have to do, at least for the time being. Nessa told herself that once she made sense of what had happened with the summoning, she would come clean to Aoife.

She didn't get the chance.

Aoife, her foul mood inflaming her impatience, leaped further into Nessa's mind, her presence overpowering Nessa's, pushing her to the very back of her own mind. Nessa had no control as her head turned, as her hand rose to pluck at her dress, pulling at the slashed and bloody fabric. Nessa had no control, but Aoife did. She was looking through Nessa's eyes, controlling Nessa's limbs.

Nessa had been possessed by her dragon.

*Stop it,* Nessa commanded.

*What...* Aoife was mystified as she peered at the chalk lines, inspecting them closely, much to Nessa's dread. *What is all of this? Why are you covered in blood? And...and is that a summoning circle? Why are you sitting in a summoning circle?*

*There's a perfectly good explanation.*

*Oh, I bet there is.*

*I was just—*

*Redecorating? Doing some art? Dabbling in something you shouldn't be?*

*Well...*

*By all the known and unknown gods and devils,* Aoife growled, *you had better not have been trying to call upon the Atheals.*

*Ah...*

*WHAT IS WRONG WITH YOU?!* Aoife screeched. *DON'T YOU REALISE HOW DANGEROUS THAT IS?! YOU COULD HAVE DIED!* Aoife's words choked off with emotion. *You could have died,* she whispered, *and if you die, then—*

*I'm fine,* Nessa rushed to say. *I'm okay. Nothing happened.*

*But why? Why chance it? The risks are too great, too many. Why would you even think about attempting something like this?*

*I was just copying a spell out of the grimoire,* Nessa knew her explanation was a weak one, but it was the best she could muster. *I just wanted to see how these things work.*

*And you thought you'd try it on your own,* Aoife said with disbelief, *without even telling me?*

*I didn't think you'd approve.*

*Of course I wouldn't bloody well have approved.* Aoife withdrew a little from Nessa's mind, allowing her to regain control over her body. *Of all the stupid things you could have done, why this? Why such a large spell? So many things could have gone wrong.*

*I made an error of judgement. I won't do it again. I can safely say that I have learned my lesson.*

*Well, at least something good came out of this stupidity-*

*induced fiasco,* Aoife grumbled, anger slowly fading. *I worry enough as it is with Hunter and Orm's antics. I don't need you adding to it.*

*I won't do it again,* Nessa promised, still shaken by the whole experience. *No more trying to call upon the Atheals and spirits. I'm done. I don't want anything further to do with that world. It's nothing but trouble.*

Aoife sensed the sincerity in her words, and Nessa could feel Aoife's relief almost as her own. Nessa meant every word of her promise. She was done with the Atheals, with Pharawynn and dabbling with forces she couldn't control. If she ever felt the need to learn more about that side of magic, it would be purely from books and in the company of Aoife.

*You're nothing but trouble, my little Rider,* Aoife murmured with fondness. *But I'm glad that you are safe, and that you seem to have come through unscathed. Well, relatively unscathed. You do seem to have ruined that dress of yours.*

Nessa looked down at herself. *At least I didn't wear my favourite one. That would have been upsetting.*

*Mmm,* Aoife was thoughtful. *I'm going to presume that that was something to do with your payment to the spirits? A blood sacrifice.*

*I believe so.*

*And what spell were you performing to require such a payment?*

*I…um…I was trying to…to…*

*Spit it out.*

Nessa sighed. She needed more time to wrap her head around what had happened during the spellcasting. She needed more time to understand. Then, *then,* she would tell Aoife everything. Just another day or two. Then she would come clean entirely.

*I was attempting to access my powers. I thought...ah... I guess I thought that if I asked nicely, then they'd help me.*

*Did asking them nicely work?*

*No. I don't think it did.* Nessa didn't feel any different. Not in any way that mattered. There was no newfound rush of power. No magic coursed through her veins, ready to be harnessed, only disappointment. Worse yet, beyond the failure to gain her powers, the mental block was still there, as strong and as impenetrable as ever. Not only were her powers still walled off, but so were her memories. Her spell hadn't worked in the slightest.

*Well, that's a pity.*

Nessa was bemused. *That wasn't what I thought you would say...*

*What's done is done,* Aoife said in a tone that suggested a shrug of her shoulders. *I'm still miffed that you tried to keep something like this from me. Make no mistake of that. But I'm glad that you're alright, and that you've learned from it. Would have been handy, though, if it had worked a little bit. Then, at least I would have an excuse to get you out of that wretched city and back by my side. Makes my scales itch knowing that you're so close to King Kaenar and his underlings.*

*Doesn't make me feel all warm and fuzzy on the inside knowing they're so close either,* Nessa agreed. *Hunter and Orm seem to like it here, though. I guess that should count for something, right?*

*Bah! Running around searching for sinister spirits one day and then transporting illegal cargo the next does not constitute a good time, in my opinion.*

*We need the money, and they do seem to be making some interesting contacts within the smuggling and gambling rings.*

*Remember the saying "it's not what you know, but who you know". Maybe that should be applied here.*

*Maybe. Maybe not. I suppose it's too early to tell if their efforts will be beneficial and pay off.*

*I guess. But I do like some of the people we've met here, whether they come in useful later on or not.*

*Like Heimaey, Bo and Luca?*

*Them? Sometimes. Mostly when they aren't whacking me with wooden implements claiming it's some kind of "training". Jerome, too.* Nessa went to mention Astrid but swiftly remembered that Aoife wouldn't know who she was, and may feel inclined to ask more questions. Nessa couldn't handle any more questions. Not when she was so tired and confused.

Aoife must have sensed Nessa's turmoil. *Into bed with you, my little Rider. You need some rest.*

Nessa did as she was told, seeing as she was struggling to keep her eyes open. She stood, leaving the summoning circle as it was—she'd clean it up in the morning—and slipped out of her dress, discarding it on the floor. She was tempted to snuggle into bed as she was, but the residual smears of blood on her chest made her pause. Knowing that she couldn't go to bed covered in sticky blood, she stumbled over to her chest of draws, half-blinded by exhaustion.

Reaching for the cloth beside the washbasin, Nessa swiftly scrubbed away the dried blood, goosebumps rising as near-freezing droplets of water ran down to her navel. Since she was right by her dresser, she took a moment to find herself a nightdress, shivering from the cold as she did so.

*You do realise that you are as naked as a newborn babe, right?* Aoife murmured, amused. *And that your window is wide open?*

*I'm on one of the top floors, and it's dark. I doubt any lookie-loos would be able to see much. Besides,* Nessa looked down at herself as she tugged the nightgown into place, *it's not like there's that much for anyone to look at.*

*Bed. Now.*

*All right. All right,* Nessa grumbled, taking a second to shut the window and pull the curtains closed before slipping beneath the bed's blankets. *Pray tell, O Impatient One, why are you so determined to have me well rested all of a sudden?*

*I am merely concerned about my Rider's health.*

Nessa's eyes were closed before her head hit the pillow. *Is that so?*

*Oh yes.* Aoife withdrew to the very edge of Nessa's mind, the level of contact through the bond minimal; they were almost separate from one another. Almost, but not quite. It seemed that Aoife wasn't willing to part from Nessa quite so soon. *I want you at your very best tomorrow.*

Nessa burrowed under the heavy blankets, seeking warmth and comfort. *Why is that?*

*Because you'll be paying me a jolly old visit, and I'll be giving you a mighty fine talking to. I might even have Hunter and Orm join us.*

*Oh no.*

*Oh yes,* Aoife said quietly with fiendish delight. *I might just tell them what you've been up to.*

*You wouldn't.*

*I might.*

*Meanie.*

*Shh, little Rider. Sleep.*

With a small smile gracing her face, and with her bonded partner hovering protectively at the edge of her mind, sleep claimed Nessa in its dark embrace, even as her hand clutched at the changed lamen resting upon her chest.

# Chapter 39

Dreams besieged Nessa. Dark and strange. Lonely and bleak. They wrapped around her like a smothering blanket, like the eye of a wild storm. She was trapped in their centre, unable to fight her way free, unable to see a way out. There were echoes of anguished screams and sinister laughter, glimpses of cruel, green eyes and of tormented blue ones. They came in bits and pieces, a jumble of images and sounds, of memories and fantasies, of truths and lies.

She was back in Pharawynn's spell room, back to the day when she had begun to doubt Pharawynn's motives for helping her. Back to the day after the night-time attack by the shadow monster. Raised voices reached her ears, an argument that drifted down the stairs from the shop above. Loud and heated, something about it pulled Nessa upstairs. Perhaps it was concern. Not so much for Pharawynn but for the other person. Pharawynn was a force to be reckoned with even in the best of moods.

Nessa had seen her slap Sissy a few times for the smallest of infractions, and once just for the sake of it. For reasons beyond Nessa's understanding, Sissy never left, never shouted back or cried. She'd just continue with her tasks like nothing had happened, like there wasn't a red handprint on her cheek.

Nessa dashed upstairs and into the creepy room behind the shop front. The voices dropped down low, hushed, just as she reached the heavy drape that divided the rooms. She paused beside it, unable to resist the allure of eavesdropping.

"You can't just ignore this," a woman unknown to Nessa said through gritted teeth. "You can't just turn your back on us. Someone is turning spirits dark. You can't just turn your back on that. Things are going to get worst. Much worse."

"Can I not?" Pharawynn hissed. "I think you'll find that I can. With ease, I might add. I'll enjoy seeing how the other half fares now that the tides are turning."

"This isn't just about the Old Bloods. It will affect everyone."

"Not everyone," Pharawynn said smugly. "Some of us will prevail. I have nothing to fear. I have been faithful to the old ways. Perhaps if you join us, you might live to see how wrong you and your kind were to abandon your ancestry, your legacy."

"Can't you see the bigger picture? Can't you look beyond petty grievances?"

"Petty grievances!" Pharawynn barked. "How dare you. How dare you call my people's suffering nothing more than petty grievances."

"That's not what I meant," the other person said, their tone softening. "And you know it. Both sides have suffered in this lifetime of warring. Perhaps it's time to put aside past differences and finally work together again."

Pharawynn snorted. "Yes, because the last time was so successful, wasn't it? No one got stabbed in the back or discarded if they weren't useful enough."

"The funny thing about you mortals," the other person said conversationally, "is that you have this strange ability to hold onto grudges for things that happened long before your time."

Nessa inched closer to the drape-covered archway, the mention of Old Bloods and mortals drawing her forwards like a moth to a flame.

"Before my time?" Pharawynn hissed. "The arrogance and the ignorance of your kind truly astounds me. It really does."

"Your self-serving bitchiness is the only astounding thing here."

Nessa's eyes went wide. One didn't insult Pharawynn under her own roof, not if one wanted to leave the place uninjured and uncursed. She moved to peer through the gap between the drape and the archway. She was able to see the figures of two people standing by the counter, facing each other over it: Pharawynn and a woman Nessa hadn't seen before.

Such was the layout of the room, the woman was standing with her side to Nessa, her hands braced on the countertop. Her bearing spoke of barely constrained anger. Her shoulders were tense beneath her black dress, and wisps of dark hair escaped from her long braid, framing her youthful face. Pharawynn, Nessa saw with surprise, stood with her back pressed up against the wall, her arms crossed protectively over her chest, trying to put as much space between herself and the woman as possible. It was unusual, seeing as Pharawynn was never one to back down in any disagreement or fight. Nessa wondered who the woman was to make Pharawynn so cautious. Fearful, even.

Nessa wondered *what* exactly the woman was.

"Bitch, I may be," Pharawynn said stiffly, her cheeks flushing pink. "But at least I stand by my promises."

"And what promises would those be?"

"To remember what happened before. To remember all those who were failed. To remember who my enemies are."

"We are not your enemies."

"I wouldn't say you are my allies. And if you aren't with me, then you're against me."

"That's a very narrow way of seeing things. Very black and white."

"Perhaps. But it keeps me focused. It keeps me on my chosen path."

"A path which makes you turn away from the suffering of my kind? A path that allows you to turn away from the chance to help, to make a real difference in what is to come?"

"I'll do unto you and your kind just as they did unto me and mine," Pharawynn snarled. "Do you think that it all stopped after you cowards ran off into hiding? The slaughter and the executions, the persecution? It didn't. It carried on regardless of whether summoners were allied with the Old Bloods or not. It carried on whether *we* were allied or not. My kind tried to help you and yours. In the end, it mattered not. The Old Bloods chose to hide where King Kaenar couldn't find them. Unable to get them, his wrath turned upon those he could find. We were punished. If we are not careful, we are still punished. We might not have a lifespan as far-reaching as halflings and Old Bloods, but that doesn't mean we don't remember. The legacy of those days runs through our blood. It's in our bones. We don't forget, Maud. We won't forgive."

"Not all Old Bloods left," Maud said heatedly. "There were those who stayed. Those who tried to aid their allies in any way they could."

"A handful," Pharawynn snipped. "A few good deeds don't undo the damage that was done. Old Bloods are and always will be my enemies. I will never help any of you."

Nessa frowned. That couldn't be true. She was an Old Blood. Pharawynn knew it and was helping her. Pharawynn had never treated Nessa like an enemy.

"We believed that we were doing the right thing," Maud insisted. "There needed to be enough of us left to aid and protect—"

"Your fabled chosen one," Pharawynn laughed, red lips twisting into a cruel smile. "The one who is to save us all."

Maud's back straightened, her shoulder's stiffening.

"Where is this chosen one? We've all been waiting. What, five hundred years? I think it's time for them to finally make an appearance, don't you? In fact, it's been so long, some of us think that your chosen one is nothing but a lie, a story to be used as an excuse by the likes of you."

"And what do you think?

"I think that I don't need to be saved by anyone."

"Fine then," Maud bit out. "I see that there's no changing your mind. I'll relay your thoughts to the others."

Maud turned on her heel, her black skirts twirling around her ankles like a fan, and strode to the front door, one hand rising to grasp at something on her chest. Nessa caught a glimpse of a gleaming pendant, one which bore a striking similarity to another Nessa had seen before.

The memory of Eliza resurfaced.

Filling Nessa's mind was the earnest look in her cat-like eyes as she had shown a medallion to her. Eliza's accompanying words whispered and echoed in Nessa's ears like a haunting spell.

*You need to be wary around others who do not bear this seal. They are your enemies...*

Those words were a catalyst, a summoning that called forth a maelstrom of fact and fiction. They twined together, merging everything into a confusing torrent. There were ravens and dragons, blood and fire, fighting and dancing. Nessa called for calm. She called to awaken from the dreams, the nightmares. But the maelstrom held her in its clutches, driving her deeper and deeper into darkness, into disorientating dizziness.

Then, with a sickening jolt, Nessa came back to herself. Her eyes snapped open as the darkness slowly receded, drawing back like theatre curtains. She stumbled, alarmed to discover that she was no longer lying in her bed but instead standing in the middle of a room.

A very large, very unfamiliar room.

Rounded like it belonged to a tower, the walls were smooth, black stone, shot through with fine threads of gold creating delicate patterns, glinting softly in the low light. Nessa gazed around, a growing sense of misgiving creeping up her spine like spiders, ticklish and unnerving. She could only think of one place that had such unusual and distinct stonework. But that would be impossible. Surely, she couldn't be *there*. She was dreaming.

Only, it didn't feel like a dream. It felt real. Too real.

The floor, smooth and threaded with gold like the walls, was cool and solid beneath her bare feet, and the air was warm and welcoming. Her eyes went to the fireplace, flames crackling in the open hearth, and then to the pair of armchairs that sat facing it. Made from elegantly carved wood and dark-blue velvet, they beckoned with the promise of comfort. The fire was the only source of light in the room save for the moon's pale rays which filtered through a great archway to Nessa's left, open to the night's sky. Gossamer curtains, coloured blue to match the chairs, covered the entrance in a fine veil. Beyond them, Nessa could see the shapes of other towers and spires in the near distance, gleaming black-gold in the moonlight. Whether the archway opened up onto a wide balcony or something else, Nessa couldn't be sure. Maybe she'll explore that later.

The vast collection of weaponry and armoury lining the high walls captured her attention. There were swords and daggers, spears and pikes. Too many to count, and a great many of them looked like they had seen combat, blade edges dented and chipped. Others were decorative, almost ceremonial in appearance. They were hung neatly from the dark walls, arranged in an order that Nessa couldn't quite decipher, each implement displayed with precision and care.

Nessa thought that Hunter would have loved to see this display, maybe Orm too. Both of them had a weakness when it came to stabby things, much like she did with plush fabrics and gorgeous gowns.

She admired the weapons from afar, then turned her attention to the suits of armour. Nessa had never seen one up close and in person before. At least, not that she could remember. Mannequins held them upright, like soldiers ready for action. They were placed at intervals around the room, dividing the weaponry into blocks. Nessa had imagined that a suit of armour would be heavy and cumbersome, ugly and sinister. These though, were elegant, each one unique, beautiful in a strange way.

Nessa slowly turned on her heel, her eyes jumping from one suit of armour to the next. They all looked old to her, although well looked after. The many different designs, the styles, felt dated by at least decades, if not centuries.

Nessa paused.

The ring of weapons and armour gave way to a large four-poster bed.

A bed that was occupied.

Nessa's eyes went wide.

"Impossible... It can't be him," she whispered as she was compelled forwards by a force unseen, a pull that tugged her closer to the bed.

Shadow was asleep, eyes closed, face relaxed. Half of his black hair was drawn back into a messy bun, the rest falling around his shoulders in raven waves, looking soft and touchable in the flickering firelight. He was reclined casually atop his velvet bedding, his back nestled against a collection of decorative pillows, wearing only a pair of dark trous.

Nessa knew she shouldn't, but she couldn't help herself. She drank in the sight of his bare chest, his chiselled abs, his strong arms. She had seen Hunter and

Orm shirtless a few times, but they were nothing compared to Shadow. He'd had centuries to hone his physique to perfection.

Her mouth had gone dry; Nessa swallowed nervously and dragged her gaze away from his body, up to his face.

Shadow looked so different asleep. He was almost another person entirely. The tension was washed from his features, transforming him, leaving him looking younger, calmer. Kinder. His handsome face was relaxed, his lips parted ever so slightly, a breath away from the faintest of smiles. His brow was smooth, uncreased by strain and thought. It was strange seeing him this way. Shadow wasn't someone who Nessa would ever envisage as vulnerable, but for some reason, that's how Nessa saw him in that moment. Vulnerable. Sweet, even. More so when Nessa spied the open book that had slipped down by his side. He had fallen asleep reading, Nessa realised with a start. How very normal. How very mundane. How very unexpected. Not at all what Nessa had imagined a villainous Dragon Rider would make of an evening. Casting spells and playing with concubines, perhaps. But reading a book...? That just seemed so very human. So very innocent.

Maybe there was more to him than just dark misdeeds and haunted eyes.

Maybe there were hidden depths to him that no one else saw, a side that gave Nessa a peculiar glimmer of hope. What if he could change? What if he could be saved?

Nessa's eyebrows pulled together as she frowned. Why would he *want* to be saved, or need to be? He was a Dragon Rider, one of the Twelve Kingdoms' strongest. What could he need saving from? Why would she *want* to save him? It made no sense. None whatsoever. And yet, she couldn't shake the idea. It was there to stay, a hushed urging at the back of her mind, quiet and unnerving.

*This is just a dream*, Nessa tried to tell herself. *And in dreams, nothing is quite right. You dream strange things and think strange things...*

A dream.

There was no other explanation. A very realistic dream, granted. But a dream nevertheless. How else would Nessa find herself in the castle, in Shadow's personal chamber? And what else could explain how she herself had changed in the moment. She was different.

When she had reached for the book, curious to see what a man such as Shadow might be reading, Nessa had paused with her hand stretched out in front of her, marvelling at its appearance, realising that she could see right through it. Nessa was a ghost, a phantom, reduced to little more than a pale shape of a girl. It was unsettling, and yet, at the same time, something about it felt right. Natural. She turned her hand this way and that, growing faintly amused at the sight of her being there, but only just.

Peering through the ghostly form of her hand, Nessa saw that Shadow's own hand, half-hidden by the book at his side, bore a strange blemish. Only the top portion of it was visible, and her eyes ran over the curling line that wrapped around his wrist and forearm.

*His Rider's Mark*, Nessa thought. But it wasn't like hers. It was different. The edges were stretched and blurred, the shape twisted and warped, making it look more like a burn scar than a shimmering tattoo. It wasn't what a Rider's Mark was meant to look like. Nessa knew that. Something had happened. Something terrible had caused it to change, to become deformed.

"What happened to you?" she whispered softly, reverently. She reached out, her fingers seeking his.

Shadow's hand twitched.

Shadow's hand clamped around Nessa's wrist.

She gasped as a wave of energy surged through her, electrifying and almost knee buckling. The pale translucence that formed her body rippled and quivered, and all at once, colour bloomed and she became as she was meant to be: solid and real, with her skin flushed pink and her heart racing. Nessa's eyes darted up and were instantly ensnared in Shadow's dark gaze.

Though clouded with sleep, Shadow's eyes, their deep depths and their sheer intensity, were not diluted. Nessa's breath left her in a rush. Reality collided with her dream. Shadow's hand, so strong and warm, slipped from her wrist and wrapped around her own, his fingers gently twining with hers.

"It's you," Shadow murmured, voice deep and groggy. "You're here." He sighed, eyes sliding shut once again. "But this is just a dream. The gods are both kind and cruel this night."

Nessa's lips parted. *He thought she was the dream? Why would he dream of her?* She tried to tug her hand free, but whilst Shadow's grip wasn't tight, it was firm. A dream or not, he was loath to part with her.

"A dream?" Nessa scoffed. "A nightmare, more like it." A really strange one. A shared one?

Maybe not one at all...

Shadow's eyes flew opened and he released her hand as if she had burned him. All visage of sleep vanished as he pushed himself upright, the warmth and comfort of his pillows forgotten.

Freed of his grip, Nessa hurriedly backed away, almost tripping on the hem of her nightgown in her haste. Any hint of vulnerability in Shadow's face was gone as he swung his legs over the side of the bed. His expression was hard, stony, as his eyes ran over her, taking in her wild gaze, her loose hair and her attire.

"Is this a trick?" Shadow mused, his voice dropping down into the familiar deep rasp that conjured a mixture of emotions inside Nessa, emotions that were too rich and complex for her to unravel, to pinpoint. "A test of sorts?"

Nessa swept her long hair over her shoulders, using it like a shroud to cover her front, and wrapped her arms around herself. Although her nightgown was long, reaching down to her ankles, and modest, she felt too exposed, too bare. "A test?"

Shadow's gaze turned from her, scanning the room as if he expected to find someone else there, lurking in the soft gloom. "Is this another of my brother's games? But then, if it were him, how could he know about you? I've kept you from him. I've kept you safe."

Nessa scowled, "Safe?" *Oh yes, he has kept me so very safe,* she thought bitterly. *Taking my memories away. Burying my powers. I've been as safe as can be, not knowing who I am and who I can trust. It's all been very, very safe...*

Shadow's eyes went back to her, confusion clear in their sapphire depths. "Or has Margan joined in with these games?"

"Perhaps you've just lost your mind," Nessa suggested, beginning to search for an escape route. It was dawning on her that, despite all logic, this wasn't a dream. She had somehow managed to transport herself into Shadow's private chamber. The idea boded ill. It shouldn't be possible.

But it was.

As soon as Shadow's hand had wrapped around her wrist, a rush of clarity had washed through her. She was there. In the castle. With him. As much as she wished, hoped, that it was a figment of her imagination, she knew that it wasn't.

The flagstones beneath her feet were cool...the fire's heat drifted through the air in lulling waves...and Shadow...Shadow drew her in, ensnaring her with his bewitching eyes. His eyes... Those eyes... They pulled her in and...and...

It was real.

It was all real.

It wasn't a dream or a nightmare.

It was something else.

*But how? How?*

"Perhaps I have lost my mind," Shadow murmured. "It wouldn't be the first time. I am long overdue for a break from sanity. But that's not the reason for this..."

"Is it not?" No, she supposed it wasn't, not unless they shared in a delusion. Nessa tightened her arms around herself, growing ever more conscious of the fact that she was in nothing but a thin nightgown and that he stared at her with a type of heat in his eyes that made her knees weak and her heart skip beats. Her gaze darted around the room, moving from the wide archway to the other entrances that were sealed shut by wooden doors. Nessa couldn't tell if they were locked or not, nor where they led.

"No." Shadow stood, his eyes deep and bright as the haze of sleep left them, and slowly stalked forwards. Nessa inched away, taking a step or two back before being ensnared by his gaze, spellbound as it locked with hers, holding her in place. "This is something else. This is something new."

"It's nothing but a dream," Nessa whispered, hoping that he would believe it even though she didn't.

His lips quirked into a small smile. "Do you often dream of me? You must in order for you to be so accepting of this occurrence."

"Of course not," she rushed to say.

Shadow looked knowingly. "Liar."

"This isn't real."

"Is it not?"

"Of course it isn't," Nessa insisted, flustered, her cheeks hot and pink. "It can't be… Unless… Unless you brought me here somehow…?" *That makes sense. Magic. He must have used a spell or something to bring me here.*

"Me?" Shadow smirked, coming to a stand frightfully close to her. Only a foot or so separated them.

Nessa was forced to tilt her head back to look at him. Her brows pulled together, and she murmured a soft confirmational "You".

"No," he said gently, his eyes running over her face as if she were a complex painting and he was trying to learn all its details, all its secrets.

"No?"

"This is all you."

"It isn't." *It can't be.*

"It isn't me, my little wildcat," he whispered, the depths of his eyes becoming as unfathomable as the deepest of oceans. "But then again. It shouldn't be you either."

"How could this be my doing?" Nessa hissed. "One minute, I'm in my bed, fast asleep, having all these weird dreams, and then…and then I'm here…with you… This doesn't have anything to do with me. This is your fault. It has to be." *It has to be,* Nessa finished silently. *Magic's involved, and since my spell failed, that means that my magic is still...*

The space between them, minute as it was, vanished as he corralled her back, boxing her in against the wall, his arms coming up on either side of her, his palms pressed against the gold-threaded stone. They were to the side of the fireplace, in a spot where the light didn't quite reach them fully, tucked between two suits of armour that stood like sentries on watch.

It felt secret.

It felt safe.

With the light only just brushing against them, soft and weak, Nessa felt as if she had been transported to another place and time, one where she could almost forget what the man before her was.

Who he was.

Almost.

Shadow was without his torc, and his Rider's Mark was out of sight, concealed by the curtain of her loose hair and the muted light. That made the illusion easier to hold onto. The only thing that broke it, though, were his eyes. Dark and deep, and unnaturally intense, they were filled with centuries of secrets and knowledge, pain and compassion, and quite a few other things besides. Things that made Nessa's stomach clench when she started to decipher them.

Shadow leaned down, bringing his face close to hers.

Nessa could feel the heat of his skin through the thin fabric of her nightgown, could feel the beat of his pounding heart, matching hers with near-perfect harmony.

"What if I were to tell you," he whispered, "that this is your doing? That I've played no part in it?"

Nessa battled against the lure of his voice, the low, hypnotising tone, at the intimacy there. It took all her strength not to allow her eyelids to flutter closed as his caressing words washed over her, soft and warm.

"I'd call you a liar."

"I'm many things," Shadow murmured. "But a liar is not one of them. Not when it comes to you. I'd never lie to you."

"Then how did this happen?" Nessa breathed. "Why am I here?"

"Why *are* you here? You shouldn't be. It shouldn't be possible. I made sure of that."

"With the mental block?"

"Just so, my little wildcat. Just so."

"But then…" Nessa's words, her thoughts, faded to nothing as Shadow shifted. The fragile barrier of heated air between them vanished.

One of Shadow's hands left the wall, sliding down to gently cup Nessa's face as he rested his forehead against hers. Their breaths mingled as their bodies pressed into each other's, moulding together in the sweetest of ways. Her arms loosened their steely hug around her waist and reached outwards, her fingers lightly skimming over Shadow's side as she made to hold him closer, his flesh hot beneath her touch; his muscles flexing, quivering. A shiver ran down his spine, and with a shuddering sigh, his chin dipped and his nose brushed against hers.

Nothing was between them, not even a whisper of air, nothing but Nessa's nightgown and Shadow's trous, which rode down low on his hips. Nessa knew that because her fingers grazed their loose waistband, toying with it, wanting it to go lower, wanting them to drop to the ground, alongside her dress… Nessa longed for there to be nothing between them but the invisible cord that was binding them ever closer together, body and soul.

"You are toying with fire, my little wildcat," Shadow growled, eyes blazing, heated and bright. He was fire, fierce and dangerous.

And she wanted to get burned.

Nessa hooked a finger into the waistband, feeling wanton and reckless. She was a different person when he touched her. Gone was the frightened, uncertain girl, plagued by doubt and insecurity. "Is that so?"

"Even though I have done all that I can to bury it, our connection is already too strong. How else can you be here? My soul calls to yours."

"Your soul?" Nessa could barely think. Barely breathe. "Our connection?"

"Even now, with the block in place, your magic still seeps out, reaching for me. Just as my magic reaches for you. I'd hoped that the block would give us more time, but it seems that fate has other ideas." He laughed grimly, little more than a huff of breath. "Who would have thought that you, my little wildcat, would be such a powerful *Sāwolwalkere*. But here you are, in full materialisation no less. We might have a chance after all."

"*Sāwolwalkere?*"

"Mmm-hmm."

His eyelids were heavy, hooded, his gaze far away. As if in a trance, his chin dipped further, and his lips grazed hers.

It was the lightest of kisses. The softest of touches.

It was hesitant, filled with uncertainty and tenderness, with sadness and longing.

Nessa savoured the slow build of heat that trickled through her veins, pooling in her stomach. It made her heart flutter, her skin tingle. She rose onto her toes, pressing her lips harder against his, earnest and hungry for more. A sound came from his chest, something between a growl and a groan. It was raw and tortured. It made Nessa's toes curl in delight.

The hesitancy left, fleeing alongside any uncertainty and tenderness, replaced by passion and a wild desire. Nessa was swept away in a wave of intensity, by Shadow's fervour. An arm wrapped around her waist, crushing her to him, lifting her. Nessa was helpless not to twine hers around his neck, burying her fingers into his long hair.

Shadow groaned again, pressing into her, crushing her spine against the wall, his lips working at hers with ardour, with expert skill that made her melt. A thumb caressed her cheek, tracing the line of her jaw, and then slid down the side of her neck, his fingers trailing over her flushed flesh, catching on the heavy chain before reaching the neckline of her nightgown. His clever fingers toyed with it, tugging at it. The fabric was pushed down just a couple of tantalising inches, and one shoulder was exposed. Nessa shivered as cool air brushed against her heated skin.

Shadow's lips left Nessa's, and she could feel his smile as he trailed a line of lingering kisses from the corner of her lips, over the fine curve of her cheekbone, to the spot just beneath her ear and beside her jaw. His lips paused there as he whispered something, and then ever so slowly, savouring it all, his lips worked their way down the column of her neck, following behind the hand that crept down over her collarbone, down and…down…

His hot fingertips ran over the bunched neckline, the fabric pulled taut by being tugged over her shoulder, and Nessa's head fell back against the wall. Shadow placed his lips against the hollow of her throat, lingering, burning. Nessa sucked in gasping breaths, his hair tickling her chin, her lips, silky and soft.

"There should be a torc right here," Shadow murmured, voice rough. "It is your right."

Nessa couldn't think clearly. She couldn't speak, unable to string even the simplest of responses together. His hand had moved southwards, his fingertips hovering over the small swell of one of her breasts. With the neckline of her gown pulled down over her shoulder, tight across her chest, an effect similar to that caused by a corset was fashioned.

Nessa grew shy, a part of her wanting to tug the neckline back in place. Not that there was all that much on display. Not that he would have been able to see if there was. Not with their secretive cocoon of pleasant darkness. A larger part of Nessa, though, didn't want him to stop. She felt nothing but pure bliss, a sheer joy caused not just by the fire of his touch, his kisses, but also by the tremors that ran through him. Nessa had one of the Twelve Kingdoms' most powerful Dragon Riders wanting her. Craving her.

It made Nessa feel powerful, to have a man such as him shake with desire, with longing and need.

It was a very powerful thing indeed.

His fingers trembling, Shadow traced the curve of her breast. It was the faintest of touches, the pads of his fingers only just skimming her skin. Nessa shivered, her breath catching in her throat.

"You'll be the death of me," Shadow groaned, his

fingers hooking her neckline with intent, slipping it lower…lower…

# Chapter 40

Nessa gasped as a jolt of pain shot through her chest, red-hot and blistering. Shadow hissed in surprise as he sprang back, reeling away from her. His hold on her was abruptly gone. Nessa was barely able to catch herself against the wall as her legs threatened to collapse, turning to jelly. One hand rose to her chest, grabbing at the hot, metal disk before it could burn a hole through her sternum.

The lamen rapidly cooled in her hand, turning icy cold in a blink of an eye. Nessa stared at it in bemusement, wondering what had happened, why it had happened. It was now the same as it had been. Nothing had changed about its appearance, nothing to indicate that it had almost been red-hot a second ago. She peered at her chest, finding that the skin there bore a small, pink mark. The pendant had scolded her.

*How strange...*

Nessa dropped the lamen, and it settled back into

place, the now cool metal soothing on the patch of stinging skin. She'd have to puzzle out what had happened later. Looking up, Nessa found Shadow standing in the middle of the room, his chest heaving, his eyes wide as he stared at his hand, at his blistering fingertips. Nessa went to take a step forwards, frowning, and his gaze snapped up, locking with hers.

Her step faltered.

The haze of longing, of passion and desire, was long gone. The spell between them had shattered. Shadow's eyes were as hard as the gemstone they resembled, filled with the glimmer of confusion and anger.

Nessa swallowed nervously and put her nightdress back to rights. There would be no more... She bit her lip, the blush in her cheeks turning from one of pleasure to one of embarrassment. There would be no more of *that*.

"What did you do?" Shadow asked, his voice dropping into a low tone that rippled with danger.

"Nothing." Nessa wrapped her arms around herself, a shield to protect from the cold that slowly seeped into her bones now that she was without his warmth, a shield to protect herself from him. "I didn't do anything."

"No?" He rubbed his reddened fingertips with his thumb meditatively, like he didn't quite believe he had been burned.

Nessa shrugged, trying for nonchalance. "Nope."

His gaze, dark and calculating, drifted over her face, seemingly weighing the truth in her words, then went to the pendant. "What is it?"

"Just something I came across." She held out her arm, displaying her torc bangle as a means of distraction. "I have a bangle too. And another necklace..." Shadow didn't pay any heed to her words, not even sparing the barest of glances at her bangle.

Nessa flinched back as he came at her, his hand snapping forwards with the speed of a striking snake, catching the pendant easily. He pulled it towards him, angling it so that the firelight caught on the sigil's raised surface. The chain grew taut, digging into the back of Nessa's neck as she fought against being drawn closer to him.

Shadow stilled. "What have you done?"

"Noth—"

"Do not lie to me," Shadow warned, his eyes flicking up from the lamen, troubled and joyless. "What have you done? How did you come by this sigil?"

Nessa blinked, taken aback by how quickly everything had been turned on its head.

"It was given to me."

"By whom?"

"I don't know."

"Liar."

"It's true!" Nessa strained against the chain, hoping that it would snap and she would be able to spring away. "I don't know who he was." *What he was.*

Shadow's hand fisted around the pendant. "How did you come to meet him?"

"I'm not sure."

Shadow growled. A muscle ticked in his strong jaw.

"I'm telling the truth!" Nessa snapped, grabbing the chain and ripping it from his grasp, a little disappointed that it hadn't burned him again. "One minute, I was in my room. The next, I'm in this bloody glowing forest, and this man appears out of nowhere. He was all glowy too and...and he changed the sigil from one of protection against the Atheals I was trying to call upon into whatever this one is." Cupping the lamen in her hand, Nessa considered it momentarily, wondering what it stood for, what it meant.

Shadow sucked in a breath, drawing her attention back to him, and Nessa found him glaring down at her with displeasure.

His throat worked. "You were trying to call upon the Atheals?"

Nessa winced. "I...uh...probably shouldn't have told you that."

"No need to tell me what you were trying to achieve with them. I can guess."

"Can you, now?"

Shadow sighed, resigned, and turned, ambling over to one of the closed doors. He pulled it open and disappeared into the black void beyond. Nessa heard a mumbled word and light bloomed from within, long rays streaking across the floor as the door swung partially shut behind him. Nessa's eyes went from the door to the open archway, seeing an opportunity and intending to take it.

"I wouldn't if I were you," Shadow called. "Bane is out there. He isn't in the best of moods tonight. He might decide to save us all some trouble and just eat you now."

"Bane?" Nessa's eyes went wide. "As in your dragon, Bane?"

There was a growl of confirmation from beyond the gossamer curtains, deep and powerful enough for the vibrations to be felt beneath Nessa's feet. She yelped and rushed after Shadow, realising that the archway was more than big enough for a large dragon to fit his head through.

Darting through the doorway, Nessa found herself

standing in the threshold of a large walk-in closet that was probably the same size as her room at Jerome's guest house, if not bigger. Shadow was rummaging around over to her left, looking for something on the clothing rails, a small orb of light hovering by his shoulder. Nessa stared at it in wonderment; then a twinkle at the back of the room caught her eye.

Neatly presented on plush, velvet cushions and metal busts, protected by a gilded-glass cabinet, was a collection of gleaming torcs.

Pulled forwards by a magnetic force, Nessa approached the tall cabinet, her breath hitching as she beheld the torcs' beauty, with their sapphire and dragon shell gems set in gold and silver. They twinkled invitingly, seductively. Nessa didn't know where to look first. Or second. Or third. Her eyes darted from one stunning neck torc to the next, drinking in the sight of precious metals and gleaming jewels, of woven threads and intricate terminals. One was familiar to her as she had seen him wearing it before, but the others...they had her spellbound.

A quiet sound of movement came from behind her, and she jumped as warm fabric enveloped her. A heavy cloak of black velvet settled over her shoulders. Nessa pulled it tighter around herself, savouring the softness, the shelter from the cool air.

"The ward is beginning to wear," Shadow said, coming to stand beside her, his little mystical orb following after him, echoing his movements. "I've been meaning to refresh it for quite some time. Especially since it will snow soon. Bane hates snow, and I hate the cold."

Nessa looked at him, quizzical. "Ward? Refreshing?"

Shadow peered at her from the corner of his eye. "You

just tried to call upon the great Atheals and yet you don't know what a ward is?" He shook his head and shrugged into a long overcoat, its dark-blue colour matching his eyes. "You are lucky not to have killed yourself. Or anyone else, come to think of it."

"Well, if it wasn't for you," Nessa grumbled, turning back to the glass case, "I wouldn't have tried in the first place."

"Not the response I was expecting."

"Oh?"

"Indeed," his tone was dry. "What you should have said was that you've learnt from your foolishness, that you will never do something so dangerous ever again. That would be the most sensible response, not trying to pin the blame on me."

"I'm not trying to pin the blame on you. The blame's already yours."

"Impertinent, little wildcat, aren't we?" Shadow turned away from the gilded case, not as enraptured by its contents as Nessa was, and faced her, folding his arms across his chest. "Humour me and explain how I am to blame for your stupidity."

Nessa only just stopped her mouth from falling open. "My *stupidity*?"

Shadow cocked a brow, amused at her growing outrage.

"I'll have you know that I only tried to call upon the Atheals to fix the problem you're responsible for."

The amusement vanished. "Your memories."

"My memories," Nessa confirmed. "The memories you stole from me, the memories you've hidden somewhere that I can't get to. If you hadn't, then I would never have needed to try and retrieve them."

"I presume that the block is still in place?"

Nessa gave a stiff nod.

"I also presume that you'll still endeavour to seek a way of having them returned?"

"Unless you would be so kind as to retrieve them for me?"

A humourless smile. "I suppose it's pointless in telling you not to do so, that you're safer and better off without them. At least for the time being?"

"Pointless and won't be believed."

Shadow sighed and looked away from her, his gaze fixing upon one of the case's higher shelves, at a row of torcs that stood out from the others. They were older and made from copper and bronze, unpolished and tarnished. They hadn't been worn in decades. Maybe centuries. Had they gone out of fashion? Replaced by gold and silver designs that the courts now favoured? Nessa wasn't sure, but she did know that a couple of them had been worn long, long ago and were now broken, the woven threads bent out of shape and dented. One torc was snapped clean in half, the wire strands sticking outwards like crazed springs. It was arranged on a thin cushion, the tarnished copper nearly black in the orb's light, the gems more purple than blue.

"I'm trying to protect you," Shadow said, staring at the broken torc with faraway eyes, his voice a rasping whisper. "I did the best I could given the circumstances."

Nessa's mouth went dry. "Circumstances?"

"Margan wanted to do to you what was done to me. I couldn't let that happen."

"What...what happened to you?"

"I was broken apart and put back together. Different. Changed. I was trying to save you from that fate."

Shadow laughed, a short, harsh bark, and waved a hand at himself. "From this fate."

Nessa was quiet, still. She gazed around, absorbing the closet that was bigger than her room at Jerome's, the wealth that was displayed by the finest of clothes and the almost full wall of precious torcs. Nessa gazed at Shadow, at his muscled arms that were left bare by his overcoat and at his deformed Rider's Mark.

If not for his Mark, stretched out and ruined as it was, and the haunted look in his eyes, one that spoke of dark memories, Nessa would have said that it didn't seem to have turned out so bad for him. But Shadow was a million miles away, and it didn't appear that he was anywhere pleasant. Nessa could feel his magic sitting just beneath his skin, fierce and poised to attack, ready to lash out like an injured animal. Hovering between them, the little, glowing orb flickered and dimmed.

"Somehow…" Shadow's throat worked, his Adam's apple bobbing as he struggled to swallow heavy emotion. "Somehow Margan discovered a secret of mine. A great and terrible secret, my truth and shame. I am beholden to him. At least, I have to appear to be for the time being. I fear that I have failed in that regard of late." He sighed wearily. "I thought that after all these years I was without weakness. Then Margan's scheming came into play and racked up a notch. It took me by surprise. I hadn't seen it coming. I hadn't expected it. And the next thing I knew…" Another humourless chuckle. "The next thing I knew, this girl was added to the mix. This small, innocent girl with the biggest, most beautiful brown eyes I've ever seen was suddenly caught in the cruellest of games, one without rules or regulations."

Nessa bit her lip nervously as questions bubbled up in

her throat. So, so many questions that she wanted desperately to ask.

*What was his secret and shame?*

*Did he just say that I have the most beautiful eyes he had ever seen?*

"This girl, though, gave Margan a run for his money. Despite being little more than a mere wisp of a thing, she managed to resist his efforts in getting her to join him in his plans. Even when he employed some of the darkest *persuasion* methods, she still refused him."

*Persuasion.* Nessa shivered at Shadow's choice of word. *What a nice way of phrasing it...*

"She even managed an escape during their latest round. At least, she came close. He caught her, of course. She hadn't made it far, and she was punished for her efforts. Something inside of me broke then. Which came as a surprise. I didn't think there was anything in me left to break. Not anymore."

Shadow looked away from the broken torc, his gaze going down to his crossed arms as if they might hold some kind of answer. His shoulders were hunched over, tense. Nessa held her breath.

"Margan is the youngest of us. He has yet to find his place amongst the King's chosen. He is quick to anger, still impulsive, and often fails to see the bigger picture. This, combined with the girl's resistance, was a dangerous cocktail. After her escape, he beat her, losing himself to his rage, his frustrations that his scheming wasn't working quite to plan. Something inside of me shattered when I saw this girl, this beautiful, innocent girl, bleeding and bruised and broken. I acted. I was helpless not to.

"It was by luck, or perhaps divine intervention, that

Margan was called back to the city before I was. At the time, I didn't know how long he would be gone for, nor how much time I had before I, too, was summoned. I was rushed. I knew..." His voice cracked, and he paused to clear his throat. Nessa stood shock still beside him, heart racing.

*Please don't stop...please don't stop.* Nessa wanted to hear the rest. She had to hear it.

"I wanted to save this girl. I needed to save her. But I knew that even if I managed to free her from Margan's clutches, she still wouldn't have been saved. Not completely. Not with the memories of Margan's torments lingering in her mind. I knew...I knew that they would never fade. So I took them away, shielding her from them."

Shadow turned to Nessa, his eyes shining bright. He looked so helpless and lost. Not at all a fearsome Dragon Rider. Nessa's heart twisted. Her lips parted but no words could be found.

"I took them from you," Shadow murmured. "But in my haste, I took not only the memories of Margan but of everything else as well. For that, I seek your understanding, my little wildcat, my little *Sāwolwalkere.*"

"But not my forgiveness?"

His smile was small, hesitant. "Are you offering it?"

"Perhaps."

Shadow moved and cupped Nessa's face, his hands warm and gentle. "But only if I return your memories?"

"The ones with Margan can stay where they are," Nessa said softly, sadly. "If they are so horrible."

Shadow stroked her cheekbone with the pad of his thumb, slowly, reverently, and dipped his chin, resting his forehead against hers. He gazed into Nessa's eyes with a kind of desperate longing, like he wanted to get lost in them, like he wanted to drown in them.

"Mental blocks are fickle things," Shadow whispered, his breath twining with hers, binding them together. "Who's to say I won't make matters worse?"

"You won't."

"And who's to say that you won't go back to hating me again?"

*Again?* "Who's to say I won't if you don't?"

"You've got me caught between a rock and a hard place, little wildcat." Shadow groaned, pulling her against him, tucking her head beneath his chin. One hand buried itself in her hair. The other slid around her back, fingers resting at the dip of her waist. "No matter what I do, I'm doomed."

Nessa closed her eyes as she rested a cheek against his chest, her hands settling there too. She savoured this more tender side of him, the warmth of his hold, the comfort she found with him for reasons unknown. Nessa listened to his heartbeat, strong and fast, steady and grounding.

*Boom.*

*Boom.*

*Boom.*

For a split second, Nessa thought she heard something over the steady beats: the squeak of a door opening, the quiet tap of booted feet on stone flooring. Her eyes flickered open, and she peered at the closet's door. When she found no one there, her eyes slid closed again.

"Can't you view this as a fresh start?" Shadow asked, voice caressing, the faintest of accents tingeing the edges of his words, rounding them. Warming them. "One where you don't see me as such a villain?"

"I have too many questions that need to find their answers on their own. I need my memories. They are what makes me, *me*. I feel incomplete without them. Don't you understand?"

Shadow sighed and leaned back. His hand slid through her hair until he cradled the back of her head. He gently urged her to look up at him. Her eyes, filled with inquisitiveness, rose to meet with his.

"I think you'll find that I understand a lot more than you can imagine."

"Then help me."

"I…" Shadow closed his eyes, wrestling with internal demons. "You really will be the death of me."

Hope bloomed in Nessa's heart. *Did this mean he's going to fix me? Undo what he has done?*

Nessa certainly hoped so.

The closet's door swung open, swinging wide. Light, blinding and white, spilled in. Nessa started and squinted, peering over Shadow's shoulder, trying to see who was there, trying to see who they had been discovered by. The blinding light came from behind them, reducing them to nothing more than an imposing silhouette standing in the archway behind Shadow.

Shadow cursed under his breath and twisted, shielding Nessa with his body as much as possible, blocking her from the intruder's line of sight.

"You have to go," Shadow hissed through clenched teeth to her, his eyes wide and shining with alarm. "Quick! Before he sees you."

A din filled Nessa's ears: the roar of blood, the racing thuds of her heartbeat, the panicked pant of her breaths.

"But I don't know how," she cried.

"Just—"

"Brother?" a voice intoned from the doorway, deep and eerily familiar. Approaching footsteps sounded out. "It is happening. It has begun. I can sense it."

"Go," Shadow whispered.

Nessa's vision wavered and the world tipped, darkened. A void opened and swallowed her whole.

*It has begun.*

༄✦༄

Nessa sat up on her bed with a strangled scream, shocked and disorientated, her eyes staring wide. The room spun in dizzying circles for a moment as she sucked in desperate breaths. Then, with painful slowness, the spinning lessened, eventually coming to a stop. Her bedroom at the guest house, swathed in the calm dimness of pre-dawn, came into focus.

A shiver crawled down her spine, and a cold sweat peppered her body. Scared and uncertain, Nessa pulled her knees up to her chest and wrapped her arms around them, her bedding pooling around her, abandoned. Forgotten.

For the second time that night, Nessa was forced to question her sanity and was left to wonder.

*It has begun…*

*…Sāwolwalkere…*

# Chapter 41

The streets were busier than usual, packed with people and noise. Small children, laughing and shrieking, darted through the slow-moving current of adults that flowed towards the main road at the end of the alley, jostling to get to the front. Parents called out cautions. Groups of youths chattered, animated and excited.

Nessa hesitated at the front door of the guest house. "Is there a street fair or something?"

Hunter looked as perplexed as Nessa felt. "Not that I'm aware of."

"Judging by the banners and flags up yonder way," Orm came up behind them. "I'd say there's going to be a procession." With a hand between their shoulders, he propelled them forwards.

"A procession?" Nessa tried to walk on her tippy-toes, attempting to see over the heads of the growing crowd. It felt as if everyone in the city was converging. Tiptoeing through a bustling crowd wasn't a particularly easy thing to do, especially when you were in a long dress and also had to keep up with your six-foot-something friend, who was particularly keen on finding out why they had been summoned by a dragon—a dragon who refused to explain why. Nessa knew what this was all about, but she wasn't going to divulge anything. She fully intended to sit at the back of Aoife's rather luxuriously decorated cave in complete silence, feeling—and looking—rather sorry for herself. Aoife can do all the talking, Nessa had decided. "A procession of what?"

"Something to do with the Twelve Houses is my best guess." Hunter was taller than her and found it easier to see up ahead.

*Procession or not,* Aoife said in all of their minds, *I expect you all to be here shortly.*

Nessa rolled her eyes. She wasn't the only one either.

The crowd grew unpleasantly dense as they neared the main street, hindering their progress as they were forced to squeeze past people who stood lining each side of the street, eagerly waiting, jostling for a better view. All Nessa could see over the heads of those around her were the flags which caught in a light breeze, metallic threads glinting in the winter sunlight. They edged either side of the main road with bold colours, hanging from buildings at regular intervals by ornate brackets, bearing the emblems of the Twelve Houses. Nessa could see the sword and crown of House Eodor, the nine-pointed star of House Hālig and the rose in flames of House Sliðen— King Kaenar's own family. All twelve of the Houses were there, even the raven perched on a branch for House Fæger. Nessa felt that flying House Fæger's emblem was a little perverse seeing as that family had been slaughtered centuries ago.

"The flags weren't up yesterday," Nessa mused. "I would have noticed."

"Indeed they weren't," Orm agreed, coming to a standstill. The crowd was too dense, too thick to move through. They were stuck in the junction where their street met with the main road.

"Must have been an impromptu thing," Hunter surmised. "Perhaps someone important is arriving. Or leaving. Hopefully leaving." He looked at Nessa, one side of his mouth curling up into a cheeky grin. "You know, one less unpleasant bugger around to bother us would be grand."

"Ah laddie, my lad." They heard a hoarse laugh to the side of them and then a breathless wheeze. "If only we were *tho* lucky." The speaker had a severe lisp.

All three of them turned to the right, where there was a wizened old woman leaning against the corner of a nearby building. In each arthritic hand, she held a cane of twisted wood, which appeared to keep her from toppling over, for her legs were as bent as saplings in a storm and her spine was folded over, keeping her trapped in a perpetual bow. Nessa's back ached just from looking at her.

"What makes you say that?" Nessa asked, clearing her throat and sharing a quizzical glance with Hunter. Orm, she saw, was looking at the woman with a pained grimace, one hand slowly rising to his mouth in a futile attempt to hide his horror. Nessa had to admit, the woman was a sight to behold, and not a pleasant one.

Milky eyes, one blue and one a faint brown, covered in the hazy film of cataracts, peered at Nessa through wisps of knotted, white hair. A twisted grin deepened the maze of cavernous wrinkles on the woman's pockmarked face.

"Oh, if it were just a *th*imple coming or going," the crone lisped from a toothless mouth, "then that would be the end of that."

"But this isn't a simple coming or a going?"

"This is just the beginning."

A shiver of warning crawled down Nessa's spine, and she clutched at the satchel's strap that ran across her chest. The grimoire's weight against her hip seemed to grow, becoming almost burdensome. "Just the beginning?"

The old crone cackled, something which made Nessa, Hunter, Orm and a few others around them share unnerved glances.

"Oh ye*th*. This is the beginning. The beginning of the end. The Veil ripples and shifts, and the mists of old are rising. The king senses this, and he sends out his puppets for a hunt."

"A hunt?"

"Oh ye*th*." The crone looked positively delighted at the prospect. "With the rising darkne*th* shall come the Child of Erith, the king'*th* bane. He has begun his hunt for the one he fears the most. The child of the divine. The one who will bring his doom. It has been foretold, and it shall come to pa*th*..." She broke off in a bitter cough powerful enough to rattle the bones.

Nessa went to go to her aid, fearful that she would topple over and fall. A hand wrapped around hers, pulling her up short. Nessa looked up at Orm, surprised and a little confused.

"It's time for us to go," he said, his golden skin growing pale. He began tugging her along, pulling her through the crowd that lined the side of the wide street in a throng of jostling bodies, everyone curious and eager to see what—who—was coming.

Hunter kept close to Nessa's back as Orm ploughed a path through the crowd, earning them more than a few glares and raised brows. Nessa looked at her companions, but neither would meet her eye, their gazes darting everywhere, scanning faces and peering up and down the street like they suddenly expected trouble.

Nessa opened her mouth, about to ask what was wrong, why the urgency to get to Aoife, but she wasn't in any particular hurry to be yelled at, or for her grimoire to become group knowledge. She was already stepping on too many toes for anyone's liking.

A low murmur rippled through the crowd, a wave of excitement and awe that quickly built in momentum and volume. The roar of thousands and thousands of voices rose into the air as a dozen dragons detached themselves from the gleaming castle in the near distance.

Nessa's questions were forgotten.

They cut through the sky like arrows, creatures born of the sky and magic, their scales, coloured diamond and emerald, ruby and tanzanite, garnet and amber, shining like the finest gems in the cold winter sun.

Nessa watched them with wide eyes, enraptured just like everyone else in the street. Like the rest of the city. The dragons were a sight to behold, both beautiful and terrible.

They were her destiny.

They were her enemy.

In the back of her mind, Nessa could feel Aoife's worry, her longing. Dragons were not solitary creatures, usually living and hunting in small groups, most often with siblings or parents until they reached maturity and found their partner, their life mate. Aoife knew no such relation or company. She was alone, the only dragon who was not sworn to the king with an unbreakable vow, with binding words of magic. Nessa reached out to her through their bond, sending all the love and comfort she could through it, reminding her that, no matter what, Aoife always had her.

There was a trumpet of horns, a steady beat of drums, and with dragons overhead, soaring high over the city of Ellor with sinister beauty and grace, the Dragon Riders of the Twelve Kingdoms appeared at the very end of the wide road, a slow procession that leisurely moved ever closer.

Rows of drummer boys and soldiers-at-arms marched in front, a splendid display of finery and synchronism. Their steps perfectly timed to the drumbeats, their armour polished, their black uniforms uncreased. They cleared the centre of the road of stragglers and dawdlers, forcing the crowd to cram against the buildings. Rogue elbows dug into Nessa's ribs, and heels kicked her shins as the front of the procession reached where she stood. She clutched Orm's hand and her satchel, fearing that she would be crushed, that she would lose him and her grimoire. Hunter stood on her other side, shielding her as much as he could.

Rows and rows of drummers passed.

Rows and rows of soldiers passed.

And then the Dragon Riders came into sight.

They rode in a long line on the backs of the finest of horses, stallions of the most prestigious lineage, with long manes and shimmering coats. There were twelve of the fourteen Dragon Riders in the procession, just as there were twelve dragons in the heavens above, large, membranous wings spread wide, riding on updrafts, souring with the barest of efforts amongst the handful of soft, white clouds.

Nessa knew who the two missing Riders and dragons were: Shadow and King Kaenar, Bane and Spite. Of course, they wouldn't be there. The king had better things to be doing than parading through the city. And Shadow... Nessa could only presume that the king's right-hand man was likewise indisposed.

Nessa was glad that Shadow wasn't there, that she wouldn't see him so soon after... Her cheeks flared pink. After last night. As for the king...in another lifetime would be too soon.

With a clatter of armour and the clear ring of iron-shod hooves on the cobbled street, the Dragon Riders of the Twelve Kingdoms moved past Nessa, power and grace coming from them in waves.

House Bismer led the way on glossy, black steeds, the twins Haelan and Maeon riding side by side, dressed in reds and golds that matched their long, fiery hair. Behind them was House Derian with the twins Daegal and Daegon. They were identical, clothing and looks. Their sable hair was styled the same, their dark clothing was the same. Even their bright, hungry smiles were the same. While Daegal and Daegon appeared to revel in the attentions of the crowd, drinking in the awed whispers and the cheering children with smug expressions on their matching faces, it was a different story with House Bismer. Haelan rode with her back straight, her countenance bored, cold. She was as unmoving as a statue, her stare fixed far ahead. Her brother was equally uninterested in the crowds, in the sights around them.

They were beneath him. Unworthy of his and his sister's attentions.

Nessa breathed a sigh of relief as they moved past. They didn't notice her amongst the awed throngs. They didn't know that she was there in the crowds. Then she spied an emerald dragon fly overhead as the next pair of Riders passed by.

And everything changed.

The blood in her veins turned to ice as she watched the creature soar and dance through the sky in a beautiful display of deadly grace and strength. It was Margan's dragon. It was Anda.

Margan.

She didn't want to look at him. She didn't want to put a face to the name. Better a faceless monster than a beautiful demon. But she couldn't help herself.

Nessa's eyes were drawn to him like a moth to a flame.

*Margan.*

He rode beside a pretty girl who looked like she could have been his sister, both of them had pale-blond hair and wore matching expressions of boredom. Braelyn of House Blēoh, one of the three female Dragon Riders who served under the king, looked as pretty as a winter rose, and as delicate as one too, all softness and regal grace. It was a facade. Nessa knew better. She could sense the power crawling beneath Braelyn's skin. She was almost able to see its aura.

Whereas Braelyn was a winter rose, Margan was ice. Cold and hard. Not even his sharp beauty could hide that. There was nothing but cruelty in his glacial-green eyes, nothing but anger in his posture.

Nessa watched him pass by, a din filling her mind.

*How could people cheer for him? For them? Do they not see what monsters they are? How cruel they are? How much pain they cause?*

*How much pain he causes?*

It was as if time had slowed down. Nessa's vision was filled with nothing but the sight of Margan. Her ears were filled with the crowd's applause and praise. A headache formed behind her eyes, a deep throb that echoed the thundering of her heart.

The ice in her veins turned to fire.

The fire was painful.

*How could they admire him?*

The fire was agonising.

*Why are they admiring him? All the pain, the uncertainty, the fear he has caused me… How? Why?*

Nessa collapsed, falling to her knees, a soundless scream ripping from her throat, her hands clutching at her head. Spikes, knives, talons, claws were being driven through her skull, fracturing it into a thousand pieces. The world around her shrivelled and shrank to nothing, becoming dark and sinister, barren and claustrophobic. She was floating in a sea of black flames, burning to a cinder, burning to ashes.

Burning…

Burning…

*Ping…*

The strangest of sensations invaded her mind, something akin to a sharp crack of crumbling glass, of something breaking. Shattering. Then there was someone else in the flames with her, someone known to Nessa yet also a stranger.

Nessa reached for them, calling for answers, begging for help.

She was drowning in a sea of fire.

Words whispered through Nessa's mind, as quiet and soft as a spring breeze, intangible and strange, echoing around in the darkness that had swallowed her whole. There was distorted laughter…crying…screams…

Promises…pleading…

Nessa fell deep within herself, pulled beneath the current of voices. Some were hers. Other weren't. Images accompanied them, flashing here and there, filling her fractured mind, showing her so many things. So many great and terrible things.

She stopped burning. She stopped drowning.

The pain vanished.

Nessa was freed from the darkness with a suddenness that made her gasp.

She felt different.

Changed.

Nessa opened her eyes, squinting up at the bright, blue sky above her, which was framed by stocky buildings on two sides. She was laid out on the cobbled ground in a quiet alley. The crowd and procession were nowhere in sight.

"Why am I on the ground?" Nessa asked, confused and a little disorientated. "Where am I?"

Hunter was crouched down beside her, and as he leaned over, messy hair fell casually over his forehead, almost hiding the concern in his amber eyes. "You collapsed," he explained. "We got you away from the crowd before you caused a ruckus."

"Yeah." Nessa turned her head and found that Orm was leaning back against the side of a building, arms folded across his chest, his gaze locked onto the alley's entrance, making sure that no one stumbled across them.

"Luckily for us, everyone was more interested in the Dragon Riders then your fainting arse."

Hunter sent Orm a warning glare.

It went unnoticed.

Nessa shot to her feet, breathing heavily. The satchel, the grimoire, was a comforting weight on her hip. *Fainting. If only it had been as simple as that.*

Words whispered through Nessa's mind. Images played on her eyelids with each blink.

"Are you feeling alright?" Hunter asked, taken a little aback as he rose from his crouch. "You look a bit off."

"Alright?" Nessa whispered, her head was overwhelmingly filled with a million thoughts, a lifetime of memories. "Am I alright?"

Nessa was changed.

She was complete.

Orm raised his brows. "I think we should take that as a no."

"You're right," Nessa said, her wide eyes darting between Hunter and Orm. "I'm not alright. I'm not alright in the slightest."

Both of them frowned in confusion. Hunter looked worried, and he took a step towards her.

"I feel hurt," Nessa continued, backing away. Backing away from them. "I feel hurt and betrayed."

"Betrayed...?"

"How could you," Nessa asked through clenched teeth. "How could you lie to me all this time? How could you keep so much from me?" Her voice rose into a shout as anger—rage—joined her rolling emotions. "How could you have the nerve to call me your friend all these months when all along you were telling me nothing close to the truth?"

All the blood left Hunter's face, leaving him as white as a ghost.

"Oh shit," Orm muttered.

Nessa swung around, eyes flashing, hands balled into fists. Orm flinched. "'Oh shit' is right, you lying son of a bitch. You've been caught out. I know everything. I can finally remember. I remember it all."

"Double shit."

"How long were you going to continue with all your bullshit? How much further were you willing to take it? Were you ever planning on coming clean or were you just going to keep feeding me lie after little lie? How much were you going to keep from me?"

"Nessie," Hunter implored, voice croaky and broken. At least he had the decency to pretend to be troubled and apologetic, Nessa faintly thought. "Please understand th—"

"I don't understand!" Nessa cried, retreating a few more steps, needing more space between them and her. She buried her face in her hands, unable to look at him, at Hunter. Everything was changing. Everything had changed. Hunter had changed. It broke her heart. Her cheeks were wet with tears, and she swiped them away angrily. Whether they were tears of rage or heartbreak, she didn't know. She couldn't be sure. "I will never understand."

"We just wanted to help you."

"By denying me everything I wanted? Everything I needed?" Nessa shook her head, backing away from Hunter as he tried to sidle closer. "You had no right. No right whatsoever."

"We just wanted to protect you."

"I don't need your protection! I didn't want it in the

first place. What I wanted was a friend, someone who respected my wishes. You did neither. You as good as stabbed me in the back. You betrayed me when I needed you the most."

Hunter looked tortured, his eyes bright with anguish. "This was never the plan. Things got too complicated."

"They wouldn't of have if you'd just told me the truth from the bloody start!"

"We had good intentions," Orm finally spoke up from where he now slouched against the wall, deflated and defeated, his face as grey as the winter coat he wore. "We never wanted to hurt you."

"But you did. You've hurt me more than you can imagine."

Hunter flinched. "Please, just let us explain."

Nessa shook her head again. "I don't want to hear it."

"*Please.*"

"There isn't an excuse good enough," Nessa spat. "Not for this. I don't want to hear any more of your lies."

*My little Rider, just listen to them. Give them a chance to explain. Give us a chance.*

Nessa recoiled, flinching away from Aoife's presence in her mind. The betrayal ran deep. *And there you are. I was beginning to think that you weren't going to make an appearance.*

*Don't talk like that,* Aoife pleaded.

*Like what? Like someone who's just discovered that the only people they know have been keeping things from them? Like someone who's been betrayed by the people she trusted the most? How could you allow this to happen?*

*I was scared and worried. We all were.*

"We just wanted to give you time to heal," Orm said quietly, like that made it okay. "As much time as we could. That's all."

Nessa stared at him, realising that Aoife had linked all their minds together, relaying what the two of them had said.

"Time?" Nessa muttered bitterly. "How much time exactly? A year? Two? Ten?"

"In all honesty," Orm started. Nessa laughed darkly at that. *Oh, the irony!* "For as long as possible. At least until you came into your powers and Aoife grew big enough for you to ride her."

"So, it wasn't for my health; it was a tactical manoeuvre."

Orm pointed a finger at her. "You're twisting my words."

"Everything's twisted," Hunter gushed. "This isn't right. This isn't how I wanted things to turn out."

"Join the bloody club," Nessa grumbled.

Hunter looked at her beseechingly. "There's more than just one reason. It's not as clear-cut as that."

"And what's your reason then?" Nessa asked him mournfully, her heart breaking in two. "And don't tell me that it has something to do with giving me time to heal or protecting me. That's bullshit. Complete and utter bullshit."

"Can't we…can't we just go join Aoife and talk about this calmly?"

"An excellent idea," Orm agreed, forcing a smile, attempting to shove aside the guilt that played upon his strong features. "We can grab a bottle of wine," he peered at Nessa's tear-streaked face, "or something stronger. Definitely something stronger. Then we'll sit with Aoife in her snug little dragon cave and discuss everything. No more secrets."

Nessa could feel Aoife sending her soothing thoughts through their bond, trying to calm her, to make her agree with Orm's suggestion.

"Tell me," she urged Hunter with a quivering voice. "Tell me why. If you were ever really my friend, then give me an honest answer."

Hunter looked torn and conflicted, standing lost in the middle of the alley, shadows and revelations crowding in on him. His shoulders sagged beneath his heavy winter tunic. His eyes were wide and pleading. "Nessie, I was against it. I swear I was." He sucked in a shuddering breath. "I know I should have gone against Orm and Chaos' idea, or just gone behind their backs and…"

"So why didn't you?"

He groaned, anguished and pained. "I guess that I didn't want to lose you again."

"Right."

*Please just hear him out,* Aoife murmured.

"But what about who I lost?" Nessa continued unrelenting, merciless. "What about those who have lost me? Did you think about that?"

"I—"

"Did you even think for a second about what must be going through my mother's head? The wondering, not knowing what happened to me must be crippling her. And having to deal with my disappearance while expecting a baby…" Nessa choked up, tears spilling down her cheeks like a waterfall. "So much time has passed. She must have had the baby by now. I missed it. I wasn't there for her. That's all I wanted. Just to be there for her. I know…I know she may not be my birth mother, but that doesn't change anything for me. Not really…"

"I made a mistake," Hunter said quickly. "A huge

one. I know that. I know that now. And I am so, *so* sorry. I am so unbelievably sorry. I just couldn't lose you too. Not to Margan. It would be too much to bear."

"You knew what was at stake for me," Nessa sobbed. "I told you everything I wanted and you completely disregarded it."

"I was trying to do the best I could."

"Well, you've messed up."

"Story of my damn life!" Hunter exploded, something in him breaking irreversibly. "No matter what I do or how hard I try, it's never good enough."

"Oh, don't try and turn this around so it's about you."

"It not about me," Hunter yelled. "It's never been about me. It about you. It has always been about you. And before…before it was about Kaya."

Orm winced. "And things go from bad to worse."

"Kaya…" Nessa had heard that name before, but where? Margan. Margan had once taunted Hunter with it during their imprisonment in Ironguard.

"Kaya was my baby sister," Hunter murmured, tears of his own starting to fall. "She was only a year or so younger than me, but there was just something about her that made me want to keep her close, to protect her from the big, bad world. You remind me so much of her, Nessie. I think that's what drew me in to start with, the similarities between the two of you. The four of us—me and Kaya, Ma and Pa—we led a good life. A simple life. We had a large farm on the outskirts of a town that was under the leasehold of House Īren. We were mostly left to our own devices, provided we paid our taxes on time and caused no trouble."

A bad feeling grew in the pit of Nessa's stomach.

"Then there was a flood one winter. It ripped through

the town, damaging buildings and shops. It ruined the fields and destroyed the crops. When it came to that year's taxes, no one in town could pay them. House Īren wanted their money, so they sent out people to retrieve it."

Hunter's throat worked. "We'd all been summoned to the town's square by the collectors, a group of merciless, highborn monsters. They demanded payment. We didn't have it. We didn't have anything. We barely had enough food to last us through the winter. Old Ottie said as much. She was the town's healer and as old as dirt. She tended to speak her mind, to put it politely. It was seen as impertinence. A lie. She was punished. Fifty lashes then and there.

"Kaya...Kaya was a kind soul. A gentle soul. She was also Old Ottie's apprentice and she loved that old woman. Loved her so much that, after the first few lashes, she demanded to take the punishment in Old Ottie's place, fearing that the old woman wouldn't survive. Those bastards accepted, even though Old Ottie was against it, and our parents were against it. Instead of giving an elderly woman fifty lashes, they instead gave them to a young girl.

"The collectors had come with a small army. There was nothing we could do. Others volunteered to take Kaya's place, myself and Pa included, but our offers were refused. We were all forced to watch; the entire town was forced to watch as those bastards tied her to a pole in the middle of the town's square and whipped her back raw."

Nessa felt sick. If Kaya was Hunter's junior, and this had happened several years ago, then Kaya had to have been even younger than Nessa was now.

"Kaya survived the lashings. But she took ill. The

wounds became infected and took weeks to heal. Old Ottie and mother nursed her, never leaving her bedside. And Pa and I...Pa and I wanted House Īren to suffer as we were suffering. We weren't the only ones. The entire town was behind us, as were a handful of other places that had been affected by the flood, although to a lesser degree."

Hunter laughed a ruined, twisted sound. "I was so young and angry, and seeing so many others feeling the same way was empowering. Hundreds of us had banded together so quickly after the incident. Within a few weeks of Kaya being brutalised, we were coming up with ideas for how to make House Īren pay. It was the most amazing thing I had seen. Somehow, I managed to persuade Ma to join the gathering that night. She hadn't left the house since it had all happened. I thought that being in such an intoxicating atmosphere would do her some good. We left Kaya with Old Ottie. They were laughing at the time. Kaya was starting to feel better. Old Ottie was telling stories of her exploits during her youth. Ma was smiling for the first time in weeks.

"What we didn't realise was that word of our little uprising had spread to not only the nearby hamlets, but also to Ironguard, and...and Margan."

Nessa closed her eyes, powerless to make Hunter stop. She had been sucked into his story, his truth. And Hunter...Hunter looked like a great and terrible weight was being lifted from his shoulders.

"I lost sight of Pa almost instantly. Dragon Fire and fleeing people separated us. I never saw him alive again. Ma and I managed to get out. Somehow. I don't know how, only that I did. I got her to safety..."

"And...and Kaya?"

Hunter sobbed. "Destroying the town wasn't enough for Margan. Nor was killing anyone who had shown any defiance. I wasn't quick enough. He got to our farm before I could. And he...and he slaughtered Old Ottie just as I burst through the door, and with her knitting needle still stuck in his shoulder—the old woman was as fierce as she was stubborn—Margan turned to Kaya..." Hunter choked and staggered forwards. Nessa didn't back away as his hands gripped her upper arms. The look in his eyes held her immobile. "I lost everything to Margan. My Pa. Kaya. My home. There's nothing left of the town where I was born and raised. Nothing but ash and bone. And Ma...she'll never forgive me for not getting to Kaya in time to save her."

Nessa's mouth was dry, and her heart ached something terrible. *So this is what the truth feels like? What it looks like...*"That wasn't your fault. There was nothing you could have done."

"I lost everything to Margan," Hunter continued, his hands shaking, his face painfully pale, his brown hair dishevelled. "I couldn't risk losing you to him as well. I just can't. I don't think I would survive it."

"I...I need to think about all of this."

"Do you understand? Do you understand that I only wanted to keep you safe, to keep you away from Margan."

"This is too much for me." Nessa shrugged out of his grip and began backing away again. "I need some time."

"*Nessie,*" Hunter begged. "*Please.*"

"I need to be alone. I need to think."

Hunter mirrored her retreat step for step, looking like he was about to grab her before she could make a break for it. Orm clapped a hand on his shoulder, leaning down to say something in his ear. Nessa didn't stay to listen to what Orm had to say. She had heard enough. She had heard more than enough.

Nessa turned and ran, disappearing into the maze of narrow streets and winding alleys as Hunter's agonised yell echoed behind her, haunting her steps, tortured and gut-wrenching.

# Chapter 42

Nessa ran without direction, lost and alone. The city's streets, its people, passed her in a blur. Tears filled her eyes and streaked down her cheeks in a never-ending cascade. Her lungs burned with sobs and gasped breaths. Nessa's mind was in turmoil, her thoughts chaotic. She once thought that discovering she was adopted would be the biggest revelation she would have to face, but Hunter's story...the lies...the secrets... She didn't know which hurt worse. The pain she felt was unimaginable. Broken bones and slashed skin were nothing compared to the agony that tore through her heart.

It had been ripped apart.

Her spirit crushed.

Her soul bruised and torn.

*How could they?*

The question haunted her, chasing after her as she barrelled deeper into the city, losing herself in the shadowed backstreets, climbing hills and narrow stairways.

*How could they?*
*How could they?*
*How could they?*

It wouldn't leave her alone.

That's all Nessa wanted. To be left alone.

Nessa wanted solitude and silence. Even Aoife had respected that wish, withdrawing from Nessa's mind even as she had built a wall of amethyst around it, sealing herself away, blocking out Aoife's sorrow, her shame. Aoife had simply told Nessa that they would be there for her when she was ready.

Nessa wasn't sure she would ever be ready.

*How could they?*

Nessa wanted to be alone.

And alone she was. She had no one she could trust. No one to turn to. Nowhere to go.

Nessa was utterly and completely alone, and that knowledge made her feel so very empty. So very cold.

Nessa stumbled to a stop, unable to take another step.

"I have no one."

It was like being in Ironguard all over again. She was back at square one, back at the very beginning. Everything had been for nothing.

"I have nothing."

Nessa felt the crushing weight of fear and uncertainty settle upon her shoulders, coiling around her chest, tight. Constricting.

"What do I do?" she wondered aloud.

The answer came as a soft whisper in the wind, the flutter of dry leaves on the stone path, the rustle of tree branches rubbing against one another.

Nessa turned, a peculiar feeling settling over her, brushing way the conflict, the crippling pain she felt. She sucked in a deep breath and wiped away her tears. None fell after them.

Something called to her.

Something was beckoning her.

She looked around, taking in the sight of trees and flowerbeds full of blooming winter plants. She was in a small park, a quiet corner of the High Quarter that was pressed up against the mountainside. A path was before her, cutting through the narrow slip of woodland, but Nessa didn't follow it. Instead, she veered off to the right, walking through flowerbeds and skirting around sleeping trees in a strange type of daze.

Nessa emerged out of the tree line, and before she knew it, she was standing at the edge of a viewpoint that overlooked the city.

A sea of rooftops stretched out before her, spreading as far as the eye could see, and Lake Nyma twinkled on the horizon, crystalline waters catching in the sunlight. The castle was to the left, presiding over it all, a hundred spires reaching high into the sky, the gold-threaded black stone shimmering with threat and sinister beauty.

Nessa spared the view the briefest of glances.

Something else held her attention.

Someone else.

A man stood with his arms behind his back, his stare fixed upon the city that was laid before his feet, at the twelve dragons flying far in the distance, twinkling like stars. He was dressed in dark clothing and wore his black hair loose, allowing it to drift around his face and shoulders, stirred by a light breeze.

A shock of familiarity coursed through Nessa. Relief

bloomed in her broken heart.

"Shadow!" she cried, running to him.

He would help.

He'd know what to do.

He turned, and Nessa caught the faintest flicker of surprise in his dark eyes as her arms wound around him, as she buried her face against his chest, the velvet of his overcoat soft and warm beneath her cheek. His hands were quick to slip around her back, pulling her against him, holding her tight.

"Hello, little one," he murmured, his voice low and silky soft. "And who might you be?"

Nessa frowned. Misgivings grew. She leaned back as much as she could, tilting her chin up, eyes taking in the familiar features until her gaze met his. The arms around her tightened.

Binding her.

Imprisoning her.

His eyes were impossibly black as they stared down at her. There was no hint of sapphire blue in them. There was nothing but darkness, a seething darkness that shot through Nessa like a lance, sharp and hard, painful and jolting.

They glimmered like diamonds, like back opal.

They were beautiful.

They were terrible.

They were the eyes of King Kaenar.

# Epilogue

He stood in the shadows, where he was secret, where he was safe. The trees' spectral limbs reached over him, blotting out the watery sunlight as much as possible in their leafless state, offering a soft sort of darkness. He wrapped it around himself, creating a blanket of cover that concealed him from prying eyes. The fine shadows were more than content to oblige his wants, curling around him like an old friend, like a long-lost lover.

They whispered a sweet promise in his ear.

*It has begun.*

The words were a faint song in the air, gentle and seductive.

He stood in the shadows. Where he watched. Where he waited with bated breath.

*It has begun.*

He had yearned to hear those words for centuries.

He had needed to hear them for the best part of two decades.

For so long, they were all he had wanted to hear.

Now. Now they offered nothing but dread.

*How,* he wondered. *How had it changed? When had things changed?* He had his orders. He had his vows.

He had for centuries. Ever since he was a foolish young man who thought that he could make a difference. A foolish young man who thought that he could put the Twelve Kingdoms back to rights.

*How wrong he had been...*

*How sorry he was.*

It had seemed so easy. So simple. So clean cut. One life in exchange for many. What was one soul versus the thousands that had suffered and that would suffer? For centuries, he had been patient. He had been biding his time.

He had chosen his path long ago.

*Oh, how he regretted his choice.*

It had seemed so clear. So effortless.

Especially before *her*.

Before Ysandre.

For almost five centuries, he knew what he'd have to do, what was expected of him. He had followed his orders. He'd had to for the sake of others, for those who had come before him and those who would come after. He had done what was needed, even if it had left a bitter taste in his mouth and his hands gloved in blood.

Then there was Ysandre.

Even now, his bones, his heart, throbbed with the echoes of the pain he had felt at her passing. Her death.

She had been the only one in his long life who had ever been able to paint the world in beautiful colour. She had been able to make him see something beyond his duty. She had been his sun and moon. His everything. She had made him forget all of the awful things he had done because of the vows he had taken when he had been young and foolish. She had made him *feel*. She had made him *see*. She had made the world bright and beautiful. She had been an artist, a creator.

She had been everything to him.

*Ysandre.*

The trees around him quivered.

The shadows that shrouded him shuddered.

Even now, the memory of her made him weak.

She still made him question everything.

Even with her gone, the memory of her lingered.

She had shown him that even in the darkest of places, a light could still shine.

She had been his light.

But she was gone.

*Gone.*

The world she had once envisioned, that she had once painted in splendid colour for him, was now faded, muted. No colour was left. It had died with her. There was nothing but the harshness of blood and fire, burning and destruction. Nothing but the bleak tones of despair and sorrow.

She had made her choice.

He had made his.

And he regretted it.

Oh, how he regretted it.

He wished he could go back in time and make a different choice. Take a different path.

But it was too late. Try as he had, there was little more he could do for Ysandre and her memory, her legacy.

Her child.

His wings, pressed tight against his back, twitching with misgivings, with the sense of wrongness that coursed through him. He longed to fly, to take to the sky and flee. He couldn't. He wouldn't. Ysandre may be long gone, but the memory of her was still alive. She lived on through him and her child.

*Her child.*

He refused to say the girl's name. Refused to even think it. The girl was too much like Ysandre. She rekindled too many memories, too many regrets. She reminded him of her mother and of the choice she had made. Ysandre had chosen everything but him. She had chosen her path, and he had chosen his.

His path was clear.

It had been for centuries.

But the memory of Ysandre haunted him. *She* haunted him.

Even now, after everything, she made him question. She made him weak.

Was that why he had tried to go against those binding vows he had once taken? Was that why he had tried to do everything in his powers to aid the girl? He had gifted the book to her. He had gifted Ysandre's grimoire to her. He had armed her as best he could. As best as he was able with those vows binding him. Yes, he may have caused strife between her and the others, her *friends*. He may have slipped into her mind and created doubts and unease, discord and conflict. But it would strengthen her. It would make her grow into the woman she was meant to be, into the weapon that was promised to the Twelve Kingdoms five centuries ago.

Maybe then, all the sacrifices he had made wouldn't be for nothing. Maybe then, all of Ysandre's sacrifices wouldn't be for nothing.

*It has begun.*

Change was coming to the Twelve Kingdoms. Whether it was for better or for worse, he did not yet know.

His glacial eyes latched onto the girl as she flew up the stairs, dark hair loose and wild around her shoulders, trailing down her back in disarray. He spied the silvery streaks of tears on her cheeks and the hopeless expression on her fine-featured face. He watched, hidden in shadows and secrecy, as she paused in the winter garden, listening to the soothing voice that was destiny.

He watched as she allowed herself to be drawn forwards towards her fate.

He watched, his heart breaking, as she walked past trees and through flowerbeds, pulled towards a man who stood at the edge of a viewpoint, looking over the city of Ellor, looking over *his* domain.

He watched, his soul splintering in two, as the girl rushed forwards, crying out a name that did not belong to the man she embraced so earnestly, so needily.

He watched, a terrible numbness creeping through his veins, as the man, as King Kaenar, wrapped his arms tight around the girl and looked up, seeing through shadows and secrets.

The King nodded to him, a satisfied smile curling his lips.

The deed was done.

His task was complete.

His vows were fulfilled.

He had, after five centuries, delivered his promise and was free.

*It has begun.*

But he wished that it was the end.

*Oh, Ysandre, what can I do to make this right?*

The answer came as a whisper on the wind, a murmur in his ear. The trees sighed, and the phantom hand of a girl he once loved touched his shoulder.

He knew.

He knew what had to be done.

*It has begun...*

Enjoyed HOUSE OF BLOOD AND BONE?
Then find out what happens next in
HOUSE OF GORE AND GOLD

Looking for something else to read while you eagerly await more of The Wyrd Sequence? Then why not try THERE IS ONLY DARKNESS?

**Death is meant to be the end. For Alfie, it was only the beginning.**

Her murder and resurrection forced her into a world invisible to humans: the Underworld, where grim things from folklore skulk in gloomy doorways and hidden corners, waiting for the perfect prey to stumble past, and where things are never what they seem.

As Alfie is pulled deeper into this sinister world, she discovers that its shadowy history is starting to repeat itself. A war is brewing; a war in which Alfie and the dark power she unwillingly possesses may have an unfortunate role to play.

*Where can Alfie run to when the man who killed her reappears, leaving a trail of bodies and chaos in his wake?*

*Who can Alfie trust in a world built from secrets and lies?*

*What can Alfie do when those she cares about most become entangled in a wicked web of deception and ruin?*

Available now in Kindle and Paperback versions.

# ABOUT THE AUTHOR

Kimberley J. Ward, aka The Creator of Curiosities, is a dyslexic introvert who grew up in rural Dorset. She loves a good ale and a decent night's sleep. When she isn't looking after her ever-growing menagerie of animals and avoiding social interaction as much as politely possible, she is either writing or making something arty or jewellery related, or having a nap.

You can find her curious creations at:

www.kimberleyjward.co.uk

Follow Kimberley J. Ward on:

Facebook @CreatorofCuriosities
Instagram @creator_of_curiosities
Pinterest @CreatorofCuriosities

✠✠✠

www.ingramcontent.com/pod-product-compliance
Lightning Source LLC
LaVergne TN
LVHW091526060526
838200LV00036B/502